SHADOWS OF THE SLAIN

ROMA

- Priano's villa
- Quirinal Hill
- Palatium Diocletiani
- Pantheon
- Viminal Hill
- Capitoline Hill
- Esquiline Hill
- Amphitheatrum
- Palatine Hill
- Circus Maximus
- Archbasilica/Lateran Palace
- Santa Prisca
- Caelian Hill
- Aventine Hill
- R. Tiberis
- Via Ostiensis
- Via Appia
- Stoldo's villa
- Basilica of St Sebastianus

Legend
- ○ Settlements
- Disabitato
- Hills
- City walls
- Roman roads
- Beobrand's journey

1 mile
1 km

SHADOWS OF THE SLAIN

Also by Matthew Harffy

THE BERNICIA CHRONICLES

The Serpent Sword
The Cross and the Curse
Blood and Blade
Killer of Kings
Warrior of Woden
Storm of Steel
Fortress of Fury
For Lord and Land
Forest of Foes
Shadows of the Slain

Kin of Cain (short story)

A TIME FOR SWORDS

A Time for Swords
A Night of Flames
A Day of Reckoning

NOVELS

Wolf of Wessex
Dark Frontier

SHADOWS OF THE SLAIN

THE BERNICIA CHRONICLES: X

MATTHEW HARFFY

An Aries Book

First published in the UK in 2024 by Head of Zeus,
part of Bloomsbury Publishing Plc

Copyright © Matthew Harffy, 2024

The moral right of Matthew Harffy to be identified
as the author of this work has been asserted in accordance with
the Copyright, Designs and Patents Act of 1988.

All rights reserved. No part of this publication may be reproduced,
stored in a retrieval system, or transmitted in any form or by any means,
electronic, mechanical, photocopying, recording, or otherwise,
without the prior permission of both the copyright owner
and the above publisher of this book.

This is a work of fiction. All characters, organizations, and events
portrayed in this novel are either products of the author's
imagination or are used fictitiously.

9 7 5 3 1 2 4 6 8

A catalogue record for this book is available from the British Library.

ISBN (HB): 9781804548646
ISBN (E): 9781804548677

Cover design: Simon Michele | Head of Zeus

Map design: Jeff Edwards

Printed and bound in Great Britain by
CPI Group (UK) Ltd, Croydon CR0 4YY

Head of Zeus Ltd
First Floor East
5–8 Hardwick Street
London EC1R 4RG

WWW.HEADOFZEUS.COM

For Simon Mann, great musician,
and both virtual and real friend.

Place Names

Place names in Dark Ages Britain vary according to time, language, dialect and the scribe who was writing. I have not followed a strict convention when choosing what spelling to use for a given place. In most cases, I have chosen the name I believe to be the closest to that used in the early seventh century, but like the scribes of all those centuries ago, I have taken artistic licence at times, and merely selected the one I liked most.

Albion	Great Britain
Bebbanburg	Bamburgh
Bernicia	Northern kingdom of Northumbria, running approximately from the Tyne to the Firth of Forth
Burgundia	Burgundy, one of the three main polities that formed the Frankish realm, together with Austrasia and Neustria
Cala	Chelles
Cantware	Kent
Cantwareburh	Canterbury
Constantinopolis	Constantinople

Deira	Southern kingdom of Northumbria, running approximately from the Humber to the Tyne
Eoferwic	York
Frankia	France
Frisia	Cross-border cultural region encompassing the north of the Netherlands and parts of northwestern Germany
Ierusalem	Jerusalem
Langobardia	Territory of the Langobards. In present-day Italy the name is preserved in the modern toponym of the Lombardy region (Lombardia)
Lindisfarena	Lindisfarne
Liyon	Lyon
Luca	Lucca, Italy
Marselha	Marseille
Mercia	Kingdom centred on the valley of the River Trent and its tributaries, in the modern-day English Midlands
Neapoli	Naples, Italy
Neustria	Frankish kingdom in the north of present-day France, encompassing the land approximately between the Loire and the Silva Carbonaria
Nobatia	Christian kingdom in Lower Nubia
Northumbria	Modern-day Yorkshire, Northumberland and southeast Scotland
Ostia	Ostia Antica, port near Rome at the mouth of the Tiber. Near modern-day Ostia

Pisa	Pisa, Italy
Placentia	Piacenza, Italy
Po	Po River
Quentovic	Frankish trading settlement. The town no longer exists, but is thought to have been situated near the mouth of the Canche River
Roma	Rome
Sona	Saône, France
Sutri	Sutri, Italy
Taurinum	Turin, Italy
Tiberis	Tiber River
Ubbanford	Norham, Northumberland

PART ONE

ROAD TO ROMA

Chapter 1

Beobrand peered through the cleft in the rocks at the men they were about to kill. The brigands below were either brave or foolhardy. At the very least they were brazen. Not expecting pursuit and, believing themselves safe in their mountain lair, they had lit a fire against the night chill. Its light would make slaying them easier.

Beobrand suppressed a shiver. They were high here, the air, thin and crisp during the day, was sharp as a blade at night. There was still snow on the towering peaks that loomed either side of the pass and the mountains' summits were often wreathed in cloud. Midsummer was close and a couple of days earlier, in the rolling hills of Burgundia, the days had been sweltering, making it too hot to travel at midday. It was hard to believe that so recently they had been sitting in the shade of a willow beside a river, cooling their feet in the stream and complaining of the stifling heat. Despite the fur-lined mittens he wore, Beobrand's hands were cold. He was glad he had listened to Fredegar. The envoy sent by Clovis, king of the Franks, to accompany them on their journey onwards to Roma had insisted they furnish themselves with warm clothing for the mountain crossing. Such precautions had seemed unimportant while sipping a mug of cool ale beside the Sona in the afternoon sun, but now, with the bitter bite of snow in the wind, Beobrand was pleased he had heeded the envoy. Besides, it wasn't as if he had needed to pay for the gloves, hats and thick cloaks. Clovis and his queen, Balthild, had rewarded them handsomely for their service to the crown. From the horses they rode, to the clothes and byrnies on their backs and the weapons in their hands, all of it was courtesy of the Frankish monarchs.

Beobrand grimaced as he watched the figures in the protected gully below. No amount of gold and silver would bring Attor and Gram back, but it was right he should be paid well after the sacrifices his gesithas had made.

The brigands' fire was large, wasteful for men eking out a meagre existence by preying on travellers and pilgrims. Flames licked high into the cold night air. The dancing light reflected off the rocks and the ruddy faces of the men. They spoke loudly, laughing from time to time. They felt secure here, unaware that their doom approached, as inexorable as the tides. Without thinking Beobrand touched Nægling's familiar pommel with his mutilated left hand. Having lost the sword when escaping Liyon, Beobrand had been overjoyed to retrieve it when passing through the city again, and now, with an enemy nearby, he was ready to test its patterned blade once more.

He squinted, trying to count the figures, but they were still some distance away and Beobrand's eyes, never that sharp, could not pick out enough detail in the dark.

Beside Beobrand, Cynan did not need to be asked for his aid. The Waelisc man knew his lord's limitations well enough.

"I count ten men," he said, his voice a hissed whisper. "And I think three women."

Beobrand grunted. The boy they had found on the mountain pass had told them five men had attacked his family.

"The women are to be spared," Beobrand said. "One of them is that boy's mother. The others might be just as innocent."

Beobrand knew he didn't need to repeat this to his men. He did not allow women or children to be harmed. The thought of what the brigands would do to the boy's mother had driven them on, following their trail even as night enshrouded the mountains.

He wished he'd brought more warriors with him, but there was nothing he could do about that now. He cursed silently at having left the brothers Eadgard and Grindan back with the boy. Wilfrid, Coenred and the envoy Fredegar were there too. Beobrand couldn't leave them unprotected. And yet, seeing that his small band would be outnumbered, he wished he had brought at least Eadgard with them. The man's prodigious strength and huge axe made him a formidable warrior.

Still, these bandits would be no match for the gesithas, even with superior numbers. They had no idea Beobrand and his men were even there. His warriors were battle-hardened killers, disciplined and deadly. With the element of surprise and attacking from the darkness, they should have no trouble besting these wolf-heads. Whatever the bandits' number, the threads of their wyrd would be cut long before the sun rose again.

Beobrand winced. It did not do to tempt the gods with such thoughts. Too many times he had believed a task to be simple, only for his plans to be shattered as easily as a skin of ice on a puddle.

Woden loved chaos.

"Take Bleddyn and Ingwald round to the other side of the gully's entrance," Beobrand whispered to Cynan, pointing over to a large boulder. "I'll give you time to get in position. Attack on my signal."

Cynan rose silently and tapped the other two warriors, Cynan's own gesithas, on their shoulders. He whispered something too quiet for Beobrand to hear. With a nod Bleddyn and Ingwald slipped into the darkness, silent as wraiths. Cynan moved his mouth close to Beobrand's ear.

"What will the signal be?" he asked.

Beobrand's teeth flashed wolfishly in the darkness.

"I'll start killing the bastards."

He watched as Cynan disappeared into the night. He moved stealthily and made little noise. A few heartbeats after the Waelisc warrior had been swallowed by the dark, Beobrand heard the rattle of a pebble slipping down the rocky slope towards the brigands' camp. It sounded very loud to Beobrand's ears, and he tensed, thinking again how Woden revelled in mayhem.

After a moment, he let out his breath. Attor would never have made a sound, he thought with a fresh pang of sadness. But perhaps the gods smiled on them this night, for the bandits did not seem to have noticed anything amiss. They were drinking wine from a clay jug, surely spoils from some previous victims. The men's voices grew louder as they joked with each other, no doubt retelling how easily they had robbed the small family on the pass.

Listening to the men's mirth, Beobrand felt his fury building. His anger, never far from the surface, had been smouldering ever since they had heard the wailing cries of the boy on the road, but now, as if fanned by the cold breeze blowing down from the snow-capped mountains, he felt that anger grow into a blazing rage. He welcomed the feeling like an old friend, relishing the imminent death of these murderers. Perhaps a blood-letting would go some way to alleviating the grief and sorrow that churned within him.

The sounds of a child's cries had reached them as they neared the highest point of the pass that afternoon. Snatches of weeping sobs carried on the icy wind. They pushed the horses up the slope, though the animals were already short of breath and blowing, and soon saw a solitary waggon on the road.

Beobrand had scanned the area, wary of an ambush. The land about was desolate. The nearest place any sizable force could hide was a cluster of boulders far from the road running over the shoulder of rock between the two enormous mountains. Judging it safe, he spurred his horse into a canter and his men followed. Fredegar shouted a warning, but Beobrand ignored him.

"Keep a watch for anyone approaching," Beobrand shouted to Cynan as they rode close to the waggon.

As he drew near, he spied the boy some way off. He was on his knees and weeping. Close to the waggon lay a thickset bearded man. He was unmoving, his kirtle dark with blood. His eyes stared vacantly into the blue heavens. Beobrand had seen enough death to know this man was beyond help, so he turned his horse towards the boy.

At the sound of his horses' hooves on the gravelly earth, the boy leapt up. He was perhaps ten or eleven, slight of build, with a head of thick chestnut hair above an angular, intelligent face. His cheeks were tear-streaked, his eyes wide with fear. Backing away from Beobrand, he stared about him wildly, as if seeing more than a lone rider approaching. After a half-dozen steps, he tripped and fell, landing hard and whimpering in pain and shock.

Beobrand slid from the saddle, clutching the reins in his right hand and holding up his left hand with its missing fingers towards the boy.

"Do not fear," he said in the soothing tone he used for frightened animals and children. "I mean you no harm." He was unsure if they were still on Burgundian soil or had passed into Langobardia. Wherever they were would make little difference, as he knew the tongue of neither land. But he hoped his soft tone would speak for itself and would put the boy at ease.

The boy's eyes widened and his face turned towards Beobrand as if seeing him for the first time.

"They took Mother," the boy said, the words catching in his throat. "Father tried to stop them…" His voice trailed off. To

Beobrand's surprise, though they were far from Albion, the boy spoke in the language of the Anglisc. There was a tale there, but it would have to wait.

"Hush," said Beobrand. "You are safe now. Who took your mother? Can you show me where they took her?" He held out his hand to the boy, offering to pull him to his feet. The boy ignored his hand, staring at the sky behind Beobrand, or perhaps at his horse.

"Bad men," he said, scrunching up his eyes as if trying to picture them in his mind. "There were five, I think. They took her that way." He pointed off to the north. "They took Osweald too."

"Osweald?"

"Our horse."

Beobrand glanced back at where his men had gathered around the waggon. The harness was empty; the traces lying limply on the ground.

"What's your name, boy?"

"Aelfwig."

"Come then, Aelfwig," said Beobrand, again proffering his hand. "Tell me all you can about these bad men. It is too late for your father, but my men and I will ride after your mother and bring her back to you if we are able."

Aelfwig again ignored Beobrand's outstretched hand, instead pushing himself up from the ground and rubbing the tears from his face. It was then that Beobrand understood why the boy did not look him in the eye. His eyes did not focus on him, or his horse.

Aelfwig was blind.

The thought of this child, alone and defenceless on the mountainside settled like a stone on Beobrand's heart. There had been no time to waste, but he had questioned Aelfwig as thoroughly as possible before heading off after the bandits. It transpired that the boy's blindness was the reason the family were there, on the mountain road between the lands of the Franks and the Langobards. They were on a pilgrimage to the holy city of Roma from Cantware in Albion. Aelfwig's mother, Wulfwyn, hoped they would find a cure for her son's affliction there. Judging from Aelfwig's plain kirtle and breeches and the similar attire of his father, and the family's small waggon, the pilgrims appeared to be simple folk. That they had made it this far was a testament to their determination and resourcefulness.

It had been late afternoon when they'd set out after the brigands. Following them had been easy. With only a blind boy behind them the bandits had made no effort to hide their tracks, and the horse they had stolen left clear signs of their passing over the thin grass and dirt between rocky outcrops. Beobrand and his warriors had left their own mounts behind, surmising the terrain would be too treacherous for riding. They were right, and it seemed that the bandits had led the horse along dangerous ridges and down steep, scree-strewn slopes where Beobrand was certain they would not have been able to remain in the saddle.

As darkness had fallen, the setting sun turning the sky behind the mountains to molten gold, Beobrand had ordered his men to press on. It would be perilous to travel in the dark. There was only a sliver of moon, but Beobrand could not bring himself to halt. As they clambered over the slopes, his lungs burning and legs aching, he could not free his mind of Aelfwig, blind and alone, his father's corpse cooling beside the waggon. The men who had done this must pay.

As Beobrand had made to leave, Fredegar grasped his cloak, pulling him back.

"You should not go, lord," he said. "These mountains are dangerous. The boy's father is dead. His mother is lost. Nothing can be gained by going after these bandits. Our path leads down there." He had pointed to the sweeping vista of verdant land to the south. "You have important messages to deliver to Roma. Important people to deliver safely. You should not risk everything for this—" He lowered his voice. "This blind ceorl's mother."

Beobrand shook off the Frankish envoy's hold on him.

"What could be more important than this boy's mother's life?" he snarled.

He had seen his men's glances at Fredegar. They shook their heads disapprovingly at the envoy, and Halinard said something softly to the man before hurrying after the lord of Ubbanford. Fredegar had stared after them, a look of confusion on his smooth, clean-shaven features. Whether the Frank understood or not, Beobrand's gesithas knew their lord would never turn away from helping a woman in distress. Such was not his way and they loved him for it.

And so they had pressed on into the gloom and cold of the mountain night, hopeful that they might be able to spare Wulfwyn the worst of her ordeal.

Beobrand stared down now into the ravine that was full of swaying shadows and the jagged laughter of hard-bitten men. He glanced over to Halinard. The Frankish warrior's face was haggard in the flame-flicker from the fire, but he nodded, indicating he was ready for action. Like Beobrand, Halinard had a wife and a daughter back at Ubbanford. Neither man could bear to stand by while a woman was abused.

Loosening Nægling in its scabbard, Beobrand flicked his gaze back to the bandit camp. He wondered whether he had allowed enough time for Cynan and his gesithas to get into position. A sudden movement drew his attention and a new sound cut the frigid dark. At once Beobrand knew the decision of whether to wait or to act now had been taken from him.

A woman was being dragged, screaming and struggling, into

the firelight. She was terrified, but her exhortations were clear enough. And Beobrand understood her words. The poor woman cried out in Anglisc for the Lord Jesu the Christ to save her from these servants of Satan.

Chapter 2

Rising up like a shadow from nightmare, Beobrand discarded all attempt at stealth. Thrusting his arm into the straps of the shield he'd had fashioned in Paris, he bellowed a challenge.

"Death!"

Like those of his men, Beobrand's shield was daubed black, an apt colour for death-dealing. Beside him Halinard stood, the firelight glimmering on the steel of his spear's tip.

"Death!" he yelled, joining Beobrand in his battle-cry.

The faces of the men in the gully stared up at them, surprise etched on their features. One of the brigands shouted something at them, but his words were cut off as Halinard's spear pierced his flesh where throat met chest. Such was the force with which the Frank had flung the spear that the man was thrown tumbling backwards into the fire.

Sparks sprayed up into the night. The man shrieked, thrashing against the burning timber and the ash-hafted spear that jutted from his body. Shadows loomed and flew around the gully as the dying man scattered the fire and the other brigands rushed to arm themselves.

Beobrand drew Nægling and leapt down into the campsite. Halinard was close behind him and in an eye-blink they crashed into the closest men. The bandits had barely had a chance to retrieve their weapons, and Beobrand and Halinard swept aside their long knives and axes on the willow boards of their black shields, hacking into the men's flesh with sharp steel.

Chaos reigned in the ravine as Beobrand hammered his blade into the head of the nearest bandit, ensuring he was dead before moving onward towards the fire. The brigands had retreated before the warriors' onslaught, leaving three dead or dying in their wake. But now they saw that although the men who attacked them brandished swords and were bedecked in iron-knit shirts and burnished helms, they numbered but two.

Wulfwyn had been forgotten, left where she had been thrown down by the fire. She now clutched her torn clothes to her body and scurried away, out of the path of the fighting men. The other women Cynan had seen had fled into the gloom.

More men came out of the depths of the gully, joining their comrades. Nine now faced Beobrand and Halinard.

"Cynan should learn to count, lord," hissed Halinard. "He said there were ten."

Beobrand shrugged.

"There are only nine of them now," he said with a grin.

The brigands' eyes glowed in the firelight. Beobrand scanned their faces. All were dirty and unkempt with the savage look of cornered animals. The youngest was little more than a boy; the oldest man's head was covered in a wispy cloud of white hair, his grey beard hanging down to his chest. A tall, broad-shouldered man with a thick thatch of dark hair and beard stepped forward, raising a vicious-looking cleaver-like blade in his meaty fist. He shouted something. Beobrand could not comprehend the words, but they were almost intelligible to him, the language strangely familiar, like the face of a distant relative seen from afar. The man, clearly the leader, spoke again, shaking the weapon in his hand. As he talked, so the others found their courage. They hefted cudgels, staves, axes and seaxes, readying themselves to fight.

Beobrand stood firm, shield held high. Blood dripped from the end of his sword's blade.

"You think we can take them?" whispered Halinard.

"Of that there is no doubt," Beobrand replied. "But when they attack, we will fall back."

Halinard nodded.

The bearded leader had ceased speaking to them now, either sensing they did not understand or believing they simply refused to reply. Instead of directing his words to them, he now turned to his men, raising his voice to build up their confidence before they rushed the two warriors. They outnumbered Beobrand and Halinard, and could surely overwhelm them, but only a fool would think the two grim-faced warriors would not slay more of them before they were through. And these men were no fools. Nor were they brave. They hesitated, cautious and nervous of the long blades.

The man who had fallen into the fire had stopped moving now and he lay nearby, his clothes smoking. The stink of roasting meat was strong. Beobrand could make out Wulfwyn's voice coming from the gloom. She was praying to the Christ, muttering entreaties and exhortations to her god.

Taking a step closer to the fire, Beobrand swept Nægling down. The blade cut deep into the burnt man's neck. His comrades, seeing his body defiled, growled and shuffled forward. Beobrand glanced down and saw the man's head was still attached by a flap of skin and sinews. Slicing down with his sword again, he severed the head from the body. Blood pumped from the gaping neck, hissing as it touched the embers of the scattered logs from the fire.

Beobrand shoved his foot under the head and with a quick

motion lifted it with a kick that sent it flying over the fire and into the group of brigands. They scattered, yelling and furious.

"Now," snapped Beobrand. "Pull back."

Halinard did not question the order. He had stood in the shieldwall beside Beobrand many times over the years. Locking their shields together, the two of them began walking quickly backwards, away from the firelight; distancing themselves from the brigands.

The brigands surged forward, finally responding to their leader's encouragement, goaded by Beobrand's treatment of their comrade's corpse, and perhaps believing the two warriors to be retreating in the face of far superior numbers.

They leapt over the burning logs that had tumbled from the fire, stepped over the bodies of their fallen friends and came on at a run. There was fury in their eyes now. They screamed abuse and insults at these interlopers and rushed towards them ever faster.

"Quickly," cried Beobrand. "To those rocks."

They backed away as fast as they were able without turning to run. Their enemies were almost upon them and Beobrand could smell the sour sweat and woodsmoke stink of them when first his heels and then his back clattered into a boulder.

He raised his shield and met the first of the brigands, the young boy who wasn't old enough to have hair on his face. Catching the boy's clumsy swinging cudgel on the rim of his shield, Beobrand sliced his sword into the lad's thin thigh, cutting deep into muscle and severing the artery. Blood spouted, splattering Beobrand's hands and face in a warm, crimson shower. The boy howled like an infant and fell back.

Beside him, Halinard had dealt with his own foe, cutting into a bald man's shoulder and kicking him back into his comrades. But they were surrounded now, their backs against the wall of stone, with nowhere else to retreat, no space to move. They could not last long like this.

Sensing their predicament the bearded leader sneered at them and laughed.

He was still laughing when he died, a Frankish throwing axe buried deep in his skull. Ingwald, who had thrown the axe, let out a great roar. Alongside him, Cynan and Bleddyn swept in from the darkness, appearing like nihtgengas, the fell creatures of mead tales, bringing doom from the black night.

"Death!" they cried. Beobrand and Halinard took up the chant once more, shoving their shields forward and thrusting with their bloody blades.

Chapter 3

The fight was over in moments.

Cynan, breathing hard from the exertions of combat and the frantic rush through the darkness to the bandit camp, glanced over at Beobrand. The dim light from the fire made his lord's face monstrous in the gloom; a glowering mask. Cynan knew him well enough to know the shadows probably concealed a furious glower.

The tall thegn of Ubbanford bent to wipe the blood from Nægling's blade on the kirtle of one of the fallen brigands. Even in the poor light Cynan saw that Beobrand's hand was shaking. It was always thus after combat. Pretending not to watch, he saw Beobrand take a calming breath, concentrating to lessen the trembling enough to allow him to slide his sword into its fur-lined scabbard.

"What took you so long?" Beobrand called over to him, a sharp edge to his voice.

Something touched Cynan's ankle and he flinched, drawing his foot back. He was close to the remains of the fire and by its light he saw the blood-smeared face of one of the bandits. The man was whimpering and clawing at Cynan. His words meant nothing to the Waelisc warrior, but from the pleading tone and the severity of the man's wounds, he assumed the bandit was asking for mercy. Cynan stooped, driving his sword into the man's chest, silencing him. Perhaps he would find compassion in the afterlife. Cynan had none to offer. He turned his attention back to Beobrand.

"Better late than never, lord," he said with a sheepish smile.

"It was almost too late," grumbled Halinard. "Did you stop for a piss on the way?"

Cynan felt his face grow hot despite the cold air on the mountain. He should have been ready sooner, it was true. In an effort to cover his discomfort he barked orders at Bleddyn and Ingwald. Bleddyn moved to the side of the weeping woman who Cynan presumed was Aelfwig's mother. Ingwald disappeared into the darkness at the far side of the camp.

"Halinard," said Beobrand, "go with Ingwald. And take a brand from the fire. There might be more lurking back there."

Halinard looked as though he wanted to contest the command, but he said nothing. With a glare at Cynan, he scooped up a snapped staff and quickly set about wrapping linen from a dead man's kirtle around it.

While Halinard made his torch, Cynan went about checking the dead. He drew his sword across the throats of two others, quickly sending them on their way from middle earth. Bleddyn knelt beside Wulfwyn and whispered to her, telling her that Aelfwig was safe. She let out a great sobbing cry, then seemed to lose all of her strength, collapsing against Bleddyn and weeping quietly.

Makeshift torch ready, Halinard set the linen ablaze in the fire and followed after Ingwald, the flame of the brand casting shadows that leapt and careened around the chasm like dark spirits.

Cynan stepped over the dead, moving close to Beobrand who stood now with his back to the smouldering logs of the fire and their red glow. He stared out into the night as if he expected an attack to come springing from the dark.

"Sorry, lord," Cynan said, his tone quiet. He had found a skin filled with wine near the fire and he handed it to Beobrand. After a moment's hesitation, Beobrand took it and raised it to his mouth. Cynan noticed that his hands no longer shook.

"What happened?" asked Beobrand, taking a deep draught of wine before handing the skin back to Cynan. "Halinard is right. We were lucky not to be killed."

Cynan accepted the wine and took a swig. It was surprisingly good, but anything tasted good after battle.

"I thought you didn't believe in luck, lord."

Beobrand grunted.

"Well, without whatever passes for such, or the gods smiling on us, I fear Halinard and I would have been slain." He held out his hand for the wineskin once more. "There were more than you'd counted too."

"Sorry," Cynan repeated.

"And you took long enough that I wondered if you and Bleddyn might have found some sheep on the mountainside."

Cynan bit his lip. When any other made jests about his Waelisc ancestry, particularly the oft-repeated jape about the Waelisc fondness for swiving sheep, Cynan would fly into a rage. But he accepted the jibe from Beobrand without complaint. He even smiled in the gloom, glad that his lord was making light of the situation. Cynan knew the outcome of the clash with the bandits could have been very different.

"The night is cold," he said, a smile in his voice, "and it might have been a nice diversion to find some warm, willing sheep, but the honest truth is we got lost."

"Lost?" said Beobrand. "How hard can it be to find the entrance to this gully? It is big enough."

"Well, I have heard tell of men who struggle to find even the largest of openings."

Beobrand snorted.

"Are we still speaking of sheep?"

Cynan chuckled, then grew sombre.

"It was harder to find our way in the dark than I would have thought possible. The land drops off down there," he pointed with his chin into the darkness, "and there are lots of huge rocks. Those whoresons chose their camp well. Even in daylight it must be well hidden. We couldn't spy even the fire's light from any distance at all. If you had not started fighting when you did, we might even now still be wandering the mountainside looking for this ravine."

Beobrand handed him the wineskin.

"Or sheep," he said, with a low laugh. "I'm glad you arrived when you did."

Cynan looked over to where Bleddyn had taken a cloak from one of the brigands and was now draping it around Wulfwyn's shoulders.

"Is she well?"

"As well as you can imagine, I suppose," said Beobrand. "She has lost her husband and feared for her life, but I do not believe they defiled her."

"That's something."

"She must be a strong woman to have travelled this far. And she has her son. She will be well enough, I think."

Halinard and Ingwald returned to the fire leading two women. They were both skinny and dirty. Their eyes widened as they took in the dead men strewn about the campsite.

"There was another one," Ingwald said. "She ran away. We lost sight of her in the rocks." He signalled for the women to sit beside Wulfwyn. Halinard found some cloaks and blankets and tossed them to the women. Then, pulling Bleddyn to his feet, the three warriors made their way to where Beobrand and Cynan stood.

"I thought you had sharp eyes," said Beobrand, looking askance at Cynan. "Your counting this night is blunter than usual. You said there were three women."

"With my good looks and battle-skill," said Cynan, "if I never made a mistake, would you believe me to be mortal?"

Beobrand scoffed, then turned to Halinard.

"Can you understand them?"

The Frank shook his head.

"They speak the tongue of the Langobards. I can comprehend a word here and there, but no more than that."

Ingwald accepted the wineskin from Cynan and took a mouthful before passing it to Bleddyn.

"What are we to do with them?" Ingwald said.

"We will take them with us," Beobrand said. "Fredegar will be able to talk to them. But for now, find food and drink and place more fuel on the fire. Clear the dead. We will spend the night here. It's too dark to travel back to the pass now. And I feel we have all earned the right of a warm fire, perhaps some meat, and some wine in our bellies."

The men moved to follow Beobrand's command. But a thought nagged at Cynan.

"Keep an eye on those women," he called out, "and for the one who ran off. We do not know if they are friends or foes, and a sickly-looking woman can gut you just as easily as a man, given the chance."

Beobrand frowned, perhaps, like Cynan, recalling Sulis and how she had been rescued from captivity and abuse, only to turn on her saviours. The thought cast a shadow over their previous mood of victory and the men, sensing it, went about the business of tidying the camp in a subdued hush.

Cynan let out a long breath. It steamed in the thin night air.

"I'll take first watch," he said.

Beobrand said nothing. With a curt nod, he walked to where Ingwald was rebuilding the fire, leaving Cynan at the mouth of the gully staring out into the darkness.

Chapter 4

Coenred finished reciting the paternoster and looked over the fire at the bowed heads of the women. They joined him each morning and evening when he prayed, sang the psalms or delivered the offices.

Mena, the younger of the two, a painfully thin girl with sharp cheekbones and eyes that seemed too large for her face, stared back at him across the flames. She was cleaner than she had been when she'd been brought back by Beobrand and his gesithas. The first stream they had seen, Wulfwyn had informed the men that she and the other two women would stop and bathe. None of the men, not even Beobrand, dared gainsay Aelfwig's stern mother, and Wulfwyn had led Mena and the other woman, Gostanza, down to the fast-flowing torrent. The women had washed as well as they were able, scrubbing their clothes in the icy water that cascaded down from the mountains and returning to the waiting men with damp clothes and wet hair, pink-cheeked and shivering. They had been lucky it was warm in the sunshine, and they had dried out as they'd walked along beside the waggon in the afternoon.

Coenred looked away from Mena. The girl's attention unnerved him. He was seldom troubled with his vow of celibacy, but he was not yet an old man and he sometimes felt the stirrings of the flesh. The absolute adoration in Mena's gaze was dangerous, he knew that. He must be wary of the temptations sent by the Devil to try him. Soon they would be in the holiest of cities and he would not falter in his faith. He would pray with Mena if she wished, but he must be careful not to allow her to believe there could ever be anything more than friendship between them.

Beside her, Gostanza was also looking at him. She was a few years older, not much younger than Coenred himself. He found her expression more difficult to read, but there was certainly none of Mena's adulation in Gostanza's gaze.

The older woman had told Fredegar, who spoke the tongue of the Langobards fluently, that she had been stolen from a group of travellers on their way homeward from Taurinum a year before. What hardships she had been through Coenred did not care to think about, but he was no fool. He understood all too well the horrors perpetrated by such men on women and what she must have needed to do in order to survive.

Gostanza, while raw-boned, was pretty enough, and the warriors watched her movements. But when any of the men came close to her, she scurried away. Seeing this, Beobrand had ordered his men to leave the woman alone. There was a hollowness in Gostanza's eyes, and it seemed to Coenred that while she went about the routines of daily life, something had died within her on that mountainside.

The most interesting of the three women was Wulfwyn. Admittedly she had been a captive of the bandits for less than a day and Beobrand seemed quite sure she had avoided the worst kind of abuse and violation, but still, Coenred thought the woman was a marvel.

When they had arrived back at the pass where Coenred and the others had made camp around Aelfwig's waggon, Wulfwyn had strode forward and embraced her son.

"Praise be to the Lord Almighty. He delivered us from evil," she said, her eyes glimmering.

Beobrand had trudged along beside her, his blood-spattered face looking weary.

"You are once again the instrument of the Lord, Beo," Coenred had said, unable to keep the smile from his face. He had been overjoyed to see all the men return, especially Beobrand, who was his oldest friend. "I should never have doubted you or the good Lord. But when you didn't return in the night I had started to fear the worst."

Beobrand told him that Wulfwyn had cried uncontrollably for a time after they liberated her from the bandits, but Coenred had not seen her weep. Ever since she arrived back with her son she had been forthright, focused and driven.

When she had seen her husband's body, wrapped in a cloak and laid carefully beside the waggon, Wulfwyn had paused, looking silently at the still form for a moment. Pulling the cloak away from the face, she had stared at the pallid features. None of the men had spoken. They shuffled awkwardly about the camp, averting their gaze and preparing the mounts for the onward journey. None of them wished to intrude on this sombre woman's grief. Gostanza and Mena had looked away too, unwilling or unable to alleviate the widow's sorrow. After several heartbeats, Wulfwyn had knelt and kissed her husband's blue tinged lips, before covering the face once more and standing abruptly.

"We will bury him here," she had said. Then, to Coenred: "You will pray over him and say the correct words." It had not been a question.

Beobrand had ordered the men to dig a grave near the road. None of them spoke as they worked the thin earth. When it was done they placed Wulfwyn's husband's corpse in the shallow hole and covered him with rocks. Coenred prayed over the grave and commended his soul to the Lord. Even then, laying her husband to rest, Wulfwyn had not cried. Her features were hard, her jaw clenched, and her eyes dry. Aelfwig wept over his father's grave and Wulfwyn placed an arm around her son's shoulders. When she deemed he had cried enough, she pulled him away and they had all headed down towards the green valley below.

After they had walked a short way, Coenred had looked back up the mountain. They hadn't gone far, but already he had been unable to make out the small cairn of rocks they had used to mark the grave.

The longer they travelled together, the more Coenred admired Wulfwyn. He was not alone. The warriors, and even Beobrand, could not stop themselves from following Wulfwyn with their eyes. She was not a beauty, but she was fair of skin with sensually full lips and she moved with a lithesome grace that drew men's attention. She reminded Coenred of the vague memories he had of his own mother. He could barely recall his mother's face and even Tata, his sweet sister, had been taken from him so long ago that he found it difficult to conjure up her features in his mind's eye. But there was something in the strength of Wulfwyn's resolve, wrapped within the soft exterior of a slender woman, that brought back ghost-memories of both his sister and mother.

Wilfrid seemed attracted to Wulfwyn in a very different way. When she bent to pick something up from the ground, or if she leaned over into the waggon to retrieve a blanket or a pot, Wilfrid's eyes roved over her curves in a very unchristian manner.

At first Coenred had said nothing. He did not wish to think ill of Wilfrid, despite what Beobrand and the others had told him of the young novice's actions in Frankia. He could not credit Wilfrid with such terrible behaviour and so he had chosen to assume that for some reason the young man had angered the warriors. He should have known better, he admonished himself. Coenred had known Beobrand and his gesithas for years and he should have trusted their judgement. Now, with his lascivious looks at Wulfwyn, Wilfrid was showing his true character.

Coenred had made up his mind that, as his elder and superior, he must confront Wilfrid. He would remind him of his vows, that he was a holy man and sent here with the patronage of the Queen of Northumbria herself. He hated the idea of conflict. The conversation would no doubt prove painful for both of them. But it was his duty. He would speak to Wilfrid after Vespers that evening.

He needn't have worried. Before he could intervene, Wulfwyn herself took command of the situation.

It was at the end of the second day after the women had been rescued. They were setting up camp in a forested glade near a stream. The mountains to the west cast their shadows down into the valley, but now that they were in the foothills, it was hot all day and warm even after dark. Wulfwyn was unhitching her horse from the waggon, when Wilfrid stepped in close, brushing against her and offering his assistance.

"If I sought help with my horse," Wulfwyn said, her haughty voice clear, "I would seek it from one of the men who knows something of caring for animals, not a child who" – she fixed him with a withering glare – "has a very different type of riding on his mind."

Eadgard laughed out loud from where he had been removing his own mount's saddle. Of all the men in the party, the huge axeman was the one who bore the strongest grudge against Wilfrid. Coenred was unsure why, but no matter how many times Eadgard had been told that Wilfrid was not responsible for Gram and Attor's deaths, the axeman refused to accept the young man's innocence. It seemed to Coenred that it was only Eadgard's oath to Beobrand, who forbade him to act on his anger, that kept his fury at bay.

Wilfrid flushed crimson.

"My lady Wulfwyn," he said, "you are sorely mistaken. I meant nothing but to help you as any good Christian man would."

"My son is blind, Wilfrid, not I," Wulfwyn said. "I see the way men look at me. Christian and otherwise. And I see what is in your mind. And lest you have forgotten, I buried my husband two days ago." She spat these words at him, her tone dripping with venom. "And if I am ever in search of another husband, let me make it clear to you now, to spare you further embarrassment, I would never settle for such a small man as you."

Eadgard was laughing so hard now that tears were streaming down his face. Several of the other men laughed too. Coenred maintained his sombre expression with difficulty. It would not be seemly to laugh at Wilfrid's expense.

For his part, Wilfrid, red in the face, stammered and stuttered, for once unsure what to say and clearly unable to use his charm to talk his way out of the predicament in which he found himself.

Eadgard wiped at his cheeks, growing suddenly serious.

"If you want me to knock some sense into the lad," he said, "just say the word, my lady." The tall gesith looked as if he would like nothing better than to be given that command.

"That won't be necessary, Eadgard," Wulfwyn said. "I think we have an understanding now. Isn't that right, Wilfrid?"

Wilfrid's mouth opened and closed but he seemed unable to speak. After a moment he nodded and strode out of the camp towards the stream. Eadgard and the other warriors' laughter followed him. By the warm glow of the setting sun, Coenred caught a glimpse of Wilfrid's face as he stalked away. The fury and hatred etched there were such that Coenred took an involuntary step backwards. He was tending towards sharing Eadgard's feelings towards Wilfrid, and he wondered whether Wulfwyn might have misjudged in making an enemy of him so openly.

Chapter 5

In the two days that followed, Coenred noted how Wilfrid studiously ignored Wulfwyn. The men spoke little with the novice, making it clear what they thought of him. Coenred did not shun him. They prayed together regularly, but Wilfrid's demeanour was stiff and awkward ever since the incident. Coenred hoped he would learn from the encounter. There was no doubt the young man was extremely intelligent and charismatic, but he was also young, impetuous and ambitious. The same traits that could lead him to rise to the heights of success could just as easily see him fall and fail in his endeavours.

The weather continued to grow hotter as they moved further into the fertile valley of the River Po. And with each passing day they saw more people on the roads. When a flock of perhaps a hundred sheep blocked their path, Fredegar spoke to the elderly man who followed along behind the animals.

"Ask him if we can buy an animal from him," said Beobrand, nudging his horse through the mass of woolly creatures and into the shade of an oak that towered near the road. "I think we'd all like some roast mutton."

Fredegar uttered a stream of words. Not for the first time Coenred was impressed with the man's ability with languages.

He could converse perfectly in Frankish, Anglisc and Langobard, and was also fluent in Latin and Grecisc.

The old man's face was wrinkled and as brown as leather and he did not look directly at the Frank as Fredegar talked, instead keeping his deep-sunk eyes on his gaunt dog. The hound nipped at the sheep's ankles, driving them along the path towards the lush pasture on the hills.

"He says he will sell us a sheep if we want, but we'll be in Placentia by dusk," Fredegar translated. "They have meat there."

"Seems we've made good time," Coenred said, riding alongside Beobrand once the sheep had passed.

Beobrand snorted.

"It is nearly midsummer and we left Cantwareburh well before the start of the year. We should have been on our way home by now, or even already back in Bernicia."

Coenred shrugged.

"You know what I mean. Gostanza said we wouldn't reach her master's hall for two or perhaps three more days."

Beobrand looked back at where the woman walked beside the waggon.

"I wonder how they will receive her after all this time."

"We'll find out soon enough."

"I know the men have enjoyed having the women with us," said Beobrand, ducking beneath a branch that protruded over the road, "but I will be glad to be rid of them. They cause strife."

Coenred glanced back to where Mena walked beside Halinard, who rode on a fine black horse. The slim girl looked up at the Frank with the same adoring expression she had frequently directed at him. Halinard had been there when she had been rescued. It was natural that she feel gratitude to the warrior. When she had noticed that Halinard was limping, the recent wound he had picked up in Liyon having not yet fully healed, Mena had taken to sitting with him in the evenings and massaging the thick slab of his thigh muscle. Coenred didn't like to admit it even to himself, but he had felt a pang of jealousy at witnessing the young woman's ministrations to Halinard. He had lain awake long into the night after watching her lie down beside the older man near the fire. Did he expect the girl to share his blankets instead? He berated himself for his weakness.

Yes, he thought, it would be good to leave the women behind, if only so that he would be separated from this temptation that had been placed before him.

"The only strife has been between Wilfrid and Wulfwyn," Coenred said. He thought Beobrand suspected how he felt about Mena, so was keen to steer the conversation away from his yearnings for the girl. "And Wulfwyn means to continue onward to Roma. I trust we will accompany her and Aelfwig all the way?"

Beobrand sighed.

"We can hardly allow her to travel alone with the boy, can we? We've seen how dangerous the roads are."

Coenred did not reply.

"Do you think Wilfrid will cause more trouble?" Beobrand asked after they had ridden on in silence for a short while.

Coenred pondered for a moment.

"I don't think he will risk Wulfwyn's ire and public humiliation again."

"Good," said Beobrand. "We've had more than enough strife on this trip."

Coenred shifted in the saddle and looked at Wilfrid who rode apart from the others. After the encounter with the bandits in the mountains he had been persuaded to remove his gold rings and the gaudy chain he liked to wear around his neck, but he still stood out from the others with his bright clothes, a gift from the monarchs of Neustria. Beobrand and the others had also been presented with fine garments of silk and linen, but favoured plain travel garb for the journey.

"I don't think he will repeat his mistake with Wulfwyn," said Coenred. "I didn't say he wouldn't cause any trouble."

Beobrand looked askance at him.

"That's what I'm afraid of. Has this journey not already been punishment enough?"

Coenred knew Beobrand was thinking about his part in the death of Oswine, King of Deira and Queen Eanflæd's cousin. It was clear to any who knew of the events surrounding the king's death that the queen, who had previously been warmly disposed towards Beobrand, had ordered him to escort Wilfrid to Roma as a form of chastisement. Beobrand had accepted the order without complaint. And Coenred knew that whatever the truth of the matter, Beobrand blamed himself just as much as anyone else for what had happened in Hunwald's hall.

Coenred looked up at the pale sky. There was not a single cloud to be seen. He groaned as he stretched his back. He ached from so much riding. Perhaps he should walk in the afternoon.

"I would say the Lord smiles on you once more, Beo," he said. "The sun shines hot and this land is pleasant." Fields lush with wheat rolled away as far as they could see. Woodland broke up the flat landscape, and lines of dark foliage marked the routes of streams and rivers. "We have left the intrigues of Frankia behind us. We are making good progress now. And you were able to rescue three women from a terrible wyrd."

Beobrand frowned. Looking over his shoulder at the waggon, he wiped sweat from his forehead.

"I feel bad that we were not able to find the other woman."

Gostanza had told them that the woman who had fled into the mountains was called Rina. She had been with the bandits before Gostanza or Mena were taken to their mountain camp, and by all accounts, she had been moonstruck. Gostanza said she would scream out and gibber, talking to herself in crazed tones. Gostanza had wondered at first if Rina was feigning madness so that the men would leave her alone, for it was true they did not seek to lie with her, fearing her rantings and worrying she might be cursed, or curse them. She had been docile enough though, and she helped prepare food, so the men kept her alive. And Mena and Gostanza came to realise Rina's mind had truly been broken. Quite what she had thought when Beobrand and the Black Shields attacked the camp, they could not imagine, but she had fled into the rocks and, no matter how much they had called for her that night and again the following morning, she did not return.

"You cannot save everyone," Coenred replied. Beobrand stiffened in the saddle. Coenred had wished to set his friend's mind at ease and he regretted his choice of words immediately. Beobrand had lost many loved ones, as had Coenred, and he knew the thegn blamed himself for every death. "But you did save Wulfwyn, Gostanza and Mena."

Beobrand said nothing.

That afternoon they rested a while in the shade of a small wood. It was hushed under the leaf canopy, sultry and humid in the sweltering summer heat. The tired travellers were glad to be out of the glare of the afternoon sun. Coenred slipped down from his horse and tottered on stiff legs to tether the animal to a rope that Grindan had already slung between two thick tree trunks. Coenred was no rider and his legs quivered. He rubbed them, bringing the blood flow back to his weary muscles.

"Shall we pray?" asked Wulfwyn. "It must be time for Nones."

Coenred looked through the trees at the sun, gauging its position. Wulfwyn was right, but his body and head ached, and a heavy lethargy had descended upon him.

"Let us rest a short while. We will pray before we leave."

"As you wish, Father," she said. He had told her not to call him that, reminding her he was no priest, but he did not have the strength to correct her again. His eyelids were heavy and his head throbbed. It was all he could do not to lie down where he stood.

Stumbling over to the far side of the clearing, he sat down with his back to the bole of a massive ash. The drone of insects drifted around him. The air was heavy with the scent of earth and leaf mould. In moments, his tiredness overcame him and he was soon asleep.

His dreams teemed with the faces of friends and loved ones who no longer walked upon middle earth. He saw Tata, not as she had been in death, but joyful and smiling. Old Abbot Fearghas stepped out of the mists of his mind, looking contented and pleased to see him. Then a figure who he thought at first was Wulfwyn stepped close. Her arms opened for an embrace. Love radiated from her. No, this was not Wulfwyn, it was his mother. He felt warm. Protected. Happily, he moved towards her, encircling his mother in his arms.

In the moment that he touched her, the warmth and light drained from the world. Gone was the lush growth of summer and the buzz of bees in the honeysuckle and wild thyme. The trees all about him were stark and bare now, chill bark rough against a dark grey winter day. His body was as cold as if he had been plunged into a frozen lake. Shuddering, he tried to pull away from his mother's arms, but she would not release him.

Panic rising within him, he strained to be free of her, but he was not strong enough. Pain sliced into his back and he realised her fingers had transformed into talons, tearing at his flesh. He jerked his face away and saw that what he had thought to be his mother was a hideous hag, eyes rheumy and black as the cold depths of a cave. Her mouth, filled with rows of sharp fangs, opened wide. The creature that held him began to chuckle, a sound of madness echoing up from deep in the back of its throat. Its breath was the foetid stink of death. The beast's maw opened wider.

Wider.

Coenred fought as hard as he could now against the foul monster's grasp. Its claws bit ever deeper, flaying the skin from him. Desperate, he screamed out for help.

Nobody came to his aid.

The mouth of the monster moved ever closer. He could not escape. A dark malevolence pervaded the place and it would never let him complete his pilgrimage to Roma. He would die here in this glade. The creature's jaws snapped down on his throat—

Coenred awoke with a start.

Sweat beaded his brow and soaked his robe. Shivering, head pounding, he pushed himself quickly to his feet. Around the clearing the travellers were dozing or sitting in small groups, talking quietly. Beobrand glanced over at him.

"Are you well?" he asked. Beobrand's voice sounded normal and there was colour and warmth in the world once more. Coenred grasped the tree behind him, relishing the reassuring scrape of the bark against his palm. It had been a bad dream. He was awake now, and yet the fiend had seemed so real. He could still feel the claws penetrating his skin, needle-sharp teeth piercing his throat.

Not trusting himself to speak without his voice cracking, Coenred raised a hand in response to Beobrand. The thegn looked at him for a heartbeat more, before turning back to his conversation with Fredegar, Halinard and Grindan.

Coenred's thoughts were settling now. Looking up at the sun, he saw he had not slept for long. Taking a deep breath, he sought to calm his racing heart. His head was throbbing and his bladder was painfully full, so he walked out of the clearing and into the dense undergrowth, not wishing to relieve himself in view of the womenfolk.

Throughout his life he had been plagued with vivid dreams and had grown accustomed to them. But this had been different. The pervasive, chilling evil that had grasped him still lingered, like the ghost image that remains in the eyes after staring at the sun. Fear yet prickled his neck, as if he was being watched. Reciting a prayer under his breath, he relieved himself into the weeds and old leaves of the wood. The unusually pungent stink of his piss turned his stomach.

As he adjusted his robe, Coenred grew certain that someone had approached him stealthily from behind. He could feel their breath on the nape of his neck. Shuddering, he spun around.

There was nobody there.

He was about to hurry back towards the others when a splash of bright red in the trees caught his sight. He hesitated. He wanted to ignore it and head back to his friends, and yet he could not turn away. He had ever been thus, frightened of the unknown, but too inquisitive to walk away from a possible discovery.

Without being aware he had made a decision he began moving slowly through the trees, peering between the trunks, trying to make out what it was he had seen. Every now and then he caught another glimpse of colour that was out of place in the muted green and brown hues of the woodland. The bright plumage of some exotic bird perhaps.

A small voice whispered to him that it might be otherworldly denizens of the forest, luring him away from his companions, drawing him into the woods so that he would become lost. Then, when night fell, the elves and goblins of the forest would fall upon him and rend his flesh from his bones, just like the creature in his nightmare.

He muttered the paternoster as he moved. He had once believed all the tales told to children, about wraiths and monsters of the wilderness, but he was a man now. Christ walked by his side and the Lord had power over all the evil that stalked middle earth. Coenred had nothing to fear.

And yet still he shivered as he moved into the densest part of the forest. Little light reached here, but Coenred found a track that led him towards the flashes of colour in the gloom. The trees were thick with ivy here, the scent of loam cloying, intoxicating. It was cooler too. The hairs on his arms rose as his skin prickled in the sudden chill.

Lances of light speared down through the canopy, illuminating the objects that he had noticed from afar. Bright strips of cloth hung from the branches of a great ash tree. Trinkets and small ornaments dangled and jangled in the dappled shade. The roots of the huge tree coiled about moss-clad rocks, delving into the earth and encircling a small, dark pond; a spring where the water pooled and then trickled away into the woodland. All about the pool hung votive offerings. Coenred saw wax formed into the shape of limbs, straw dolls resembling children. From the depths of the pond's waters gleamed coins and other items of value.

Coenred stepped back, wishing he had not given in to his insatiable appetite for knowledge. He had seen such places before. Unholy shrines, revered by the folk of the countryside. They would come to make sacrifice to their old gods in such hollows, making offerings to the sacred trees, begging the spirits of the land to bring them a strong harvest, to heal their sick, or to help them find love.

Coenred backed away from the ribbon-bedecked ash and the black pond beneath it. This was the presence that had come to him while he slept. He could feel the strength of it, making it difficult to draw breath. A malignant force older than time itself. A horror that hated the one true God and His son the Christ. A dark spirit. An evil power.

It was then that Coenred noticed that the shapes nestled in the roots were not moss-covered rocks. Dark eye-sockets stared at him and with a stab of fear, he realised the truth of what he saw.

The foot of the tree was dotted with skulls. He saw the long angular shape of horse skulls, and what might have been dogs or wolves, with their curved, sharp teeth. He was praying more loudly now, hoping that the Lord's Prayer would fend off this evil, but the words died on his lips as he spotted the domed shapes, large eyes and slit-nose cavities of human skulls. How had he mistaken them for rocks? There were so many of them; skulls of all ages, from the fragile skulls of infants to heads that seemed too large even for a tall man.

Stumbling away from the dark glade, Coenred crashed through the undergrowth. He knew the Almighty had the ultimate power over even the oldest of spirits, but no matter how much he told himself this, his terror did not abate. He ran without care, branches scratching at his face, believing that at any moment the claws of a beast would snatch at his robe, dragging him back into the depths of the forest where his skull would join those of the sacrifices made beneath the gnarled tree.

But he ran on unhindered. No hand grabbed him. Moments later he burst out of the trees and into the glade where the rest of the pilgrims were readying the horses and preparing to leave.

Coenred's breathing was ragged and he was drenched in sweat. As he looked about the clearing, he wondered at the expressions of consternation on his companions' faces. Was he the only one who felt the evil in this place?

"Are you quite well, brother?" asked Wilfrid.

Coenred snapped around to stare at the young man. He grasped at Wilfrid's linen kirtle, shaking him. He must listen. Coenred wanted to shout that they must leave. That to tarry might see them fall foul of the malevolent entity that resided there. But his voice would not come. Wilfrid was saying something, but Coenred could not make out the words. Other sounds reached him, voices raised in concern, but they were muted and muffled, as if underwater, and he could not understand them.

Was he too late?

His mind was loud with his cries. *Flee! Fly from this place!* And yet he made no sound. His warnings were trapped in his throat. His vision began to swim and blur.

Wilfrid stared at him uncomprehending.

Battling against the darkness that threatened to engulf him, Coenred searched for Beobrand. He would listen. They had been through so much together and Beobrand trusted him.

The tall warrior was striding towards him, concern on his scarred face. But still Coenred's voice would not respond to his commands and, just as Beobrand reached out to him, the world closed in and darkness swallowed up all light and sound.

Chapter 6

Beobrand leaned in close to Fredegar.
"What is it that Guduin is asking? Does he enquire about Coenred?"

Fredegar tilted his head in acknowledgement.

"That he does, lord Beobrand. I note that the tongue of the Langobards is becoming easier for your ears to hear."

Beobrand shrugged. He was surprised by how much meaning he was able to glean from the people of Langobardia. Though to do so required concentration, and the noise in the hall made it more difficult.

"I hear some words that sound familiar to me, but I doubt I will ever understand it as you do."

Fredegar grinned.

"Well, I have an advantage, lord. Your mother was not from Taurinum. Shall I tell lord Guduin that Coenred is improved?"

"Please do," Beobrand said, nodding in thanks to the portly lord who sat on a magnificently carved chair at the high table. "And thank him for his concern." He waved his hand to encompass the bustling hall. "And for this feast."

They had arrived before dark. Coenred had ridden in the waggon, where Mena had tended to him, bathing his brow with cool water and fanning his face. When he woke, Mena had seen that he drank plenty of water, and by the time they had reached Placentia and the hall of lord Guduin, Coenred was already feeling much better. He complained of a dreadful headache and was still adamant that he had sensed a terrible evil in the forest. But Mena and Gostanza said he had merely spent too long in the sun with his head uncovered. That made sense to Beobrand. The sun was painfully hot at midday and, like Cynan, Coenred, with his pale skin, suffered dreadfully. The Waelisc warrior had taken to wearing a broad-brimmed straw hat, but Coenred had not thought to protect his head and he had paid the price for his carelessness.

Still, Beobrand could not deny that seeing his friend raving and crying out about a dark evil that would slay them all had unnerved him. The others too had made the sign of the Christ rood, spitting and touching the hilts of their swords and whatever amulets and charms they wore. Beobrand had clutched the Thunor's hammer symbol he wore on a leather thong around his neck next to the ring Erchinoald had given him. He wished to believe the women were correct and Coenred's behaviour could be explained by having spent too long in the heat, but Beobrand knew the gods and old spirits walked hidden, secret paths within ancient forests. He was glad to leave the trees behind.

His heart had lifted when crenellated stone walls came into view. The sky above the walls was smudged with the pall of cooking fires. This was Placentia, just where the shepherd had said the city would be, on the southern bank of the River Po. As soon as they were in sight of the place, Gostanza had become more animated. Placentia was larger than Beobrand had expected, and with its memories of past glories present in the high walls, brick buildings, marble statues and straight cobbled streets, it reminded him of Liyon, though it was decidedly less grand than that great city.

Gostanza's eyes had sparkled with a new life as she pointed

out sights that were familiar to her. There, visible over the walls, was the tower of the basilica of Saint Antoninus, and behind a line of soaring cypresses outside the walls was the cemetery that she said had been used for countless generations. At the western gate, they had been halted by half a dozen guards. The leader, a greasy-haired man with a bulbous nose, had begun to question Fredegar, but Gostanza had snapped something. The guard had stared at her suspiciously, and Gostanza had spoken at length. Eventually, the guard had stepped aside and ushered them into the city. At Gostanza's insistence he'd even sent a man running ahead to announce their arrival.

As they'd passed through the stone-flagged market square, Gostanza had told them about the imposing bronze statue that stood there. It had been made long ago, and depicted a muscular, bearded man. Nobody remembered who the man was, she'd said, so the locals called him simply the "old one". She clearly knew this place well and directed them unerringly to Guduin's hall. It was situated at the centre of the city within a walled compound.

Beobrand swept his gaze around the hall once more, taking in the throng of people and the linen-draped boards, laden with sumptuous platters of rich meat pottage, roast guineafowl and spiced sausage.

The bones of the building were evidently ancient, brick and stone, and the roof was tiled with red clay. But inside, dark timbers lined the walls and stout wooden pillars had been erected. The columns bore intricate carvings and were painted in vibrant colours. It reminded Beobrand of the halls of Albion.

Guduin was speaking at length, and Beobrand turned his attention back to their host, not wishing to offend him by appearing uninterested in what he had to say.

He gathered that Guduin was talking about the food and that it had been prepared not for Beobrand and his party, but for his other distinguished guests. Beobrand glanced to Guduin's right. The man who sat there returned his gaze, but offered him no smile. The man's unblemished skin was the warm tone of seasoned oak. His hair was black and long, the ringlets oiled and falling to his shoulders in what looked to Beobrand a style that would have better suited a woman than a man.

The man had been introduced as Deusdedi, envoy of Olúmpios, most holy Exarchos of Ravenna. Beobrand wasn't certain what that meant exactly. That he was a man of considerable power was evident not just from his sumptuous attire and the jewelled rings that adorned his fingers, nor even the large retinue of aides and crimson-cloaked guards who accompanied him. What truly spoke of his influence was the way in which Guduin, lord of Placentia and clearly a man of import himself, showed him respect and had provided a feast befitting a king.

Wilfrid had instantly sensed where the power resided in the hall and had managed to seat himself near Deusdedi. Wilfrid, as clever as he was ambitious, was able to converse with the emissary using one of the languages he knew.

Fredegar's voice interrupted Beobrand's thoughts.

"Guduin says you are fortunate to have arrived at the same time as the messenger from the Exarchatus. God has blessed him indeed to have two such distinguished guests in his hall on the same night."

Beobrand smiled at the lord of the hall. Guduin nodded in return, his long beard almost dipping in the gravy from a dish of stew on the table. He was perhaps a dozen years Beobrand's senior, broad of girth as one who enjoys feasting more than fighting. Soft now perhaps, contented and fattened by years of rich food, but Beobrand noted Guduin's hands were large and strong, his forearms scarred with the memories of battles past.

"The honour is mine," he said.

Fredegar translated Beobrand's words and Guduin's response.

"Nonsense. You are a noble guest and I thank you for bringing

Gostanza back to us. We had believed the poor girl dead long ago. My wife never truly got over losing her."

Guduin's wife, a woman of about Gostanza's age, had been overjoyed to see the servant. The two women had wept as they embraced. They had retired from the hall, chattering loudly through their tears. Mena had gone with them, swept along on the wave of emotion of the reunion. Shortly after they had left the hall, a plain-faced, serious-looking maid had returned to order refreshments to be taken to her lady's quarters. Beobrand recognised her as the servant who had been attending the lady of the hall when they'd arrived. Following the surprise return of Gostanza, the maidservant had looked bewildered and on the verge of tears. Beobrand felt sorry for her. No doubt she had been secure in her role and now saw how she would be quickly replaced by her mistress's trusted confidante.

"We were in the right place at the right time," he said. "I am glad we were able to rescue Gostanza, and the other girl, Mena. Perhaps you could find a space in your household for her too."

Guduin listened as Fredegar relayed Beobrand's words, then waved his hand dismissively.

"Of course, of course." He made the sign of the Christ cross. "You did a good deed, no doubt. But I thank the Lord Almighty for guiding you to the lair of those bandits. You say you brought down God's vengeance on them all?"

"We killed every one of them."

Guduin nodded.

"That was well done," he said. Beobrand understood that, without the need for Fredegar to translate, and nodded grimly. Guduin continued talking and now Beobrand lost the thread of the man's meaning.

He looked to Fredegar.

"Lord Guduin says those men were as wolves. There could be no mercy for such men."

"Wolf-heads," Beobrand said. "That is what we call such men. Outside of the law of man. Nithings."

Guduin glanced over to where Deusdedi conversed quietly with Wilfrid. He lowered his voice slightly, though not perhaps as much as he thought, given the quantity of wine he had imbibed.

Fredegar relayed Guduin's meaning, also speaking more quietly now.

"We are warriors, you and I. We know there is nothing to be done with animals like that but slay them. I attend Mass and take the Eucharist as God decrees, but I never understood the idea of offering the other cheek when one has been struck. In that I sometimes think our forebears had the right of it. If a man crosses you, face him with steel. Take his life and he will not wrong you again and others will think twice before standing against you."

Beobrand was about to reply when Deusdedi broke off from his conversation with Wilfrid and, turning towards Guduin, uttered a few words in a sneering tone. Guduin stiffened. Those sitting nearby fell quiet and a hush rippled across the room until nobody spoke.

Guduin, beard bristling and cheeks flushed, scowled. Beobrand noticed the man's meaty hands were bunched into fists on his lap. The lord of the hall took a deep breath, controlling himself with an effort before speaking. When he did it was in a soft, conciliatory voice Beobrand had not expected.

To Beobrand's surprise, the emissary from the Exarchatus let out a barking laugh at the bearded lord's response. Guduin flinched as if slapped.

"What are they saying?" Beobrand hissed to Fredegar.

The Frankish interpreter was pale.

"The emissary accuses lord Guduin and his people of not being true believers. He says they are heretics."

"Heretics?"

Fredegar searched for an explanation.

"They do not worship God in the right way."

Guduin had raised his hands and ordered his servants to pour more wine, clearly in an effort to smooth over the disturbance caused by his guest's rude words. He lowered his gaze while Deusdedi mocked him. The emissary turned back to Wilfrid and muttered something under his breath. Wilfrid laughed. Guduin's face was crimson. He took a deep draught from his goblet of wine, then looked back to Beobrand apologetically. He spoke briefly and Fredegar translated.

"The Exarchatus and Langobardia disagree on some of the finer points of the teachings in the good book." He shrugged. "The messenger is here under truce," he added by way of explanation for his actions. He was embarrassed that a guest had spoken to him thus in his own hall without reproach.

Beobrand looked at Deusdedi. The oil lamp light gleamed in his shiny black hair. Wilfrid said something quietly, and the emissary sniggered in return with a knowing nod.

Without warning, the fire of Beobrand's anger, which he usually kept banked deep within him, roared into a raging inferno.

"Tell that greased cockscomb to apologise for his rudeness to our host," he said, his voice as hard and sharp as splinters of granite.

Fredegar was aghast.

"Lord Beobrand," he hissed, "I cannot. He is the envoy of the Exarchatus of Ravenna. You do not understand."

"I care not who he is. He could be Woden himself. He eats and drinks from Guduin's table and has no right to insult him. Tell him what I said, or I will go to where he is sitting and make my displeasure understood in a more painful manner."

A pair of burly guards stood behind Deusdedi. It would be no easy matter to reach the man. Beobrand wondered why he needed such protection. Perhaps he frequently insulted those he dined with.

"Lord Beobrand," said Wilfrid, having overheard. "This man is the emissary of the Exarchatus. He is a powerful man. It would not do to make an enemy of him. It would behove you better to befriend him."

Beobrand shook his head, suddenly weary.

"Did you learn nothing in Frankia, boy? There are more important things than power."

Deusdedi spoke. Wilfrid translated.

"He asks why you are angry."

"Tell him I do not like to see our host insulted."

"I do not insult lord Guduin," Deusdedi said, using Wilfrid to voice his words. "I merely state the truth. The people of Langobardia are heretics and barbarians. Much like the men of Albion, it would seem, apart from a few notable exceptions like young Wilfrid here." The young novice at least had sense enough to appear embarrassed when he translated this last sentiment.

Beobrand stared at Deusdedi. The man met his gaze with a twisted smirk. Beobrand placed his palms on the table. His muscles bunched and flexed.

Guduin touched his arm and gave an almost imperceptible shake of his head. The man's meaning was clear. Guduin did not wish him to take this further.

Beobrand took a deep breath, drained his goblet. That was enough wine for one night. The drink must be stronger than he had realised. It was folly to allow his ire to get the better of him like this. He was unsure why Deusdedi's words had infuriated him so. Perhaps it was that the man reminded him of Dalfinus and Annemund, the *comes* and bishop of Liyon. Not in any physical sense. The man's body and features were unlike either of those brothers, but there was something about his demeanour and the way he addressed those around him, so certain of his own worth and secure that he was right, that brought them to mind. The fact that Wilfrid had gravitated to the man so readily had only served to reinforce that impression, and had further angered Beobrand. Wilfrid's actions in Liyon had ultimately led to the deaths of Gram and Attor, and the wound of their loss was still raw and far from healed.

"I am sorry," Beobrand whispered to Guduin, trusting that Fredegar would translate.

Setting aside his goblet, Beobrand rose quickly to stand towering over the men seated at the high table.

The red-cloaked guards behind Deusdedi tensed, readying themselves to protect their master. Deusdedi himself seemed momentarily nervous. Beobrand was pleased to see fear flicker across the man's handsome features.

"Remember," Deusdedi stammered, Wilfrid translating his words, "I am here under the banner of truce."

Beobrand fixed him with a hard stare.

"I swore no truce with you."

He waited for Wilfrid to convey his meaning. Deusdedi's throat bobbed convulsively as he swallowed nervously. Beobrand offered him a wolfish grin and made a sudden movement as if he planned to launch himself at the emissary of the Exarchatus. Deusdedi's guards stepped to intercept Beobrand and Deusdedi gave such a start he almost fell from his chair.

But Beobrand did not attack. Without waiting for an answer, he turned away from the cowering Deusdedi and made his way out of the hall.

Stepping into the warm summer darkness, he drew in a long breath. Quick footsteps followed behind him. He listened, wary of danger, but he did not turn back. He recognised the sound of that step and had expected it. Beobrand smiled to himself in the dark, striding past the door wardens and into the night, certain that Cynan would follow.

Chapter 7

Cynan shook his head at the memory.

"I thought he was going to leap over the benches and attack the man," he said.

Coenred, still pale-faced and wan, was shocked at what he heard.

"By all that is holy, Beo," he said, "you cannot make an enemy of every man you meet."

"He seems to make a good effort of doing so," Cynan said.

"But this is the emissary for the Exarchatus," replied Coenred.

"So everyone keeps saying," replied Beobrand. "Not that I know what that is. Besides, I don't only make enemies. I was friendly enough with lord Guduin. He seems a good man."

The three of them were seated in a small room in a solid-looking stone building that lay the other side of a cobbled courtyard, just across from the hall. The place was lit by a single oil lamp. By the flickering light Cynan could make out a simple pallet and a wooden chest that doubled for a table beside the bed. Servants had brought Coenred food and drink. A plate covered in breadcrumbs rested beside a jug of water and a wooden cup.

Beobrand and Cynan occupied the two stools in the room. Coenred was sitting up in the bed, his back propped against the whitewashed stone wall.

"The Exarchatus is like a kingdom," Coenred said. "It lies south of Langobardia, between here and Roma."

"Who rules that kingdom?"

"The Exarchos. He is the governor of the territory."

"He is the king?"

"No, he governs in the name of the emperor."

"The emperor of Roma?" asked Cynan. He had heard of such a man in tales.

"The emperor of *Nova Roma*," Coenred said. "New Roma."

"Not Roma then?" Beobrand said. He sounded as if his head pained him. Cynan was not surprised. It had been a long day, this was confusing and the wine had been strong.

"No," said Coenred, smiling, "not the city of Roma that we are travelling to. New Roma is another name for the city of Constantinus, *Constantinopolis*. It lies across the sea. To the east. They say it is the greatest and richest city in all the world."

Beobrand reached for the jug of water and filled the cup.

"And this Exarchatus is a vassal state of *Nova Roma*?"

"In a manner of speaking."

"And the people of the Exarchatus are not friends of the people of Langobardia?"

Coenred shrugged.

"How friendly are any neighbouring kingdoms?"

Beobrand raised an eyebrow, conceding this was a good point.

"Both kingdoms worship your Christ god."

"Yes, they do."

"But Deusdedi spoke with disdain of the way in which the people of Langobardia worship God."

"Ah, yes," Coenred said, holding out his hand for the water. Beobrand refilled the single cup and handed it to him. "I recall some of this. The men of Langobardia believe in the teachings of

Arius, whereas such is deemed heresy by the Patriarch of *Nova Roma*."

"The Patriarch?"

"The head of the Church."

"Is that not the—" Beobrand hesitated, trying to remember the correct term. "The Pontifex Maximus? I thought the high bishop of Roma was the head of the Christ followers."

Coenred blew out a long breath and drank some water.

"That matter is complicated. The Patriarch of Constantinopolis and the Pontifex of Roma do not always agree on the finer points of the scriptures. Though I believe they both agree that the teachings of Arius are heresy."

"What are those teachings? And what makes them heresy?" asked Cynan.

"The short answer is that, as I understand it, Arius said that Jesu was created by God, but was not God himself."

"Why is that a problem?"

"Most Christ followers believe that Jesu and God the father are part of the same divine being."

"I don't understand."

Coenred sighed.

"I am not sure I do either. And I don't think I have the strength to try to explain it fully. My head is pounding."

"We should let you sleep," Cynan said.

"Indeed." Beobrand took Coenred's hand. "I am glad to see you feeling better. You scared me." He grinned, his teeth flashing in the lamplight. "And you know that is not such an easy thing."

"I will wear a hat tomorrow," Coenred promised. "And drink plenty of water."

"You have had no further bad dreams?"

"I'm not so sure they were dreams," Coenred said, his voice not much louder than a whisper. "It felt so real."

"Whatever it was," said Beobrand, "we have left that grove far behind us and we will not rest there on our return journey. I know better than to ignore such visions. We have seen too much together, you and I."

Beobrand squeezed Coenred's hand and stood. Cynan watched as a silent understanding passed between the two men. He wondered what they were remembering. They had known one another for several years before Beobrand had rescued Cynan from a life of thralldom in Mercia.

Coenred lay back down on the pallet.

"No doubt Deusdedi would say belief in such things is heresy."

Cynan rose.

"I think perhaps Deusdedi sees heresy in many things," he said. "Rest well, Coenred."

At the doorway, Beobrand paused.

"You know, I can never understand you Christ followers," he said. "You speak of peace, love and forgiveness, and yet you cannot even agree with each other. The Langobards are heretics; the wrong sort of Christ follower. And you tell me even the Bishop of Roma and the Patriarch of Constantinopolis are in dispute." He shook his head and sighed. "It is madness. Woden and the old gods are simpler. All they want is sacrifice and tribute. That I can understand."

Chapter 8

Coenred awoke before dawn. He was attuned to life in the minster on Lindisfarena and once his body had recovered from the heat he found it difficult to remain abed.

He rose, splashed the last of the water from the jug onto his face, then made his way outside. The sun was just colouring the eastern horizon. It was still cool, the sky clear of clouds, but it would be another hot day. In the distance, a cockerel crowed, welcoming the approaching sunrise. A dog barked somewhere far off.

Across the courtyard, the shadowed shape of a servant came into view. It was a young woman carrying two buckets suspended from a yoke across her shoulders. She ignored Coenred and disappeared into a building from where sounds of activity drifted.

"Are you feeling better, Father?"

The voice startled him. It was very close and for a fleeting moment he was gripped by fear. Was he dreaming once more? Had the evil spirit from the forest crept inside the walls of Placentia during the night?

He turned to face the voice and instantly felt foolish. It was Wulfwyn, looking fresh-faced and rested. Beside her stood the boy Aelfwig.

"Much better," he said. "Thank you." It was true, he realised. His headache had vanished in the night. In the dim wolf-light of the dawn, Coenred saw that Wulfwyn's waggon was in the courtyard and the horse, Osweald, was already hitched.

"I do not wish to keep lord Beobrand and the others waiting," Wulfwyn said, as if he had questioned her.

"Beobrand has given his word to escort you and your son to Roma," Coenred said, suspecting there was more to her early morning preparations. "He will not abandon you."

"He thinks we are a burden," she said with a sigh.

"Nonsense," said Coenred, though he knew she was right. "We are all happy to have you and Aelfwig with us. Now, if you can leave the waggon unattended for a short while, would you wish to accompany me to the church? I was going to say Prime there."

Already there was more movement in the courtyard. Hostlers were bringing out horses and people were talking quietly. The clatter of cooking utensils was joined by the scent of food being prepared for the breaking of the night's fast.

Wulfwyn hesitated.

"There is plenty of time," Coenred reassured her. "And they will not leave without us, I promise you."

"Very well," Wulfwyn said at last. "It would be a nice change to pray in a church."

They made their way down the hill through the awakening settlement. Wulfwyn held Aelfwig's hand, and, as ever, Coenred was impressed with how self-assured the boy was in spite of his blindness.

The church was empty of people but filled with shadows. The sky was lighter now, the sun about to crest the horizon, but little illumination found its way through the small windows. The building was made of stone and it was cool inside.

Kneeling on the cold flagstones, Coenred led them in prayer, the familiar words of Prime comforting him and soothing away the remnants of the horrific visions that had beset him in the forest. When they had finished, he stood, feeling lighter of spirit and filled with a new vigour. Wulfwyn too seemed less anxious and as they stepped from the church into the golden light of the sunrise, it seemed to Coenred that some of the worry had fallen from her features. She offered him a small smile. Unnerved by her radiance, he turned away and looked up the hill.

When they arrived back at the hall, Deusdedi and his entourage were leaving. Deusdedi swept past, mounted on a white stallion. Some of the warriors stared hungrily at the widow beside Coenred as they rode by. Wulfwyn seemed not to notice, but Coenred was pleased when the party from the Exarchatus had filed out of the courtyard.

"We wondered where you had got to," said Cynan, coming across the cobbles towards them, stepping around the steaming piles of fresh manure. Behind him, their horses were being harnessed by the busy stable hands. "There is some food set aside for you inside." He nodded back towards the hall. "But do not tarry. We are leaving as soon as the horses are saddled."

By the time they had eaten bread and cheese, and drunk some watered wine, Beobrand and the others were mounted.

Wulfwyn and Aelfwig climbed into their waggon. Bleddyn led Coenred's mare over to him and handed him the reins.

Thanking him, Coenred climbed into the saddle with Bleddyn's aid. He was acutely aware of the stares of all those gathered in the courtyard as he struggled to take his seat. Finally, cheeks flushed and hot, he was mounted and ready to go.

Beobrand, via Fredegar, thanked Guduin again for his hospitality. The older man bowed graciously.

"You are always welcome in my hall, lord Beobrand," he said. "And I pray that if you ever return we will be able to feast without the likes of Deusdedi spoiling our appetite."

Beobrand listened as Fredegar translated his words, then chuckled.

"It would take more than that worm to lessen the warmth of your hall, or to sour your good wine. I look forward to our next meeting."

And with that, he turned his horse's head to the south and trotted out of the courtyard. The air was loud with the hooves of the steeds and pack animals, the creak and jangle of harness, and the rumble of the waggon.

Coenred waited for the men before him to ride away, content as ever to follow along at the rear of the group. Before he could nudge his horse into motion, a touch on his ankle drew his attention. Looking down he saw it was Mena, her eyes bright and wide as she stared up at him. In her hands she held the wide-brimmed straw hat he had agreed to wear. So early in the morning it was not yet hot and he had forgotten that he had left the hat in the room where he'd slept. He glanced up at the sky. It was a pure, pale blue with only the thinnest wisps of cloud far off to the north. It would be a hot day, with many to follow before they reached Roma. He would have regretted leaving the hat behind.

"Thank you," he said, accepting the hat from Mena. Her slender fingers caressed his hand. She said something as he placed the hat upon his head, but he did not understand her. "Thank you," he repeated. "God be with you." He made the sign of the rood.

"Come on, Coenred," said a loud voice close to him. It was Halinard, sitting easily on a large grey gelding. "We have a long road ahead of us. No time to dally with Mena, much as you might like to."

Coenred felt his face grow hot again. He nodded once more to Mena, then kicked his mare's flanks, getting the animal moving behind the others. Looking over his shoulder he saw that Halinard had reined in his own mount. He was leaning out of his saddle, conversing quietly with Mena. Coenred felt afresh the stab of jealousy at the bond between the Frankish warrior and the girl. He looked away, ashamed of himself.

After a short time, Halinard trotted up beside him.

"I think we are both going to miss that girl," he said in his thickly accented Anglisc.

Coenred did not reply. Halinard was right, but he did not wish to admit it. He would miss Mena, but as they rode south towards the spectres of distant hills that loomed far on the edge of sight, he was also relieved that the girl, and the temptation she embodied, was behind him.

Chapter 9

Beobrand was glad to be on the road once more. The encounter with Deusdedi had stirred dark emotions within him, memories from Frankia that were too fresh to examine. He had slept fitfully in Guduin's hall. He could feel his resentment and anger simmering deep inside him and he knew from bitter experience it would take little to blow the embers of his ire into terrible, raging life again. Once he would have revelled in that fury, seeking out a way to vent his anger, picking a fight with one of the guards from the Exarchatus perhaps. Or even confronting the envoy himself, as he almost had. He was older now. Mayhap he was wiser too, he pondered. His mission was to reach Roma safely with Wilfrid and then return northward. He had allowed himself to become embroiled in the intrigues of Frankia, he would not make the same mistake again. Whatever he thought of Deusdedi, the man and his obsession with the perceived heresy of others was no concern of his.

Beobrand had awoken feeling lighter, as if the weight of his anger had been lifted in the night. He felt rested despite his disturbed slumber and was pleased to find Coenred recovered and ready to travel. He used some of the Frankish silver to pay Guduin for provisions, which he had loaded onto Wulfwyn's waggon and strapped to the backs of the pack mules.

Guduin waved them off with a cheerful smile and honest words of friendship. Beobrand liked the bearded man. He spoke plainly and without deception. He had offered to resupply Beobrand's party at no cost, but Beobrand would not hear of it. He was certain the offer was made in good faith, but while the lord was wealthy, the cost of the feast would not have been insignificant. When Beobrand had insisted, pressing a pouch of silver into the older man's callused hand, he knew at once he had made the right decision.

"You might not be a good Christ follower," Guduin said with a wink, "but you are more generous than that bastard from the Exarchatus. Despite all his silks and jewels and his belief he is as holy as a saint, he keeps his purse strings tied as tight as a virgin's cunny."

When asked how far they were from Roma, Guduin had said with good weather and a fair wind, a man on horseback could make the journey in under a week. Encumbered as they were, he thought a fortnight would be more likely.

Two weeks until they reached their destination. Beobrand thought of this as they rode, allowing his horse's swaying gait and the warm sunshine to lull him into a doze. He wondered how long he would need to remain in the city before he could begin the journey home. A week? Two? Then how long would the return trip take them? It was not yet midsummer. With luck they could be in Albion again before the autumn storms. Even then, they would have been away for close to a year.

Beobrand grew maudlin as they trudged up into the forested hills. He missed Ardith and thought of how old her child would be. Did he have a grandson or granddaughter? He had hoped Coenred might bring news of this, but his friend had not known.

They stayed that first night in a steading Guduin had told them of. The master of the place, a tall, gangly man with a long face, was Guduin's cousin and he welcomed them warmly enough. His welcome became more effusive when Beobrand gave him some hack silver, and the man grinned, ordering his wide-hipped wife to bring out a clay jug of their finest wine.

Beobrand was careful not to drink too much, but the wine was good, as was the food and the company. Guduin's cousin was quick to laugh and Beobrand was pleased that his own morose mood had left him. He vowed he would do what he could to keep his ill humour at bay. Dwelling on the past and fretting about the future would make him a miserable travelling companion, and he might as well try to enjoy the warm weather and rich food of this region.

As they moved up into the mountains, they became wary of bandits. Beobrand ordered Cynan and Halinard to scout ahead. Guduin's cousin had warned them that brigands often attacked lonely travellers and even merchants, but he doubted there were any bands brave enough to confront the men from Albion, who were mounted, well-armed and looked more than capable of defending themselves.

They slept under the stars shortly after passing the highest point of the mountain. These peaks were not as high as those that separated Langobardia from Burgundia, but still it was cold up there, and snow yet clung to deep crevices where the warmth of the sun barely reached. Beobrand ordered the men to keep watch, but he allowed them to light a fire. If there were thieves up in these mountains watching the roads, their existence would already be known. There was no need for their night's rest to be uncomfortable.

They spent a pleasant enough night. The men played knucklebones and told riddles. Aelfwig sat with them, laughing and joking with the warriors. The boy had a sharp wit and the men had quickly taken to him. Wulfwyn seemed pleased that her son was accepted by the men and she sat some way off from them, watching their interaction with her boy. When the riddles became too bawdy for her liking, she stepped in, admonishing Grindan, who she appeared to think was the serious one of Beobrand's gesithas and should know better.

For her part, Wulfwyn brought something different to the group. The food she prepared was tasty and wholesome, and she appeared genuinely happy to serve the men. Halinard, who usually cooked for them, saw the task as a chore and was glad of the respite from the work.

Wilfrid had got over the embarrassment of Wulfwyn's rejection and once again prayed morning, noon and evening with Coenred and the widow. Ingwald, Bleddyn and Grindan would sometimes join them.

They fell into an easy routine and as they moved down from the wooded slopes to the fertile plains beyond, the pilgrims' mood was buoyed somewhat. The recent deaths of loved ones were still too recent for them to be truly content, but a sense of comfortable camaraderie had enveloped them that made the journey agreeable.

Leaving the mountains behind, Beobrand was happy that Guduin's cousin had been proven right and they had not been attacked. They had passed through the shaded oak and beech forests and over the mountain passes without incident. And now they travelled through more densely populated lands. Farms and hamlets dotted the landscape and Beobrand marvelled whenever he spied one of the stone buildings constructed by the men of Roma generations before. In Albion, to find such buildings in good repair was rare, but here they were often still inhabited, and had no doubt been so since they were originally erected centuries earlier.

They came to a most memorable ancient construction four days into their journey. The mountains were now vast shadows on the horizon behind them and the road was often busy with merchants, traders and all manner of travellers. They had crossed fertile, well-irrigated land, through fields thick with rye and millet, and found themselves travelling alongside a wide river. In these lowlands the sun beat down hotter than ever, and the previous day they had all decided to rise before the dawn and to travel until midday. When the sun was at its zenith they would find shade to rest and wait out the hottest part of the day before travelling on some more until making camp or finding a settlement in which to spend the night.

And so it was that they were walking in the early dawn glow of the day, while mist yet curled over the waters of the meandering river. The world was still and nobody spoke, not even Aelfwig who loved to chatter with anybody who would listen and quite often with those who did not wish to. They had been awake only a short while and it was as if they were all still dreaming, the land about them washed in the gold of the summer dawn and the air hazed with the mist from the river. The road for as far as Beobrand could see was empty.

A large stand of ash trees grew beside the river and as they approached a haunting melody came to them. It was the music of a pipe, lilting and trilling, soaring and blending with the chorus of birdsong from the trees. There was something otherworldly about this tune.

Beobrand looked at the faces of his companions. They all felt it too. They were smiling and wide-eyed, such was the music's beauty. He glanced at Coenred, wondering if, after his encounter in the forest a few days earlier, he might say this was the tune of some evil spirit, but the monk was smiling too. There was no fear on his face.

Beobrand spurred his horse on, wondering who the musician might be. As he rounded a bend in the river, a wonderful sight came into view, causing his breath to catch in his throat. He reined in his horse, content to watch and not wishing to interrupt the music or shatter the quiet spell cast by the melody and the scene.

From the trees rose stone columns, impossibly tall to Beobrand's eyes. Atop them rested a finely sculpted and decorated stone pediment. The trunks and branches of the trees grew between the pillars of the portico, giving the impression the building had grown with the wood. But as he looked more closely, Beobrand saw that part of the roof of the once magnificent building had collapsed. It must have fallen a long time ago, for the trees had taken root in the broken marble steps and now grew as tall as the roof itself. Statues of men and women posed on plinths and peered out from niches, clothed in ivy and nettles.

At the foot of the ancient temple's weed-clogged steps sat a man. In his hands he held a long reed flute which he played with effortless ease, the music at once earth-bound and heavenly. At the man's feet grazed half a dozen deer. Crows, jays, blackbirds and doves pecked at the long grass, oblivious or uncaring of the man's presence. The beasts were close enough for him to reach out and touch if such had been his desire, and yet he merely watched them and played his doleful tune.

As Beobrand watched, the sun rose over the mountains, turning the morning mist into cobwebs of spun gold and further enhancing the sensation that what he was witnessing was not real, but part of a dream. The others halted around him and they all stood, transfixed, while the man played his flute and the animals ate calmly at his feet.

Wilfrid started to speak, but Eadgard hissed at him. Moving his mount close, he shook his head and grasped the novice's reins. Wilfrid fell silent, abashed.

"What is it, Mother?" said Aelfwig, his child's voice loud in the hush.

Noticing them for the first time, the man on the steps stopped playing and looked up. Instantly, the deer ceased cropping at the grass. Raising their heads, they sniffed the air. Then, seeing the travellers on the road, as fast as thought the animals bolted into the forest with a flash of white rumps and bounding legs. The birds took notice of the deer and flapped quickly into the air, away from this new danger.

The man on the steps stood and stretched, yawning widely, as if awakening from slumber. He was slim and muscular with short-cropped white hair atop a weathered face. He wore a plain linen robe, tied at his waist with a rough hemp cord. The wrinkles around his eyes spoke of someone accustomed to smiling. He reinforced that impression by grinning broadly, walking down the crumbling steps and making his way towards them, arms outstretched as if he meant to embrace them all.

He said something in a musical voice. Fredegar moved his horse to the front of the group and replied.

"He says his name is Nardo," Fredegar said. "And that the weather is good for travelling."

"It will be too hot soon," Beobrand said.

Fredegar translated and Nardo laughed, a warm, welcoming sound.

"That is what the shade of a tree is for," Nardo replied, speaking through Fredegar. "And the cool waters of the river."

"Alas, we cannot spend all day sitting in the shade playing the flute," Beobrand said.

Nardo shrugged.

"This is what is wrong with the world," he mused. "Men find time for all the wrong things. I play the flute here every morning and can think of nothing more important."

"What is this place?" Beobrand said, looking up at the towering columns and the magnificent statues with their foliage robes.

"It was once a temple of Mithras, the bull-slayer. Now it is home to the animals of the forest."

"Is he a monk?" Beobrand asked Fredegar.

When Nardo heard Fredegar's translation he chuckled and shook his head.

"I am just a man who likes to play his flute to the deer and the birds. My father played for them here, and his father before him."

"And do you have a son who will play the flute after you?"

Nardo's expression turned wistful.

"Ah, times are changing," he said, his tone sorrowful. "My son longed for the noise and excitement of the city. I have not seen him for years."

"I have heard it said sons are given to test us," said Beobrand, thinking of Octa.

"Perhaps," Nardo said. "But if so, I care nothing for this test. I would just like to have my son home with me again. It matters not to me now if he plays the flute or no." He sighed. "It seemed important once."

"Maybe he will return," Beobrand said. "One day."

Nardo nodded sadly.

"Maybe," he said, and walked back to the temple steps. His plaintive melody followed them as they rode past. Beobrand turned in his saddle when they were some distance away and saw Nardo still sitting cross-legged on the cracked marble, the grass before him once again thronged with birds and deer.

The following day, as they approached the town of Luca, with its imposing walls and large stone buildings, they passed a group of pilgrims, all dour-faced and walking in silent contemplation.

Their leader was a silver-haired man whose skinny legs looked too weak to support even his meagre weight. His bare feet were dusty and smeared with blood from cuts and scratches. Beobrand noticed that none of the pilgrims wore shoes. Their faces were sombre, their shoulders bent as they leant on their staffs, looking down at the rock-strewn path before them, marking the distance to Roma one painful step at a time.

Coenred dismounted and made the pilgrims understand that he wished to treat their lacerated feet. He spoke to them in Latin, which they understood well enough. There was some debate and they talked at length.

"What are they saying?" Beobrand asked, impatient to move on. They would reach Luca soon. They had heard tell of the place from other travellers and Beobrand was looking forward to a night under a roof, some good food and a cup or two of wine.

"Coenred wishes to clean and bandage their feet," said Wilfrid, his disdain for such an idea clear in his tone. "They believe the pain is part of their penance."

"Penance?" queried Beobrand.

"A task they have undertaken to atone for their sins. Like a sort of punishment."

Beobrand scowled. This whole trip felt like penance.

"Come, Coenred," Beobrand said. "Leave them to their torment and let us ride to the town."

"No," said Coenred. "It may be their penance to walk barefoot all the way to Roma, but God is good and has placed me in their path for a reason. I am skilled at healing, and I cannot ride by without aiding these God-fearing people."

Beobrand recognised that tone and knew his friend's stubbornness. They would not be leaving until Coenred had done what he believed to be his duty. Beobrand dismounted and ordered Eadgard to collect some firewood from a nearby copse, and for Grindan to light a fire. The pilgrims might not know it yet, but they too would lose this argument with Coenred.

Beobrand was right. Shortly afterwards, the pilgrims acquiesced to the monk's request, allowing him to clean their feet with freshly boiled water, to apply foul-smelling salve he carried with him in a small earthenware jar, and then to bandage them in clean strips of linen cut from one of Wulfwyn's dresses. She was content to offer her help and to sacrifice the garment, while Beobrand and the warriors sprawled drowsily in the shade of the tall pines that grew beside the road.

Wilfrid sat apart watching Coenred and Wulfwyn with a mixture of envy and consternation on his youthful features. Gods, how Beobrand wished they had never embarked on this journey. Wilfrid irked them all and Beobrand knew he was not alone in wanting to be done with the young man.

Reminding himself of his previous promise, he pushed such pointless thoughts from his mind, instead imagining the food they would eat in Luca. That morning a drover had told them of a place in the town that served salt fish on a toasted flatbread. The way he had described it, his face lighting up and his eyes growing dreamy and distant, had made Beobrand and the others excited to try this delicacy. It was true that the journey had been long and at times fraught with danger, but these last few days had been a pleasant routine. Their bellies were always full, they had not been cold or wet, and they had suffered no further attacks.

As they waited for Coenred and Wulfwyn to finish with the pilgrims, a small band of travellers, of four men and four women, came along the road heading north from Luca. They carried leather bags on their backs and leaned on long walking staves. One of them had a cut lip and a swollen eye. It was clear he had sustained the injury recently for the bruise had not yet grown dark.

Coenred offered to look at his injuries, but the man declined. Beobrand thought there was little to be done anyway. It was not serious and the man would heal soon enough. The group were anxious to be on their way, but Fredegar spoke to them briefly. They were pilgrims from Frankia, heading homeward after having spent several days in Roma.

They spoke in hurried, gasping breaths, their agitation clear. The women's eyes were red, their cheeks tear-streaked. As they hurried off, Halinard told Beobrand what they had said.

"They were robbed."

"On the road?" asked Beobrand.

"In Luca. They spoke of the place as if every street was lined with devils."

"We'd best be careful," Beobrand said.

"Aren't we always?" Halinard asked, with a lopsided smile.

Leaving the pilgrims hobbling along behind them, still in pain, but much improved, thanks to Coenred and Wulfwyn, they reached the walls of Luca just as the sun was setting over the distant mountains.

Fredegar asked a man lounging near the gate for directions to the inn the drover had mentioned. The man waved his hand, rattling off a stream of instructions. They headed into the shadowed streets, following Fredegar, who seemed confident. After a few missed turnings, they eventually found what they were looking for. The twisted streets all seemed to spiral out from the old stone Roman arena. It was smaller than the great amphitheatre of Liyon, but it was still a formidable structure, with some of the terraced seating yet intact. Their destination was situated on one side of the arena. The smell of toasting bread and boiling fish was thick in the evening warmth, the stone of the building golden in the last rays of the sun.

Beobrand felt as though his stomach was shrivelling as they passed beneath an archway and onto the floor of the amphitheatre itself. Recent events in Liyon washed back into his mind. The arena was busy. Beobrand looked about at the inquisitive faces of the locals who peered at the mounted group and thought of the warnings of the pilgrims on the road. He remained wary, but the master of the inn, a friendly, round-cheeked, pot-bellied bald fellow, was not one to allow anybody to stay sombre for long. He called for boys to see to the travellers' animals, then proceeded to bring out platter after platter of delicious food. Beobrand did not allow himself to drink too much, but as the evening wore on, the good food and the wine did their job, and he felt himself relax.

In the morning, Beobrand strolled around the shaded arena while the others finished breaking their fast and readying the horses. As always, he marvelled at the ingenuity of the men who had built such massive edifices, buildings that remained centuries after their builders had vanished from the world. As a young man he had thought that tales of his battle-skill and exploits might live after him, captured in scops' songs. A warrior's renown was worthy of pride. But now, looking up at the arched openings high above him, the rising sun spearing down into the shadowed interior of this ancient arena, he wondered if perhaps this was not a more worthy legacy to leave behind. Not to be immortalised in song, but in stone.

Coenred came and stood for a time beside Beobrand, taking in the building and admiring its cunning construction.

"This place is a lasting reminder of the greatness and evil of man," he said.

Beobrand thought of its original use. Men, women and beasts slain for entertainment. He shuddered to recall Dalfinus' hunt in Liyon.

"I suppose it is," he said. "Such beauty in the name of death."

Coenred moved closer. He tapped Nægling's pommel where it jutted from the sword's scabbard hanging from a baldric over Beobrand's shoulder. "Like so many things made by man," he said. "Beauty and death combined."

Beobrand looked down at the sword. It was a thing of exquisite craftsmanship, gold and garnets interlocked in a delicate pattern. Without needing to draw it from the tooled leather scabbard, he could picture the patterned blade. It too was beautiful, like the skin of a serpent, or the waves of the Whale Road.

Coenred said no more. He walked back to the others, leaving Beobrand alone with his thoughts.

They left Luca shortly afterwards and continued on their way. The sun was still hot, but the inhabitants of the farms and houses they passed were always happy to sell them a jug or two of wine, salty ham and dried sausages, and to provide them with somewhere shady to rest in the hottest part of the day, or overnight. Despite their worries about Luca, they had not fallen foul of cut-purses, brigands or mountebanks. They had eaten well and the food and wine was every bit as good as the drover had led them to believe. The days after Luca were warm, sultry and peaceful and Beobrand began to believe they might reach Roma without any further incident.

Thus, when the armed men stepped out from behind the trees, arrows nocked and aimed at them, Beobrand rebuked himself for tempting the gods with his complacency.

Chapter 10

As soon as Cynan saw the men, he readied himself for a fight. There were ten of them, enough that they might be brave enough to confront the riders. And they had chosen their location well, stepping out from the shade of a stand of beech and fir trees situated at the top of a long, steep incline.

The horses were blowing, the riders sweating and tired from the morning in the saddle. Luca was six days behind them and the journey had been easy since then. This was the highest point of the road, crossing a band of hills, dotted with large lakes. Glancing down to the south, Cynan could see the flash of sunlight on another body of water. They had hoped to be down from these hills and able to camp beside the cool lake that night. Cynan had been looking forward to bathing and washing off some of the dust and sweat from the road. But the chance of a wash and another peaceful night under the heavens was blocked by the men who spread out across the path.

Cynan took them in quickly with a warrior's eye. They were young men, sinewy and darkly tanned. They did not wear armour, but four of them bore hunting bows and he had no reason to doubt they knew how to use them. The archers were positioned in pairs either side of the road, on one side atop a steep slope strewn with boulders, and on the other amongst the trunks of the trees, but with a view of the path. Six other men were spread out across the road. All of them carried a weapon. The two largest men held stout wooden cudgels, three others had long knives on their belts, hands resting on the hilts. One man, whom Cynan assumed was the leader of the band, was armed with a sword. The swordsman was tall and whip-thin with a shock of unruly brown hair and stubble on his cheeks that almost concealed the blemish of a long scar.

The leader stepped forward, holding up his hand and snapping a curt command. Cynan watched the man's eyes. They were pale and, despite his apparent ease and relaxed posture, they flicked and darted from left to right, taking in the riders and the waggon that still lumbered up the slope behind them. He was evaluating the men from Albion in much the same way that Cynan had assessed the bandits. What he saw were six mounted men with hard faces and swords at their sides. Eadgard, the largest of the Black Shields, was helping Wulfwyn with the waggon. Wilfrid, Coenred and Fredegar had the look of soft men. They did not carry weapons, nor were they armoured and Cynan sensed the bandit dismiss them as no threat. Whatever danger he perceived from the other riders, and only a fool would have believed them to be anything other than warriors, he evidently did not believe them to be too menacing to rob. Cynan thought the man's assessment might well be right. They were outnumbered by a force armed with bows. And none of the Bernicians was armoured. It was much too hot to wear heavy iron-knit shirts. Their byrnies, helms and shields were stowed on pack animals or in the waggon.

"I can imagine what he wants," said Beobrand, reining in his horse, "but translate his words nonetheless, Fredegar." There was no fear in Beobrand's tone. To Cynan's ears he sounded more weary, or perhaps even disappointed at the interruption to their journey.

"He says you are to pay for the right to use this road," Fredegar said.

"Is that so?"

"It is what he says, lord."

Beobrand looked about him. He raised his eyebrows at Cynan.

"And how much does he think we should pay?" Beobrand asked Fredegar.

Fredegar exchanged a few words with the bandit leader.

"He says show him what you have of value and he will decide."

"And if I refuse?"

"He says he will kill us and take *all* we have."

Cynan was watching Beobrand closely and saw his shoulders tense almost imperceptibly. The lord of Ubbanford stared at the bandit, then he scanned the other men spread across the road, taking in the archers on either side. Finally making up his mind, he nodded and held up his hands.

"Tell him there will be no need for any killing."

"Lord?" Fredegar sounded uncertain.

"Tell him we will pay," said Beobrand. "Cynan, Grindan. Fetch the largest chest from the waggon. Leave it close to me and far from the whoresons on the road."

Cynan hesitated.

"Do as I say," snapped Beobrand, then as if still speaking of the chest, he pointed at the waggon that was even then just pulling to a halt. "Give no sign of what I am saying, but be ready to rush those bastard archers. Grindan, take the ones in the rocks. Cynan, with me. The rest of you, do what you can."

Cynan nodded and slipped from the saddle. Grindan dismounted too and followed him towards the waggon.

"What is this?" said Eadgard, stepping from behind the waggon where he had been pushing. He was soaked with sweat, his hair plastered to his forehead, his kirtle dark.

"Give nothing away, brother," Grindan said in a quiet, even voice. "But be ready. Wulfwyn, when the fighting starts, hide with Aelfwig in the back of the waggon."

Wulfwyn's eyes were wide as she took in the men blocking their path.

"What is it, Mother?" said Aelfwig.

She hushed the boy and whispered quietly to him.

Eadgard was a huge man, and his face bore the marks of many fights. People often mistook him for slow or stupid. He was neither. He had listened to his brother and without a word he had slipped around behind the waggon where he could not be seen. There, out of sight of the bandits, he was already pulling a shield and his large axe from the pile of gear.

The bandit leader shouted something.

"He is growing impatient," said Fredegar, nervousness in his voice. "He says if you make him wait much longer, he will let his men have the woman."

"Come on," shouted Beobrand, "do not keep the man waiting."

Cynan and Grindan hefted the chest. It was heavy.

"Do you think he'll get us out of this?" hissed Grindan as they carried the box between them with difficulty.

"With some of his luck," whispered Cynan. He gave another furtive look at the archers. "And if you run fast enough. It's going to be a close one." Cynan smiled thinly. "But by Tiw's cock, I wouldn't wish to be that big-mouthed bastard with the sword."

Grindan's eyes narrowed and he nodded. They both knew how Beobrand felt about men who threatened women.

They spoke no more as they approached Beobrand. Danger crackled in the air like lightning in a storm. They were unsure what would occur next, but they had fought countless times beside the thegn. They trusted him with their lives, as he trusted them.

"Put it there," Beobrand said, taking a step closer to the bandits and pointing at the ground. There was no sign of anxiety in his voice. Beobrand and his gesithas had overcome worse odds in the past, and yet Cynan thought it unwise to dismiss the threat posed by these bandits. The Black Shields were formidable foes, but an arrow would pierce a strong warrior just as easily as a weak one.

The bandit leader was protesting, signalling for them to carry the chest to him.

"Put it there and step back," said Beobrand, ignoring the man's protests.

Cynan felt exposed. His skin prickled. He imagined arrows singing through the warm air and burying themselves in his flesh. Grindan and he placed the sturdy box on the packed earth.

The brigand was still complaining loudly. Fredegar began to translate, but Beobrand cut him off.

"Tell him if he wants his payment, he can take it, but I will not carry it for him too." He dismounted, handing his horse's reins to Fredegar. Stooping, Beobrand opened the chest. The summer sun gleamed on the silver heaped within. The bandits gasped.

The leader's eyes widened and he licked his lips. He barked out an order.

"He says for you to get back," Fredegar said.

"Tell him not to take it all," Beobrand said, moving away from the chest and ushering Grindan and Cynan with him. Fredegar had already distanced himself. He relayed Beobrand's words. The bandit leader merely laughed and sent four of his men forward, two towards the open chest and its shining contents, the two cudgel-wielding brutes flanking them. Nobody spoke now. The bandits watched their companions walk towards the coffer and its treasure. They were open-mouthed and hushed. Cynan thought they had probably never before seen such a hoard of silver. Such wealth was beguiling. It could make men mad.

Or distract them.

"Ready to run, Grindan?" whispered Beobrand, his voice so low Cynan was barely sure he had heard him. "Cynan, you're with me."

Cynan did not answer. Neither did Grindan. Beobrand knew their worth. Whatever he planned, they would be ready.

The bandits reached the chest. The pair of smaller men bent to examine the contents, the two club carriers staring balefully at Beobrand and the others. Beobrand met their gaze unblinking. His hands were at his side and, several paces away as he was and under the watchful eyes of the archers, he surely posed no threat. The two burly bandits glowered at him for several heartbeats, while their companions muttered and whistled at what they saw within the box.

Beobrand did not move until the bandits' eyes were inevitably drawn down to the precious metal. In that instant, he burst into a flurry of motion so sudden that even Cynan was surprised.

Before anyone could react, Beobrand produced the seax that hung from the back of his belt. With deadly force and unerring accuracy he threw the heavy knife at the tallest of the cudgel carriers. The sharp iron blade punched deep into his chest.

The next nearest bandit was bending over, greedily staring at the contents of the box. Without hesitation, Beobrand sprang forward with the speed that made him such a deadly enemy. Dragging Nægling from its scabbard as he moved, he covered the distance in a heartbeat, hacking the sword-blade into the man's skull. The bandit collapsed face-first into the treasure, overturning the box and sending the silver across the road in a glittering scatter.

Cynan had been ready for action, but was still taken aback by the speed of his lord's attack. He rushed forward now, the merest moment behind Beobrand. Aware that Beobrand was fighting, and that Grindan had sprinted off to the left, Cynan kept his focus on the man with the large club before him. The bandit was thickset, with arms like the knotted trunks of trees. He was fast too, and raised his club, ready to meet Cynan. The man was skilled with the sturdy wooden weapon, that much was clear to Cynan in his stance and fluid movements. Against most men, he would surely have been a terrifying opponent, but Cynan was no fearful peasant to be brushed aside.

Cynan parried the wooden weapon easily, though the man's power caused him to grunt in surprise. Splinters flew as his blade bit into the cudgel, the shock of the blow thrumming along his arm. Still, the stocky bandit with his oaken club was no match for Cynan, warrior of Bernicia, bearing a polished patterned blade. Twisting his wrist, he stepped to one side and flicked out with his sword. The sharp steel flashed, tearing out the man's throat in a spray of blood. Cynan danced back out of reach of the dying man, looking for his next adversary.

The hill was utter confusion now as men reacted to the sudden violence. The bandit leader was screaming at his men. He was hurrying forward, sword in hand and bellowing at the archers. Cynan could not understand the man's words, but his sentiment was clear. The bowmen were to bring down these men who dared stand against them.

Cynan watched in dismay as the archers on the slope drew back their bow strings. Grindan was rushing up the slope. Eadgard, red-faced and panting, was lumbering up after his brother, shield and axe in hand. The first bowman loosed in haste, perhaps torn between shooting at Beobrand and the men storming up the hill towards him. Whatever the reason, his aim was off and the arrow drilled into the hard earth near the overturned coffer and the dying man, whose blood was pumping over the spilt silver.

The second archer did not flinch, maybe gauging he still had time before Grindan could reach him. Sighting down the arrow shaft directly at Beobrand, he let fly. The afternoon was clear, with little wind, and the archer's aim was true. The arrow sped towards Beobrand. It happened so quickly there was nothing Cynan could do. He did not even have time to call out a warning.

Cynan gasped. He had thought he would see the sharp arrowhead strike his hlaford, but instead he once more witnessed Beobrand's uncanny speed and what many deemed his luck. The first man he had hit with his seax still stood, clawing at the knife in his chest and staggering as if drunk. As quick as thought, Beobrand grabbed him, dragging him close into a desperate embrace. The man stiffened as the arrow lanced into his back. Beobrand wrenched his seax from the man's body, shoving him away savagely and turning to confront the last of the four men who had been sent for the chest.

"Go," he shouted. "Get the archers in the trees."

The bandit leader was closing, flanked by another young man carrying a wicked-looking dagger. Cynan hesitated. He did not wish to leave his lord to face three men, especially exposed as he was to the archers.

"Go!" repeated Beobrand, sweeping his blood-drenched blade in front of the closest adversary, sending him stepping back.

Ingwald and Bleddyn were running forward now, swords in their hands. Halinard, limping, came on as fast as he could behind them. Beobrand would not be outnumbered for long. Cynan made his decision.

"Bleddyn," he shouted, "with me."

He ran into the woods to the right, hearing Bleddyn close behind. Ahead he saw a flash of movement and an arrow thudded into the bole of a fir tree near his head. Cynan understood then why Beobrand had insisted on placing the chest where he had. Its location had prevented the archers from getting a clear shot.

Another arrow whistled past and Cynan dodged to the right, then cut back to the left, not slowing his pace, relying on his speed and movement to keep him safe. Bleddyn, crashing through the undergrowth close by, let out a curse.

"Are you hit?" Cynan called out.

"Just a scratch," Bleddyn panted.

They rushed on towards the position of the archers, shouting their battle-cry as they went.

"Death! Death!"

No more arrows came and after a short while Cynan slowed to a halt, leaning against the trunk of a beech and drawing in great lungfuls of the cooler air beneath the trees. Bleddyn came skidding up next to him. A deep cut scored his cheek and blood ran down his face. His eyes shone with battle-rage.

Cynan peered further into the forest, holding up a hand for quiet. Behind them they could hear shouting, but it was impossible to make out what was being said or by whom. He could see no sign of movement ahead of them, but the sound of men hurrying through the foliage was clear. The archers were already far off and receding quickly.

"We won't catch them," he said. "They know this land."

Bleddyn reached up and touched his face, bringing his fingers back slick with blood.

"Pity," he said, "I was going to take great pleasure in ramming their bows where this warm sun's light never reaches."

Cynan laughed at that.

"It is no surprise to me that they fled like cravens," Bleddyn said, following Cynan as he turned back towards the road.

"And why is that?"

"We are formidable, of course. I sometimes wonder if this is because we were both once thralls." He rubbed the blood from his fingers onto his breeches. "Or perhaps the opposite is true."

"I do not understand your meaning," Cynan said, not liking to be reminded of his time as a slave.

Bleddyn gave Cynan a lopsided smirk.

"I wonder if we are such skilled warriors because we were once thralls, forbidden to bear arms. Now we must make up for lost time. The other possibility is that we Waelisc were not permitted to wield weapons because they knew we were such formidable warriors."

Cynan shook his head, but returned Bleddyn's smile. They stepped out from the shade of the woods and into the bright afternoon sunshine. There was no fighting now.

On the road, Wilfrid was busy collecting the spilt silver, plucking the pieces from the blood pooling and congealing beneath the man Beobrand had killed. Flies already buzzed and flitted over the bodies, settling in the gore. Some way from the three corpses near the chest, lay a fourth body. Cynan and Bleddyn walked over and looked down at it. It was the leader of the bandits, his face pale, eyes wide and looking shocked that death had come to him so quickly on this sunny day.

"The archers?" Beobrand asked.

"Ran away," said Bleddyn. "Too scared to face two Waelisc men."

"It seems none of them had much of a taste for fighting," Beobrand said. He prodded the leader with his foot. "This one had some courage, but it was misguided. He thought he might best me with a sword."

"He will not make that mistake again," said Cynan. "Any losses?"

"No, but Eadgard caught an arrow."

Near the waggon, Grindan looked on as Coenred tended to his brother. An arrow jutted from the big man's left shoulder. He groaned as Coenred used a sharp knife to cut his flesh and free the arrow's metal head. Blood flowed freely down Eadgard's arm and Coenred called to Wulfwyn for her aid. She hurried over, bringing freshly torn strips of cloth to be used as bandages.

"At this rate she will have no dresses left," said Beobrand. He pointed to Bleddyn's cheek. "This savage Waelisc warrior bears the only other wound. These bandits were of some danger with bow and arrow, it seems, but less so when forced to fight like men. Go and have Coenred do something for that cut."

Bleddyn made to walk towards the waggon when a sudden shouting brought him to a halt. They all turned towards the sound. There, standing atop a large boulder on the slope where the archers had been, stood Fredegar. His back to them, he was screaming abuse and insults into the distance at the retreating bandits. To the Black Shields' amusement, the Frankish envoy seemed drunk with their victory and he raved and yelled, spitting and screaming. They could only imagine the insults he uttered, and they all laughed when, in a paroxysm of rage, he lowered his breeches and turned his bare arse in the direction of the robbers, slapping his buttocks like a drum to punctuate his furious diatribe.

Wulfwyn blushed to see Fredegar's antics, looking away quickly to continue helping Coenred with Eadgard's wound.

"Perhaps at times," murmured Bleddyn to Cynan, "Aelfwig's blindness is a blessing."

Chapter 11

The day after the encounter with the bandits, they arrived in Sutri, another ancient settlement of pale limestone buildings with red clay tile roofs jumbled inside sturdy walls. As they passed through the town's northern gate, Coenred turned in his saddle and looked back at the hills.

Since the attempted robbery in those hills, they had all been tense. After dispatching the four bandits and scattering the rest, they had camped beside the lake, but they had been unable to relax. Beobrand had set double guards through the night and they had been relieved when the sun rose, shining on the waters of the lake as brightly as the silver in the chest. It felt good to reach Sutri's walls and Coenred welcomed the sense of safety they brought.

A barefoot boy with a dirt-smudged face stepped out from where he had been loitering in the shade of the wall. Fredegar spoke briefly to the urchin, then handed him a small silver coin. The boy stared at the coin for a moment, eyes wide, then he nodded gravely and beckoned for the travellers to follow him.

"He'll take us to a place to stay," Fredegar said. "He says it is good."

Eadgard, astride his large horse, ducked under the gateway.

"If it serves drink and meat, I say lead on."

Nobody disagreed and they followed the young boy, who could have been no more than ten years old, through the narrow alleys and lanes. It was mid-afternoon and the town was quiet, the inhabitants drowsing in the afternoon heat. When the sun lowered and the temperature dropped, Coenred was sure the people of the town would emerge from their houses to conduct their business. The settlement would be filled with life and noise until the cloak of night drew about it. They had seen the same pattern in Luca and the other settlements they had passed through. The afternoon sun made it too hot to do much more than doze.

The men were content to do just that. Fredegar haggled for a short while with the obsequious master of the inn the boy led them to, but soon they had agreed a price and the middle-aged innkeeper brought them dry-salted ham, cheese and slightly stale bread, along with jugs of passable wine.

The building was stone, with thick walls, and two stories high. There was a walled courtyard and a small stable, within which a few horses already stood in the dusty shadows. No doubt the inn had been a palace once; a villa for a wealthy Roman. Now it provided lodging for travellers to and from the holy city.

Inside, the main hall was shaded, the shutters half-closed against the heat of the day. The floor was flagged with hard stone, which also helped keep the temperature bearable. The innkeeper bowed apologetically and explained that most of them would have to sleep in the main room. There were three rooms on the floor above the hall. One was for him and his family, another was occupied by three silk merchants, who were evidently out of the inn on their business in Sutri. The third room was small and Beobrand insisted that Wulfwyn and Aelfwig should have it. The widow protested a polite amount, but acquiesced quickly enough to make it clear she was pleased to have the room away from the warriors.

For his part, Beobrand didn't mind having to throw down a blanket in the inn's hall. They had slept in many less comfortable surroundings. He ordered the men to carry in everything of value from the waggon. They placed the chest of treasure in the corner furthest from the inn's entrance and positioned the benches and tables around it to further prevent anyone from accessing the silver.

As the afternoon wore on, Wulfwyn and her son retired to their room. The men snoozed or conversed in hushed whispers.

Coenred sat quietly for a time, but he found that the food and drink had revived him somewhat. And yet, despite the shutters and the stone floor, the inn was still dreadfully hot. Sweat trickled down his spine and he stood up, restless and uncomfortable.

Sensing movement in the hall, the innkeeper shuffled in from the kitchen, raising his eyebrows inquisitively.

"Is there a church nearby?" Coenred asked him in a low voice. He spoke in Latin, which he was pleased to note most of the people they now encountered used to communicate. The language they spoke was perhaps not as florid and precise as what Coenred had learnt from the study of classical texts, but he could comprehend it and make himself understood well enough.

The innkeeper smiled broadly.

"There is indeed a true wonder of a church in Sutri," he said, clapping his hands excitedly. "It is built into the cliffs at the south of the town. *The Madonna of the birth*. Carved from the very rock itself. A marvel. You must visit."

"Is it cool?" Coenred asked, fanning himself with his large hat.

The man laughed.

"It is summer. Nowhere is cool. But it is not as hot as the street. And probably cooler than even my fine inn."

Coenred yearned for solitude, to be away from his companions for a while, and the thought of praying in the quiet cool of a cave appealed. But when Beobrand saw him preparing to leave, he called him back.

"You cannot travel alone," he said. "Grindan will go with you. Bleddyn too."

"I would see this cave church too," said Wilfrid, rising from where he had been sitting in a corner by himself.

Coenred sighed. So much for tranquillity. But Beobrand was right. However peaceful this land appeared in the still of the afternoon, they had found danger lurking wherever they went.

Outside the inn's gate, they found the same urchin who had guided them from the city walls. After Fredegar's silver coin, the boy was keen to lead them to the church in the hope of more riches.

It didn't take long to get there, and Coenred could only agree with the innkeeper: the church was cooler than outside and it was an impressive place. Several ancient tombs, cut into the rock, dotted the cliffs. And one of the elliptical amphitheatres, so common across the lands the men of Roma had once ruled, had been hewn from the rock.

Like the tombs, the church was carved into the cliff face. An arched doorway led into a long grotto, lined with openings along one side that let in the light. A colourful fresco depicting the Virgin Maria, the swaddled baby Jesu in her arms, decorated the wall at the end of the church. Upon the altar stood a golden cross.

Coenred knelt and prayed before it. The others joined him. Coenred was pleased that Wilfrid seemed subdued by the serenity of the place. He made none of his scathing comments, apparently content to worship the Lord in peace.

When they rose to return to the inn, Grindan looked back at the ornate gilded rood on the altar.

"I can scarcely believe nobody has stolen that," he said. "With that much gold a man could live in comfort the rest of his days."

"The people hereabouts fear God," replied Wilfrid haughtily. "They would not risk eternal damnation by stealing from the church."

When they returned to the inn, the sun was setting and they were all looking forward to resting after the taxing days they had spent on the road. The innkeeper had already brought out more pitchers of wine, and from the volume of the laughter and conversations that came from the hall when they arrived, Coenred judged the warriors had already drunk ample. He knew better than to comment though, and he resigned himself to a long evening filled with the raucous chatter, singing and riddling of the Black Shields.

The night was young and the men still relatively sober when the sound of screams and a scuffle reached them from outside in the street. Coenred had just dipped a slice of fresh bread into a pungent fish sauce and was in the process of lifting it to his lips. At the anguished cries from outside, he halted, shocked and appalled at what he was hearing.

Beobrand did not pause. He leapt to his feet and rushed out into the darkness, followed by Cynan, Halinard and the rest of the men, who overturned benches and knocked cups and plates from the boards in their haste.

Coenred set down the bread and looked over at Wulfwyn. They could hear shouts and the sounds of fighting now. He wanted nothing more than to run in the opposite direction, or at least to remain inside, away from the violence taking place in the night. Shaking his head, Coenred rose. He knew himself well enough to know he would not stay where it was safe. His insatiable curiosity would not allow it, and he found his attention dragged to the open door.

"Stay here with Aelfwig," he said, then, almost reluctantly, he slowly made his way outside.

The gate to the courtyard was open and Coenred could see the shapes of the men fighting in the street. By the time he reached the edge of the yard, the fight was almost over. It was gloomy in the narrow lane, but there was still enough light in the sky for Coenred to survey the road and ascertain what was happening.

As he watched, Beobrand sent a bone-crunching punch into a man's face, splitting his lip and sending streams of blood down his chin. The man's face was already bloody and now his head lolled. Beobrand hit him again, this time in the stomach, and the man would have collapsed if he had not been held upright by Grindan.

Against the far wall of the lane, Eadgard was hammering blows into another man. The huge warrior, uncaring of the arrow wound to his shoulder, had pinned his opponent against the wall with a massive hand around his neck, while he slammed his meaty right fist over and over into the man's bloody face.

"How do you like that?" he bellowed. "Pick a fight with a man next time, you worm!"

A third man was curled into a ball on the muck-strewn cobbles. He struggled to protect himself from the vicious kicks Cynan was delivering first to his midriff, then, sickeningly, to his face.

Fredegar stood watching beside the inn's gate.

"They were forcing themselves on those girls," he said, nodding to where two women cowered in the shadows. They were both slender and young. The dress of one of them had been torn, and she held the material tightly around her. The other one's face was bleeding and she was sobbing.

Beobrand landed another solid punch into the face of the man

Grindan was holding. The man's nose crunched and his head snapped to the side.

"Beo," Coenred said, "you'll kill him."

These men had chosen the wrong place to attempt to violate women, Coenred thought.

"Perhaps I should at that," Beobrand snarled, raising his blood-smeared fist.

"They are done," Coenred said. His stomach churned at the violence that had erupted so suddenly. "I can see these men are guilty, but surely they do not deserve death."

Beobrand trembled, such was his rage. His knuckles were split and covered in blood, but he was oblivious of the pain.

"Such men do not deserve to live," he said.

"No, Beobrand," Coenred replied, forcing calm into his tone, "that is not the way. They should be made to pay the weregild for what they have done. Silver to the women's kin would benefit them more than their deaths."

"Would you feel thus if they had attacked your kin?" Beobrand hissed. "Your wife? Or your sister?"

The bitter words stabbed at Coenred, but he drew in a deep breath.

"You know I have never condoned such violence," he said, keeping his voice soft. "It should be for the law to decide their fate. And for God."

For several heartbeats Beobrand did not move. Then, shaking his head as if to clear it, he stepped back and looked about him.

"Enough!" he shouted. "Bring them into the courtyard where we can see them better. And Coenred, tell those women they have nothing to fear from us. Then fetch Wulfwyn."

Coenred hesitated, wondering if perhaps Beobrand meant to kill the men as soon as he left. He immediately dismissed the thought. If Beobrand had meant to slay them, Coenred's protestations would not have stayed his hand.

He called Wulfwyn out to the courtyard and shouted at the innkeeper to heat some water. They would need clean cloths and bandages too.

Wulfwyn came out, Aelfwig by her side. They were followed by the innkeeper carrying an oil lamp. As the light fell on the unconscious men the gesithas had dumped in the middle of the yard, the innkeeper let out a cry.

"What have you done?" he exclaimed. "These men are my guests! They have paid for their room in advance. And now you have killed them."

When Fredegar translated his words, Beobrand scoffed.

"Tell him they'll live, but if they have any sense, they will be far from here come morning. I do not wish to see their faces again." He turned to Wulfwyn and Coenred. "Tell the women to come in out of the street. Wulfwyn, would you tend to their injuries and perhaps help them with their clothing?"

"Of course, lord," Wulfwyn said.

The girls remained in the entrance to the inn's yard, as if frightened to enter. Wulfwyn and Coenred went to them and he translated Beobrand's assertion that they meant them no harm.

The young women were still pale and clearly shaken, but they had composed themselves. One of them had a bruise swelling on her cheek. After listening, the prettier and younger of the two women shook her head.

"Please thank your lord," she said, "but we need no further assistance."

On hearing this, Wulfwyn beckoned them into the yard.

"At least let us clean your cuts. And I have a needle and yarn. I can mend that dress."

Coenred translated and the bruised woman, not much more than a girl he saw now by the faint light of the lamp, shook her head again.

"No, no," she said, a firmness in her voice that surprised

Coenred. "We must leave. We will be safe. Those men are strangers. None of the people of Sutri will harm us."

When Coenred told Beobrand what they were saying, the tall thegn strode forward. The women stared at him, eyes wide, but without fear. The younger one squared her shoulders and met his blue gaze almost defiantly. She repeated that she thanked him, but needed nothing further.

Beobrand appraised her for a time. It was obvious she had made up her mind. He turned back into the yard. Wulfwyn and Coenred followed his gaze.

"Grindan, Halinard," Beobrand called, "accompany these girls and see that no further ill befalls them."

When they turned back, the two women were already hurrying away. Beobrand called out, but they did not slow their pace. He made to follow them, but Wulfwyn placed a hand on his arm.

"It may be for the best," she said. "Would you have Grindan and Halinard confronted with the girls' kin when they arrive home in the dark, bruised and bleeding?"

Beobrand watched the two slender forms disappear into the night. With a frown, he gave Wulfwyn a small nod.

"Perhaps you are right," he said, then stalked back through the gate into the yard.

He did not halt there. Ignoring the innkeeper's angry shouts, he crossed the courtyard and entered the inn, calling for Grindan and Halinard to follow him.

Moments later, the three of them returned, arms filled with bags, sacks, an assortment of clothing and a bolt of fine blue silk. These items they threw down beside the insensate forms of the men they had beaten. The innkeeper continued to protest angrily.

Beobrand held up a hand for silence.

"Tell him we will take the empty room," he said to Coenred. "It has a stout oak door and can only be accessed from the narrow stairs. It will be a perfect place to store our silver." He smiled. "You can share the room with Fredegar. You might even get some peace that way."

Coenred began to translate, surprised by the turn of events, but also warmed that Beobrand should think of his comfort, even in such a moment. The innkeeper was not pleased, and was making that very clear to Coenred. Beobrand touched the monk's shoulder.

"I will give him more silver for the room. All he has to do is serve us more wine and stop his complaining. My patience is all but spent. Tell him that."

The innkeeper's face blanched as he looked at the three bloodied merchants slumped and unmoving in his yard. He bit back his retorts, swallowing his anger, and swept his gaze across the stern-faced northerners who had inflicted such a terrible beating on the men. With a nod, he ceased his griping at the change in lodging arrangements and hurried back inside.

Beobrand and the warriors returned to their drinking with renewed vigour. Beobrand told them not to drink too much, but the men had been energised by the fight. They needed to release some of the tension from the road. Beating the silk merchants had gone some way towards achieving that. Wine would help too.

Coenred finished eating, lost in his thoughts, while the men around him grew more strident by the moment. He watched Beobrand drain another cup, then, not heeding his own command for moderation, calling for more wine. The innkeeper obliged, quickly refilling any empty cups. Beobrand's trembling had stopped and now he was listening, red-faced and sweating, to one of Grindan's riddles. Wulfwyn and Aelfwig had gone to their room soon after the fight, and without their presence in the hall, the men's riddles, songs and jests were becoming increasingly ribald.

Beobrand leant back and laughed at a pithy comment from Bleddyn. Coenred wondered whether he would ever understand his friend. The fight had left the monk unnerved and on edge. Frowning, he watched as Beobrand slapped the table, making the plates and cups rattle.

No, thought Coenred, Beobrand had always been a mystery to him, and would surely remain so for the rest of their lives. Just when it had seemed they would be able to rest after the tiring days on the road, Beobrand had once again found himself in a confrontation that ended in blows and blood. Coenred smiled without humour at the thought. Beobrand would never change. He knew that. Beobrand had done what he always did. He had heard someone in distress and had rushed to their aid. Coenred abhorred violence, but he could not deny Beobrand's bravery. Nor could he deny that, despite frequently disagreeing with his friend's methods, Beobrand was often right to intervene. The results of his actions were evident. He had rescued Gostanza, Mena and Wulfwyn from the brigands in the mountains. This evening he had freed another pair of women from violation in the alleyway beside the inn.

It was not Coenred's place to pass judgement on Beobrand, any more than it was the thegn of Ubbanford's to judge the merchants for their actions. That was better left to God. Stifling a yawn, Coenred pushed himself to his feet.

"Rest well," said Beobrand, raising his cup to Coenred.

"God willing," Coenred replied. "At least some good came of you beating those merchants."

Beobrand chuckled.

"You do not approve of my actions, old friend," he said, "but I do not see you complaining about the bed you now have upstairs."

"Who am I to complain?" said Coenred with a grin. "Or to question the Almighty's plan?"

Chapter 12

Coenred lay on the mattress and stared up at the whitewashed ceiling. It was swelteringly hot in the small room. Thin moonlight from the small window pooled on the ceiling. If there was any breeze in Sutri, none of it reached the inn.

He had imagined sleep would come easily, but he had lain there for a long time, his thoughts roiling and churning, keeping slumber at bay. He went over the attack on the two girls and the subsequent beating of the silk merchants. Briefly he wondered what caused men to behave that way, but he knew the answers well enough. They were bolstered by being in a group and emboldened with drink. On seeing the young women, they had believed themselves strong enough to take what their base passions desired without consequence. That had proven a terrible miscalculation on their part, and yet Coenred wondered how many such assaults were happening in that very moment, in other alleyways and halls all across middle earth. Such things were commonplace and men like Beobrand were few.

When he had tired of that saddening subject, disgusted at the weakness of men who should know better, Coenred's thoughts turned to that afternoon. Though still awake, his eyes barely registered the dim splash of silver moonlight above him as he thought about the church and the golden cross. He had to agree with Grindan. It was remarkable that men's fear for their souls kept the treasure safe. Would that men's conscience was as strong when it came to all sins committed against others. His mind wandered back to the attack on the hill and the four men who had been slain there. And for what? A few handfuls of silver.

When he had left Albion he had not imagined this journey would be so perilous. He realised now how naive he had been. When had the world around him not held danger? He only felt truly safe and at ease in the minster on Lindisfarena. He took some comfort from the knowledge they were almost at Roma. He was looking forward to witnessing the sights there, to standing in the steps of martyrs and saints. To seeing their tombs and praying to them, where they might listen to his petitions.

From below came the sound of the men's chatter, every now and then punctuated with raucous laughter. Coenred reached for the jug of water the innkeeper had given him. He longed for sleep, but with the noise from below and the stifling warmth in the room, it seemed a long way off. He wiped sweat from his brow and poured himself a cup of water. Perhaps he should have remained below with the others, but he truly wanted to be alone.

Ever since his strange vision in the forest, he had been apprehensive, unsure of himself in this strange land with these violent men. He did not dislike them, and he loved Beobrand as a brother, but he had long since had his fill of killing and bloodshed. He had forgotten how death seemed to follow in Beobrand's wake, sweeping all those who travelled with him along in its waves of violence. He knew it was unfair to blame recent events on his friend. Beobrand could not be held responsible for the actions of others. And without Beo and his warriors, Coenred knew he might well be dead. It had ever been thus with him and Beobrand. They were connected by their shared past, yet separated by the paths they had chosen in life. Coenred knew the world needed men like Beobrand; those who would defend the weak. That understanding did not make him enjoy witnessing it.

Splashing some of the water from the jug on his face, Coenred lay back on the thin mattress. His face was cool for a time, but quickly, the water warmed and dried and he once more lay in a sheen of sweat, listening to the merriment in the main hall beneath his room.

Coenred's mind was finally drifting, sleep at last beginning to wrap its soft arms about him, when steps on the stairs pulled him awake. There was a gentle knock on the door. With a sigh, he rose and drew back the locking bar. Fredegar staggered in, the warm glow of lamplight spilling into the room with him. The noise from the men below was louder than ever. Coenred leaned out of the door.

"I'm trying to sleep up here!" he shouted down the stairs.

This was met with an uproarious barrage of drunken laughter. Coenred slammed the door in disgust, replacing the bar and flopping back onto his bed.

Fredegar was already lying on the other pallet.

"Surely they will sleep soon," Coenred said. "They must be weary."

Fredegar's reply was a loud snore. The man had awoken him only to fall asleep instantly. Now Coenred would need to contend not only with the heat and the noise from the hall, but with the Frankish envoy's snores too.

Coenred recited the paternoster quietly to himself a couple of times to calm his anger at Fredegar. After that, he moved on to the Psalms. Some way through the fourth Psalm, his weariness caught up with him, overpowering the cloying heat and the noise, and he fell into a deep sleep.

★

The moment Coenred opened his eyes he knew something was wrong. The room was dark, but something had disturbed his sleep. A movement perhaps. The creak of a floorboard, the rustle of clothing. He held his breath. There was a presence there. He shuddered, fearing the entity from the forest had returned to haunt his slumber. A voice he did not recognise whispered in the darkness.

There was someone in the room. Not an evil spirit, but someone who should not be there. He was certain of it. But how could that be? The door was barred. Had Fredegar opened it?

Coenred lay as still as he could, listening to the inky dark, his senses alert.

The scrape of a foot. A sibilant whisper. There were two of them. Moving stealthily on the other side of the room. Intruders. Despite the heat, Coenred was suddenly cold. He knew he should cry out; warn Beobrand and the others that they were in danger. But still he could not move. He was sure that if he made a sound the men would strike him dead where he lay.

He could smell their sweat, hear their murmured whispers as they crept carefully about the room. It was as if… In a flash of clarity he knew what the strangers were doing. They were searching. As the realisation struck him, so Fredegar awoke.

"What are you doing?" he said, his words slurred with sleep and wine. "Who are—"

A quick movement, brutally savage, cut off Fredegar's questions. He struggled against the unseen assailants, making no further sound beyond guttural grunts. Coenred listened with his mouth open, motionless in his terror. At last the struggle ended. Fredegar let out a moan, at once gurgling and breathy, rattling deep in his throat.

In the stillness, the sound of heavy breathing was loud. The sound did not issue from Fredegar.

Unable to stand it any longer, Coenred let out a small cry of fear. He must alert the others. Beobrand and his warriors were his only chance of surviving through the night. He drew in a deep breath, ready to scream for help, but he had left it too late. Something hard struck him behind his right ear, sending him tumbling out of the bed and onto the rough timber floor.

Groaning, he tried to push himself to his knees, but something heavy weighed him down, preventing him. Another blow to the head dazed him. A hand grabbed a fistful of his hair, yanking his head painfully up from the floor. The cold steel of a blade pressed against Coenred's throat.

His strength fled. So this is where he would die. He would have loved to have seen Roma before the end. But there was nothing more he could do now than commend his soul to the Lord and accept his death. He closed his eyes and prayed.

One of the voices, louder now, but still quiet, hissed something Coenred could not make out. A moment later the knife at his neck was withdrawn. He breathed a sigh of relief. Perhaps God meant to spare him after all. Then, without warning, a sudden burst of pain engulfed him, and he knew no more.

Chapter 13

Beobrand's knuckles hurt. He sat up. Wincing, he looked at his hands. They were swollen, and blood caked his fingers. That large whoreson's teeth had ripped the skin.

He should wash, perhaps soaking his hands in cool water before travelling. Maybe he should have stopped hitting the man sooner, but the sight of the three of them, all tall, well-fed and strong, looming over the cowering girls had really ignited his anger. He had been content to let it rage.

To think he had believed a few days ago they might reach Roma without further problems. Now they were only a day or two from the city. Surely they'd had their fill of trouble. Beobrand groaned as he flexed his fingers, causing the scabs on his hand to crack and start bleeding again. He shook his head, thinking about what Coenred had said last night.

"Trouble follows you as if it is your shadow."

"I did not tell the nithings to force themselves on those girls," Beobrand had replied.

Coenred conceded the point with a nod.

"I know, Beo. And they are safe because of you. But I would welcome a single day without strife."

"I'll see what I can do," Beobrand said with a smile.

He hoped Coenred's wish would come true. He was tired.

Wilfrid believed that in Roma they would be given lodging in one of the palaces of the Pontifex. Surely then they would be able to rest without fear of attack. Beobrand looked forward to that.

He rose and stretched, groaning at the bright light lancing in through the inn's open door. He had drunk more wine than he had planned and was suffering for it now. Coenred was right. There had been too much death on this journey, but Beobrand could not bring himself to be upset about what had happened the previous night. Or in the hills north of Sutri. They had lost none of their wealth, had suffered only two minor wounds, and had even made the roads slightly safer for other travellers.

Beobrand wandered towards the door as the others began to rouse themselves from where they had slept. The hall was a mess. The tables and benches had been pushed up against the walls and the men stretched out on the stone floor, wrapped in blankets, cloaks, or just as they had fallen.

Blinking, he stepped into the morning light. Cynan was leaning on the wall.

"Here," he said, handing Beobrand a cup.

"Wine?" Beobrand asked, his stomach tightening at the thought.

"Water."

Beobrand took the earthenware cup and drank its contents.

Cynan hawked and spat.

"Thought we weren't going to drink much," he said.

"It would appear drunkenness must be added to the list of things I cannot seem to avoid," said Beobrand.

He looked about the yard. In the stables Eadgard's big gelding poked its head out of a stall, interested to see whether it was time to be fed. Outside the confines of the inn, the town was awakening. People shouted. A donkey brayed. The rattle and creak of a cart accompanied by the clopping of hooves passed by in the street nearby. The smell of baking bread and woodsmoke hung in the air. In the centre of the cobbled yard lay the blankets, bags and clothes of the three merchants. Beobrand half-expected to see them still lying there jumbled with their possessions, but on closer inspection, all three of them had gone. He was surprised to realise he was glad none of them had died in the night. What they had done, and what they had intended to do, was despicable, and it had been right that they had been soundly beaten and thrown out of the inn. But death would have been a harsh punishment.

"You think they learnt their lesson?" he asked Cynan.

Cynan scoffed.

"I doubt it. Their sort rarely learn. But they'll be more careful next time. Perhaps it will make them think twice."

"Maybe that's all we could hope for."

"Maybe."

Beobrand was still staring at the merchants' belongings. He frowned.

"It is passing strange that they have left without their things," he said.

"Scared of us, I'd wager."

Beobrand smiled.

"Terrified of the Waelisc warriors, eh?"

"Terrified of anyone and everything after last night," Cynan said. "Like whipped curs."

Beobrand grunted. He trudged to the far corner of the yard where the men had taken to relieving themselves once the wine began to flow. It was early still, the day not yet as hot as it would be, but the air here was pungent, the acrid bite of piss catching in the back of his throat. He brushed away flies that flitted about his face, and made water quickly, keen to be away from the stink.

Cynan had not moved. On his way back towards his friend,

on a whim Beobrand turned to the stables. He patted Eadgard's gelding's snout and peered into the gloomy interior.

"Their horses are still here," he called over to Cynan.

"What?"

"The merchants' horses. They're still in the stable."

Cynan walked over to check for himself.

"I know my eyes are not as keen as yours, Cynan," Beobrand said, "but I can still recognise a horse tethered in a stable."

Cynan looked, then nodded.

"You're right," he said.

"Of course I'm right," Beobrand replied. "I drank too much wine, I didn't go blind or lose my wits."

"I meant nothing—" Cynan's words were cut off by a loud scream. It came from inside the inn.

Beobrand shook his head. Not even one day without trouble, he thought. Coenred was right. The scream came again and Beobrand started running. There were words in that scream; garbled, terrified words that were lost in the distance, but Beobrand recognised the voice. He had just been thinking of its owner.

Coenred cried out again as Beobrand cleared the doorway. There was a desperate, pained quality to the monk's wailing and fear gripped Beobrand's heart. The hall was full of movement as the men roused themselves, looking about them in confusion, taking up discarded weapons in case this screaming signalled an impending attack from some unseen assailant.

Beobrand ignored them all. Headache and tiredness forgotten, he bounded up the stairs two steps at a time. Grindan had reached the top before him. He was hammering on the door.

"Coenred," he shouted, "open the door."

Coenred continued screaming for several heartbeats, then his voice dropped to an almost inaudible whimper.

"Coenred," said Beobrand in a soothing voice, pulling Grindan aside. "It's me, Beobrand. Can you open the door?"

There was silence for a time. Beobrand saw Grindan's expression mirrored his own. They both wondered what they would find in the room. As others began to crowd up the stairs behind them, shouting and enquiring what was happening, they heard the locking bar being drawn back.

Beobrand pushed the door open. His seax was in his hand, though he was not aware of having drawn the weapon. Grabbing Coenred's robe in his left half-hand, he pulled the monk from the room, shoving him behind, out of danger, to where Grindan caught him.

Beobrand stepped into the room without hesitation, but not before he had caught a glimpse of Coenred's face. Both of his friend's eyes were blackened and bruised and there was a large, swollen welt on his jaw. Beobrand tensed, raising his seax against whoever was in the room.

He swept his gaze around the small chamber. Enough light came through the window to illuminate the space well. He lowered his seax. He would have no need of it here. There was but one other inhabitant of the room and he posed Beobrand no threat. Fredegar would never threaten anyone again. The Frank's body lay on the mattress to the left of the room. The straw and bedding was soaked dark with blood. Beobrand let out a long juddering breath, looking back at what rested in the centre of the timber floorboards.

Fredegar stared back at him, his severed head resting in a small pool of thick, congealing blood.

"What happened here?" Beobrand asked, turning to Coenred. "Who did this?" He knew without question that Coenred was free from guilt. The monk hated violence. Coenred shook his head, opening and closing his mouth, unable to articulate his thoughts.

There was movement on the stairs. Wilfrid pushed his way past the others there and peered into the room, taking in the dreadful sight.

"Coenred," Wilfrid said, placing his hand on the monk's shoulder and making him flinch. "Who killed Fredegar?" He looked through the doorway again, moving his head from left to right as he took it all in before turning back to Coenred. "Who killed him?" he repeated, anger colouring his voice. "And who took my silver?"

Chapter 14

Cynan pulled Beobrand away from the innkeeper.

"He knows more than he is telling us. I am sure of it," Beobrand said, struggling against Cynan's grasp.

The innkeeper shook his head and spoke rapidly, desperate to assert his innocence. The man was frightened, and no wonder. He had seen what Beobrand was capable of, and now one of the scarred warrior's men had been slain in his establishment.

"He might know something," Cynan said.

"He does. See how nervous he is?"

"Perhaps that's more to do with you looking as if you are about to gut him."

With a sigh, Beobrand relented and allowed Cynan to lead him back down the stairs. The innkeeper followed them at a safe distance, muttering apologies.

"Bring wine," said Wilfrid.

The man bowed low, pleased to be given a task that would take him away from the scowling warriors. He scurried off.

"How could they have taken everything?" said Beobrand, beginning to pace back and forth across the hall. "How did not one of us notice anything?"

Fredegar and Coenred had noticed, thought Cynan, but he kept this to himself.

"They used the window," Grindan said. "There is no doubt." He had just returned from the street where he had examined the wall outside. "There are scratch marks on the stone outside, where men's boots scraped, or perhaps where our things hit against the wall as they were being lowered down."

"And they did this without making a sound?" said Beobrand. "Impossible."

The innkeeper returned with a flagon of wine and enough cups for them all. Ingwald, his usually tanned face somewhat wan from the after-effects of the evening's drinking coupled with the shock of what they had found, poured the wine and handed a cup to Beobrand.

"They had no need to be silent," he said, filling a cup for Cynan, and then himself. He handed the flagon to Eadgard and moved away to sit on a bench, his back against the wall. "They could have banged a drum and we would not have noticed."

"But Coenred says they came in the night, when everyone was sleeping. He heard them."

Cynan sipped his wine. "He did. But he had drunk little. It would have taken much to rouse me after all that wine."

Wilfrid, still pale-faced from the shock of losing the treasure he had acquired in Frankia, accepted a cup of wine from Halinard, but after looking into its depths for a short while, he set it aside without drinking.

"Could it have been those merchants?" he asked. "They knew the room and that we had placed our belongings there."

Beobrand shook his head, dismissive of the idea.

"They were not small men. I cannot imagine them scaling that wall and slipping through that window, even if they had been hale. After last night, I doubt they could stand, let alone climb."

"So where are they?" Wilfrid asked.

It was a good question, but none of them had an answer.

Since the grisly discovery in the room, Bleddyn had been quiet. Now he rose from where he had been sitting.

"Are you going to drink that?" he asked Wilfrid.

The handsome novice wrinkled his nose as if he had noted a bad smell, then shook his head. Bleddyn took the cup.

"There was more to this than theft," he said, raising the cup to his lips and drinking deeply.

"It seems to me," said Halinard, "the theft and killing of Fredegar are bad enough."

"Bleddyn is right," said Wilfrid. "The way in which Fredegar was killed. It is a message."

"Why not kill Coenred too?" asked Beobrand. "I thank the gods my friend yet lives, but why kill one and not the other?"

"I don't know," admitted Bleddyn. "But they risked taking the time to cut off Fredegar's head for a reason."

Cynan rubbed a hand over his face. There was sweat on his forehead. The day was rapidly growing hot. He thought of Fredegar and how the man liked to drink and laugh with the warriors. He recalled his savage glee at the victory over the brigands in the hills, how he had taunted them as they fled.

"Could it be that the bandits followed us down from the hills?" he said quietly, turning the idea over in his mind.

"Surely they were just brigands," Beobrand said.

"Perhaps. But we know at least six of them were unharmed. They lost their leader. No man likes to lose. To have his brothers killed. To be insulted in defeat."

"And they knew of the silver," mused Beobrand. He continued to pace and for a time nobody spoke. Cynan could hear Wulfwyn's voice, quietly praying with Coenred. She had taken him into the kitchen, where she had tended to his injuries and served him watered wine and some bread and honey. Coenred had been appalled by Fredegar's murder and he had taken a bad blow to the head, but he was resilient. Stronger perhaps than even he knew. He would recover in time.

"But if it was them," Cynan said, "Beobrand is right. Why not kill Coenred too? Why only beat him senseless and risk the noise alerting us, or him coming to sooner and raising the alarm?"

They thought on this for a time. Beobrand paced. Wilfrid called for more drink. The innkeeper brought bread, cheese and a fresh jug of wine.

"I have been asking myself the same question."

They all turned to see Coenred standing in the doorway, Wulfwyn and Aelfwig at his side. The skin of his face was distended and discoloured where he had been hit. Where there were no bruises, his skin was as pale as curds. He had a hand on Aelfwig's shoulder for support.

"You should rest, my friend," said Beobrand.

"There will be plenty of time for rest later," said Coenred. "I was thinking of the church of the Madonna of the Birth. We were surprised the gold rood remained there."

"I wish they had taken that instead of robbing us," growled Beobrand.

"Ah, but the cross is safe there, for it is on the altar of the Almighty."

Understanding dawned on Wilfrid.

"You think that is why they allowed you to live? Because you are a man of God?"

"I can think of no better explanation," said Coenred. "Not that it brings us any closer to finding the men who murdered poor Fredegar."

"And stole our things," added Wilfrid.

"It is all gone?" asked Wulfwyn. "My things too?" Wulfwyn had entrusted the small number of coins and pieces of hack silver she possessed into their care, believing her treasure would be safer that way.

"I am sorry," Cynan said, unable to look her in the eye. "They were thorough. We believed the room to be safe. They took all of the silver and anything of value we had stowed there for safekeeping." He glanced at Beobrand who had commenced pacing once more. "They even took lord Beobrand's sword," he whispered.

"My eyes may not be as sharp as they once were," snapped Beobrand from the far end of the hall. "But my ears still work well enough. Yes, those whoresons, whoever they are, took all of our wealth and made off with Nægling too." He scooped up an empty cup from one of the tables and stared at it for a time. Cynan thought he was going to fling it against the wall, but after a while, Beobrand sighed and placed it back on the board. He strode back towards Coenred, Wulfwyn and Aelfwig. "There is no denying that Nægling is a rare blade, but I can find another sword," he said. "I could replace your silver if we were in Bernicia, but here, it is not so easy. I'm sorry."

"It can't be helped," Wulfwyn said. "We must pray for Fredegar's soul and rejoice that the Lord saw that we were spared. While we yet live there must be hope."

Cynan marvelled at the woman's fortitude. She had lost so much on this pilgrimage and yet she still managed to see things in a good light.

Coenred stiffened, as if recalling something.

"What of the letters?" he asked.

"The letters?" replied Beobrand.

"Letters of introduction from Clovis and Balthild. And Bishop Landericus of Paris."

Wilfrid moved closer, a look of horror on his face.

"And from Queen Eanflæd and Archbishop Honorius of Cantwareburh. Tell me they are not lost."

Cynan shook his head. He did not need to utter a word for his answer to be clear.

"By the thorns of Jesu's crown," shouted Wilfrid, furious at this loss on top of the theft of their treasure. "This journey is cursed."

Eadgard slammed down his cup with a resounding crash.

"Since the moment you joined us," he said, glaring at Wilfrid and rubbing at his bandaged shoulder.

Aelfwig sniffed. None of them had been paying the boy any attention, but Cynan now saw that tears were streaming down his cheeks.

"What is it, Aelfwig?" he asked.

Aelfwig spoke so quietly Cynan could not make out any of the words. The men fell silent, chastened by the sight of the weeping blind boy.

Beobrand knelt before Aelfwig and placed his hands on the boy's shoulders.

"Speak up, lad," he said, using the tone he employed with skittish horses.

"I heard them," Aelfwig said, sniffing back his tears and cuffing at his cheeks.

"The men who did this?"

Aelfwig's face was a mask of despair. He nodded.

"Why did you not speak out?" Beobrand said, his voice rising.

Aelfwig's crying intensified. Wulfwyn put her arm around him, pulling him close and away from Beobrand.

"I didn't know what it was," Aelfwig whimpered. "Ma was tired. We couldn't sleep for a long time. You were making such noise."

Beobrand clenched his fists. Cynan, knowing well his lord's temper, shuffled forward a pace, ready to intervene. He would not allow Beobrand to strike the child. After a few heartbeats, Beobrand stepped back, taking a deep breath, and controlling his growing anger with difficulty.

"None of this is of your doing, Aelfwig," he said, his words clipped. "Forgive me." He looked to Wulfwyn as he spoke. Slowly, she nodded.

"What is it you heard?" she asked her son.

"It is as Coenred says. I think there were three men in the room. More in the street below. They spoke in whispers and I could not understand them. I listened but after a time they were quiet and I fell asleep." Tears welled up in his eyes once more, then slid down his cheeks. "I did not know…" Aelfwig's small voice cracked. "I did not know… what they were doing to Fredegar." He began to tremble, sobs shaking his fragile form. Wulfwyn wrapped her arms about him, her hair covering his face.

Beobrand turned away, his jaw set. His eyes burnt with a cold rage.

"We will make those responsible pay the blood-price for what they have done," he said.

Cynan recognised the look of fury that gripped his lord. It was his determination for vengeance and justice that made him one of the most feared warriors in all of Albion. When Beobrand of Ubbanford set after someone with that iron resolve and simmering ire, his quarry would do well to run as far and fast as they were able.

"That is good," said Cynan. "There is only one problem."

"What is that?" Beobrand asked, his tone as sharp as the blade of his seax.

"We have no idea how to find them."

Chapter 15

Coenred used his sleeve to mop away the sweat that trickled down his face. The sun was still hot, but it was low enough in the sky now that many of the narrow streets of Sutri were in shade. Not that it made much difference to the heat. He removed his hat and ran his fingers through his sweat-soaked hair. He winced as his fingertips brushed the bruises and welts from the beating he'd received in the night.

His head ached and, from time to time, his vision blurred, objects swimming out of focus as if he had been drinking. He did not mention this, hoping it would pass once he was able to rest. Beobrand, clearly anxious for him, had told him to stay in the relative cool of the inn, but Coenred had been adamant. He needed to help. He told himself he was not responsible for Fredegar's death, but that did not stop the waves of guilt that he yet lived while the Frank's corpse was already beginning to rot in the summer heat.

"I'm sorry, Beo," Coenred said, turning away from the baker he had been speaking to. "He says he knows nothing of what happened."

Beobrand shook his head and scoffed.

"Nobody heard or saw anything and not one person in this town has any inkling who might have done this thing."

"So it would seem."

As only Wilfrid and Coenred could converse with the locals, they had split into two groups, aiming to cover as much of the settlement as possible. Wilfrid had gone north with Ingwald, Cynan and Bleddyn. Coenred had accompanied Beobrand, Halinard and Eadgard and covered the southern streets of Sutri. Beobrand had ordered Grindan to remain with Wulfwyn and Aelfwig for their protection. The dangers in this place were very real and Beobrand was not about to let anything happen to the widow and her son.

The only way Beobrand and his companions could think of discovering who had stolen from them and killed Fredegar was to ask whoever they could find for information. Someone must have seen something. The town was not so large that such an audacious crime would go unnoticed. At the very least the locals would have some idea who might carry out such an act. But though they had questioned dozens of tradesmen, merchants, shopkeepers, labourers and several women they had met about their daily business, traversing the squares, streets and alleyways, none of them had offered up a single name or direction to follow.

Beobrand hawked and spat.

"They know something," he said. "It is plain on their faces."

"They all have the look of fear about them," said Halinard, "like the innkeeper. That boy was right."

"But he told us nothing of use."

Sometime earlier they had come across the boy who had led them to the inn and guided them to the church the day before. He had been watching them from the shade of an awning that hung over a stall selling pottery. It was Eadgard who'd spotted the dirty boy and beckoned him over. Not wishing to be questioned, the boy had turned, meaning to slip away, but before he could disappear into the warren of alleys, Beobrand sprang after him, his long legs eating up the ground between them. Catching him by the collar, he'd dragged him back to where the others waited.

The boy denied all knowledge of what had happened, but he had let something slip while he was professing his innocence.

"Nobody will speak to you," he said. "Their silence keeps them alive."

"What do you mean?" Coenred asked.

"It is the *humilitas*."

"They are humble?"

"More than that," said the boy, struggling in vain against Beobrand's iron grip on his stained kirtle. "People know if they talk they will be killed, just like your friend."

"Who will kill them?" Beobrand asked, shaking the skinny boy. "Who did this?"

The boy was still defiant, but his eyes now bore the tinge of fear they had seen on the faces of others.

"If I told you, they would kill me too. It would be best for you to leave while you can."

"*I* could kill you," snarled Beobrand.

"You could," admitted the boy, staring into Beobrand's angry face, "but you won't, I think. You are not the kind to kill a boy."

Coenred admired the child. And Beobrand liked him too. He could tell. With a final shake, Beobrand had released him. The boy had not hesitated. He dashed off into an alleyway, vanishing before the huge northerner could change his mind.

Beobrand sighed.

"All we learnt is that an urchin told us what we already surmised. The people are scared to speak up. We still know nothing of who has them cowering so. Come," he said, "let us return to the inn."

They trudged through the streets, the sun-baked stones of the buildings radiating heat and making the town feel like the inside of a bread oven. A breeze had picked up in the afternoon, but when a rare gust reached them in the maze of streets, it was as warm as the air from an open forge and did nothing to cool them.

"I pray Wilfrid has had more luck," said Coenred, longing for the cool of the stone-floored hall and a cup of watered wine.

When they arrived at the inn, they found Wilfrid and the others already there. Coenred noticed that the merchants' horses and belongings had still not been taken.

Slumping down on a bench, he accepted a cup from Wulfwyn with a pinched smile. His head throbbed and he was glad to be in the shaded interior of the building. His lips were parched. He sipped from the cup, enjoying the taste of the watered-down wine.

"Any tidings?" asked Beobrand.

Cynan shook his head.

"Nobody told us anything of interest. But if I had to place a wager on it, I would say they know who did it."

"They are frightened," said Ingwald. "Whoever did this thing, the people fear for their own heads."

They all sat, tired and dejected after the long, hot day traipsing Sutri's streets. For a time the men muttered and murmured quietly amongst themselves. They glanced at Beobrand as he drank a cup of wine and then held it out for Wulfwyn to refill. Coenred could sense their uncertainty. They trusted the lord of Ubbanford, but they were far from home and none of them knew how he could resolve the problem of the stolen treasure.

With a grunt of barely contained anger, Beobrand pushed himself to his feet and began pacing around the hall once more. Coenred felt sorry for his friend. Beobrand had never been comfortable leading men, but he had accepted the mantle of lord many years ago. Men looked up to him, turned to him for answers when none were apparent. The responsibility was not an easy weight to bear.

Wulfwyn came and sat close to Coenred. Her weariness was plain on her wan face, but it did nothing to diminish her demure beauty. He offered her a thin smile, trying not to dwell on her closeness.

"Perhaps it would be best if we were to leave Sutri and head for Roma," she whispered. "We cannot bring Fredegar back and I fear if we stay, things might only get worse."

"You might well be right," Coenred said, speaking in a hushed tone he hoped would not carry. "But Beobrand is not one to flee from danger. Nor will he leave while the debt of Fredegar's murder remains unpaid. Whoever did this does not know Beobrand as well as I. He will not rest until he has his vengeance."

Wulfwyn made the sign of the cross.

"God help us," she said.

Coenred reached up and gingerly touched the bruises on his face.

"And God have mercy on those who did this. For Beobrand will show them none."

From the far side of the hall, Eadgard spoke up, his rumbling voice like the echo of thunder in the far-off hills.

"If we believe it might have been the bandits we faced in the hills, why don't we head back there? We could track them to their camp, as we did those who had taken Wulfwyn in the mountains."

"The hills are more than a day's travel," said Cynan. "And even if it is the same men who attacked us, their trail is cold. I can track a fresh path, but I do not have Attor's skill at the hunt. We would walk around the hills for days until we starved. Those men know the land and would never allow themselves to be seen."

Eadgard's face darkened and he massaged his shoulder.

"I cannot bear to think they might have got away with killing

Fredegar and taking our belongings." He reached for a jug and sloshed wine into his cup, spilling some on the table. "It is not right," he grumbled, falling silent.

Grindan clapped his brother on his uninjured shoulder in commiseration.

"What of those merchants?" he said. "Did you see or hear anything of them in the town?"

"Nothing," said Bleddyn.

Halinard scratched at his beard.

"It is strange indeed," he said.

Wilfrid rose and moved to the open door, peering out into the hot afternoon shade of the courtyard.

"They have not come for their things?" he said.

"Not even their mounts," replied Grindan. "There are good quality clothes in their gear too. And one of them left a pair of calfskin boots. And those horses are hale animals. Not to mention the harness and saddles. Not cheap."

Beobrand frowned.

"We did not beat them so badly that they would not be able to return for their things," he said. "We are no thieves that we would keep what is theirs."

"They don't know that," said Coenred. "Perhaps their fear of you is greater than their desire for their possessions."

Beobrand scoffed.

"Perhaps. Yet it seems passing strange to me that there was no mention of them on the lips of any of the townsfolk."

Without warning, Wilfrid stepped back from the door.

"Someone approaches," he hissed.

The gesithas stiffened. Eadgard and Cynan stood, hands on the seaxes that hung from their belts.

Into the gloom of the hall stepped two men. Both were young, tanned and handsome. The first through the door had hair as black as a raven's wing and a sneering quality about him, as if everyone within the inn was of less worth than he. The second man had a more open face. Beneath a mop of auburn hair, his eyes twinkled and his lips curled in a twisted smirk.

Beobrand raised himself up to his full height, stepping forward to intercept these newcomers.

"Ask them who they are," he said to Coenred.

Before Coenred could reply, the second of the two men spoke in Anglisc.

"My name is Lucifrido," he said. "This pretty boy is Perteradi."

At the sound of his name, the first of the strangers glared about him at the staring men. He puffed out his chest, his clean-shaven chin jutting. He wore an expensive-looking red tunic and reminded Coenred of the cockerels that strutted about the minster buildings on Lindisfarena, looking for another bird to fight, or a hen to mount.

"You have told them who I am," the man said to Lucifrido, clearly not understanding Anglisc, but recognising his own name. "Now tell them they are to come with me."

Lucifrido bowed his head in acknowledgement of the order.

"Are you Beobrand?" he asked.

Beobrand met his gaze, squaring his shoulders.

"How is it you come to know my name?" he asked. "And how can you speak my tongue?"

Lucifrido grinned. Perteradi snapped at him, asking what Beobrand was saying. Smiling still, Lucifrido ignored him.

"As to the first," he said, his tone light, "your fame precedes you." His grin widened. "Or perhaps it is that you have told your name to everyone in Sutri." He winked at that and Coenred found himself warming to the young man in spite of himself. "As to your second question, my mother was from Albion. To tell the truth, it feels good to speak in my mother's tongue. There is seldom a chance for me to converse with anyone interesting. May I?" Without waiting for an answer, he picked up a jug, turned over a clay cup that was resting on the table and filled it.

"Tell them now," said Perteradi in Latin, his voice sharp. "This is not the time for your foolishness." He looked at Lucifrido with undisguised contempt.

Lucifrido drained his wine in one swallow. He offered Perteradi a wide smile.

"My excitable friend here would like you to accompany us to visit his father."

Beobrand scowled, unsure how to take the two men, the one angry and preening, the other at ease and grinning.

"Who is his father?"

"He is a man of great import in these parts," Lucifrido said. "Believe me, you will be glad to accept his offer of a meeting. Few are granted such an honour." He was still smiling. Coenred was not sure if he was making fun of them, or if he was amused at the prospect of them meeting Perteradi's father. Perhaps both, he thought.

"Why would I want to meet him?" Beobrand asked.

"Oh, I almost forgot." Then in Latin to his companion: "Perteradi, show him."

The black-haired man glowered. A flash of anger passed over his features, like a cloud scudding across the sun. Perteradi did not like being given orders it seemed. But after a brief hesitation, he pulled aside the cloak he wore to reveal a sword hanging from a baldric slung over his shoulder. With a fluid motion he drew the blade. The warriors on the benches, sensing the threat emanating from the young man with the naked steel in his hand, jumped up. Cynan pulled his own blade from its scabbard, moving to stand between the pair of strangers and Beobrand.

"Halt," said Beobrand, his voice slicing through the tension like an axe through new cheese. None of the men moved. Perteradi leered, holding the sword up for all to see. Lucifrido chuckled to see the men's reaction. He seemed pleased with the excitement Perteradi and he had caused.

Beobrand stepped closer, to stand beside Cynan.

"That is my sword," he said.

Coenred gasped. Now that Beobrand had said it, he saw it was true. He could make out the garnets and gold mounted in Nægling's pommel.

"I can think of only one way for you to have that sword in your possession." If Perteradi's demeanour carried a certain danger, Beobrand's tone conveyed a deadly threat. There was death in the air now. A misstep would see blood spilt in an eyeblink. "Give me a reason not to kill you both now."

Lucifrido's smile wilted somewhat. He was clearly no fool.

"We bring you the sword as a token of good faith, lord Beobrand," he said. He whispered something to Perteradi. For a long moment, the angry young man did not move, then, suddenly, he lowered Nægling, taking the blade in his hands and offering the hilt to Beobrand.

Beobrand locked eyes with him, unsure if this was a trick. Having made up his mind, he stepped close and took the sword. He examined it, then held out his mutilated left hand to Perteradi. Clicking his fingers, he nodded at the baldric and tooled leather scabbard. With a scoffing curl of his lip, Perteradi slipped it off and tossed it to Beobrand. He caught it, sheathed his blade and slung the baldric over his shoulder.

Turning away from Perteradi, he addressed Lucifrido once more.

"Again, if you have my sword, you must have killed my friend and stolen our things. Why should we not slay you both?"

"I did not kill your friend," said Lucifrido, holding his hands up. "Nor did I rob you. But Perteradi's father would speak with you. He has the information you seek, and it would not do to keep him waiting." He offered Beobrand a half-smile. "You could surely kill us, but then you would never learn what we have to tell you." He turned to leave, nodding at Perteradi. As they walked towards the door, he looked back over his shoulder, beckoning to Beobrand to follow. "And," he said, grinning once more, "if you slew us, you would certainly never leave Sutri with your life."

Chapter 16

Reluctantly, Beobrand followed Perteradi and Lucifrido out into the yard. He caressed Nægling's pommel. The familiar feel of the sword anchored him, but did little to soothe his frayed nerves.

"This could be a trap," Cynan whispered to him.

Beobrand looked up at the sky that was reddening in the west.

"To what end? They already have our treasure."

"I know not, lord. But I have a bad feeling about this."

"I feel it too," said Beobrand. "But what would you have me do? They have offered this token of truce. I say we follow them and see where they lead us."

Cynan bit his lip.

"That smiling one is too cocksure," he said. "The other looks in need of a beating such as we gave to those merchants."

Eadgard, who had just stepped out of the inn, clenched his fists and chuckled.

"I would gladly oblige," he said.

Beobrand halted, holding up his hand for his gesithas to stop. They gathered round. On the far side of the yard, by the gate to the street, Lucifrido and Perteradi paused.

"Come," called Lucifrido, "it will be dark soon and Perteradi's father does not like to be kept waiting."

Beobrand ignored him. He had to agree with Cynan. Lucifrido's self-assurance and constant smirking were tiresome, and yet, despite his infuriating grin, the man was instantly likable. Perteradi on the other hand, with his pouting good looks and swagger, made Beobrand want to slap him. With a sad grimace, Beobrand realised the young man reminded him of his own son, Octa.

"Grindan and Halinard, I would have you remain here with Wulfwyn, Aelfwig and the priests." The two warriors began to protest, but Beobrand cut them off. "There is no time for debate. I will not bring them with us. We know not what dangers lie ahead and we have travelled too far to lose Wilfrid now. If we do not return, take them on to Roma as quickly as you are able."

"Surely it will not come to that," said Grindan, frowning.

"Let us hope not. But if I do not come back, I free you of your oaths."

"Don't look so glum, brother," boomed Eadgard, taking Grindan's forearm in the warrior grip. "These little men won't stop us coming back." He hefted his axe, resting it on his shoulder, and set out across the cobbled yard.

"Take care, lord," Halinard said, nodding seriously.

Beobrand smiled without conviction.

"Don't I always?"

As they reached the street, Cynan tapped Beobrand on the shoulder. He nodded behind them, towards the stables and the midden pit. There, slinking out of the shadows from behind the buildings, stepped several men. Beobrand looked over at the inn itself and saw more men appear from where they had been concealed. Beobrand counted a dozen. All the men were armed.

"What is this?" he called out to Lucifrido.

The man turned, taking in the armed men with a glance and grinning.

"Friends of ours," he said. He tapped his forehead. "To keep your thoughts focused."

Beobrand recalled the man's deadly warning in the hall, delivered with a warm smile. It seemed he could make good on that threat. A dozen men would not be easy to beat. With a twist in his gut Beobrand worried about leaving Coenred, Wulfwyn and the others. But there was nothing for it now. The dozen armed men strode behind them, cutting off any chance of retreat. His skin prickled. He could feel the men's eyes on him, but he did not look back again. He would show no sign of weakness.

"Ignore them," Beobrand growled at his gesithas.

With the twelve men walking menacingly behind, they followed Lucifrido and Perteradi through the twisting streets. The sun was setting, the roofs and the tops of the higher buildings bathed in the ruddy glow of the dying day's light. The men and women of Sutri were packing away their stalls, sweeping out their small shops, closing shutters and readying themselves for the night. At the sight of Perteradi and Lucifrido, the townsfolk halted whatever they were doing and bowed low. Beobrand had seen similar reactions in the past, but only for nobility, kings, queens, bishops and ealdormen.

At a crossroads, a leathery-skinned man with wisps of white hair, seeing the group approaching, shouted at his oxen, swiping at them with a switch. The beasts, hauling a cart piled high with barrels and earthenware amphorae, now halted, lowing and shaking their huge heads. They were travelling uphill. It would take stern words and goading to get the animals moving again. But the old drover did not complain. He lowered his gaze as Lucifrido and Perteradi walked by without slowing their pace.

"Who are these men?" hissed Cynan.

Beobrand shrugged.

"We will find out soon enough." He wasn't sure they would like what they discovered.

They continued through the labyrinth of lanes and alleys, the setting sun at their backs, for some time till they came to the edge of town. They passed beneath the eastern gate and walked out of Sutri. The shadow of the walls stretched before them, long on the land.

"Where are we going?" asked Beobrand.

"Not far now," Lucifrido said, smiling. He lifted his chin and sniffed the air. "We will be there soon enough. Can't you smell it?"

Beobrand drew in a deep breath. He could smell the hot dust of the town, the resiny scent of the pines that grew on the slope overlooking Sutri. He could make out the smoke from the many cooking fires of the inhabitants, and he could detect the smell of roasting meat on the warm breeze.

"What should I be smelling?" he asked.

Lucifrido grinned.

"You'll see. Come. We are almost there."

Perteradi said something to Lucifrido, who laughed. Beobrand could not tell if he laughed with the man, or at him.

"We were right," whispered Cynan as they set off once more, walking along the dusty road towards a line of trees on the nearest hill.

"What do you mean?"

"These are the men who tried to rob us in the hills. At least some of them are."

"You are sure?"

Cynan rolled his head to loosen his neck muscles as Beobrand had seen him do countless times when he was tense, or preparing for battle. Cynan kept his eyes forward, and gave a small nod.

"There is no doubt. At least one of them was among those we fought in the hills. I had a look when we stopped by the gate. I thought I recognised one of them in the yard at the inn. Now I am certain of it. The whoreson knew me too. Couldn't stop staring at me. If his eyes were blades I'd be as dead as Fredegar now."

Bleddyn walked close to them.

"I've seen two who were in the hills," he whispered through gritted teeth.

Beobrand clenched the muscles in his jaw.

"So the bandits returned and stole what they had failed to take on the road, and killed Fredegar too. But why come to us now? Why return Nægling and bring us here?"

Ingwald had moved near. His face was sombre.

"Perhaps they want to finish what they started," said Ingwald, his tone bleak. "Somewhere outside the walls, where our screams will not keep the children awake."

Beobrand placed his hand on Nægling's pommel, steadying himself with its touch. Ahead of them, Lucifrido and Perteradi passed under the canopy of the pines. The smell of cooking meat was stronger now.

"If they wished simply to kill us," said Beobrand, "why waste time?"

As if in answer, a cry echoed down from the trees. Rising in a howl of pain and fear, it was suddenly cut off. The abrupt sound startled them. Beobrand and the others came to a halt. That was a human scream the like of which Beobrand had heard before. It was a sound of abject horror and agony such as hangs in the air after battle, when ruthless leaders release their victorious warriors to descend on the defeated and defenceless, giving free rein to the foulest passions of men.

Lucifrido turned, an apologetic expression on his handsome face.

"Do not fear," he said, "that poor nithing's fate is not yours."

Beobrand did not move.

"I fear nothing," he said. "But I will not lead my men to their torture and death." He dragged Nægling slowly from its scabbard. "If you plan to kill us, do it now and we will see what wyrd has in store for both you and I." Beside him, Cynan, Bleddyn and Ingwald all drew their own swords. Eadgard brandished his axe. There were only five of them, but they were formidable and would take many with them to the afterlife if the sword song began to play.

The twelve men behind them produced blades of their own, but Lucifrido held up his hands. "If you wish, Beobrand, we can fight now. You are strong warriors, but you are few and we are many."

Beobrand gave the dozen men spread across the road a contemptuous glance.

"We have overcome worse odds."

"No doubt. No doubt," said Lucifrido. "But no matter how many men you can kill, you will die here. Your men too."

"So sure are you?"

"We are close to the house. If I shout, another dozen men will be here in moments. Even the great Beobrand cannot kill everyone."

"I can try," Beobrand whispered.

"Think for a moment," Lucifrido said, serious now and unsmiling. "We have not brought you here to cause you harm. Why would we give one such as you a sword, if we planned to fight? Why allow your men to bring their arms?"

Beobrand glowered at him.

"It has been a trying day and my patience has gone," he said. "Tell me plain. Where are you taking us? And who is that poor wretch we heard?"

Lucifrido nodded. Perteradi, his voice carrying the sharp edge of annoyance, spoke quickly. Lucifrido replied without taking his eyes from Beobrand. Perteradi did not look satisfied. He was about to speak further, but Lucifrido addressed Beobrand once more.

"These are reasonable questions," he said. "Beyond those trees is Perteradi's father's house. The man you heard is an enemy."

"Enemy? Whose enemy?"

"Perteradi's father's," Lucifrido said. "And yours also."

"You speak in riddles," Beobrand said, "and I grow weary. Tell me clearly. Who is this enemy you speak of."

Lucifrido smiled again, his tone soft, conciliatory.

"Trust me a moment more and all will be made clear."

"I do not trust you," said Beobrand.

Lucifrido's smile broadened.

"That is honest," he said. "I cannot tell you all there is to know yet. I serve Perteradi's father, and I must obey his orders. Follow me up to the house and he will tell you all you wish to know."

For several heartbeats Beobrand fixed Lucifrido with an icy glare.

"He does not wish us harm?"

Lucifrido did not blink.

"He does not," he said. "Trust me."

"I've already told you," replied Beobrand, feeling the slightest of smiles tugging at his own lips, despite the situation. "I do not trust you."

It was true, he thought. He did not trust Lucifrido, Perteradi or any of the men behind them. But the man was right. They outnumbered Beobrand's small group by almost three to one. If Lucifrido could truly call on more men from the building close by, escape with their lives would be next to impossible.

"Lead on," Beobrand said at last. "But if you cross us, know I will slay you first."

Lucifrido smiled and turned back to the wooded hillside. Perteradi said something to him. Lucifrido replied, his tone curt. Beobrand had no idea what either man had said. He almost wished he had brought Coenred with them. His knowledge of languages would have proven useful.

"You think he is telling the truth?" asked Cynan.

"I have no idea," Beobrand said. "If he is, we might live to see tomorrow."

"And if he is lying?"

"We might well die tonight." He wanted to spit, but his mouth was dry. He licked his lips instead. "But if we stand and fight here, I think death will find us quicker."

Cynan looked back at the men following them.

"Choosing the slower death seems like sound judgement, lord."

Ingwald shook his head.

"If there is a choice, I would prefer no death."

None of them laughed at Ingwald's poor attempt at humour. They walked on behind Lucifrido and Perteradi, more conscious than ever of the men following behind them. Under the shade of the trees it was slightly cooler, but sweat streaked Beobrand's forehead and he felt rivulets trickle down his spine. Flying insects droned in the wood, flitting through the fingers of dusty golden light that scratched through the branches to pierce the gloaming.

The path turned sharply and the incline of the slope steepened. They trudged upward through the trees until the path turned back on itself. Panting from the exertion and sweating profusely from the heat, Beobrand gazed up. There was a stone wall up there. As they moved closer he saw a pair of stout timber doors set into the wall. What had looked like a wooded hillside from Sutri was in fact a steep crag. Perteradi's father's house was perched atop it, hidden from view by the towering trees. The wall was solid and as high as two men. With only the one steep path up to the gate, it reminded Beobrand of Bebbanburg. He took a deep breath, thinking of the terrible wailing cry and again wondered who Perteradi's father might be.

As Lucifrido and Perteradi neared the entrance, a voice called down to them. A face peered out from a small window in a watch tower beside the gate. Perteradi barked something and the man disappeared from view. A moment later the tall, iron-bound timber doors swung open. The smell of roasting meat and other food being prepared greeted Beobrand and the others as they arrived.

Perteradi had already entered, but Lucifrido awaited them.

"Our destination," he said with a flourishing wave of his hand. "You will see I did not play you false."

"I hope you did not," said Beobrand. "I have no wish to kill you."

Lucifrido laughed, a warm, welcoming sound.

"Come, come," he said, ushering them through the open doors.

They stepped into another world. Gone was the dusty forest of the steep hillside. It was replaced with straight-edged beds of flowers, bright colours vivid in the last light of the sunset. Bushes trimmed into cunning shapes lined the gravelled path that led to a large house. But truly it could not be called merely a house, not even a hall, such as that built by Beobrand at Ubbanford. This was a palace, fit for a king. Like most of the buildings in Sutri, it was constructed from the warm pale local stone and its roof was tiled with red clay. But this place was built on an altogether grander scale, with a colonnade along one wall of the terraced garden, marble statues staring down at them from niches and a portico decorated with lush scenes of ripe fruit and harvest. The high walls encircled the entire area at the top of the rocky outcrop. Within the walls, the ornate gardens spread for as far as Beobrand could see. Some way off the copper-coloured sky was mirrored in a large rectangular pond. Over the scent of cooking hung the heady aroma of lavender, rosemary, chives, parsley and thyme.

In front of the house's main entrance, a large group of people was gathered. Even from this distance, Beobrand could see they were dressed in finery, bright silks and linens. And as he walked nearer, gold and silver flashed on the wrists, necks and ears of the women, and on several of the men too.

"Perteradi! Lucifrido!"

A stocky man in a dark robe held out his arms and walked towards them down the sloping path. Four armed men detached themselves from where they had stood inconspicuously beside columns and statues and hurried after him. Their hands rested on sword pommels and their eyes darted warily over Beobrand and his gesithas.

The man who approached was not tall, but he exuded a relaxed power. His hair was dark, his close-cropped beard streaked with grey. His face had the ruddy complexion of a man who spent much of his day outside. Perhaps in this garden, thought Beobrand.

Noticing the men following him, the man paused and waved them away. One of them voiced his displeasure, but the short man insisted. Grudgingly, the four guards waited where they were as their master made his way towards the new arrivals. They glowered at Beobrand and the other men of Albion, clearly not trusting them.

His order given and obeyed, the man ignored his guards. Reaching for Perteradi, he kissed the young man on both cheeks. Perteradi began to speak quickly in an angry tone, but the man, who Beobrand assumed to be his father, held up his hand, silencing him. He sent him towards the gathered throng with a flick of his wrist, then, shaking his head, he turned to Lucifrido.

They spoke quietly, then the older man turned and smiled at Beobrand. He held out his arms in expansive welcome. He addressed him at length, then nodded to Lucifrido to interpret his words.

"This is my master, Perteradi's father, Tanualdo. He bids you all welcome to his home. He says that his guards are not happy to see you all bearing blades. This is not a normal thing and could be seen as an insult. Perhaps you would leave your weapons by the gate."

Beobrand's eyes narrowed. He glanced over his shoulder. The dozen men who had followed them were now amassed on the path not ten paces behind them.

"Tell him we will keep our weapons for as long as his men have theirs. I mean him no insult, but we are surely not friends."

Lucifrido relayed Beobrand's words. Tanualdo smiled and nodded.

"I assured my guards you will cause no trouble," he said, Lucifrido translating his words. "I understand your misgivings, but let us get the unpleasantness of the past out of the way so that we may feast and talk about the future."

Beobrand bridled.

"One of our party has been slain," he said, anger colouring his voice. "All of our silver and wealth stolen. We recognise some of the men who tried to rob us in the hills amongst those who escorted us here. Your men. These things cannot be so readily forgotten."

Tanualdo listened to Lucifrido, nodding gravely.

"There have been some unfortunate actions," he said, "carried out by young, foolish men. We have all been young once, eh? I apologise on behalf of my family. But the past cannot be altered. And I would now set things right between us."

Beobrand scowled. The man's demeanour baffled him.

"You do not deny your family's involvement in my friend's killing, nor the theft of our goods? Why bring us here now? And why seek to make peace with me? Your man here says you do not mean us harm, and yet we are surrounded by your warriors."

Again Tanualdo listened patiently. When Lucifrido had finished relaying Beobrand's words, the older man beckoned for Beobrand to follow him.

"Your men should remain in the gardens," Lucifrido said. "We will have food and drink sent to them."

"I don't like this one bit," said Cynan.

"Nor I lord," rumbled Eadgard, leaning on his axe.

Beobrand looked after Tanualdo. The man had paused, waiting for him to follow.

"I do not like it either," Beobrand said, "but we have come this far, and we must not hide from the truth. If Tanualdo meant to kill us, he could surely have done so already. I will go with him. Do not give up your blades." He leant in close to Cynan. "Be careful not to give any of these whoresons reason to feel threatened. So many swords in one place does not bode well for a peaceful evening."

"Are you sure about this?" Cynan whispered.

"Not at all," Beobrand replied, and headed after Tanualdo and Lucifrido.

The four burly guards made way for them to pass, then fell into step behind them. Beobrand looked back and saw servants bringing stools and trellises from the shade of the colonnade that ran the length of the south wall. They began to set them up around the pond. The dozen warriors stepped back, giving Cynan and the others room. Beobrand watched as they walked somewhat tentatively towards the pond. He let out a breath. He was still on edge, and yet surely Tanualdo would not bother to feed the men of Albion if he meant to have them slain.

Fleetingly, he thought of Dalfinus and Vulmar. At times the actions of powerful men made little sense to him. Power did not bring a sense of honour to most men. Too often it seemed to engender a taste for causing suffering and pain. Tanualdo was a powerful man, no doubt, but there was something about him, a sombre open quality, that made Beobrand believe he would keep to his word. He did not fully trust the man, but he thought once

Tanualdo had given his word that he meant them no harm, they would be safe for the time being.

Beobrand was aware that all of the people crowded before the entrance to the villa were staring at him. Some glowered with distrust, others with open interest. There were grey-beards there, and women of all ages. Children played, peeking out from where they hid in the flowerbeds. The place had the air of a festival. This was heightened by the rich smells of the food that had been laid out on huge platters on boards set up before the house. Off to one side, servants turned a boar on a spit over a fire pit. Its grease splashed into the embers and flared in the dying light. Beobrand's stomach growled. It had been a long time since he had eaten roast boar, his favourite meat.

A couple of thralls, barefoot and wearing the simplest of drab tunics went to the fire pit, dipping brands into the coals until they flashed into life. Then they set off around the garden, lighting the torches and lamps that dotted the area.

Beobrand took all of this in, again wondering at the wealth and power of Tanualdo and his family. How many warriors did he have at his disposal? How many servants and thralls? Surely this man must be the lord of Sutri and the surrounding area. Why then would his men be robbing travellers on the road like common wolf-heads? It made no sense to Beobrand.

Lucifrido was signalling for him to follow Tanualdo to the left of the entrance. Beobrand pulled his gaze away from the people and the piles of sumptuous foodstuffs and saw another table heaped with bags, sacks, a chest and a scattering of other smaller items. It took Beobrand a couple of heartbeats to recognise the possessions that had been stolen from Fredegar and Coenred's room.

"So you did steal our things?" he said. Despite what he had said to his gesithas, he placed his hand on the hilt of his sword. He had not wished to believe that these men had been responsible for killing Fredegar and taking their treasure, but now there could be no doubt. The guards tensed. One half-drew his sword from a black scabbard.

Tanualdo stopped the man with a command, then spoke to Lucifrido.

"Tanualdo again apologises for the headstrong actions of some of the young men of the family. They did not act on his orders and they will be punished for what they did. Tanualdo does not wish to be enemies. He offers you your things."

"Why?" asked Beobrand. "Why return what was taken?"

When Tanualdo heard Beobrand's question, he called over to the throng of people. A figure stepped out of the crowd and walked towards them. It was a young woman. With a start, Beobrand recognised her as one of the women he had rescued from the merchants. She stepped close to Tanualdo and he wrapped a solid arm around her shoulders, pulling her tightly to him.

He spoke and Lucifrido again interpreted.

"You have already met my youngest boy, Perteradi. This is Nezetta, my only daughter. She looks so much like her mother." The girl's dark eyes peered at Beobrand coyly through her lashes. When he had last seen her, her face had been blotchy and tear-streaked. Now he could see she was a pretty thing, plump-cheeked and smooth-skinned, tanned like her father. "Do you have children, lord Beobrand?"

"I do. A son and a daughter."

"Then you know the great service you have done me. If anything were to happen to my Nezetta..." His voice trailed off and he allowed Lucifrido to speak his words in Anglisc.

Beobrand thought again of Vulmar and the men who had taken Ardith. He understood well what a father would do for his daughter. A thought came to him then.

"Whose was that scream we heard?" he asked.

Tanualdo shrugged and let out a sheepish sigh.

"You had weakened him with your hands," he said. "He was not so strong. The other two are inside still. I will keep them alive until they are recovered. I would have them suffer more for what they did. Before they meet their god."

He spoke the words with a chilling lack of passion. Beobrand felt a scratch of anxiety run along his spine. Nezetta's expression did not change. She gave no sign she had heard her father's talk of torture and murder. Giving his daughter a soft kiss on the cheek, Tanualdo sent her back to the rest of the family.

"Now you see why I return your things to you," he said. "With a small levy deducted, of course. It is customary to pay tribute to my family when staying in these lands."

On hearing these words, Beobrand's anger began to bubble up.

"A levy?" he said, incredulous. "Are you saying the man has the nerve to steal openly from me?"

Lucifrido grew sombre.

"Lord Beobrand," he said, lowering his voice. "You would do well to think about where you find yourself. You have killed men of the family and Tanualdo has let you live. Do not defy him on this, he is not a man to argue, no matter what you did for his daughter."

Beobrand seethed with fury. By Woden, he would like to draw Nægling and lay about him with the blade. When he was younger he might have done so, but now he held his infamous temper in check. He would surely die if he was not careful. His men too. This was not the time for anger and heroic deeds. He was not a simple warrior who could throw away his life for vengeance. He must think and act like a lord of men. With difficulty, he swallowed down his rage, and glared at Tanualdo.

The man moved to the table, picking up a small piece of silver from the chest and examining it studiously. He acted as if he was unaware of Beobrand's outburst and the conversation taking place with Lucifrido. He uttered some words in a laconic tone.

Lucifrido repeated them in Anglisc.

"He says he hopes you can be friends, you and him."

Beobrand took a calming breath.

"Thank him for our possessions," he said, "but I fear we cannot be friends. His men killed one who travelled with us. He was an envoy from Clovis, King of Neustria himself. He had been good to us and I cannot ignore his death so easily."

Tanualdo set down the piece of silver and met Beobrand's gaze. His eyes were black, devoid of emotion. He did not blink.

"You killed four young men in the hills," he said, his voice rasping now with the sharpness of steel. "All four were dear to me, with mothers and fathers, sisters and brothers. One of them was my cousin Agiperto's boy. You think Agiperto is pleased that I am letting you live?"

He looked towards the gathering outside the house. A thin man with unruly grey hair and stubble on his cheeks was at the edge of the group. When Beobrand followed Tanualdo's gaze, the man's eyes met his. There was such hatred in those eyes that Beobrand knew instantly this must be Agiperto, the father of one of the men he had slain. He tried to recall the faces of the men he had killed, searching for a resemblance, but he could not. He had seen them for only a moment before they had been killed and there were too many dead in his past to hold all their faces in his mind. They would return to him in his sleep though. Of that he was certain. His nightmares never forgot the faces of the slain.

Agiperto, distraught and shaking, began to shout. He spat towards Beobrand, aiming gestures of insult in his direction. He moved closer, raving and screaming, his fury and grief driving him mad, emboldening him. Beobrand turned to face the man, placing his hand on Nægling's pommel. No matter the man's sorrow, Beobrand would not allow Agiperto to strike him.

Tanualdo snapped an order. Two of his guards stepped in to restrain Agiperto. The grief-stricken father struggled for a time, then allowed one of the men to lead him away. The sound of his sobbing was loud in the hush that had fallen over the gathering.

Tanualdo waited patiently until Agiperto had been led into the house. A woman clothed in black glowered at Beobrand with red-rimmed eyes, then followed Agiperto and the guard. The people gathered before the entrance were silent. Some of them stared with undisguised dislike at the large fair-haired stranger who conversed with their leader. Beobrand did not shy away from their baleful looks. These people were no friends of his.

Tanualdo clapped his hands and shouted something at his family. Slowly, first one, then the rest of them, began to speak in hushed tones. Soon, the hubbub of chatter filled the warm garden once more. Beobrand glanced over to where his men were eating and drinking by the pond. Dusk had settled over the land and the shadows were dark now. But he could make out Cynan's anxious expression well enough, lit by the flames of one of the guttering torches. Beobrand held up a hand to show there was no need for concern. He hoped he was right.

When he looked back at Tanualdo, the older man's previous goodwill seemed to have vanished with the last rays of the sun. He scowled at Beobrand and spoke in a clipped, quiet voice that was vastly more disconcerting than Agiperto's raving and shouting fury.

Lucifrido hesitated before translating his words. He asked Tanualdo a question. The man's answer was brief and curt. It was clear his patience had worn thin.

Lucifrido was no longer smiling.

"Tanualdo says he has considered your plight. The Frank was your guide and interpreter, was he not?"

Beobrand nodded, unsure of the path the conversation was following.

Lucifrido sighed.

"Then my master says he will send you one who can guide you, who knows the streets of Roma and speaks your tongue too."

Lucifrido stared at him, as if expecting a reaction. Slowly, the young man's meaning dawned on Beobrand.

"You," he said.

A hint of his infectious smile flickered over Lucifrido's features.

"The same."

Beobrand snorted.

"Tell Tanualdo that the envoy of the King of the Franks cannot be so easily replaced."

Lucifrido did not immediately interpret his words.

"You would do well to accept his offer," he said in a voice not much louder than a whisper, "and be thankful."

Beobrand was still furious. He could see no way to exact any vengeance for Fredegar. To leave here with most of their belongings and a guide was truly better than he had hoped for, and yet he still felt the need to goad Tanualdo.

"Tell him," he said.

With a sigh, Lucifrido spoke. Tanualdo listened without expression, then fixed Beobrand with his dark stare as he gave his reply. Lucifrido translated his words. All the while, Tanualdo kept his unblinking eyes on Beobrand.

"He says he is done talking about this, and I urge you not to push him further." Lucifrido's smile had vanished. He was deadly earnest now. "Tanualdo is grateful to you for protecting his daughter's honour, but he warns you to take what he has given you and to go in peace. He will not abide you haggling with him as if you are trading horses."

Beobrand looked from Lucifrido to Tanualdo. He might as well have been staring into the stone face of one of the statues in the garden, for there was no give in the older man's gaze.

At last, Beobrand gave a slight nod and turned away. He knew he should be thankful for what he was taking with him, but as he walked stiffly back towards his waiting men, his mouth was sour with the bitter taste of defeat.

PART TWO

RELICS OF RUIN

Chapter 17

Coenred's skin prickled. He suppressed a shudder.
"It is cool down here," he said, rubbing his arms.
"It is," replied Marsiglio, without looking back.

Coenred hurried after his guide. Oil lamps dotted the path they were following through the catacombs. The flame of the small lamp Marsiglio held flickered, making the shadows in the niches and arches loom and bob.

After the dusty heat of the midday sun, these subterranean corridors and rooms were indeed cooler, but Coenred knew that was not the only reason for his shivering. To think that behind each of the niches they passed lay the mortal remains of some long-dead martyr or noble of Roma. Coenred could not help imagining all the lamps suddenly blowing out and becoming lost down here, alone in the darkness; nobody for company but the dead.

He murmured the paternoster as he followed the light in his guide's hand. It was foolish to entertain such thoughts. These were the resting places of good Christ-followers. The bones of many saints lay buried in these tombs and he was blessed to be able to come here. Few men were so fortunate and he must not allow such fearful thoughts to taint his experience. This was the destination of the pilgrimage that had taken him all the way from Lindisfarena. Conant and Comdhan had been so envious of him when Coenred had been given the messages to carry to Hereswitha in Cala and then to His Holiness Martinus, the Pontifex Maximus himself. They would be desperate for details of what it was like to tread in the footsteps of such holy men. He would not disappoint them.

Marsiglio stepped out into a wider area. Several lamps burnt there already. Coenred had begrudged the fee requested by the man at the entrance to the catacomb, but he supposed oil was expensive and keeping the lamps burning was no small task.

It was the man at the steps into the catacombs who had planted the seed of fear within Coenred's mind.

"Stick to the lit areas and all will be well," the man had said, accepting the piece of hack silver and handing a lamp to Marsiglio. "Do not stray. Nobody knows how far these tunnels stretch. Some years back a man was lost down there for three days." Coenred had thought he had been exaggerating, trying to frighten a gullible visitor to the city. But the longer they had been down here, the less sure he was. The labyrinth of tunnels seemed to go on forever.

"This is the crypt of Saint Lucina," Marsiglio said, turning to face him with a smile. Marsiglio's head was shaved in the tonsure of the monks of Roma, a circle of baldness, surrounded with hair to symbolise the crown of thorns. Marsiglio was a member of the Pontifex's household and had been given the task of guiding Coenred's pilgrimage around Roma by Martinus himself. Marsiglio was about the same age as Beobrand, but other than their age, the monk could not have been any more different. He was short and slender, dark of skin and hair, as was the way of the people from far-off Nobatia. His features too were soft, his eyes tender and thoughtful, where Beobrand's were flinty and cold.

"If you desire," Marsiglio went on, "I could leave you alone for a time to pray." His eyes twinkled in the lamplight.

"I am happy to contemplate the holy place with you," Coenred replied.

"That is good," said Marsiglio. "But when you wish to head back to your companions, I will be happy to do so. I do not relish being underground so much. I think perhaps this was His Holiness' jest at my expense. He knows I find these old catacombs... disturbing. I think he finds my unease amusing."

Relief washed over Coenred.

"I am pleased to hear you say such a thing," he replied. "Not about the Pontifex Maximus jesting with you." He felt his cheeks grow hot and was glad the darkness would hide his embarrassment. "But I am not wholly at ease here myself. I know these are holy places and I am overjoyed to be here..."

"Of course."

"And yet..." He struggled for the words to best describe how he felt. He did not know Marsiglio well and did not wish to give a bad impression of himself. "And yet I cannot seem to stop thinking about the bones of the countless people buried here." He sniffed.

"The air is not so sweet down here, is it?" said Marsiglio.

"I am sure I can smell all of the deceased," said Coenred. The air was stiff with the sickly scent of decay and perfume.

"Well, if you are happy not to linger, I will lead us back to the surface forthwith."

"That would be good," said Coenred. He pointed to an earthenware jar beside one of the lamps. "Is that oil?"

Marsiglio removed the wooden lid.

"Please," he said. "Fill your *ampulla*. It is there for that very purpose."

Coenred took the leather bag he carried slung over his shoulder and rummaged within. Setting it on the ground, he took one of the small flasks he had purchased and unstoppered it. Within the jar of oil, there was a small metal spoon, and he used this to fill the vial, before replacing the wooden stopper.

Coenred slipped the *ampulla* into his satchel, careful not to break it or any of the other flasks. He had bought several empty *ampullae* at Marsiglio's urging when they had visited the Basilica of Saint Lorenzo.

"It is the fashion now for pilgrims," the monk had said, pointing to several sellers with collections of the flasks on display. "You fill each one with the oil from the lamps in the different tombs of the catacombs. In that way, you can take back to your home a small piece of the essence of the saints' resting place."

The cost of the small flasks had seemed exorbitant to Coenred. He had haggled for a time, but in the end he had relented and paid more than the things were worth. He had a small amount of silver and he doubted he would ever return to the decaying majesty of Roma. The labelled *ampullae* would make wonderful gifts for his brothers in Christ. He would reserve some of the rarest, those from the most potent saints, to be gifted to Queen Eanflæd. He had suggested as much to Wilfrid, but the young novice had scoffed at the idea.

"You can take your pots of oil back to the queen," he said. "I will return with relics of much greater worth." Wilfrid had come with them to the Basilica of Saint Lorenzo, but after that, he had found places to visit he deemed more likely to provide him with what he sought. With his usual nose for power, Wilfrid had already become acquainted with some of the cardinals and bishops they had met at the Pontifex Maximus' residence, the Lateran Palace. Marsiglio insisted it was not a palace, but a *patriarchium*, the home of the patriarch. With its cool marble floors, soaring arches and ornate gardens, it certainly looked like a palace to Coenred.

It was much too grand for his liking, but no doubt Wilfrid

dreamt of building a residence on that scale. Wilfrid's attitude aggrieved Coenred. While it was true that Wilfrid had access to far more silver than Coenred following his encounter with the monarchs of Neustria, Coenred could not abide his rudeness. Whenever he dealt with Wilfrid, it was all he could do to remain courteous and Christian. He quite understood Eadgard's desire to beat the young man; his ambition and disregard for others was enough to incense even the most forgiving of men. Coenred prayed that in time God would lead Wilfrid to a better, more compassionate understanding of His word. Coenred also implored the Almighty to give him the strength never to strike the foolish young man, no matter the provocation. Coenred deplored violence, but he knew from his own bitter experience that even the most peaceful of men could be driven to lash out. And it seemed to Coenred that at times Wilfrid took pleasure in goading others. He had best be careful, thought Coenred. For surely Eadgard would not be praying for guidance and temperance of his ire where Wilfrid was concerned.

Marsiglio replaced the lid on the jar. His dark skin shimmered like basalt in the lamplight.

"The crypt of Lucina, you say?" Coenred asked. "You must remind me when we get back to the palace so that I can scribe the label."

Marsiglio bowed his head.

"Of course. It is said that Lucina listens to prayers here. She was most blessed among women and helped collect and bury the bodies of many holy martyrs. God sent her a vision so that she could find Saint Sebastianus' remains. It is said she was a great healer in life and in death is still able to cure all manner of ailments."

"Then I fear we must tarry here a while longer," said Coenred. "I would not be able to look Wulfwyn in the eye if I did not pray to the holy Lucina asking that she restore Aelfwig's sight."

"Quite so," said Marsiglio, taking a few steps back. "There is a place to kneel there, before the tomb."

Coenred knelt. The stone was smooth and cold. Closing his eyes he offered up a prayer to Saint Lucina, asking that she petition the Almighty to return Aelfwig's sight. Wulfwyn had wanted to accompany them, but two days after arriving in the city she had been taken ill with a fever.

She was not the only one of their party to succumb. Eadgard too had complained of watery guts and had spent the last few days on a mattress in their quarters in the palace, shivering and bathed in sweat. It was unclear what had caused the illness or how grave it might prove to be. The arrow wound had not festered and was healing well.

His Holiness Martinus had called on his own physician, Zanobi, to attend them both. Zanobi had assured Coenred it was the ague, which was common in these parts. Wulfwyn and Eadgard were both young and strong, he said, and the trembling and sweats should pass in time. Coenred hoped Zanobi was right. He could not bear the thought of Aelfwig coming all this way only to lose his father in the mountains, and then his mother in Roma itself.

Coenred added Wulfwyn and Eadgard to his prayers. Once he had finished praying, Coenred stood and rubbed his knees.

Marsiglio smiled. "I prayed too," he said. "For the boy and his mother."

"I give you thanks. You did not also pray for Eadgard?"

"The big man? Yes, of course, but I could not recall his name." Marsiglio beamed, his teeth gleaming in the gloom. "Still, I think that one does not need our prayers so much. He looks as strong as an ox."

Coenred chuckled.

"He is," he said. "As stubborn too."

"With his strength and stubbornness, our prayers, and those

of the Pontifex himself, I would say Eadgard has a good chance of recovering."

"I am not sure that he understands the honour it is that Martinus would take an interest in his plight. Wulfwyn though was overjoyed."

Coenred recalled the widow's tears when she had heard that the Pontifex would hold her and the axeman in his prayers. More importantly for her, he had promised to pray for Aelfwig as well. Coenred marvelled at that. Surely the Almighty listened to the prayers of the Pontifex Maximus, the Bishop of Roma himself, above those of other men.

Coenred remembered his first meeting with Martinus with a mixture of awe and reverence. Coenred wasn't sure what he had expected, but the patriarch of the Church of Roma was not the imposing figure that his vaulted office might have suggested. He was an elderly man with a full, greying beard, quietly spoken and thoughtful. While he lived in luxury, surrounded by guards, artefacts, polished stone and silver and was waited on by a staff of priests and servants, the Pontifex was humble, approachable and kind. He reminded Coenred of both Fearghas and Aidan, which should not have come as a surprise, for they had both been touched by the hand of God.

Martinus had welcomed the pilgrims from Albion warmly, wanting to know all about their long journey. He seemed genuinely interested in not only tales of their travels and exploits, but in the pilgrims themselves, as people, members of his flock for whom it was his duty and honour to shepherd in all things spiritual.

Of all of them, only Wilfrid had appeared somewhat disappointed in the Pontifex's calm and attentive demeanour. The young man believed a leader of the Church should be ambitious, reflecting the power he wielded in the name of God with lavish displays of pomp and ceremony.

Marsiglio raised his lamp, leading the way out of the crypt and into a narrow tunnel. Wilted roses, violets and sprigs of greenery littered the niches to either side, where people had commemorated the dead.

"I find it hard to believe Grindan is truly Eadgard's brother," Marsiglio said over his shoulder. "They have little in common."

"It can look that way," Coenred said, following close behind. The shadows stretched and warped the shapes of the sarcophagi they passed. "But when you see them fight, you see they are forged from the same iron. They are both formidable warriors."

Marsiglio made the sign of the cross. There were no flames burning here. The only illumination came from Marsiglio's lamp. The light flickered, giving tantalising glimpses of carved inscriptions in Latin and Grecisc. Part of Coenred wanted to pause, to decipher the secrets of these tombs, but he did not ask Marsiglio to halt. He'd had plenty of these catacombs for one day. He had slowed to look at the carvings and the darkness now threatened to swallow him. He hurried to keep up.

"You have seen much fighting then?" asked Marsiglio. "You are braver than I."

Coenred laughed.

"Brave is not a word many would use to describe me. As to battle, I have seen too much of it. It always terrifies me."

They entered another larger space. There were lamps burning here, and from the other side of the chamber, the narrow passageway continued. Marsiglio lofted his lamp. The light shone on the inscriptions. There were paintings here too; depictions of angels, a shepherd carrying a lamb on his shoulders, a basket of loaves and fish.

"There is always call for good men willing to stand and fight the enemies of God," he said.

Coenred was distracted as he read the words chiselled into the rock above the large tomb to the left.

"True," he said absently. "The resting place of Cyrinus," he read aloud. The name had brought a thought to the forefront of his mind.

"Yes. That tunnel will lead us back to the steps."

Coenred slung his bag from his back and pulled out a folded parchment. Unfolding it carefully, he held it close to the nearest lamp.

"Wait a moment," he said, scanning the scratched writing that covered the vellum. "Ah yes," he said at last. "It is as I thought. We cannot leave so soon. The guide says I should visit the tomb of Flavianus."

Marsiglio gave a lopsided smile.

"If the guide says so, who am I to disagree?"

A Grecas merchant had sold the parchment to Coenred outside the Basilica of Saint Lorenzo. He had watched as the monk from Albion had bought the *ampullae* from another trader and then he had sidled up to Coenred.

"A guide to all the sites spiritual and holy of the most sacred Eternal City of Roma," the merchant had said, bowing obsequiously and proffering the paper in both hands.

Marsiglio had snatched the parchment from the man, rapidly perusing the crabbed writing.

"The text seems real enough," he whispered to Coenred. "But what he is asking for it is as bad as robbery."

Coenred had talked the Grecas man down, but Marsiglio had rolled his eyes at the size of the piece of silver he had parted with in the end. After that first day travelling around the churches and tombs, Coenred had learnt that his silver would not go far in this city.

"You know the way to the tomb of Flavianus?" Coenred asked.

"I do," Marsiglio replied, "and I thank the Almighty it is not far. I would see the light of day again soon. Come, follow me."

He made his way to the tunnel at the far side of the crypt. Coenred fancied he could see movement down there. Shadows drifted in front of a light. Whispered voices echoed from the stone. He shivered, again thinking of the dead and feeling afresh the memory of the terror that had gripped him in the forest.

Marsiglio smiled.

"No need to look so frightened," he said. "We are not alone down here, but those we can hear are other pilgrims. The man at the entrance said there was another party here. If I am not mistaken, they are in the very tomb you wish to visit next. Perhaps they have the same parchment to guide them."

Feeling foolish, Coenred followed Marsiglio into the tunnel.

"You have known the lord Beobrand a long time?" Marsiglio asked. Since they had descended the stone steps into these catacombs, the man had barely stopped speaking. Coenred wondered whether Marsiglio was doing so for Coenred's benefit, attempting to keep him from dwelling on his fears. Or perhaps it was his own nervousness that drove him to chatter so.

"Since I was a novice," Coenred said, deciding he did not care why Marsiglio was asking so many questions just as long as it kept his mind busy. "I can barely recall a time when I did not know him."

"You are friends then?"

Coenred thought for a heartbeat before answering.

"Yes, we are friends."

"He is another man of war, it seems."

"A great warrior."

"But a man of Christ."

Coenred was unsure what to say to that. The whispered voices of the other pilgrims were louder now. He could see their shadows shifting and moving ahead. He licked his lips.

"He is a good man," he said at last.

Marsiglio glanced at him askance, as if he understood Coenred's unspoken meaning.

"And his men too?"

"They are all good men," Coenred said awkwardly. It was not for him, he thought, to divulge whether the warriors were devout followers of Christ or if they chose to worship the old gods. They were his friends. That was all that mattered.

They were nearing the tomb now. Coenred thought he could detect the tongue of the Franks being spoken in hushed reverence.

"That Lucifrido is a strange one though," Marsiglio said before they reached the end of the tunnel.

"What do you mean?"

Marsiglio shrugged.

"A feeling," he said. "He smiles too much."

"You smile a lot too."

Marsiglio smiled.

"True, but my smile hides nothing."

"You think Lucifrido is hiding something?"

Marsiglio raised his eyebrows.

"You don't?"

Lucifrido and Grindan had accompanied them to the catacombs from the Lateran *Patriarchium* where they were staying as Martinus' guests. They had decided not to descend below ground with the monks, instead content to doze in the shade of the cypress trees that dotted the cemetery. Lucifrido said he had visited the catacombs before and did not need to see them again. Grindan had seemed torn, but in the end decided to stay with Lucifrido. Coenred thought perhaps Beobrand had ordered him to keep an eye on the man from Sutri. Beobrand certainly did not trust Tanualdo's man.

Coenred touched his face. The bruises had faded and were no longer tender, but the lump on his head remained, though it was smaller now. Not for the first time he wondered whether

Lucifrido had been one of the men who had killed Fredegar and beaten him. Even if Lucifrido had not actually been in their room that night, he was of the same clan, a man who made his way in life by preying on the defenceless.

And yet he was friendly enough and had been nothing but courteous in the ten days since he had joined them in Sutri. He had apologised to Coenred for what had happened, but his words had been such as to leave Coenred wondering at his true meaning. Was Lucifrido confessing his involvement? Coenred had wanted to ask him, but could not summon the courage. So much for his bravery, he thought.

Beobrand had not warmed to the man, despite his affable nature and the ease with which he conducted himself. The rest of the men were perhaps not close to Lucifrido, but in the days since his arrival, they had grown to accept him within their ranks. And there could be no denying that his knowledge of the road from Sutri, and then of Roma itself, had proven beneficial to them.

Coenred thought of the day they had arrived at the great city. He had been open-mouthed with awe. The place was vast, beyond any other city he had seen before. He had once believed Eoferwic to be too crowded, its tall walls and jumble of buildings oppressive and stifling. Then he had visited Paris and the even grander Liyon, with its Roman bridge, huge amphitheatre and splendid palaces. But those cities were nothing when compared to the Eternal City of Roma, sprawling over its seven hills, the broad Tiberis river coiling through its centre.

But as they'd drawn closer and eventually traversed the streets, Coenred had seen that much of the city had fallen into ruin and disrepair. Marble columns and bronze statues jutted from marshy pasture dotted with grazing red cattle. Once lavish temples to ancient gods were surrounded now by briars, brambles and twisted trees.

Coenred had stared about him, marvelling at the grandeur

of the buildings that remained standing and even those massive structures that had collapsed. A great covered bridge of stone arches cut across the fields. Several of the arches had been broken, rocks and tiles tumbled in the scrub, overgrown with weeds.

The rest of the pilgrims had looked around them as if in a dream. Wilfrid alone seemed unhappy with what he saw.

"Is this it?" he'd whispered, almost to himself. "Is this the great Roma?"

"This is the *Disabitato*," Lucifrido had said. "The uninhabited part of the city."

"How has it been left to fall into such abandon?" Coenred asked.

Lucifrido shrugged.

"War. Famine. Floods. The years have not been kind to Roma."

"But the Pontifex resides here," Coenred said, aghast. "This is the holy see of the Bishop of Roma."

Lucifrido spat into the nettles that grew beside the paved road. A sudden movement caught Coenred's eye. A rat scurried over a pile of weed-smothered rubble, disappearing as quickly as it had appeared. Lucifrido grinned.

"Christ does not mend buildings," he'd said. "Or rebuild aqueducts, it seems."

"Careful," whispered Marsiglio, bringing Coenred back to the present.

Stepping out of the tunnel, Marsiglio bowed his head to avoid the low archway. Coenred ducked behind him and entered the area beyond. It was larger than the tunnel, but cramped by the presence of four men. They were sombre, their pale faces turned towards the newcomers. On seeing the two monks, they visibly relaxed. The oldest of them, a slight man, with a thin, grey beard, made the sign of the cross and nodded in welcome.

"God's blessing be upon you," Marsiglio said.

"And upon you, brother," replied the man. His accent was strong, but his Latin was fluent. He bit his lip, embarrassed. "I am glad to see you are men of God. We were scared you might be thieves. We have heard such terrible tales of the bands of ruffians that prey on the faithful."

"No," said Marsiglio, offering them a wide smile, "not thieves."

"I told you," said a younger man. He resembled the first, but his beard was black, his shoulders broader. "There is nothing to fear down here." He rapped his knuckles on the sealed entrance to one of the tombs set into the wall. The sound was hollow and shockingly loud. "The dead can cause us no harm."

"Hush now, Fridolin," said the old man. "It is not the dead I am worried about." He looked with a pleading expression at the other men in his party. They scowled and shook their heads in outrage. "Come now," the old man continued. "These men wish to pray to Saint Flavianus. Let us leave them in peace in this holy place."

"They are welcome to it," said Fridolin. "The stink of it fills my nose. I would wash the taste of the dead from my throat with some good wine."

The older man sighed. Shaking his head he said, "My name is Sergius and I apologise for my son. He is weary."

"No need to apologise," said Marsiglio. "We had planned to leave the catacombs after our visit to this tomb. We are heading back to the city after that. There are guards waiting for us outside. You are welcome to join us if you wish. Your son is right that there is nothing to fear from the dead here, but it is also true that the roads outside the walls are not safe."

"That is kind of you," said Sergius. "We would be honoured to accept your offer."

"Nonsense," said Fridolin. "We have no need of these monks. I wish to take a drink at that vineyard we saw on the way here."

Even in the flickering light of the lamps, Coenred could see Sergius' cheeks flush. He was clearly ashamed of his son's contemptuous tone, but he forced a smile at Marsiglio and Coenred.

"We will leave you to pray and will await you outside the entrance."

"We will not be long," replied Marsiglio, with a slight bow.

They waited until the small group had left, their voices and the echoing scuff of their feet vanishing into silence once more. They had been able to hear Fridolin's angry berating of his father long after the light from their lamps had disappeared into the gloom.

"You never know who you will meet in Roma," Marsiglio said. "Pilgrims come from all over the world. For many different reasons."

"I would imagine," said Coenred, "that some pray for the Lord to grant their sons more grace, and that they might show more respect for their elders."

Marsiglio snorted.

"Do you think they will indeed be waiting for us when we leave?" he asked.

Coenred pondered a moment before answering.

"That man's son will never allow himself to be kept from the wine he craves. No. I believe we will be travelling back to the city without the company of those pilgrims."

"You know," said Marsiglio, "it may not be very Christian of me, but I hope you are right."

Chapter 18

Coenred breathed a sigh of relief as he climbed the steep steps out of the catacomb. The afternoon sun fell hot on his face, but the air was fresh, devoid of the stagnant reek of the decay of centuries, the sharp bite of quicklime and the sickly scent of old perfume, that pervaded the catacombs. Looking about the cemetery with its gravestones and faded tombs, he was pleased that his hunch had been correct. There was no sign of Sergius, Fridolin or the other pilgrims.

Pulling his hat from the satchel over his shoulder, he placed it on his head. He blinked against the brightness, taking in the small stone church on the rise. Seeing Marsiglio and Coenred emerging from the catacombs, several men came out from the shade of the building and hurried down towards them. In their hands they held the items that Coenred had become familiar with. Slivers of bone, trinkets, *ampullae*, parchments and anything else they thought they might be able to sell to unsuspecting pilgrims.

"You look like a man of learning," crooned one of the men with a weather-beaten, lined face. His grin exposed several missing teeth. Those that remained were as yellow and twisted as the tomb markers that dotted the graveyard. "I have one of the finger bones of Saint Caecilia herself."

Another man, as dark-skinned as Marsiglio, but much taller, shouldered the first seller aside, crowding close to Coenred.

"Forget finger bones," he crowed. "I can sell you a splinter of the True Cross. I even have Saint Synon's skull, for a man of worth such as yourself!"

He thrust a bleached skull towards Coenred, dark eye sockets yawning, teeth long and unusually clean. They were more numerous than the teeth of the man trying to sell him the finger bone. Coenred recoiled.

Lucifrido appeared, striding down from the church.

"Begone!" he shouted. "Out of the way!"

Grindan walked beside him, hand on his sword pommel. The hawkers dispersed, grumbling, and returned to the shade of the church.

"Vultures!" spat Lucifrido. "Selling pig bones and twigs."

"That skull was from no pig," Coenred said.

Lucifrido spat.

"Look about you," he said. "If you wish for a relic, go back down and take one. These carrion crows are as bad as the thieves on the road."

"I am content with my *ampullae*," Coenred said, patting his bag. He looked sidelong at Lucifrido. "You know much about the ways of these men."

"Enough to keep you safe," Lucifrido said.

Coenred smiled.

"And I thank you for it."

He did not push for further explanation. They all knew what manner of man Lucifrido was. But whatever his failings, Coenred was glad of the man's company. Grindan's too. Like all Roma's catacombs, the catacombs of Saint Callixtus were some distance outside the city walls and there were many stretches of the road where travellers were vulnerable to attack.

"Have you finished all of the wine?" Coenred asked. Fridolin had been right in one thing at least, the stink of the catacombs did linger in the throat.

Grindan handed Coenred the skin they had bought at a small vineyard that morning.

"We saved you a little," he said.

Coenred weighed the skin in his hand.

"Little indeed," he said with a raised eyebrow. He took a mouthful. The wine was warm and tart. There was not much left, but the rich flavour revived his spirits immediately. He passed the skin to Marsiglio.

"Be thankful we saved you any at all," said Grindan. "It is hot out here and we were both thirsty."

Lucifrido began walking down the path. The hills of Roma rose in the haze of the distance.

"Come," he called, "there is plenty of wine in the city."

They passed between fields of vines and rye. Far-off to the right, peeking above a stand of cypress trees, was a large building.

"That is the home of Stoldo," said Lucifrido. "A powerful man."

Coenred shielded his eyes from the sun's glare. He could make out the baked-earth red of the roof and the gleam of whitewashed walls.

"A farmer?" he asked.

Lucifrido smirked.

"Farming is an honest living," he said cryptically. "This land is Stoldo's. He has many interests."

They trudged on along the dusty cobbles of the *Via Appia* for some time, each lost in his own thoughts. Sweat trickled down Coenred's neck and the heat from the stones of the road permeated the thin soles of the sandals he wore, hurting his feet.

"This heat is intolerable," he muttered.

Marsiglio smiled.

"The day is not so hot, brother," he said. "There are days here when you could cook an egg on these stones. And even that is nothing when compared to the land of my birth."

"Well I am glad we are not there then," grumbled Coenred. "I feel as if my feet are being cooked in an oven."

Ahead of them several tall, wide-canopied pines grew either side of the road, where it passed over a stream. Grindan pointed ahead to the puddle of shadows beneath the trees.

"Perhaps you can bathe your feet and rest in the shade there."

Lucifrido shook his head.

"Best if we press on," he said. "The walls of the city are not so far and the palace not much further beyond that."

Grindan glanced at him.

"You think it unsafe to stop?"

Lucifrido sniffed, wiping the sweat from his brow with the back of his hand.

"I would rather we did not tarry on Stoldo's land. That is all."

Grindan met his gaze, then nodded.

"Then we will not pause."

As they neared the small stone bridge, Coenred saw that it arched steeply over a bed of pebbles. A thin trickle of water snaked between the dry stones and the sandy banks. No doubt in the winter this was a raging torrent. So close to midsummer, it was practically dry.

A cry of alarm cut through the still afternoon, shocking Coenred to a halt. They had seen few people on the road, and the path ahead of them had appeared empty. But now, without warning, a figure stumbled over the bridge towards them. With a start, Coenred recognised him.

"Sergius!" he exclaimed.

"You know him?" asked Lucifrido.

"A fellow pilgrim," Coenred said, his mouth dry. "We met in the catacombs. We offered him to travel with us. For safety."

In the glare of the afternoon sun, he saw bright blood on Sergius' face. The steep arch of the bridge and the shade of the pines had hidden him from their view, but now as they drew closer, Coenred saw that the other three pilgrims were also there, on the other side of the stream. They were surrounded by four men. Sunlight gleamed from the naked steel in their hands.

Lucifrido sucked air through his teeth.

"He should have accepted your offer," he said. "Come, I know another path that will take us back to the city. They'll leave us alone if we hurry. They have what they came for."

Sergius ran towards them, arms outstretched.

"Help us!" he wailed.

Ignoring the man's pleas, Lucifrido was already turning away.

Coenred grew cold despite the heat. He thought of what Marsiglio had said about needing men who would fight to defend others.

"We must aid them," he said, his voice smaller than he would have liked. His stomach churned at the thought of placing themselves in danger. But even as he thought of the peril to himself, he broke into a sprint towards the bridge. He could not abandon these men to their fate.

Behind him, Lucifrido cursed loudly.

"Come back!" shouted Grindan.

But Coenred did not halt.

"Help them," he cried, his voice a croaking bark. "In the name of Jesu Christ and all the saints, help them!"

His sandals slipped as they slapped against the stones of the Appian Way. The satchel thumped against his back with each step. He could hear the fragile *ampullae* rattling inside. Fleetingly, he hoped they would not break.

Behind Sergius now came two of the armed men. On seeing them, a sliver of reason pierced Coenred's thoughts. What could he do to stop brigands armed with knives and swords? His running steps faltered and he slowed down. He did then the only other thing he could think of. He prayed.

He whispered fervently to Lucina and Flavianus, desperately hoping that the oil in the *ampullae*, taken from their tombs, would make them more likely to hear his entreaties.

Please aid these poor Christian pilgrims. By the grace of God, help them.

As if in answer, Grindan and Lucifrido sped past. Both had their swords drawn. At the sight of them, the men on the bridge halted.

"Let them go," shouted Lucifrido, stopping several paces from the bridge. He hauled Grindan back too and both of them stood there in the afternoon heat, panting, sweat soaking their kirtles.

"These pilgrims are ours," called the shorter of the two men on the bridge. His head was bald and looked as hard as a boulder. His red face had seen many fights, his nose twisted and misshapen.

Sergius had crossed the bridge now. He staggered along the road towards Grindan and Lucifrido. His eyes were dazed. He seemed unsure what was happening.

"You've had your fun, Vico," Lucifrido said. "Now let them go."

The ugly man's eyes narrowed.

"How do you know me? You have seen me fight?"

"No, I have never seen you fight," replied Lucifrido. "But I have heard your fists are like boulders. We met a couple of years back. In Sutri."

Vico peered at Lucifrido, trying to place him. He whispered something to the man beside him. The other man nodded, replying in a hissing whisper too quiet for Coenred to hear.

"You are Tanualdo's man," Vico said.

Lucifrido bowed slightly.

"I am."

"You are far from home."

"I am working."

"Looking after monks and pilgrims?" Vico sneered.

"Something like that."

"Stoldo will not like you being here without him knowing. You should have paid homage to him."

"We have only just arrived," Lucifrido lied. "As soon as I have these men settled in the city, I will pay him a visit." He slid his sword into its scabbard. "I will come tomorrow."

"How about you come now?" Vico said. "All of you."

Lucifrido smiled and held out his hands in a show of peace.

"They are expected at the table of the Pontifex Maximus himself. They would be missed if they did not return for the evening meal."

"If these men are the guests of His Holiness, he should send more guards with them."

"I will pass on the advice," said Lucifrido. "And I will pay my respects to Stoldo. Tomorrow." He whispered something to Sergius. The old man looked bemused. He shook his head, but did not speak. Lucifrido grabbed his shoulder, shaking him and hissing urgently. Sergius' eyes cleared somewhat and he replied in a whisper. Lucifrido nodded curtly then addressed Vico again. "Until then, please accept half of what those pilgrims carry, with our thanks as a gift to your leader."

Vico scowled.

"We could just kill them and take everything," he said.

"You could," said Lucifrido, "but it would prove... troublesome. These men are friends of Tanualdo, as well as of His Holiness, Martinus."

Vico conferred briefly with the taller man, then nodded.

"Very well," he said, "but see that you come to the villa tomorrow."

Chapter 19

Beobrand stared up at the massive columns supporting the portico. Baducing was right, the columns were larger than many of the edifices they had seen that morning, but it was yet another colonnade topped with a triangular stone pediment. Beobrand rubbed at the back of his neck. It was slick with sweat. Above the church the sky was congealed with clouds. The day was stiflingly hot, but unlike the last fortnight, it was now humid, the air thick with the threat of rain.

"I'm thirsty," Beobrand said, turning to Cynan, Bleddyn and Ingwald for support. "I fear I have seen enough old buildings for one day, my friend."

Baducing chuckled. He was a young man, whose stocky physique and broad, strong hands belied his noble upbringing, his studious nature and his quick wits. Ever since meeting Baducing the year before in Cantwareburh, Beobrand had liked the young novice.

"I understand how Roma can overwhelm the senses," Baducing said. "With treasures all around. The buildings, the statues, the relics, the catacombs, not to mention the scriptures and rare books that line the libraries of the palaces. But trust me on this," he offered them all a grin, "we will rest our feet and seek some ale and wine soon, but you have not seen anything like the *Pantheum* before."

"Very well," said Beobrand with a sigh. "Lead on."

He followed the thickset monk up the steps. Baducing still limped, though it seemed less pronounced now. He had broken his leg badly the previous winter, necessitating a stay in the north of Frankia over the winter while he recovered. Aculf, the leader of the gesithas who had accompanied him from Albion, walked beside Baducing. The five warriors had been sent by Baducing's father to guard him, and Aculf was quietly watchful, always looking for threats. They had heard, from what had happened to Coenred and the others, about the dangers of travelling through the *Disabitato* and outside the walls, but given the number of armed men in the party, Beobrand thought they would be safe enough. They had traversed the *Disabitato* that morning from the Lateran Palace without incident and now they were in the inhabited part of the city, where richly dressed men and women walked accompanied by only a small number of guards.

It was good to see Baducing, Aculf and the other warriors who had travelled with them from Cantwareburh. They had remained together for several weeks in Liyon before Baducing had finally grown weary and frustrated. His destination had always been Roma and after quarrelling with Wilfrid, he had headed south with his father's gesithas, accompanying a group of merchants. Beobrand did not blame Baducing. They should have gone with him, he mused, frowning as he traipsed up the steps behind Baducing and Aculf. If they had left Liyon sooner, Gram and Attor would both still live.

When they had been reunited the night before in the Lateran Palace, Baducing had been overjoyed to see them. He had embraced them each in turn, and Beobrand had been reminded how much he liked the man, and how different Baducing was from Wilfrid. They were both clever, with a great knowledge and interest in written teachings and the word of their god, but where Wilfrid was conniving, petty and ambitious, Baducing was thoughtful, caring and true.

Baducing had been dismayed to hear the details of what had happened in Liyon and later in Paris, and filled with sorrow to learn of the deaths of Gram and Attor. The latter in particular shook him.

"He had so looked forward to visiting the holy city," he'd said, tears welling in his eyes. "I will show you some of its most important churches tomorrow. You have travelled all this way, and you must tour the city before you leave. It would be my honour to guide you."

Beobrand had been pleased to accept, wishing to see more of the churches, basilicas and other great buildings. He had always marvelled at the skill of the men of Roma and the constructions they had left behind. Once he had even wondered whether giants might have been responsible for the huge Wall in the north and the imposing arena that housed the slave market in Cantwareburh. Here, at the heart of the old empire, memories of Roman genius were everywhere. He had commenced the morning full of enthusiasm, but as the day grew hotter and the clouds smothered the sun, his endurance had waned.

Baducing and Aculf passed into the shade of the portico, walking swiftly towards the towering bronze doors that stood open. Taking a deep breath, Beobrand strode after them. He would complain no more of the heat or his tiredness. Attor had wanted nothing more than to visit this place. Now Beobrand would take in every detail and commit it to memory. He owed it to Attor's spirit.

Several vendors lurked in the shadows beneath the colonnade and they called out to Beobrand and the others, recognising strangers to the city and potential marks. Beobrand ignored them. The hawkers did not approach. The tall, fair-haired thegn did not need to say a word. One look at his scarred face and sharp, ice-blue eyes was enough to dissuade them.

Baducing waited beside the bronze doors with Aculf. As Beobrand, Cynan, Ingwald and Bleddyn reached him, Baducing stepped inside. Remaining outside, Aculf gestured for Beobrand and the others to enter.

Beobrand stepped beneath the lintel. The doors were at least three times the height of a man. Inside, Baducing swept his arm about him.

"Behold," he said, "the *Basilica Santa Maria ad Martyres*."

Ingwald let out a long whistle. Beobrand's breath caught in his throat as he looked around the interior of the church. Bleddyn produced a sound half way between a sob and a laugh, as if he wasn't sure how to respond to what he was witnessing.

The Waelisc man turned on the spot, looking about him, his face bright from the light streaming in from the circular hole in the centre of the domed roof.

"Just when you think you've seen all that Roma has to offer, you step inside something like this."

Baducing was beaming at the reaction the church had provoked. He was clearly delighted to be the one to show them this wonder and looked as proud as if he had built the place himself.

"There are many fabulous buildings in the Eternal City," he said. "But you will find no other like this. It has been a place of worship for over five hundred years."

Beobrand gazed upwards, unbelieving of the enormity of the dome. It was covered in square indentations of such perfect regularity, each picked out with the shadows caused by the light tumbling through the circular opening at the roof's apex. The floor and walls were polished marble and the whole place felt impossibly large. Bleddyn's reaction was understandable.

"How is it possible?" Cynan said, voicing a question that was also in Beobrand's mind. "There are no pillars holding the roof up. And it is made of stone."

"Not stone," said Baducing, "but *opus caementicium*. It is used in many of the constructions of Roma. But none greater or more impressive than this dome."

"But what is it, if not stone?"

"It was like liquid stone that hardened when dry. I believe those square indentations held the frame upon which it was cast."

Cynan shook his head.

"It is hard to believe," he said.

"The men of ancient Roma knew this place as the *Pantheum*, or *Pantheion*, which means 'temple of all the gods'. It is circular so that each of their gods could have their own shrine." He walked them around the edge of the great circular building. Every few paces they passed an alcove hollowed into the massively thick wall. Each of the niches held a different altar or gilded statue. "Now," said Baducing, "where once there were demons, there are saints and the blessed mother."

Beobrand circled the building. It was peaceful and cool here, the sounds of their steps and the voices of the others in the church echoing and calming. He thought of all the men and women who had come here to worship over the centuries. His mind could not fathom how many that might have been.

When they had walked from the palace through the large areas of pasture and farmland of the *Disabitato*, Baducing had told them some of the history of the city. Beobrand's mind still swirled with the information. Centuries before, all of the area within the walls had been inhabited. Where cattle now grazed and vines grew, houses had once stood. Beobrand had seen the decaying city of Lunden on the Temes, but that was nothing compared to the scale here.

"Where did all the people go?" he had asked.

"The way of all people," Baducing had replied. "When the city was overrun by *barbaroi*, many people were killed."

"*Barbaroi?*"

Baducing had smiled.

"It is what the men of Roma called uncivilised races. Men with beards. Those who worshipped different gods to the Romans. Savage men, from the north. *Galatae. Germani.*" He shrugged. "Men like you and me."

Beobrand shook his head in amazement.

"They must have been formidable warriors indeed to destroy all of this and kill everyone who lived here."

"Much more than the attacks of the *barbaroi* led to the city you now see. There have been several wars and yes, many Romans were killed. But there has also been pestilence, floods, even tremors of the earth itself that caused buildings to collapse."

"For a city you call holy," said Beobrand, "it seems as if your god has abandoned it."

Baducing acknowledged Beobrand's words with a nod.

"Some have called it cursed," he said. "And yet there is still much good here. I have learnt more than I would have believed since I arrived. And I have visited the shrines of many important martyrs."

"I have heard these martyrs mentioned many times. They are holy men?"

"Holy men. Women too," said Baducing. "Killed for their faith."

"And the bones of these dead are sacred to you?"

"Very much so," replied Baducing, his tone solemn.

Beobrand shivered. He did not comprehend the desire to worship the bones of long-dead men and women. Coenred had been excited to visit the catacombs; tunnels of the dead. Beobrand had drawn the line at that.

"There is nothing to fear," Coenred had said before he had headed off the previous morning.

Beobrand had shuddered, imagining skeletons piled high in cavernous crypts.

"I am not afraid," he said. "Nor am I a follower of your Christ god, so I will remain above ground with the living."

Coenred had smiled at that, but when he had returned late in the afternoon, he had been shaken and scared. When Beobrand heard of what had happened, he had been angry.

"I should have gone with you," he'd said, his fear for his friend making his tone sharp. He would never have forgiven himself if Coenred had been hurt by the brigands on the road.

"We are unhurt," Coenred had said reassuringly. "By God's grace Lucifrido was with us. Besides, you were right."

"How so?"

"I am pleased that I have visited the catacombs where so many martyrs are interred, but even I was unnerved to be surrounded by the dead far below ground."

"Even you?" said Beobrand, raising an eyebrow. "You speak as if you are seldom afraid."

"Well, I found it difficult enough to journey into the catacombs. You would most likely have been frozen in terror." He grinned at Beobrand.

"Is that so?"

"Yes, and I am not sure I would have been able to carry your bulk from the darkness."

Beobrand had laughed with the rest of them. He was glad Coenred had returned safely, even though the old pilgrim Sergius' wounds were testament to the dangers he had faced. But Beobrand was secretly pleased he had not ventured into the subterranean tombs.

He was still thinking about the conversation and Sergius' injuries when they stepped out of the domed church. Aculf and the other gesithas were waiting by the doors. They all walked together into the overcast heat of the afternoon.

"I promised you ale and wine," said Baducing, clapping his hands, "and I will not disappoint my friends. Follow me."

He limped off down a street that Beobrand thought led towards the river.

"You seem to be at home here," he said, glancing at the magnificent buildings. "Amongst all this grandeur."

Baducing followed his gaze.

"When I first arrived, I could barely concentrate on the books I found in the libraries. My mind was filled with visions of the temples and palaces." He scratched at the stubble growing on his head. "I am still in awe of the city, but like anything, I have become accustomed to it. It remains inspiring and full of wonder, but it no longer seems strange to me."

Beobrand wondered whether the great city could ever seem normal to him.

"What of the people who live here?" he asked.

"There are men and women from every part of middle earth," Baducing said. "There aren't the numbers of citizens there once were, but you can find anything in the world within the walls of Roma."

"And outside the walls?"

Baducing looked at him sharply.

"You speak of what occurred to Coenred?"

Ahead of them, a man began bellowing at a heavily laden donkey. The creature's back was piled high with crates and sacks and the animal stood in the middle of the cobbled street, refusing to move.

"What do you know of this Stoldo?" Beobrand said, watching as the man tugged at the donkey's rope, shouting furiously.

Baducing seemed not to notice the man and the stubborn animal.

"Enough," he said, "to know that if your friend Lucifrido is known to him, you would be well not to trust him too far."

Beobrand frowned.

"Lucifrido is not my friend."

Baducing turned to look at him quizzically.

"Indeed?"

Beobrand did not wish to go into the details of how they had met. Not now. He was too hot and tired. They were close to the donkey and its irate owner now. The man was straining at the animal's harness, trying to move it by brute force.

"Lucifrido is merely our guide," Beobrand said. "Nothing more."

The man had finally managed to get the donkey moving, but after a couple of tentative steps the animal stumbled and fell to its knees. In his frustration, the man kicked the animal, and then proceeded to whip it about the face with a twig switch.

Cursing, Beobrand made his way to the stricken beast.

The man, face crimson, bald head drenched with sweat, continued to berate the donkey loudly, swiping at it with the long twig. With every blow the man dealt the defenceless animal, Beobrand's anger grew.

Unaware of the tall thegn's approach, the man raised his switch again. Beobrand grasped his wrist. The man gasped, turning and directing his rage at this stranger who had dared interfere with his affairs.

The man struggled against Beobrand's hold. He was not weak, but he was no match for Beobrand's strength.

"Tell him the animal is overloaded," Beobrand said, not releasing his grip on the man's arm. "Tell him," he repeated to Baducing.

Baducing spoke to the man. Furious, the owner of the donkey screamed at Beobrand, spittle flecking his lips and spattering Beobrand's face.

Beobrand squeezed the man's wrist, applying pressure so the bones crunched together. The man gasped in pain.

"Tell him," Beobrand said, his voice cold and hushed, "that if he keeps shouting at me, or hitting the donkey, I will beat him with that switch."

The man's sweaty features paled as Baducing relayed the message. He looked at the ten warriors thronging about him. He was no fool. The tallest and strongest of them all had a tight hold of his arm and seemed content to snap it if he was not careful.

The man spoke rapidly, lowering his tone and ceasing his struggles. He bowed his head as he talked.

"He asks for your forgiveness," Baducing said. "He only has the one animal, and must get these pots to the river before sundown. There is a barge coming."

Beobrand nodded. He drew in a long breath and released the man, who pulled away, rubbing at his wrist.

"Are we heading to the river?" Beobrand asked.

"Yes," replied Baducing, "I am taking you to a small tavern I know there. The wine is good. The food too."

Beobrand took another calming breath, forcing his anger back down with an effort. Perhaps this poor tradesman did not deserve to suffer Beobrand's infamous wrath.

"Tell him we'll help him to carry his wares," he said. "But I hate seeing an animal maltreated. If he keeps beating that poor donkey like that, he'll not only have no animal at all, but he'll have to answer to me." He glowered at the tradesman while Baducing translated.

The man listened with suspicion in his eyes, but he knew there was nothing he could do, confronted as he was by so many determined men, all of whom, apart from Baducing, were armed and looked ready to use their weapons.

Without delay, the men of Albion removed most of the crates of pottery from the wretched creature's back, distributing the items amongst them. Beobrand whispered to the donkey in a soothing voice. Taking hold of its harness, he hauled the skinny creature up. It rolled its eyes and lowered its ears, but after a heaving effort from Beobrand, it rose and remained standing.

"There you go," Beobrand whispered, patting the creature's dusty cheek and handing the lead rope to its owner.

Beobrand turned away from the donkey, ready to continue on towards the river when he felt a searing pain in his upper arm.

"Tiw's cock!" he roared, swinging around with his fists raised, ready to strike his assailant, only to find it was the donkey that had bitten him.

With difficulty he checked himself and did not strike the beast. The men, sweating under their new loads, couldn't keep themselves from laughing and Beobrand felt his face redden. The donkey's owner was unable to hide his smirk as he led the animal away.

"That will teach you to help cantankerous animals," said Cynan, chuckling.

Beobrand grumbled, rubbing at his bruised arm as they continued down the road.

It didn't take them long to reach the Tiberis. Trees lined portions of the bank and the chattering of starlings roosting in the canopy filled the air. The river was wide and several timber jetties, jumbled with moored vessels, jutted out into the water.

The men set down the goods they carried on a stone wharf. The red-faced trader bowed low to Beobrand, unable to meet his gaze. He mumbled his thanks.

Beobrand massaged his arm, a twisted smile on his lips.

"Tell him only to beat the donkey as much as is needed," he said.

"How much is that?" the man asked, with Baducing interpreting his words.

"Enough that it doesn't bite me again!"

They all laughed and they left the man and his donkey standing beside the pile of his goods on the wharf. Baducing led them north along the riverbank to a small timber building set some way back from the wharfs and quays. Large sheets of sail cloth had been stretched over frames outside the building to provide shade. Beneath the awnings were several benches and rough tables. It was late afternoon and there was nobody seated there.

"It does not look like much," said Baducing, "but the food and drink is every bit as good as Genofeva's."

They sat and a fat man with a stubbly beard waddled out to meet them. He wore a grease-stained apron and his forearms were scarred with many burns, both old and new.

He addressed Baducing warmly. Baducing spoke quickly, ordering food and drink for them. The fat man nodded and made his way back into the timber shack, shouting at someone inside as he went.

Cynan watched his huge frame squeeze through the door.

"The food might be as good as the widow Genofeva's," he said, "but I doubt he has such pretty daughters."

"Less temptation that way," said Baducing with a wink that made the men laugh.

They had all enjoyed eating and drinking in Genofeva's tavern in Liyon, and the presence of her older daughters was certainly one of the attractions.

A sallow-looking youth with lank, greasy hair, and cheeks covered in boils and white-headed spots, came out of the building bearing a tray stacked with wooden cups and two large earthenware jugs. He set them down on the table without a word.

"No daughters, but that is his son," said Baducing, provoking guffaws from the men.

One pitcher contained wine, the other ale. The men served it up and soon they each had a cup. Beobrand drank deeply.

"You were not lying when you said the ale was good," he said. "Even the view isn't all that bad." He waved his hand to take in the green water of the river. In the distance a great stone bridge spanned it. A broad-bellied barge was passing beneath it. On the other side of the river loomed a great stone fortification, surrounded by a huge circular wall. The sky was bruised and thick with cloud above the castle.

Cynan grinned.

"Just as long as the master of the house and his son remain out of sight."

The men sat back, content to sip their drinks and chat in the shade of the sailcloth awning.

Baducing drank some wine, then leaned forward.

"You suspect Lucifrido is not a man to be trusted then?" he said, picking up their conversation as if it had not been interrupted.

"More than suspect," said Beobrand. "I know it. His master is a man called Tanualdo. In Sutri. Do you know him?"

"I do not, but if he is acquainted with the likes of Stoldo, I can well imagine the kind of man he is."

"This Tanualdo appeared to be the lord of Sutri, though it seemed to me that the dooms of the land do not apply to him or to his men. They are little more than brigands and thieves. But Tanualdo has a great palace." He took another mouthful of the ale, enjoying its cool bitterness. "He owns the town. The people are frightened of him and his family."

"I cannot say I see much difference with what you say about this man and the lords of any hall in Albion, Frankia or elsewhere," said Baducing. "The powerful take what they will and answer to no man."

Beobrand scratched at his beard.

"Apart from their king."

"Yes," agreed Baducing. "And God."

Beobrand lifted his cup again, only to find it empty. He held it out for more, but when Bleddyn lifted each of the jugs in turn, neither contained any liquid. Baducing shouted for more drink.

"It seemed to me," said Beobrand, "that Tanualdo perhaps answers to nobody but himself."

"Stoldo is such a man too," Baducing said. "There are several such families in Roma and in the lands about here. They have become rich and powerful over the years. Ruthless and rich as kings."

The pimply boy hurried out carrying two fresh pitchers.

"The Pontifex does not govern Roma?" Beobrand asked, accepting a refill from Bleddyn after the boy had scurried off with the empty jugs.

"It is not so simple," said Baducing. "The Emperor Constans is the true ruler of the lands," said Baducing. "Martinus is the shepherd of the souls of men. But Constantinopolis is a long way from here, and the fathers of the families of Roma are never far from any decision. They are even welcome at the tables of bishops and cardinals."

"You think Stoldo will be at the feast tomorrow?"

The previous evening Wilfrid had relayed the invitation to Beobrand and Coenred to visit a priest by the name of Eugenius. Wilfrid had met Eugenius on their third day in Roma and had spent much of his time since at Eugenius' residence.

"I think it unlikely," said Baducing. "But I know little of this Eugenius."

Beobrand sipped his ale and stared down at the river. In the distance he could just make out the shapes of several figures crossing the bridge towards the fortress.

"I know nothing of this priest," he said, turning back to Baducing, "but if Wilfrid has fallen in with him I would vouch he has power. Or something else of value to Wilfrid. I have never met a man with more ambition."

"Eugenius comes from an old family and his church is one of the oldest in Roma. Santa Prisca, on the *Collis Aventinus*, the Aventinus Hill. Martinus wears the red mantle of Pontifex Maximus, but there are those who say Eugenius eyes his throne."

"I can imagine Wilfrid would fit in well in this Eugenius' household."

Baducing smiled.

"Wilfrid is not so bad," he said. "He is ambitious, true, but I believe we both want the same things, him and I."

Beobrand raised his eyebrows.

"And that is?"

"To return to Albion with greater knowledge of the Lord's word and to carry back with us books and relics, that we might spread His word and glorify His name."

Beobrand thought there was only one name Wilfrid wished to glorify, but he did not voice his opinion.

Instead, he asked: "When do you think that will be?"

"Return to Albion, you mean?" said Baducing.

Beobrand rubbed a hand over his face, smoothing his moustache and beard with his fingers.

"I have done my duty to my queen," he said. "But this is not where I belong. And you heard that man Rothad. It is not the first time we have heard such tidings from the north. If war is coming to Northumbria, my place is there."

Outside a church that morning, they had met a man from Frisia, who had introduced himself as Rothad. He had heard them speaking and recognised them as hailing from Albion. When he learnt they were from Northumbria, Rothad told them he had spoken to a sailor in the port of Marselha who had said the new king of the Picts was harrying the frontier of Oswiu's kingdom, forcing the King of Northumbria to march north. Beobrand's stomach clenched at the thought. If it were true, weeks, or even months might have passed since the events in the north of Albion had taken place. What would have happened to Ubbanford and Stagga if there was war? What of his people there? His family?

"I understand," said Baducing, his expression sober. "Do not tarry here on my account. It is my plan to collect what I can in the next few weeks and then head home before winter. I cannot speak for Wilfrid, and…" He hesitated, looking away. "And it is between you, your queen and God what oath you swore."

Beobrand gritted his teeth. He did not like to be reminded of his oaths, especially ones he might break. He had long wondered whether he might leave Wilfrid behind without sundering his word to Eanflæd. She had commanded him to escort Wilfrid to Roma. Beobrand did not believe she had ordered him to remain here with the young man. To think thus made him angry with himself. Lesser men played with the meaning of words in such a craven manner. He knew that the correct course would be to see that Wilfrid was escorted safely homeward, but at what cost? Was his oath to Oswiu not just as binding. Surely an oath to a king was above all others.

Seeing Beobrand's consternation, Baducing went on.

"Perhaps your quandary will be lifted from you," he said.

"I cannot see how," Beobrand said.

"Mayhap Wilfrid will spend all of his treasure soon, buying what items he can in a few days." He grinned suddenly, his teeth flashing bright. "He certainly has a knack for finding the best libraries wherever we travel. He told me last night that Eugenius has put him in contact with someone who possesses a collection of very interesting relics. This man will be present at tomorrow's feast. With God's grace, I hope we will be able to convince him to part with some of his holiest artefacts."

Beobrand emptied his cup of ale. He felt as though the sky, with its turgid clouds, was pressing down upon him, crushing the breath from his lungs.

"I wish I could believe such a thing were possible," he said.

"But you were at Liyon. You saw how Wilfrid revels in being surrounded by power. He will be in no hurry to leave Roma."

Beobrand understood Wilfrid and Baducing wishing to make alliances with powerful men of the Church, but he could not fathom the Christ god's magic, with its reliance on seemingly worthless splinters of wood, rusty nails, broken thorns, slivers of bone and all manner of other items that could well have been collected from a midden heap. The Christ followers put great store by such things, often parting with fortunes to purchase the smallest trinket.

And yet who was he to scoff at their magic? Coenred and Baducing had prayed together over Wulfwyn and Eadgard the previous evening, clutching the small vials of oil that Coenred had brought back from the catacombs. In the night, the patients' fever had broken, and this morning, they had both woken, pale and weak, it was true, but much restored.

The raised voices of the gesithas interrupted Beobrand's thoughts. From the ramshackle building came the fat man, followed by his skinny son. What they carried had caused the excitement amongst the hungry men. Despite his misgivings about being here, far from home while danger might be closing in on his hall and loved ones, Beobrand felt his stomach rumble in anticipation as he saw the platter that the older man carried. It was piled high with coils of boiled sausages. The man's son bore a similar sized plate, but this one covered in loaves and small bowls of sauces.

The men set to with gusto. The food was sumptuous. Baducing, in this at least, was proven correct. It was every bit as tasty as anything on Genofeva's table. Beobrand thought it less likely that Baducing would be proven right about Wilfrid. He could not imagine the young man being ready to leave Roma any time soon. But with each passing day, Beobrand felt the pressure within him grow.

Taking a deep breath, he made up his mind that he would speak with Wilfrid the following day when they met at Eugenius' residence. He would tell Wilfrid that his duty lay in Bernicia, defending the land and their king. *And the queen*, a small voice whispered within him. The thought of seeing Eanflæd again made Beobrand's skin tingle.

Yes, he would tell Wilfrid that he would wait in Roma no longer.

He felt lighter of spirit than he had in weeks. Tomorrow he would begin preparing for the long journey home. It would take a few days, but it felt good to have made a decision.

Cutting off a piece of sausage from the platter, and tearing off a hunk of warm, coarse bread, Beobrand dipped the food into one of the sauces and ate. He smiled, savouring the salty tang. For the first time in weeks, he looked towards the future and what tomorrow might bring.

Chapter 20

Cynan wiped sweat from his face with the back of his hand. They had started early, but the sun was rising in the sky now and the day was heating up. The pines that grew around the edges of the plaza provided some shade, but even free from direct sunlight, the day was hot. And Eadgard, still recovering from his sickness, was the only one of them sheltering beneath the tall trees.

"Enough now," panted Ingwald, coming to a stop beside Cynan. The older man was bent double, hands on his knees, drawing in great lungfuls of air.

Cynan handed Ingwald a waterskin and nodded towards Beobrand.

"Are you going to halt before he does?" he said.

After taking a quick drink from a leather flask, their hlaford tossed it onto the pile of their kirtles, and set off at a run once more.

"Come on," Beobrand called, seeing Cynan and Ingwald talking. "Time to burn off some of that fat." He slapped his own flat stomach. "We have grown soft. I don't want weaklings by my side when we return home."

With a groan, Ingwald threw down the waterskin and stumbled after Beobrand.

"If I run much longer in this heat," he moaned, "I won't be going anywhere. I'll be dead!"

Cynan jogged along beside him. He looked at the red faces of the others. They were all soaked in sweat, their torsos shining, the waists of their breeches stained dark. Halinard, like Ingwald, was struggling, dragging his injured leg. He had tripped and stumbled more than once. Cynan was pleased at the change that had come over Beobrand, glad that they were finally readying themselves to leave Roma and begin the long journey northward, but Ingwald was right. There was no point in pushing them too hard.

He looked up at the sky. It was still thick with clouds that seemed to act like a blanket for the world, holding in the heat that emanated from the stone buildings of the ancient city. The air felt as thick as soup. He had been awoken in the night by the rumble of distant thunder. The room he shared with the other warriors was stuffy and terribly hot. He had gone outside, hoping to find relief from the heat in the palace gardens, but although it was marginally cooler out in the darkness, no rain had fallen. Flashes of lightning illuminated the sky, as if God himself was striking sparks from a giant flint, but the night had remained dry.

Shortly after dawn, Beobrand had ordered them all to come here, to the square of open space before the great basilica attached to the palace, to run and to practise with shield, spear and sword. They had already run several laps of the square and then spent some time sparring, before going through their shieldwall positions, moving smoothly and quickly into each formation at Beobrand's barked orders. There were not enough of them to form much of a shieldwall, but the skill with which they executed each move was gratifying and all of them had been pleased to see the admiring stares of passers-by.

After they had practised the shieldwall for a time, Beobrand had commanded them to run once again. After the snappy controlled movements of the shieldwall formations, some of the servants and clergy who worked in the palace had congregated to watch them. They began to drift away as the bare-chested warriors ran.

Cynan ignored those that remained, pushing himself to greater speed. His lungs burnt and he was awash in sweat as he caught up with Beobrand.

"It is growing too hot, lord," he said, his voice coming in rasps.

Beobrand, breathing hard but too proud and stubborn to admit he too was struggling, said nothing.

"Remember what happened to Coenred," Cynan said.

Beobrand flicked a dark glance his way.

"Coenred is no warrior," he said, his tone gruff.

"He is not, lord," replied Cynan. "But he is a man. And so are your gesithas."

They approached Eadgard now where he sat, his back to a tree trunk.

"I'll run with you tomorrow," he called out to them, grinning. He had lost weight in the days of his illness and his skin still bore a sallow pallor, but already he looked stronger than the day before when his fever had mercifully withdrawn.

"Yes, you will," shouted Beobrand with a smile. "You've spent quite long enough lazing about."

Cynan thought Beobrand was going to ignore his words. He knew how he needled his hlaford at times and he worried that speaking out might have had the opposite effect than that intended; that in his stubbornness, Beobrand might actually decide to push their endurance even further. But as they reached Eadgard and the scattered waterskins and heaped clothes, Beobrand came to an abrupt halt.

"That's it for today, lads," he said.

Bleddyn and Grindan were the first to arrive and they threw themselves down in the shade. Halinard limped up to where Cynan held out a waterskin for him. Ingwald ceased running and trudged over to the group of men. His face was dark. He looked spent.

He drank deeply, then staggered behind a tree to vomit noisily.

Beobrand spat and moved close to Cynan.

"Thank you," he said, his voice low.

"What for?"

"Making me see what should have been clear to me. There is nothing to be gained by breaking the men."

"We could all use some training," replied Cynan, patting his own belly and smiling ruefully. His stomach was firm and well-muscled, but he thought he detected a new layer of fat that had not been there previously. "The exercise will do us good. But there is a difference between whetting a blade and snapping it."

"Well put," Beobrand said.

Cynan peered down the path that led to the south. The sun was bright, making him squint, but he recognised the figure that approached, even though he was still a long way off.

"He's back," he said, gesturing with his chin towards the lone rider trotting along the road.

Beobrand's eyes narrowed, but Cynan knew his sight was not sharp enough to pick out the details of the horseman.

"Lucifrido?" Beobrand asked.

Cynan took another drink of the warm, sour water from a skin. It tasted of leather.

"The same," he said.

Beobrand's breathing had slowed now and he stood tall, his muscular chest and arms slick from the exertion. He stretched and Cynan thought how his physique was like that of some of the ancient statues of Roma. Just as those marble carvings had been damaged over the centuries, bearing witness to the city's struggles in their cracks and snapped limbs, so Beobrand's body carried the memories of past battles in the twisted tracery of scars across his chest, arms and shoulders.

"I had hoped he might not return," Beobrand said.

"He said he would come back," Cynan replied, "but I had wondered."

Beobrand retrieved his kirtle and pulled it over his head.

"What do you think he has been doing since yesterday when he set out to this Stoldo's villa?"

Cynan shrugged, picking up his own kirtle from the ground. He wished he had brought a cloth to wipe some of the sweat from him. He hoped he would be able to bathe before evening.

"Why not ask him?"

"I will, but do you think he'll give an honest answer?"

"That is a more difficult question," Cynan said.

"I don't trust the man," Beobrand said, not taking his eyes from the approaching rider.

"I think that is wise, lord." Cynan hawked and spat, trying to rid his mouth of the rank flavour of the waterskin. "But he did save those Frankish pilgrims. And Coenred and Marsiglio said that if it had not been for him, they too might well have been robbed or worse."

Beobrand grunted.

"Yes," he said, "by the very men in whose company Lucifrido has spent the last day and night."

Cynan tugged his kirtle on.

"Grindan likes him."

Beobrand looked askance at Grindan for a moment. The warrior was sharing a jest with Eadgard, who let out a bellow of laughter that sounded more like a bull than a man.

"By the gods," said Beobrand. "Grindan likes his brother too. His judgement cannot be trusted."

Cynan chuckled. In spite of his misgivings about Lucifrido, Beobrand's mood was light. It was good to see.

The horse's hooves were loud on the stone road as Lucifrido reined in near them. He grinned and swung down easily from the saddle.

"I am glad to see I missed whatever it is you have been doing," he said, his tone relaxed. "The day is hot enough as it is without running about like madmen."

"We are warriors," said Beobrand. "Like any weapon, we must be kept sharp."

Lucifrido stifled a yawn.

"I prefer to think of myself as a cudgel that only gets taken up when absolutely needed. Certainly not on a hot day like today, if I can avoid it."

Cynan noticed Beobrand's shoulders tense.

"You also avoided returning last night," Beobrand said, "as you had said you would."

Lucifrido lifted a hand.

"My apologies," he said. "You are right, of course. I did mean to leave before dark, but Stoldo can be a very persuasive host."

"And what did he persuade you to do?" asked Beobrand, suspicion colouring his tone.

Lucifrido laughed at his stern expression.

"Nothing," he said. "Nothing bad at least. Unless missing a night in your company could be thought of as a bad thing."

Cynan snorted. Beobrand looked at him sharply.

"All he persuaded me to do," Lucifrido went on, "was not to ride back to the city last night. Stoldo's wine is strong and I had drunk more than was good for me." He winced and rubbed at his temples. "Which is why I have such a thirst now. I have never understood how it is that the more you drink, the greater your thirst."

"It is a mystery," replied Beobrand.

Cynan could see him struggling not to lose his earlier good humour.

"I think we would all welcome a drink," he said, trying to move the conversation along. "Some food too. We have not broken our fast yet. And I would like something to wash away the taste of that leather skin."

"Yes," said Eadgard, shoving himself to his feet. "I am tired just from watching you all. And I too made the mistake of having a mouthful of that water. It tastes like a mule's ball sack."

"Well, brother," said Grindan, grinning widely, "you are a brave man to admit you recognise that flavour!"

They all laughed at that. Even Beobrand. Cynan was glad to see Ingwald joining in with the mirth. His tanned face was yet flushed, but he sipped water from a skin and was standing upright. He caught Cynan's eye and gave him a small, reassuring nod.

"Come then," said Cynan. "Let us see if we can find some provender."

They picked up their belongings and made their way back towards the palace. Lucifrido led his horse.

"I will take a drink of wine," he said, "but I do not believe I can face food yet."

"And so the circle of the drunk begins again," said Grindan with a chuckle.

As they walked, the men laughing and chattering, Cynan looked to Beobrand. He laughed with the rest of them, but a small frown quickly returned to his brow as he watched Lucifrido.

Chapter 21

It seemed to Beobrand that there were too many people in the hall. At the end of the long table, where he sat in a place of honour near to Eugenius himself, there was some space to move, but further down the board, many of the guests could barely raise their elbows without knocking their neighbours' arms, spilling drinks and whispering embarrassed apologies.

The large room was oppressively hot. Even though the sun had set some time before, the temperature had not dropped. The doors were wide open, and the windows high up on the walls let in air from the night, but if the hope was that a breeze would flow through the gathering and cool the diners, it was a vain hope. Beobrand swatted away a moth that had flown too close to his face. Night insects flitted and fluttered in swirls around the candelabras and oil lamps that glimmered from the sconces attached to the carved stone pillars.

The table was covered in plates and goblets, one of each for every guest. And these were not simple earthenware or wooden vessels. All the items on the linen cloth were polished silver and the table gleamed in the flickering light of the candles and lamps. The food being expertly dished out by the numerous servants added many vibrant colours to the image of luxury.

There were platters of glistening broiled lobster, bowls

of olive-oil poached fish and braised leeks. There was even a magnificent display of a roast swan, its white plumage brilliant and shimmering.

At the table sat priests in dark robes and men who must be local dignitaries, with their silk clothes, gold rings flashing on their fingers and immaculately dressed and perfumed women at their sides.

Sipping his wine, Beobrand smiled to himself. He had been right about Eugenius. The man had welcomed him cordially enough and had seated him near his own high-backed chair, but the priest carried himself with the confidence of one born to lead, accustomed to be followed without question.

He was younger than Beobrand had thought he would be. The way others had spoken about him, Beobrand had imagined he would be an old man, over fifty years of age like Martinus, but Eugenius' hair was black, his face yet smooth. He could not be more than two or three years older than Beobrand, and whilst he sometimes felt old, particularly on cold, damp mornings when his aching body remembered every injury received in countless battles, he was not yet forty.

After their midday meal, Marsiglio and Coenred had joined them, and Beobrand had asked what manner of man Eugenius was.

Marsiglio had accepted a cup of watered wine with a smile of thanks.

"He says his throat is dry from praising the Lord," Coenred said, interpreting the dark-skinned monk's words. Coenred frowned, seemingly disapproving of his new friend's comment.

Beobrand chuckled, amused by Coenred's discomfort.

"It does not surprise me," he said. "You spend much of your time singing."

The two of them had just returned from one of the frequent, seemingly interminable masses in the vast stone church close to the palace. Marsiglio had told them its full name, but Beobrand could only recall that it was the *Archibasilica*, the most important Christ church in the whole of middle earth. Beobrand did his best to avoid attending the services, but he did sometimes stop whatever he was doing to listen to the chanting song of the Christ believers. He did not comprehend the words, but he found the melodies soothing.

Marsiglio told them that Eugenius had been born to a wealthy family from the Aventinus area of the city where he now ran the church dedicated to Saint Prisca, one of the countless martyrs of Roma. With so many believers tortured and killed for their faith, Beobrand wondered why anyone would wish to worship the Christ. Then he thought of Eadgard and Wulfwyn and the strong magic that had healed them. Perhaps the Christ god's followers had so many enemies because they feared the potency of his magic.

Looking down the long table, Beobrand saw evidence of Eugenius' wealth everywhere, from the sumptuous silverware and the elaborate delicacies, to the gilded bronze statues that gazed down upon them from their plinths in arched niches. The residence was far from as grand as the papal palace, that Coenred called the Lateran *Patriarchium*, and Eugenius' church, the *Titulus Priscae*, was tiny by comparison to the *Archibasilica*, but that Eugenius was rich and powerful was in no doubt.

Beobrand pulled the collar of his kirtle away from his neck, blowing downward in an effort to cool himself, but it was no use. Sweat trickled down his spine. He was glad he had bathed that afternoon before riding the short distance to this villa, otherwise he feared he would reek like a swineherd. He longed to be able to rid himself of the linen tunic he wore. It was a gift from Balthild, the fabric smooth and soft, its cut good, but the heat made his skin prickle and he only stopped himself scratching like a flea-ridden dog with an effort of will. He already suspected how he looked to the sophisticated clergy and nobles. He saw how they observed him; the men with disdain and more than one of the women with hungry interest, but all of them with a touch of alarm. Fear of the unknown, of one of the uncouth *barbaroi* from the far north, and he did not wish to cement their opinion that he was no more than that.

He looked to the welcoming darkness through the open doors at the far end of the hall and imagined leaving. They were near the river. Lucifrido had told them so when he'd led them to Eugenius' residence late that afternoon. Perhaps after the feast, they could go down to the water and refresh themselves. Or maybe it would finally rain, and the world would be cooled somewhat. Beobrand took a swallow of wine and vowed silently that if the clouds did finally disgorge their contents, he would go outside and stand beneath the rain.

A voice to his right cut through his thoughts. Coenred was seated there and had been conversing for some time to the man next to him. As Beobrand only understood a few simple words of the local tongue, he had been content to sit back, eat the food, drink the good strong wine, and let the evening wash over him like a dream. But it was clear that the man, who had been introduced as Lutozzo, was now addressing Beobrand rather than Coenred.

Beobrand turned his attention to the man. He was of middling age, a few years older than Beobrand, with a hard face, a hawk-like beak of a nose and smudges of grey in his black hair where it receded at his temples. He was smiling. Coenred listened intently, and then translated.

"Lutozzo asks if it is too hot for you here."

Beobrand returned the man's smile, nodding and fanning himself with his right hand.

"Tell him that in Bernicia the number of days each year when the sun shines hot in the sky can be counted on the fingers of one hand." He held up his left hand with its missing fingers. "This hand!"

Lutozzo laughed when he heard Coenred's translation.

"Are you the lord of large estates in Albion?" he asked.

The question unsettled Beobrand. He was proud of Ubbanford and the hides of land he had been given, first by King Oswald and then his brother, Oswiu. But when compared to the palaces and sprawling vineyards and olive groves he had seen on his travels, he had come to understand he was but a minor lord, a warrior who had made his fortune with his battle-skill and the edge of his blade. Nothing more.

"I have land," he said, his tone awkward. "A hall. A comitatus. Some good sheep land."

Lutozzo nodded.

"The riches you see around you here are beyond what most men can dream of."

"I'm not so sure," Beobrand replied, with a lopsided smile. "I can dream of a lot."

Lutozzo laughed again, but something in his eyes told Beobrand he was not truly amused. There was a guarded, simmering anger about him, as if the wealth surrounding them offended him.

He spoke gravely, and Coenred, frowning, continued to interpret.

"And why should you not?" Lutozzo said. "A man should have all he desires, if he is strong enough, and clever enough to take it." Coenred shook his head and Beobrand wondered if he might voice his disagreement with Lutozzo's comments, but in the end, the monk bit his lip and carried on. "He asks how you came by your land."

"It was gifted to me," Beobrand said. "By my king."

Lutozzo leaned forward.

"What did you do to deserve such a gift?"

Beobrand shrugged, embarrassed to be speaking about himself.

"I fought for him. I captured the king of our enemies."

Lutozzo laughed and clapped his hands together. Other diners turned to see what the disturbance was. Seeing nothing amiss, they returned to their conversations and the murmur of their voices quickly filled the hall once more.

Lutozzo grinned.

"Your strength and your sword brought you wealth," he said. "Good. Good. This is as it should be." Again Coenred hesitated, but chose not to interject. "A man should be able to make a life for himself and his family."

"Does Lutozzo have land?" asked Beobrand.

Coenred interpreted the question. Lutozzo nodded and waved a hand, as if Beobrand would be able to see what he was referring to outside of the hall. Beobrand listened to Coenred as he translated.

"He has land in the *Disabitato*," he said.

"And he was not born into this land?" Beobrand asked.

Lutozzo showed his teeth and shook his head ferociously. The movement made Beobrand think of a dog shaking a rat in its jaws.

"No, no," he said. "I took it." He snatched at the air with his hand as if grasping some invisible treasure.

Beobrand was intrigued by this man. When they had first arrived, taking in the sumptuous decorations, he had dismissed Lutozzo as just one more of the gaudily dressed guests. But there was something unnerving about his intensity. He was opening his mouth to ask more, when he was interrupted by Wilfrid, speaking loudly from the other side of the table. Beobrand's eyes narrowed in annoyance at the young man's rudeness.

"I don't believe you have been formally introduced," Wilfrid was saying, stretching out a hand to indicate the man sitting beside him. Beobrand recalled the man from their arrival, with his sculpted, oiled beard and receding hair that he wore slicked back from his face. He searched in his memory for the man's name. There had been so many presentations in those first moments that they were a blur.

"Priamo, wasn't it?" he said at last, content that he had dredged out the name.

"*Priano*," Wilfrid corrected him. His supercilious tone was infuriating. The man was as insufferable as the heat. Beobrand was reminded why he had been glad the young novice had decided to remain at Eugenius' residence these past few days.

Beobrand said nothing. He stared at Wilfrid.

After an awkward silence, Wilfrid smiled.

"Priano is the collector who has promised to show us his treasures. I hear he has one of the nails from Christ's cross and a piece of the sponge in which vinegar—"

"I have little interest in such things, Wilfrid," Beobrand said, cutting him off. "But Coenred and Baducing told me they are eager to see all that Priano has to offer."

Priano was taking in the interaction, his cool grey eyes unblinking as he looked from Beobrand to Wilfrid, the slightest of smiles on his lips. Now he spoke up, his voice as smooth and rich as the silk tunic he wore.

"Not all I possess is for sale," he said in Anglisc. "But I will be happy to show your friends some of my more interesting pieces."

Beobrand was surprised. Apart from Lucifrido and a handful of pilgrims around the sacred sites of the city, they had met very few people who could speak their tongue.

"You speak the language of my people well," he said, meaning it. Priano's deep voice had the lilting sing-song quality of the locals, but his pronunciation was clear and perfectly intelligible.

Priano preened, pleased at the praise.

"I believe a man can learn much from the tongue of a people.

I have studied many languages, though I confess the tongue of the men of Albion is one I practise rarely." His smile widened. "I cannot deny that the chance to speak Anglisc made my decision to welcome Wilfrid and his companions to my humble home an easy one. And it has led to an interesting proposition."

"Priano is a great man," interjected Wilfrid, keen to rejoin the conversation he had started. "He is a scholar of all things and a collector of artefacts from all over the world. He has travelled all the way to the Holy Land."

Priano shook his head, smiling indulgently at Wilfrid as an uncle might look upon an eager nephew.

"Wilfrid," he said, "the lord Beobrand has already told you he is not interested in my collections." He lifted his silver goblet of wine, raising it towards Beobrand before sipping from its contents. "And I doubt a man such as he wants to hear of my studies."

Beobrand stiffened, sure there was a cloaked insult in the man's words.

"I am no expert in such matters," he said, forcing a smile. "I was talking to Lutozzo here about land and power." He could hear Coenred translating his words to Lutozzo as he spoke. "You are clearly a man of worth. How did you come by your wealth?"

Wilfrid scowled, disapproving perhaps of Beobrand's bluntness, but Priano laughed.

"If not already clear from your appearance," he said, and again Beobrand sensed the man was insulting him, "the cut of your words leaves no doubt you are a warrior."

Wilfrid muttered something in Latin, but Priano waved him away like an insect that buzzes too close to one's ear.

"No need to apologise for Beobrand," he said. "The question is fair and a man of learning should never – how do you say – hide from questions. To answer you, Beobrand, my father left me a large estate. Rich farmland. This was fortunate for me.

By God's grace, I have used the land well and it has brought more riches. My..." he hesitated, searching again for the right word. "My prosperity allows me to indulge in my interest for the *exōtikos*..." He turned to Wilfrid for help with the word.

From beside Wilfrid, Baducing said: "Foreign things, from strange lands."

Priano smiled his thanks.

"Just so," he said. "I have travelled to many lands, bringing back items others might not see as valuable."

Beobrand sniffed.

"So, you are a merchant of relics," he said, still annoyed at Priano's implied insults.

Priano laughed again.

"I believe I am," he said. "Among other things." Beobrand searched his face for any sign of annoyance, but he saw none. The man seemed genuinely amused by Beobrand's jibe. Priano took another sip of wine. "Pray tell, lord Beobrand, how does..." He turned to Wilfrid. "What was the lady's name?"

Wilfrid flushed crimson.

"Well?" Priano pressed.

"Wulfwyn," Wilfrid muttered.

"Yes," Priano went on, "how is the lady Wulfwyn?"

Before Beobrand could respond, Coenred replied. The confusion in Coenred's voice at the question echoed Beobrand's own.

"Wulfwyn is much improved," Coenred said. "It is good of you to enquire as to her health, but forgive me, how do you know of the lady?" Wulfwyn was still in the Lateran Palace and had not left its environs, despite her recent recovery.

"It is not so complex," Priano replied, chuckling at their confusion. "Wilfrid spoke to me of her, and her son. The blind boy."

Wilfrid's usual composure had slipped considerably. His

cheeks were blotchy and red and he was biting his lip. It was obvious he had not meant for the conversation to head in this direction, or if he had, he had wished to steer it there himself.

"And what did he tell you about them?" Beobrand said, keeping his voice low and his eyes on Wilfrid. It was good to see the young man squirm.

"That the widow is devout and hard-working. And the boy, apart from his affliction, is gifted with a sharp mind."

"What interest do you have in them?" Beobrand could not keep the edge from his voice now. There was something in Priano's gaze that reminded him of other rich men. Men used to getting whatever they desired.

"Lord Beobrand," said Wilfrid, regaining some of his composure, "it is not befitting to look upon Christian charity with such contempt. Priano is a generous man, and when he heard of Wulfwyn's plight, he said he would offer her a position in his household."

"I asked Priano," hissed Beobrand, "not you."

Priano leaned forward conspiratorially, as if he and Beobrand were accomplices in some game.

"Again," he said, his eyes twinkling in the candlelight, "I cannot pretend that I had no more motive than Christian duty to a poor lost widow woman."

Beobrand scowled. He cared nothing for the man's sneering tone, or his honeyed words. He was tired and hot. He could feel the sweat running in rivulets down his spine whereas Priano, despite being corpulent and some years older, seemed not to be bothered by the heat in the slightest. His silken tunic was not damp and darkened. His hair was oiled and immaculately combed, and there was no trace of the sweat on his brow that Beobrand constantly had to wipe from his own forehead.

"What other motive do you have?" Beobrand asked.

Priano picked up an oyster. Lifting the shell to his mouth, he sucked the flesh and juice from it.

"As I said, I would like the opportunity to practise the tongue of the Anglisc."

Beobrand suspected he knew what Priano really sought and how Wilfrid aimed to use Wulfwyn to gain favour with him.

"You can find nobody more suitable for the task than Wulfwyn?"

Priano laughed again. It irritated Beobrand, but once more, the man's humour seemed genuine.

"I do not mean the good lady, though I will happily converse with her too in her mother tongue. No, I was speaking of her son."

"Aelfwig?" Beobrand and Coenred blurted out as one.

Priano grinned, rankling Beobrand even more.

"I always have use for keen minds," he said. "And I like the idea of a boy who I can talk to freely, teaching him whatever I need, while knowing he will not see anything I want to remain a secret."

Again Beobrand thought of how much he disliked the man; the easy arrogance and knowing smile, and the belief that he could have whatever he wanted. Priano had neither said nor done anything to indicate any wrongdoing, but Beobrand had seen his kind before in men like Vulmar and Dalfinus. He could not bear the thought of Wulfwyn and Aelfwig at Priano's mercy.

"Perhaps Wulfwyn will not wish to stay in Roma," he said.

"Perhaps. Perhaps." Priano shrugged, taking a honeyed quince from a bowl and popping it into his mouth. He chewed appreciatively, speaking with his mouth full. "But she came all this way for her son, to pray at the shrines here that he might see once more. And I am the owner of some of the most powerful relics in all the world. Maybe one of them will restore Aelfwig's sight."

"But if that happened," said Beobrand, "you would not have your blind boy with whom to practise the Anglisc tongue."

Priano sighed, still smiling.

"True. True. And I would of course rejoice with mother and son if the boy's vision returned. I will pray with them for just such a miracle." He drank more wine, wiping his moustache delicately with his fingers. "But if that does not occur, at least Wulfwyn and Aelfwig will be provided for, and if the boy proves himself adept at learning, he will have a bright future." He shook his head and chuckled, as if embarrassed at his choice of words. "Perhaps not bright, but prosperous in his constant darkness."

From the head of the table, Eugenius addressed Wilfrid and Priano. The priest had been deep in conversation with the man immediately to his left. Beobrand could not recall his name, simply that he had been introduced as an envoy of the Exarchatus of Ravenna. As Eugenius spoke, his tone quiet but carrying easily over the hubbub of the hall, the envoy stared at Beobrand with dark, suspicious eyes. His oiled hair, rich silken clothes and aloof bearing reminded Beobrand of Deusdedi, the haughty emissary they had met in Guduin's hall.

Eugenius stopped speaking and Wilfrid translated for Beobrand's benefit, as he was the only person at the table who could not converse in Latin or Grecisc, the two tongues prevalent in Roma.

"Eugenius thanks you for your visit," Wilfrid said.

Beobrand forced down the anger that had been building within him. He would be leaving Roma soon and there was no need to make new enemies. He had enough waiting for him in Albion.

"Please thank him for me," he said, "and tell him it is always interesting to meet those who hold the power in any place. To wield power in such a magnificent city as Roma must be a difficult task."

Wilfrid interpreted, listened to Eugenius reply, and translated it.

"Eugenius says he has scant power. Though you are right that those with whom you have been speaking are as powerful as any men in Roma."

"It pays to keep table with powerful people," Beobrand replied.

Eugenius smiled.

"You know of what you speak," Wilfrid translated for him. "You are no stranger to power yourself, I hear. You reside with the Pontifex Maximus himself and Wilfrid here tells me you are close to the kings and queens of both Albion and Frankia."

Beobrand watched Eugenius as he spoke, trying to infer from his bearing and tone what manner of man he was. His wealth and influence was clear from the feast and those who sat at his table, but beyond that, Beobrand could not make out any more about the man.

"I wouldn't go so far as to say any kings or queens think of me as their friend," Beobrand said, "but it is true that I have served several rulers."

"And from what I hear, you serve them well. You are a formidable man, lord Beobrand. And as one who serves, you will understand now that I must bid you good night. I have urgent matters to attend to."

Before Wilfrid had finished translating these words, Eugenius rose from his high-backed chair and stepped away from the table. Offering a quick farewell to his guests, he turned and swept from the hall through a door in the rear. Without a word, the envoy from the Exarchatus stood and followed him.

Beobrand was wondering the real reason for his invitation here. Had it been to meet Eugenius, or these other men he had been sat with? And if it had been for him to meet Lutozzo and Priano, to what end? He was too hot to care, and despite Lutozzo intriguing him, he would rather be far from the airless hall than continue these conversations. They would be gone from Roma in a few days and he would be glad to leave these powerful men to their games and plots.

Draining his cup of wine, he pushed himself to his feet.

"Coming?" he said to Coenred.

Coenred shook his head.

"Baducing and I are going to stay as Eugenius' guests. On the morrow we are going with Wilfrid to Priano's villa."

Priano raised his goblet in a toast towards Beobrand.

"It has been a pleasure to meet you," he said. "Will you convey my offer of employment to Wulfwyn?"

Beobrand met his gaze for a time, but said nothing.

"Please thank Lutozzo for his company this evening," he said to Coenred at last, before walking the length of the hall and leaving through the open double doors. He could feel the eyes of the diners upon him as he walked, but he did not look at any of them.

Outside was marginally cooler, but it was still unbearably hot. Still no rain fell. Moths and midges flitted around torches that burnt in the patio. Bats swished silently out of the darkness, flapping and turning through the flying insects, having their own summer's night feast.

Beobrand followed the sound of coarse voices and laughter and found Cynan, Lucifrido and his men sitting with the guards and servants of the other guests. The men had been fed simpler food, served on a large trestle table in the yard and they appeared relaxed, talking and laughing amiably. Beobrand felt a stab of envy. He wished he had been able to eat out here. The food looked more to his taste, and the company certainly was. And it was cooler than inside too.

He stood with his back to the torches and the men, looking out into the night, while Lucifrido and Cynan went to collect their mounts. The moon was up, its glow diffuse through the clouds, but it gave enough light to pick out the silvered waters of the Tiberis where the river looped around the Aventinus Hill below them. He thought again of heading down to the river to bathe, but discarded the idea. He was tired. Tomorrow he could bathe at the palace.

They rode in silence for a time. The journey back would not take long. They reached the building Lucifrido had told them that afternoon was the circus, where chariots and horses used to race for the delight of roaring crowds. The bulk of the great building loomed huge and dark, a deeper shade in a world of shadows. Beobrand let out a long sigh.

"Bad night?" asked Cynan, riding close. The clop of their horses' hooves were loud in the night, reverberating from the arches of the circus.

"Not bad," said Beobrand. "Hot and tiring. I will be glad when we are on our way home."

"We all feel that way," Cynan said. "There was nobody of interest in the feast then?"

"That depends on what you mean by interesting," Beobrand replied. He recounted his conversations with Lutozzo, Priano and Eugenius. As he described the evening he could not shake the thought that the other men had been involved in some form of game. Like tafl, but where they moved all the pieces and he was oblivious of the rules.

Lucifrido nudged his horse nearer.

"Well, it cannot be said that Eugenius does not have interesting people at his table," he said.

"You know them?" Beobrand asked.

"By name, yes, I know them. Many know of Priano, who is rich and mixes in such circles. But I think everyone in Roma and beyond knows the name of Lutozzo. I have never met the man."

Lucifrido pushed a hand through his hair in a nervous gesture. "To be honest, I would be frightened if I had."

Beobrand felt a scratch of unease down his spine.

"Who is he?" he asked.

"Lutozzo is the head of one of the five families of Roma."

"You mean like Stoldo?"

Beobrand saw Lucifrido's shoulders rise in the gloom.

"In some ways, yes," he said. "But he is more powerful by far. His is the most powerful of the families. They call him the real ruler of Roma."

Chapter 22

"By the Blessed Virgin and all the Saints," whispered Coenred, "the priests in Roma are not like those back home."

His head was throbbing and the morning light made him squint. It was bright, in spite of the thick clouds that still covered the sky and hid the sun.

Baducing, ashen-faced and appearing as fragile as Coenred felt, nodded.

"There is more feasting here, that is for sure," he said, keeping his own voice to a hissed murmur. "But they do not always indulge quite as much as last night. Or if they do," he said with a twisted smile, "I have not been invited before."

They were hurrying across the courtyard towards the church. Wilfrid had woken them moments earlier. They were late. It had been years since Coenred had overslept. His body was attuned to the routines in the minster of Lindisfarena, but after weeks of travel and last night's copious drinking, something else he never did at the minster, he had slept soundly until Wilfrid had angrily shaken him awake.

"If they drank that much regularly," Coenred said, "they would never manage to get to Mass." He turned to Wilfrid who annoyingly seemed as fresh as ever in the warm light of day. "Can you imagine what Abbot Finan would say?"

Wilfrid scoffed.

"I can imagine," he said, almost running across the cobbles so that Coenred and Baducing struggled to keep up. "But I would rather not. When I have my own church, I will host feasts such as those we have seen here. Surrounded by men and women of power and knowledge. The church must be at the centre of things, not on some island in the middle of nowhere."

Coenred and Baducing exchanged a glance. Wilfrid's ambition was tiresome. He was young and had much to learn about life and the world. And yet Coenred could not deny that Wilfrid's mind was sharp and, in spite of his misgivings about the young man, he would not be surprised to see him fulfil the destiny he believed awaited him. For his part Coenred was content to pray, praise the Lord, work the land and learn more about God's word. There was much he loved about the world and his part in it, but he did not long for more than he possessed. As it was, he considered himself blessed with good friends, and life had seen him able to travel here, all this way to this holiest of cities. What more could he ask for?

The sound of singing wafted from the open door of the church. The smell of incense was strong in the air.

"Come on," hissed Wilfrid, rushing the final steps across the yard. "Prime has started."

Baducing shrugged, meeting Coenred's eyes with a smile. Together, they trotted after Wilfrid.

Coenred's stomach churned, sour and unsettled, as they entered the cool interior of the building. The singing was loud here inside the stone walls of the church of Saint Prisca and Coenred recognised the liturgy instantly. Without thinking, he added his voice to the words of the fifty-seventh Psalm as they made their way to a place near the rear wall. He noticed that Baducing and Wilfrid were also chanting. Whatever he thought of Wilfrid, he could not question the young man's dedication. He knew the rituals and scriptures as well as anyone.

When the service ended, Coenred was feeling slightly more clear-headed. As people filed out of the church and into the overcast, clammy heat of the day, Priano approached them with a cheerful greeting. He too seemed unaffected by the previous night's indulgence.

"Good morrow to you all," he said, beaming. Behind him walked four stout men. Two wore short swords on their belts, the other two bore heavy cudgels of gnarled and twisted, polished wood. Priano glanced up at the sky.

"It looks to me," he said, speaking in Latin, "that what we most crave today will elude us once more." On seeing their confusion, he laughed. "Rain, my friends! To wash away this heat and the dust. When it comes, the streets will flood no doubt. You would do well not to be in the low parts of the city then. The sewers overflow and some of the roads turn into disgusting rivers of excrement. But do not fear. I live on a hill! And if we ride fast, the breeze will cool us."

"I am no rider," said Coenred, wondering if he could keep his seat on a horse and not shame himself by vomiting.

"You rode all the way from Albion, did you not?"

"Yes, but—"

"Then you can ride," said Priano, clapping him on the shoulder.

Priano's guards helped bring out the horses and soon they were all mounted. Unsure and uncomfortable, Coenred clung to the saddle of the brown mare he had ridden since Paris.

"Do not look so glum, Coenred," Priano said. "Just think of the wonders I will show you!" With that, he dug his heels into his black stallion's flanks and set off at a canter.

The other horses sprang forward, eager to follow the stallion. Coenred took a deep breath, attempting to hold his mount back while he built up his nerve. But it was no good, and a heartbeat later, he gave the animal its head and they loped off after the rest of the party.

Coenred's head ached with each pounding step of his horse, but after a time he forced himself to relax somewhat and to take in the buildings they passed. Priano had been right about the ride. The breeze against his face was cooling and it helped to clear his mind. Priano had been nothing but charming to them ever since they had met the previous evening. After Beobrand had left, Priano had regaled Baducing, Wilfrid and Coenred with tales of some of the places he had been, the things he had witnessed and the relics he would show them at his villa. He had made no comment about Beobrand's behaviour, but Coenred had been embarrassed for his friend. It was clear that Beobrand had taken a dislike to Priano and was distrustful of his motives. Given what had happened in Frankia, Coenred could understand that, but he couldn't help feel that Beobrand had treated Priano unfairly.

Fleetingly, Coenred wondered whether Beobrand was concerned Priano might be a predator such as Cormán, the bishop whose depraved actions had seen him sent away unceremoniously by Oswald. Coenred shuddered at the dark memories of Cormán's caress, his hot breath, his lascivious leer. But Priano was surely not such a man as Cormán and whatever possible dangers the future held for him, Aelfwig would have his mother close by to watch over him.

Priano's offer to Wulfwyn was a generous one, and his plans for Aelfwig, while unusual, would give the boy something that he had no right to expect. Most people afflicted with blindness became a burden, beggars sitting at the doors of churches, crying out for a crust. Coenred recalled when he had first met

Beobrand. The young warrior had been injured in battle and for a time he had feared he would lose his sight. Beobrand had fretted for days, living in terror of the life he would be forced to lead without sight. And well he might fear such a life. He had been young, not many years older than Aelfwig, and to be struck blind would have been to live in a cage of darkness, shunned by all, with nothing to offer to others apart from another mouth to feed. Priano could give Aelfwig so much more than that. The boy was quick-witted and if he applied himself and took to helping Priano as the man hoped, he could look forward to a life of relative luxury. There were certainly worse things than to work for a rich man.

When they reached Priano's villa, Coenred slid from the saddle with a groan. His legs buckled and he almost fell to his knees, but one of the guards caught him and heaved him upright. The man chuckled to himself as he led the horse away. Coenred pushed aside his embarrassment. There was much to be pleased about. He had told them he was not a good horseman, yet he had stayed in the saddle as they crossed the city and climbed up the slope of *Mons Quirinalis* through groves of oak and pines before entering the walled grounds of Priano's residence. His legs might be trembling after the fast ride, but at least he had not disgraced himself.

He offered up a silent prayer of thanks for that small mercy. But his head still throbbed and he staggered, stiff-legged, into the shade of the building. In the rush he had forgotten his hat and even though the sky was wreathed in cloud, he could feel the heat of the sun on his shaved forehead. For a fleeting moment he recalled the horror of the vision of evil that had burnt in his mind in the forest outside Placentia. Mena and Gostanza had been certain it had all been a bad dream caused by too much sun, and he had almost convinced himself of the same, but every now and then, he remembered the sibilant whisper of evil and could feel the creature's hot breath on his neck. Shuddering, he pushed the thoughts out of his mind and turned to Priano.

The owner of the villa was standing with his back to Coenred. Beside him Baducing and Wilfrid were looking out over the city. Pale stones shone between dark green patches of woodland and far off, the cloud-veiled sun gleamed on the waters of the Tiberis.

"The view is wonderful, is it not?" said Priano.

"It is magnificent," said Wilfrid. "You are blessed to have this villa, and we are equally blessed that you have invited us here. I thank you on behalf of us all."

Baducing turned to Coenred and raised an eyebrow. Coenred grinned at Wilfrid's transparent need to flatter and inveigle himself with those he believed might help his advancement.

Priano seemed not to notice. Turning away from the vista, he beckoned for them to follow him into the house.

"I sent word ahead for victuals to be prepared," he said over his shoulder. "When we are refreshed, I will show you some of the wonders I have acquired."

He led them beneath a tiled entrance between columns of polished marble and into a secluded courtyard. It was lined with potted plants and beyond the greenery, a shaded colonnade. The floor was covered in tiny coloured tiles cunningly arranged to depict images of sea creatures, leaping and swimming through the waves of the ocean. Long tables had been set up, draped with white cloth and festooned with silver platters of food. Large cushions were scattered around the tables. In the centre of the atrium was a fountain in the shape of a leaping fish. Water gurgled from its mouth into a small pool.

"Once, such things were commonplace in Roma," Priano said. "But I had to bring a man all the way from Neapoli to get that fountain to work. You cannot imagine the cost. But it was worth the expense, I think. Don't you agree?"

Wilfrid stepped close to the fountain, walking around it and gazing at the clear water bubbling from the lead-lined mouth of the stone fish.

"Indeed it is, Priano," he said. "It is a marvel."

"There are greater marvels than that within my Hall of Relics, but first we eat and you must try some of my family wine."

Coenred was in awe of the affluence on display. The fountain, the beautiful mosaic floor, the tables heaped with colourful and sweet-smelling food, all spoke of a wealth that was hard to comprehend. Beobrand had called Priano a merchant. The truth was he lived like a king.

It was cool here and Coenred was glad to be in the shade. His head ached and his stomach roiled. He lowered himself onto one of the deep cushions and settled there, closing his eyes for a moment.

"You are tired, my friend," said Priano. "Here, try one of these."

Plucking a dainty pastry from the nearest table, Priano brought it to where Coenred was slouched on the soft cushion. Coenred tried to sit up straight, but the cushion was covered in sheer silk and stuffed with soft feathers. Coenred thrashed about, struggling to right himself, his face hot with embarrassment. He regretted his decision to slump onto one of the cushions, but he could not change that now. Priano loomed over him and, resigned to the fact he looked a fool, Coenred sighed and held out his hand so that their host could pull him to his feet. To his dismay, instead of helping him up, Priano handed him the sticky morsel.

"Make yourself at ease, Brother Coenred," Priano said, his smile broad. "There is no need to hurry. And I know well how comfortable these cushions are. They are filled with the softest goose down." He clapped his hands and instantly a young woman stepped out from the shadowed interior of the building. "See that my guest has a selection of all these dishes."

"That's not necessary," Coenred mumbled. He wasn't sure he could eat much without his stomach rebelling. If being trapped on a cushion was embarrassing, he did not want to imagine the shame of vomiting up the rich provender.

Priano ignored his protestations and the servant hurried to the tables, filling a silver plate with food.

Wilfrid glared at Coenred.

"I thought we might see the relics before we ate," he said.

"Too late for that," replied Baducing. He had already taken several items from the table, filling a plate for himself. "But perhaps best if you remain standing, so that you can help us up when we are done."

Baducing flashed Coenred a smile and flopped down onto an embroidered pillow that was just as plump and soft as the one that had enveloped Coenred.

"There will be time for relics and books soon enough," said Priano, lowering himself gracefully onto another cushion. "Before we nourish the mind and spirit, the flesh must be tended to."

The servant came to Coenred and handed him a plate piled high with food. She was a pretty thing, with large green eyes and dark hair. As she bent down to where Coenred sat, he could not help but notice that her simple dress was cut low at the neck, giving him a brief, but tantalising glimpse of her ample breasts. He felt his face burn red and he looked away. All the while she kept her eyes averted. The moment he took the plate from her the servant scurried away. Wilfrid watched her as she moved past, his gaze lingering on the curve of her hips and the pale, smooth skin of her legs.

Priano too saw the young man's lustful look and he chuckled.

"Yes, the flesh must be tended to," he repeated. "I see you have taken a fancy to Basina. She is from the tribe of the Thuringii. They are a simple people from the far north. But their women…"

He raised his eyebrows suggestively. "Perhaps after we dine you might care to… rest. There are many rooms in my home, with soft beds and clean sheets. Basina would be all too willing to accompany you."

Wilfrid licked his lips.

"You are too kind," said Coenred, flustered, "but that won't be necessary." He did not care for the direction of this conversation. Not one bit. "Once we have eaten our fill of this wonderful repast, if you would be so good as to show us some of the wonders you have promised us."

"Of course," replied Priano, winking at Wilfrid. "The flesh must sometimes wait. The expectation makes the final tasting all the sweeter."

Coenred glanced at Baducing. The younger man shrugged, but looked as shocked as Coenred felt. Perhaps Beobrand had been right in his estimation of Priano. The thegn was certainly more worldly and altogether less naive than Coenred, so it was foolish to dismiss Beobrand's intuition.

Another serving girl was moving between the men with a tray of goblets. Coenred accepted a silver cup with a smile, careful to keep his gaze from the revealing cut of her dress. She did not respond. Keeping her eyes downcast, she departed the atrium quickly.

A sadness came over Coenred as he watched the girl hurry away. He had been excited to see what Priano had to offer. He still wished to hold the nail from the holy rood and see the pages of the God-spell of Iacobus, but the day's lustre had been tarnished. Beobrand had been right. Priano was just like other rich men. Constantly yearning for more than he had, and taking whatever he could, no matter the harm or suffering caused. He was nothing more than a merchant, seeking the highest price for what he sold. All that separated him from the men hawking their trinkets outside the churches and catacombs was the vastness of his fortune.

Coenred nibbled the pastries, slices of meat and fruit on his plate, all the while observing the others. The food was sumptuous, the cakes dripping with honey, the thinly sliced ham salty, the fruit tangy and tart. Sipping the wine, he found it exquisite, light but full-flavoured, and so smooth it did not need watering down. Coenred was surprised to find that his headache had receded and after the first tentative mouthfuls of food, his stomach's churning had eased too.

It appeared that, in this at least, their host had been right. The food and drink were making him feel better. Coenred remained silent, watching the man and wondering about him. Priano reclined against his cushion, leaning effortlessly on one elbow. He was talking about Ierusalem, speaking of the heat there, the beauty of the temples and the endless desert sands of the Holy Land. Wilfrid interjected with questions every now and then, listening in rapt adoration, eyes wide. Baducing was more reserved in his reaction to Priano's tales, but he smiled and nodded as he ate and drank. After the excesses of the previous night, he too had regained his appetite, observed Coenred, for Baducing's plate was soon clean and a serving girl stepped up quickly to offer him more food. Baducing seemed to bear Priano none of the ill will that had begun to sour Coenred's mood. This gave Coenred pause. Perhaps he had been hasty in his judgement of the man. Maybe he was wrong to allow Beobrand's obvious dislike of Priano to colour his own feelings.

But as Priano spoke of the relics he had brought back from the Holy Land, Coenred found himself wondering how he had procured them. These were holy objects, unique items that bore great power. They should not be bought and sold like amphorae of wine or tanned hides in a marketplace. It was not right;

unseemly. That such a wealthy man as Priano should profit from holy artefacts saddened Coenred.

"You are very quiet, my friend," Priano said, turning to Coenred. "Do you feel quite well? Or are you reconsidering the offer of a bed to lie on for a time?"

"I am much recovered," Coenred said. "I thank you for the food. You were right. This wine is a marvel. It has rebalanced my humours." Setting aside his plate on the tiled floor, Coenred rolled over and unceremoniously pushed himself to his feet. The strength had returned to his legs and he was pleased he did not stumble. "I am ready now for your Hall of Relics. I have had quite enough expectation." He forced a smile, trying to rekindle the excitement he had felt earlier. "Now I would see the items with my own eyes and hold them with my own hands. Perhaps it is sinful of me, but I am envious of you, that you have such things in your possession."

"Perhaps soon enough some of my relics will not only be in your hands, but also in your possession."

"I pray it is so, but I fear the church of Lindisfarena is not as wealthy as those of Roma. I worry that I will not be able to meet your prices."

"Forgive me for saying so, Coenred, my friend, but I get the impression you worry too much. You should have more faith. I am no saint, for sure, but I try to be a good Christian, and I would not see my brothers in Christ from far-off Northumbria leave without items that will bring their congregations great joy."

Priano rose from his cushion, making the movement appear effortless. Baducing and Wilfrid both clambered to their feet with the ease of the young, though Baducing did let out a small groan, making Coenred wonder if his leg still pained him.

Blinking, Wilfrid stretched and ostentatiously stifled a wide yawn.

"I too wish to see the relics you have spoken of with such

passion, Priano. But alas, I fear your wine is stronger than I'd imagined. Perhaps you would be so good as to have one of your servants show me to a room where I can rest a while as you suggested."

Priano chuckled deep in his throat. It sounded almost like a growl.

"Of course," he said, "it is easy to forget how young you are. I am sure that after a short rest you will feel much more ready to peruse the relics." Priano beckoned to the serving girl with the green eyes. "Basina, take my guest to the *locus nubium* and see that he has everything he desires. When he is... rested, accompany him to the Hall of Relics. We will await him there." He chuckled again, grinning at Wilfrid. "I doubt he will need to rest for long. He is young and will recover his strength rapidly."

The girl's face was expressionless as she took Wilfrid by the hand and led him away.

"Wilfrid!" Coenred said, his tone hard. "Remember yourself."

Wilfrid's cheeks were flushed as he looked back.

"I'll return soon," he said, and then he was lost from view.

Baducing watched in open-mouthed disbelief. Coenred shook his head, also shocked by Wilfrid's behaviour. Beobrand and the others had informed him of the young man's actions during their travels, but still it amazed him to see the novice so openly giving in to the lustful urges of the flesh.

"Ah, youth," said Priano with a wistful smile, "the most priceless of commodities."

Still reeling, Baducing and Coenred exchanged a glance, then followed Priano through an open door, into the interior of the building. Coenred had thought it cool in the patio by the fountain, but inside the villa itself, the temperature was pleasant and by some cunning of the windows and doors of the place, a breeze flowed through the corridors.

Such was Coenred's disquiet at Wilfrid's flagrant disregard

for decorum and propriety that following behind Priano he barely took in the statues and ornately painted plastered walls. The muscled forms of the marble busts and the glimpses of the pictures of cavorting naked men and women only served to reinforce his discomfiture as he imagined Wilfrid's antics with Basina. He thought of the green-eyed girl and felt shame. He would remonstrate with Wilfrid when he got the chance. The novice's behaviour was unacceptable and could not be ignored.

They came to a door made of stout timber and bound in iron. Before it stood a tall man. He was broad of shoulder with heavily muscled arms. His craggy face was hard and devoid of emotion, as if it were carved from the same stone as the villa's many statues. A short sword hung from his belt. Without a word, the guard stood aside. Priano produced a large key from a chain around his neck and unlocked the door. The mechanism must have been expensive and well-oiled for it opened with only the slightest click.

"Behold," said Priano, with a sweeping gesture, "my Hall of Relics."

It was a long room, with candelabras and sconces positioned along its length. At night, with all the candles and lamps lit, Coenred imagined there would be ample illumination, but none of the flames burnt now. There were areas of shadow, but despite the sky being overcast and smothered with grey clouds that teased the promise of rain, enough light still lanced through the high, barred windows for Coenred to make out the details of what lay within the hall.

Tables and benches lined the walls and Coenred wondered if this had once been intended as a feasting hall. But no food would be served on those boards now. They were covered in all manner of items, in all shapes and sizes. At the far end of the hall, the wall was hidden behind shelves holding countless scrolls and books.

Coenred's mouth was dry. The air was strangely familiar to him, redolent of the Scriptorium, with its sour tang of parchment and ink, but there were other scents here too. Aromas he could not place, but that somehow conjured images in his mind of distant lands and almost forgotten times.

He followed Priano and Baducing further into the room, staring about him, slack-jawed in amazement. He could feel his wonderment smothering his shock at Wilfrid's actions and overcoming his reticence to deal with Priano. This was a hoard of priceless objects, and if he could convince the man to part with some of them, Coenred would leave contented. And, a small, selfish voice whispered inside him, he would not need to compete with Wilfrid, at least not for a while.

He pushed that mean-spirited thought away, but the truth was Wilfrid was increasingly far from Coenred's mind as he stared about the hall. Everywhere he looked there were boxes and crates, ranging in size from small enough to house a piece of jewellery to large enough to contain a bundle of spears.

"Ah, the sandals of Jesus Christ," said Priano, seeing him looking at a particularly ornate casket. It was fashioned of bone of some kind, carved with intricate patterns and people and animals in bas-relief. It was no more than three hands' breadths across and Priano lifted it from the bench. He opened the lid and held it toward Coenred to reveal a pair of silken slippers. They were flattened and dusty with age, but the stitching was wonderfully delicate and they were decorated with intricate embroidery. "I found these in a small village near Ierusalem," Priano said. "The man who owned them had no idea of their true value."

"They are beautiful," whispered Coenred, and it was true. The casket alone would be worth a fortune, but to think that the relics inside had been touched by Christ Himself.

Coenred reached out his hand, then drew back, frightened.

"I would have thought the son of a carpenter would wear something less... ornate."

"Not just the son of a carpenter though," Priano whispered. "The son of God! These shoes were made for the *Messias*! Touch them. Feel their power."

Coenred swallowed. His queasiness had returned. Cautiously, slowly, he moved his hand towards the relics. He could sense Baducing watching him, but he could not draw his gaze away from the silk slippers. As his fingers grew close, he held his breath.

"You can feel it," hissed Priano, "can't you?"

Coenred simply nodded. He wasn't sure he would be able to speak. The hairs on the nape of his neck prickled. Holding his breath, he offered up a prayer and touched the stiff fabric of one of the shoes. Letting out a small gasp, he quickly withdrew his hand. His fingers tingled, as if his hand had been slapped.

"See?" said Priano. "There can be no doubt they were once worn by Jesu himself."

Coenred's gaze lingered on the shoes for a time. He could not deny that he had felt something. His hand trembled. He imagined Comdhan and Conant's faces if he were to return to Lindisfarena with such precious and powerful relics. The shoes could be housed alongside the arm of King Oswald. Pilgrims would travel from all over Albion, perhaps from further afield still, to pray before such things. Enticing as the idea might be, he dismissed it before it could take hold in his heart. He knew instinctively he did not have enough silver for such priceless relics. He would have to be content to have been in the shoes' presence and to have touched one of them. He closed his eyes, praying to the Almighty for guidance, that he would not be overwhelmed, surrounded as he was by so many sacred wonders.

Looking about him, he saw that Baducing had wandered along to the books. Coenred would go there soon and he hoped that Priano would allow him to visit again and read from the tomes while he remained in Roma, for he thought it unlikely he would be able to afford to buy any of the manuscripts. Perhaps he could negotiate to borrow some for the monks of Lindisfarena to transcribe. He was keen to see the books in Priano's library, but before he could follow Baducing, Coenred's eyes drifted to the largest box that rested atop a trestle in the middle of the hall. A shaft of dusty light from one of the small windows fell upon it, demanding he give the box his attention.

Priano saw where he was looking. "That is the body of Saint Melania the Younger herself," he said, his tone reverent. "Let me show you."

Uncertainly, Coenred followed him towards the box that he now realised was the dimensions of a coffin. His breath came fast and shallow and he recalled the terror that had gripped him in the catacombs. There was nothing to fear from the dead, he told himself, particularly not a saintly martyr.

Approaching the timber coffin, he noted a sickly, cloying smell and, without thinking, he held his breath. Priano raised the lid, lifting it up and setting it aside.

"Isn't she something?" he whispered, gazing down at the body within. "I have commissioned a lavish tomb for her. She will be enshrined in the *Archibasilica*, my gift to the Pontifex Maximus."

Still not breathing, Coenred stared into the wizened face of the saint. Her skin was desiccated and wrinkled, the empty eye sockets shadowy pits. Dark leathery lips pulled back from long teeth. For a stabbing heartbeat, Coenred recalled the sharp pain of the fangs of the creature he had sensed in the forest, the talons raking at his flesh.

Staggering back from the coffin, he let out a strangled cry.

"I pray that Martinus has a more agreeable reaction to her," said Priano.

"I apologise," Coenred mumbled, feeling foolish.

"No need. It is said she was a beauty in life, but death has done her no favours."

Coenred's head pained him, and the food and wine were heavy in his belly.

"How did she come to be here?" he asked, forcing his voice to remain steady. "Was she not interred in a church or a catacomb?"

That Priano traded in holy artefacts, trinkets with a connection to Christ or His saints, was bad enough, but to disturb the dead, removing their mortal remains from their eternal resting place, sparked a fresh anger within Coenred.

"Do not fear," said Priano. "I am no grave robber. The church where the holy Melania the Younger was buried was destroyed in battle with the accursed Saracens. I merely rescued her body. Would that I could have done the same with all the good Christians there. But alas, I am but one man and my fortune is not boundless. The rest of the bodies were dragged from the crypt, broken and scattered. Dogs and jackals feasted on the bones." He made the sign of the cross, then, as if a thought had just come to him, he bent over the coffin. "I could save no more of the bodies, but there is no reason why the saint's power should not benefit the brethren of your minster as well as those of the *Archibasilica*." Priano reached into the casket, and Coenred watched in disgust as he took hold of one skeletal hand. Deliberating for a heartbeat, Priano made up his mind, and with a splintering snap, he pulled off one of the saint's thumbs.

"Here," he said, holding out the dry brown thing, "a gift from me to the brothers of Lindisfarena."

Coenred felt his gorge rise and for a terrible moment he thought he might puke.

"Take it," said Priano, "while I find a suitable box in which you can transport it. It will be a fabulous relic for your minster."

Coenred did not wish to touch the object, but saw no way of

avoiding it, so, taking a breath through his mouth and hoping his stomach would settle, he allowed Priano to place it on his palm.

It weighed nothing. Coenred stared at it in horrified awe. The skin was parchment thin and had torn where Priano had separated it from the hand. A pale, yellowing bone jutted from it. The other end was tipped with a blackened nail.

Priano rummaged through the contents of a nearby table.

"Ah, here it is," he said, returning with a small box of cedarwood inlaid with a pattern picked out in mother-of-pearl. Removing the lid, he held the box out to Coenred, who placed the shrivelled thumb inside. He resisted the urge to wipe his hand against his robe.

"A small cushion inside to protect the relic would be a good idea," Priano said, "but I think that box suits well, and now your brothers in Christ on the holy island will feel the power of Melania the Younger."

"Thank you," Coenred said. "They will be most grateful." He swallowed against the dryness in his mouth. "As am I."

Priano grinned, then moved to replace the lid on the casket that housed the body of Melania. Coenred could not prevent himself from letting out a sigh of relief as the hideously dried corpse was covered once more. If Priano noticed the reaction, he said nothing.

"Come, let me show you a nail from the one true cross."

Coenred followed obediently as Priano walked him around his jumble of relics and wonders. He showed him pebbles from the Sea of Galilee and straw from the manger where Christ had slept as a babe. Coenred sniffed richly scented Frankincense and Myrrh, both, said Priano, remnants of the gifts the Magi had offered the Blessed Virgin Maria. With awed reverence Coenred stroked a stained piece of soft fabric that Priano said was taken from the hem of the dress worn by Christ's mother on the day of His crucifixion. Again Coenred felt the thrill of hidden power tingling on his fingertips.

A sliver of doubt crept into Coenred's mind then. He could imagine Beobrand's disdain at seeing these things. The thegn would ask how anyone could prove these items were authentic. What stopped men from merely saying such objects were from saints, the Blessed Virgin or Jesu himself? But Beobrand had no faith, Coenred told himself. He could not comprehend the mysteries of God. And if these things were not real, what could explain the power Coenred had sensed at their touch?

Coenred had felt the shiver of energy as his fingers brushed the silk shoes and the hem of the Blessed Virgin's dress. His faith was strong. Nevertheless, he felt himself becoming less enthralled by the relics and increasingly attracted to the scrolls and books at the end of the hall. The knowledge and learning stored within those parchments called to him. There could be no question as to the tomes' value, and their power. Wisdom set down in ink, words captured in silent repose on the vellum pages, and given life by each reader anew. This unique power possessed by books always left him giddy with excitement.

"Make yourself comfortable," Priano said, ushering him towards the shelves and tables that were strewn with leather-bound tomes. "I see you and Baducing are both men of letters."

Baducing was already seated with a large book open before him. In the afternoon light spearing down from the high windows, he was holding a small bone pointer to track the letters on the page, his lips moving as he silently mouthed the words.

"I thank you," Coenred said. "I believe you have more books than our Scriptorium. I could spend days here."

"And you would be welcome, of course," Priano said, airily. "Is there any particular tome you are interested in?"

"I will be content to look at what lies on your shelves, for I am sure not to have seen most of what you have on offer."

"Of course, of course. Choose whichever book interests you the most. I have been reading Aristoteles' *Protrepticus* recently and found it to be most enlightening." He indicated a book that lay open on a reading stand. "I will call for more refreshments. Reading can be thirsty work."

Coenred smiled absently, but barely heard Priano. The spell of the books was already taking hold of him. He went to the book Priano had mentioned and began to read from the page on which it was open. The penmanship was exquisite. So too were the words. Such elegance and grace in the poetry.

Setting down the box containing Melania the Younger's thumb, Coenred sat and was soon lost in the timeless brilliance of Aristoteles.

Sometime later a man with thinning grey hair and a sombre demeanour entered the hall. On a table near where Baducing and Coenred were reading in silence the man set down a tray bearing a flask and silver cups.

"Would you like me to serve, *dominus*?" he said, his tone low and respectful.

Priano had been leafing through a copy of Strabo's *Historia*, but had seemed to Coenred increasingly uneasy, nervously fidgeting and glancing at the door.

"No, Turco," Priano said. "That won't be necessary. Go to the room of clouds and see whether our other young guest has had his fill of resting."

Until now Priano had not once mentioned the cost of any of the items in his hall. This had pleased Coenred, but now he wondered whether perhaps Priano was anxious to move on to the negotiations. Coenred sighed. He had become engrossed in the works of a poet called Publius Ovidius Naso. He had never read anything by the man before and while the subject of the poetry was enough to make Coenred blush, the beauty of the language and the intelligence behind the words enthralled him.

He had pushed thoughts of Wilfrid from his mind. Now his anger at the young man's behaviour came rushing back.

Turco bowed and left the hall. Coenred watched him leave, noting how the light from the windows was a different hue now and the sun had slid far across the sky. They had been at Priano's villa for quite some time and they would need to leave soon, if they were to return to the Lateran *Patriarchium* before dark.

Priano poured a pale liquid from the flask and handed a cup each to Baducing and Coenred.

Holding up his own cup, he said, "To new friends."

"New friends in Christ," Coenred said, lifting the cup to his lips and tasting the contents. It was a wine as sweet as honey and light as cherry blossom. "This is perhaps even better than your other wine," he said. "I must be careful not to drink too much. Otherwise the ride back to the *Patriarchium* will be torture."

"That is easily remedied," said Priano with a chuckle. "You should stay here tonight. I have plenty of space and Wilfrid will attest that the beds are soft." He winked.

"I thank you for the generous offer, but I cannot accept." While the prospect of uninterrupted access to Priano's books appealed, Coenred did not wish to stay where Wilfrid would be open to further temptations.

"Oh, but it is no trouble for my new friends," Priano said. "You simply must stay."

Coenred searched for a good reason to decline. After a brief hesitation, he said, "I have promised lord Beobrand to help with his travel preparations tomorrow." It was a poor excuse and he saw Priano mulling over whether to question it. In the end, to Coenred's relief, the older man nodded.

"Of course. When we have concluded our business I will have some of my guards accompany you. The roads are not safe, particularly after dark."

"You have my thanks," said Coenred. He had been worried

at the thought of riding through the overgrown thoroughfares of the *Disabitato* without an escort. "You have been a most generous host."

"Do not judge me so quickly," Priano said with a mischievous smile. "We have not begun the dance of the haggle yet. And friends or no, I take that dance most seriously."

Coenred's heart sank.

"Don't be too hard on me," he said. "My minster's purse is not heavy."

"Do not fear, Coenred," Priano said, "whatever else you take with you, you will not leave my home empty-handed."

Baducing looked up from his book. "You have bought something already?"

"No. A gift." Coenred picked up the small nacre-decorated cedarwood box. "The thumb of Melania the Younger."

Baducing raised his eyebrows.

"I see I missed out," he said. "I was perhaps too quick to begin perusing these books."

"No, no," said Priano. "There are plenty of items I think you will be interested in. When Wilfrid returns we can begin to see what you might take with you back to Albion." The door to the hall opened. "Ah, here he is now."

But it was not Wilfrid. The grey-haired Turco, flushed and plainly flustered, was alone and he hurried along the length of the room.

"What is it?" snapped Priano. "Where is Wilfrid?"

The old man bent and whispered in his master's ear. Priano's face paled and he surged to his feet.

"How can this be?" he said, his voice strident. "That room is locked."

"Perhaps," said Turco, his tone apologetic, "someone forgot to lock it."

Priano glowered at him.

"If you left the door unlocked, you will be punished," he said.

Turco cowered, as if he expected his master to strike him. And such was the anger washing off Priano, Coenred thought it quite possible.

"Sorry, *dominus*," Turco mumbled, not daring to look up.

"I will deal with you later," hissed Priano. "Now, come with me."

He began striding along the hall, Turco hurrying in his wake, when he suddenly halted.

"Wait here," he said to Baducing and Coenred. "I will be back with Wilfrid soon."

Without waiting for a response, Priano practically ran from the room with Turco trotting at his heels.

Chapter 23

The heavy door slammed shut, then swung slightly ajar, such was the force with which it had been closed. Coenred heard a hissed exchange outside and then the sound of footsteps receding down the corridor.

Baducing let out a breath.

"What do you make of that?" he asked.

"Wilfrid has somehow caused this," said Coenred. "I know not what he has done, but this is his doing." In a sharp motion he swallowed down the rest of his sweet wine and slammed the empty cup onto the tray with a clatter. "The man is a menace. He lusts like a rutting stag, uncaring for how his actions harm others. I just pray his foolishness has not gone too far."

Neither of them could think of reading now and they stood in uncomfortable silence. Baducing awkwardly sipped his wine.

"Priano has been the best of hosts," he said suddenly. "I was hoping to be able to come back and read as many of his books as possible. You know he has copies of epistles from Paulus I have never heard of before? And the Almighty alone knows what other treasures can be found on those shelves. Whatever Wilfrid has done, I do hope it doesn't colour Priano's feelings towards me."

"You mean beyond bedding the man's thrall?"

Baducing shrugged.

"In Wilfrid's defence, Priano did offer."

"The Devil comes in many guises," said Coenred, scowling. "Both you and I stood firm in the face of the same temptation."

Baducing tried to emulate Coenred's sombre look, but eventually gave up and laughed.

"Interesting choice of words," he said. "I imagine Wilfrid stood firm too!"

Coenred shook his head.

"Let us hope we can all laugh about this later."

"From the sound of it," said Coenred, "I am not so sure that will be possible."

From the open door the sound of raised voices reached them. They could not make out the words, but they recognised Priano's voice. He was clearly furious. The second voice was quieter, less shrill, but it was loud enough for them to place it as Wilfrid's.

The angry exchange continued for some time, becoming louder and more intense with each passing heartbeat. As Wilfrid's senior in the Church, Coenred felt it his duty to find out what Wilfrid had done and see whether he could intercede.

"Come," he said, "let us go and see what is happening." It might be his duty, but he felt nothing but anger towards the young man who caused trouble wherever he went. He knew he should be more forgiving, but it was not easy. The voice of Priano had reached such an intense pitch now that Coenred began to fear this might escalate beyond all reason. Men of Priano's standing, with wealth and power, did not take well to being crossed and he had many guards in his employ. Could Wilfrid have offended him so much that it might end in the shedding of blood?

Stomach churning once more and his headache returning, Coenred rushed to the door and pushed it open. The guard was not there. Perhaps he had accompanied Priano and Turco when they had gone to find Wilfrid, or maybe he had been drawn to the shouted voices and their ever increasing anger. Those voices echoed along the painted corridor, making it easy to know in which direction to turn.

They did not need to go far. Rounding a corner in the passageway, they saw a similar door to that of the hall, fashioned of stout timber and bound in iron. It was wide open and the furious voices emanated from within.

Coenred pressed on. He loathed confrontation, but such was the heat and depth of rage in Priano's voice, he feared what might happen if he did not intervene. Taking a deep breath, he stepped into the room.

Turco, white-faced and nervous, lingered near the entrance. The room was much smaller than the Hall of Relics, but had a number of similarities. The left side of the chamber was also crammed full of crates and boxes. On the right were shelves containing half a dozen books. A handful of scrolls rested on a narrow shelf above the leather-bound tomes. In the centre of the room was a table and chair. Priano and Wilfrid stood facing each other across the table. Priano's face was mottled and red as he yelled at Wilfrid. The novice was rigid and pale, just as angry as their host, but perhaps, thought Coenred, taking in the scene at a glance, for different reasons. The burly guard they had seen earlier held Wilfrid. His huge hands gripped the novice's thin arms, meaty fingers pressing into the flesh hard enough to bruise.

Coenred was still unsure of the exact nature of the dispute, but the object of their confrontation seemed plain. For on the table between Priano and Wilfrid was a book.

And what a book!

It was closed and Coenred had no inkling of what resided within the pages of that tome, but if a book could be judged by the value of its cover, this book must be worth a king's fortune. The room was drab and dusty, with little of the gloomy late afternoon light filtering through the two small barred windows, and yet still the book appeared to glow.

Intricate golden bindings glimmered. Jewels winked in the mote-swirled light. Gemstones held in the ornate golden scrollwork gleamed. At the centre of the tome's cover a blood-red stone shone as if lit from within. Golden threads flowed away from it like roots and connected to a solid strip of gold.

Coenred's mouth was dry. He had no knowledge of what was written within that book, and yet he had never in his life wished more to own something. He wanted to reach out and touch the jewel-laden cover, and his heart fluttered at the thought of opening the tome and reading the secrets it promised to hold within.

Beside him, Baducing gasped, and Coenred knew the younger man must have felt the same strange and powerful longing. With a great effort he dragged his attention from the book. There were more pressing matters to deal with first. On their entry into the room, Priano and Wilfrid had fallen momentarily quiet and Coenred decided he could not allow them to begin shouting again.

"I see Wilfrid has offended you, Priano," he said. "I know not what he has done—"

"I have done nothing wrong!" interjected Wilfrid, but Coenred cut him off.

"Silence!" he barked. He seldom showed his emotions in this way, so his voice carried more weight, and both Wilfrid and Baducing tensed. "Whatever Wilfrid has done, I apologise."

"I fear this has gone beyond an apology," said Priano. "I welcome you into my home, offer you treasures and pleasures, and you betray me like this!"

Priano's voice was rising again, fanning the flames of his anger into fresh life.

"This is madness," replied Wilfrid, an edge of desperation in his voice. "All I did was offer to buy this book." He reached out to stroke the bejewelled cover. Priano lunged forward, slapping Wilfrid's hand away.

"Hold him," he snapped. The guard tightened his grip, pulling Wilfrid roughly away from the book. "You offer to buy something that is not for sale. A book you would never have seen if you had not been skulking about my villa like a thief."

Shock strained Wilfrid's features.

"The door was unlocked," he said, frustration giving his voice a whining tone. "I entered thinking this was where you were waiting for me."

"You lie!" raved Priano. "I can see it on your face. You desire the book. Did you come for it all along? Was that your game? How did you know of it?"

Wilfrid gave Coenred a pleading look.

"I meant no offence," he said. "I saw this door and entered. When I found books inside, I could not resist opening one and reading. And when I read what was inside the covers, I wanted to read more." He turned again to Coenred. The light from the gems and gold shone on his face. "You should read it, Coenred. Baducing, you too. It is—"

"Never!" spat Priano, silencing Wilfrid with his fury. "The book is mine and you will not have it."

Coenred appraised the man anew. Spittle flecked his lips and insanity tinged his voice. Coenred glanced at the book, again feeling its pull. He made the sign of the cross, wondering what devilment was at play here.

"I know not what book this is, Priano," Coenred said, keeping his voice calm and low, "but I think Wilfrid tells the truth in this. He can be a fool, of that there is no doubt, but in this I believe him."

"Then you are a fool too," Priano hissed. "You are in league with him, no doubt."

"I may be a fool," Coenred said, "but I promise you I am in league with nobody. We came here in good faith and you have been a most generous host. Again I can but apologise for Wilfrid's actions." He cast a glaring look at Wilfrid then, urging the young man to offer his own contrition to the apology.

For several heartbeats Wilfrid met his gaze. His lips were pressed together in a scowl and he was shaking with anger and frustration. Coenred did not blink and was thankful when Wilfrid finally let out a long breath and turned to face Priano once more.

"I too apologise," he said, his words clipped and sharp as slate. He glanced at Coenred, who nodded for him to proceed. "You have been generous and I am sorry for my part in this... misunderstanding."

Priano scoffed. "You mean you are sorry you were caught."

His anger had not vanished, but Coenred let out his breath as he detected that the man's rage had lessened. Wilfrid looked ready to respond, but Coenred shook his head.

"Again, let me offer you my apologies," Coenred said. "Perhaps it would be best if we departed now."

"Yes, that would be best," said Priano. He signalled for them to move to the door. The guard prodded Wilfrid in that direction. The others followed. Coenred noticed how Wilfrid's eyes lingered on the book and he felt his own gaze drawn to the tome even as they left the chamber. He felt a stab of jealousy that Wilfrid had seen inside those fabulous covers and vowed to ask him what wonders he had read within its pages.

Soon they were outside the door. Priano locked it with the key he wore on a chain.

"Do not let it be said I am not a man of my word," he said, turning to face them. His cheeks were flushed, but he was visibly calmer now. "As promised I will lend you my guards to escort you from here. And you may take with you the thumb of Melania the Younger."

Coenred offered him a small bow.

"I thank you," he said. He was relieved. Moments earlier he would not have believed such an outcome might have been possible.

"But know this," Priano said, an obdurate edge entering his voice. "You will never return to my villa. You are no longer welcome here. I have seen the darkness that resides within Wilfrid and unless you wish to see it burnt from him, you will stay far from me and my lands from this day forth."

Chapter 24

Beobrand accepted the bridle of his horse from the hostler and led the animal past the rock positioned near the stables. It was broad and flat-topped, with a couple of shallow steps carved in the side closest to the building. It was used for the purpose of mounting. Beobrand's legs were stiff from the previous morning's training, and if he had been alone, he might have used the stone, but there was no way he was going to give Cynan an extra chance to comment on his age. Woden knew he felt old enough as it was, without his gesith reminding him. Taking a deep breath and a handful of the stallion's mane, he swung himself up and settled himself in the saddle with a grunt.

Cynan was already mounted and while he was waiting for the others, he cantered about the yard, loosening up his horse's muscles. Halinard allowed the hostler to lead his gelding to the mounting rock. Limping up the two steps, he climbed easily into the saddle.

Cynan reined his horse to a clattering halt beside the Frank.

"I hope you are not going to expect help getting into the saddle when we are on our way home," he said.

"I will manage," replied Halinard, his tone gruff. "But I see no reason to tire myself unduly now when this rock is here. I am sweating as it is."

The day was already hot and it would be unbearable soon. That was why Beobrand had chosen to ride to Eugenius' residence shortly after dawn. He looked eastward over the broad canopies of some of the pines that grew all over the city. The sun was hidden behind dense cloud, but Beobrand knew it would be as hot as a forge by midday.

It had been that way for several days. Each day following the same pattern. A warm sunrise leading to insufferable heat and a sweat-soaked, restless night. Those who followed the Christ god prayed to the Almighty, His son and His saints for rain. Beobrand had buried a piece of silver in a grove of ash trees and begged Thunor to send his chariot across the sky. A storm would clear the air and blow away some of this accursed heat. And yet, despite a few small squalls of rain and wind that blew the dust in spiralling clouds that got in their eyes and scratched at their faces, none of the gods seemed willing to heed the wishes of the mortals who roasted amongst the hot stones of the palaces, hovels and temples of Roma.

The three riders rode out of the courtyard and turned south along the cobbled road, glad of the lightest of breezes on their faces. None of them wore armour, but all carried their shields slung across their backs and their swords in scabbards hanging from baldrics.

Beobrand had been meaning to visit Wilfrid for several days. But each new day found him busy with the preparations for their upcoming journey homeward. In the mornings, he trained, pushing his aching body, running with his men and drilling them in the spear-skill and sword-craft that made the Black Shields such a force to be reckoned with. He was determined that when they returned to Bernicia, they would still be the most feared warriors in all of Albion. Ever since the chance encounter with Rothad the Frisian trader, Beobrand had worried about what might be happening in his homeland. More than once he had awoken from nightmares drenched in sweat, biting back a scream of terror at the thought his loved ones might be under attack from the Picts. He saw the faces of Torran and Broden in his dreams. The sons of Nathair mac Gaven were long dead, but still the memory of them brought back times of great anguish and he didn't need a cunning woman or shaman to explain his dreams' meaning.

With each passing day his anxiety and disquiet grew. He recognised these feelings and threw himself into getting ready to leave. After training with the gesithas, there were always other tasks to occupy the long, stifling summer days. He oversaw the replacement of horses that were lame. He bought a new waggon to transport their provisions and any other items they had purchased in Roma. He found Halinard good at helping with such work. He was quick-witted and when problems arose, his solutions were effective and practical, his manner decisive. Coenred too came with him on many of his errands, acting as interpreter.

But the monk did not ride with him today.

"You think Coenred will ever forgive Wilfrid?" Cynan asked, glancing at Beobrand from beneath the wide brim of his straw hat. His once pale skin had taken on a light golden hue.

"If any man can forgive Wilfrid," Beobrand said, shielding his eyes from the hazy sun to look over at the huge stones of the circus, "it is Coenred. But that does not mean he wishes to see him."

"If he comes with us to Albion, he may have no choice."

Beobrand scowled.

"I know," he said. "It will not make for a pleasant journey."

"In my experience," said Halinard, turning in his saddle, and grimacing, "no journey with Wilfrid is good."

Cynan sniffed.

"If Eadgard had been at Priano's, I don't think we would be having this conversation."

Halinard's gelding shook its head, then halted without warning and proceeded to let out a gushing stream of piss. The others reined in without comment.

"More likely," said Halinard, waiting patiently for his mount to finish, "we would be discussing where Wilfrid should be buried."

The gelding stopped urinating and walked on. Beobrand kicked gently at his stallion's flanks and fell back into step beside Halinard.

"Then we must be glad Coenred was there," he said, "for to hear him tell the tale, Priano might well have taken the young fool's life."

"And we should be glad of that?" scoffed Cynan.

"Do not forget," said Beobrand, "I swore an oath to protect Wilfrid."

"How could we forget?" said Cynan. "That oath has caused us much grief."

Beobrand felt a spark of anger flicker deep within him. He did not wish to be reminded of how they had come to be on this gods-forsaken mission. He squinted into the already-light sky and watched a buzzard take flight from atop a ruined column, jutting from a tangle of parched brown weeds and long grass. The bird flapped languidly eastward, stark against the pale cloud-heavy sky, to be lost in the shadows of a stand of trees.

"As I recall," Beobrand said, "we both had our part to play in being sent south on this pilgrimage." He gave up trying to spy the buzzard in the trees and let out a long breath. "But there is nothing to be gained from blowing air on those coals. It is too hot already to be angry."

"Indeed, lord," said Cynan. He did not say sorry, but Beobrand knew him well enough to understand that the Waelisc man regretted bringing up the memories of events that had led to their journey to Roma.

They rode in silence for a time. Ahead of them two peasants with staves trudged behind a herd of ruddy cattle, leading them down to water no doubt, before it grew too hot. A squat dog trotted along in the shadow of the large animals.

The men stooped and touched their hats to the passing horsemen. The cattle milled about on the road, ignoring the horses and their riders. Beobrand pushed one away from his mount with his foot. The cow rolled its eyes at him, lowed gently and moved aside.

They had climbed the Aventinus Hill and the silver ribbon of the Tiberis was visible in the distance. A few boats already dotted the water. Closer to the riders rose the solid shape of the church of Santa Prisca.

Beobrand was surprised at how quickly they had reached their destination. He bit his lip. He did not blame Coenred for not wishing to see Wilfrid, nor could he hold it against Halinard and Cynan that they felt animosity towards the man. Wilfrid had caused more trouble than he was worth and Beobrand fervently hoped he would decline to join them on their return journey to Albion. But no matter his personal feelings about the man, he felt his oath demanded of him that he at least make the offer. What Coenred had told them of Wilfrid's conduct at Priano's villa, coupled with his behaviour in Frankia, was bad enough, but Beobrand could not recall ever having seen Coenred angrier than when he heard about Wulfwyn and Aelfwig.

After the feast, Beobrand had decided not to tell the widow of Priano's offer, nevertheless somehow, perhaps from one of the warriors, Wulfwyn had heard about it. She was feeling much recovered from the ague, but recent events and her illness must have unnerved her, making her consider what might happen to Aelfwig should the worst occur. The chance of a rich patron who promised to teach her blind son had been too good an opportunity to ignore. Beobrand wondered if she suspected there might be more to Priano's offer, that mayhap he would ask of her more than she would be willing to give. But if she had such misgivings, they did not sway her decision. With Grindan, Eadgard and Lucifrido as escorts, she had left for Priano's villa the very afternoon following the feast.

The next morning, Coenred had come to where Beobrand and his gesithas were training on the open ground before the *Archibasilica*. First he had angrily recounted what had transpired with Wilfrid. When he heard about Wulfwyn and Aelfwig, he had been distraught.

"Why did she not wait?" he asked, pain and worry in his voice. "Why would she hurry to the man's villa without even bidding me farewell?"

"She knows we plan to leave Roma soon," Beobrand said. "She wishes to stay and must think of Aelfwig. Besides, she thought they would find you there. At the feast you all seemed to be Priano's closest friends."

"Well," Coenred said, his face ashen, "we are friends no longer. But I do not understand how we did not cross paths. She had not arrived when we left."

"I know not. Lucifrido, Grindan and Eadgard returned after dark, but they said Wulfwyn and the boy were made welcome at the villa."

Coenred fell silent for a time.

"I was furious with Wilfrid," he said. "I did not wish to remain in his company, so we rode to Eugenius' hall before coming back here. That is how we missed them. What cursed bad luck."

"Could it not be that this was in God's plan?" Beobrand said the words with a smile, unable to resist the jibe. Coenred did not find it amusing.

"I fear what will befall Wulfwyn and Aelfwig in Priano's hall," he said.

Beobrand grew serious.

"I didn't like that man," he said, "but you said yourself that until Wilfrid betrayed his trust, Priano was a good host. Perhaps he will treat them both well. The gods know Wulfwyn and the boy are easier to like than Wilfrid."

"True enough," Coenred said with a sigh.

But he had not been able to ignore his fears, and two days later, Coenred had set out with Eadgard, Grindan and Marsiglio across the city to Priano's villa.

They returned late that afternoon. After Vespers, Coenred had visited Beobrand in the palace gardens. Beobrand had taken to sitting outside most nights in an attempt to avoid the worst of the heat. Coenred found him sipping from a skin of wine in the darkness. Cynan was nearby, but both men had been contented in the silence that had descended on them with the dusk.

Beobrand had watched Coenred approach, flitting between the shadowed rows of bushes and trees. At the sound of the monk's footsteps crunching on the gravel path, Cynan rose slightly from where he was sitting and peered into the gloom.

"It's just Coenred," Beobrand whispered.

Cynan took another look, then, satisfied that this was no threat, he relaxed again.

Beobrand struggled to make out any details as Coenred approached. His eyesight was worse than ever in darkness. However, he had known Coenred for most of his life and recognised his shape and gait. He could tell from the set of his shoulders and the speed of his step that he was less troubled than when he had set out that morning.

"Thirsty?" Beobrand said, offering Coenred the wineskin as the monk reached him.

After the briefest of hesitations, Coenred accepted it.

"In this heat, always," he said, then took a long draught.

"Good day?" Beobrand asked. He took the skin back and poured some of the liquid into his mouth.

Coenred thought for a short while before answering.

"Good is perhaps too much to say, but I have spoken to Wulfwyn, and she is well enough."

"Priano let you in then?"

"Oh no, he was not at home and his servant, Turco, had orders not to allow us entry."

"After what Wilfrid did, you cannot truly blame the man."

"Indeed," said Coenred, sitting beside Beobrand and holding out his hand for the wineskin once more. "This wine is good. I'll miss it when we return to Bernicia."

"I have a taste for it too," said Beobrand. "Perhaps Oswiu will sell me some of his, though I don't believe I have tasted wine as fine as this in Bebbanburg. So this Turco did not let you in, but allowed you to speak with Wulfwyn?"

"In the end he relented and allowed us into the stable yard. He even had food and drink sent out for us. Wulfwyn and Aelfwig met us there."

"And they are well?"

"They are," Coenred said. "Priano has already begun to teach Aelfwig, and Wulfwyn seems happy enough with her lot as servant."

"I am glad," Beobrand said, and he meant it. He had been uncertain about Priano. Something made him distrust the man. He was pleased to find his qualms appeared unfounded.

That had been four days ago. Since they had met them in the mountains, Beobrand and his companions had grown accustomed to having the widow and her son with them and now they missed them both. But their days were busy and everyone could feel the building expectation of their pending departure.

Now they rode out of the shade of Santa Prisca and across the yard towards Eugenius' residence. Their horses' hooves clacked against the smooth, dressed stones, attracting the attention of a group of dark-robed men standing beneath the portico of the church.

Beobrand recognised Eugenius, and the man from the Exarchatus of Ravenna. Close to those men of influence and power – just where Beobrand would have expected him to be – was Wilfrid.

He waved to the young man. Wilfrid raised his hand in reply, detached himself from the group and hurried over. Beobrand felt no joy at seeing him again and would be glad if he never laid eyes on Wilfrid after this day, but he had put off this visit as long as he could and they were ready to leave. He could not imagine facing Eanflæd and telling her he had abandoned her pet priest in Roma without giving him a chance to travel with them.

Wilfrid called out before he had even reached them.

"Is Coenred not with you?"

"He is not," replied Beobrand. Sliding down from the saddle, he handed his reins to Cynan. "No need to unsaddle them," he said, his voice low enough that it would be heard by Wilfrid. "We shall not be staying long."

Wilfrid halted before them. His eyes were bright and his cheeks flushed.

"Perhaps it is for the best Coenred has not come," Wilfrid said.

"Perhaps so," said Beobrand. "I am not sure he has forgiven you yet."

Wilfrid scoffed. "I don't care a fig for Coenred's forgiveness, lord Beobrand. He is a little man and his mind is veiled in darkness."

Beobrand frowned.

"Coenred is my friend," he said quietly, a warning sheathed in the softness of his words.

"And mine," added Cynan, who had dismounted along with Halinard. The two of them were about to lead the horses over to the stables where there were water-filled troughs.

Wilfrid ignored the two gesithas.

"I will not hear Coenred insulted," growled Beobrand, feeling his anger kindling.

"Of course, of course," said Wilfrid quickly. "I meant nothing by it."

Unspeaking, Beobrand glowered at him.

"I am sorry," muttered Wilfrid.

"It is Coenred who needs your apology for what happened at Priano's."

Wilfrid cocked his head as if listening to a far-off sound.

"Perhaps," he said.

The men who were gathered before the church called out to Wilfrid. He turned to them, shouting something in Latin. Beobrand wished he had brought Lucifrido to interpret for him.

"They are waiting for you?" Beobrand asked.

Wilfrid seemed distracted.

"No, no. I have told them not to tarry on my behalf. I have somewhere else I need to be anyway."

There was a sly undercurrent in his tone, a strange excitement.

"A lady?" asked Beobrand, surmising the reason for Wilfrid's nervous energy.

"Oh no," Wilfrid said. "Something much better than any momentary pleasure. You would not understand."

Beobrand bristled.

"I am but a warrior," he said. "And it is true I do not readily comprehend the ways of monks and priests."

"You cannot be blamed for that, lord Beobrand. You have

your own strengths. And a sword is often valued highly in this earthly realm."

Beobrand shook his head. There was an unusual quality to Wilfrid's mood that he did not recognise. Wilfrid had always been arrogant, but there was a directness to him now that Beobrand had not witnessed before. The young man was full of pent-up energy, like a warrior before standing in his first shieldwall.

"I came here today with a sole purpose," Beobrand said, pushing aside his annoyance at Wilfrid's dismissive tone.

Wilfrid appeared unable to stand still. He was practically trembling with excitement, shifting his weight from one foot to the other, like a child desperate for a piss.

"And what would that be?" he asked.

"I bring you a message."

"Well speak it, man," Wilfrid snapped, "or is it a written missive?"

Beobrand clenched his fists at his side. He imagined punching Wilfrid. But instead he gritted his teeth and forced himself to take a long, calming breath. He had given his oath to his queen to protect Wilfrid, but the gods alone knew how difficult it was proving to honour that vow.

"I bear the message, but I am not merely the messenger, but the sender too. I came to tell you we are leaving."

Wilfrid blinked.

"Roma? When?"

"We have all we need for the journey. We leave the day after tomorrow. We will be heading back to Albion by the most direct route and will not linger along the way." Beobrand did not wish to speak the next words, dreading Wilfrid's reply, but he swallowed back the bitter taste in his throat and pressed on. "You are welcome to join us."

"Oh no," said Wilfrid. "I do not plan on leaving Roma soon. I still have so much to learn here."

Beobrand let out his breath slowly.

"Well," he said, feeling the sudden lightness of relief, "I know how much you enjoy your books."

Wilfrid grinned. The broad smile looked out of place on his fine features.

"Some books more than others," Wilfrid said, lowering his voice but unable to hide his elation.

Beobrand could not recall seeing such a gleeful expression on the young man's face before.

"Coenred told us you found a particularly special tome at Priano's," he said.

"Oh yes." Wilfrid's eyes glittered and he seemed to thrum with his passion. "Such a book. Filled with the most wondrous things." Without warning he blurted out a snigger, before abruptly cutting off the sound with what sounded like a stifled sob. He held a delicate hand up to his mouth.

"Are you quite well?" asked Beobrand. He wondered if perhaps Wilfrid had been imbibing a little too much of Eugenius' good wine.

"Better for having found that book," said Wilfrid.

"I know little of these things," Beobrand said, "but Coenred has not stopped talking of the libraries in the city. I'm sure you will find other books."

"I have no need for other books now," Wilfrid said. Then, as if he had heard a voice calling him, he looked over his shoulder furtively. "I must go."

"Books to read?" asked Beobrand.

"Just one!" Wilfrid turned to leave.

Beobrand placed a hand on his shoulder, halting him. In spite of himself, he felt a strange sorrow wash over him at the thought of leaving this young novice behind.

"Wilfrid," he said. "We have not been easy travelling companions on this journey, you and I, and the gods know too much death has followed us. But I wish you no ill. Be careful of angry husbands and may your stay in Roma be fruitful." He held out his hand and after a brief pause, Wilfrid took it. "Maybe one day we will meet again."

Wilfrid looked directly into Beobrand's eyes. All sign of mirth had vanished from his face.

"I have no doubt of that, Beobrand of Ubbanford," he said, then turned on his heel.

Frowning, Beobrand watched Wilfrid, his robes flapping about him like wings as he almost ran across the courtyard and disappeared into Eugenius' residence.

Chapter 25

"Do you think we will reach the *Archibasilica* in time for Vespers?" Coenred asked. He wiped sweat out of his eyes and hurried to keep up with Marsiglio, who was setting a gruelling pace. During the long afternoon in the tranquil cool of the library he had almost forgotten how hot the city streets were.

They walked out of the shadowed street and into an open area where their route crossed a larger thoroughfare. Coenred blinked at the brightness. Marsiglio glanced to the west.

The sun was low in the sky, the red orb casting its ruddy glow beneath the thick cloud that had cloaked the city for days.

"If we hurry," he said. "We really should have left some time ago."

"I'm sorry," said Coenred. "I did not want to leave before completing my transcription of Hippolytus' treatise on the determination of the date of Pascha."

Marsiglio smiled widely, his teeth gleaming.

"No need to apologise, friend," he said. "I know you are sorry to be leaving."

It was true. Beobrand had announced that they would be setting forth on the morrow, which made this Coenred's last chance to obtain access to some of the priceless books dotted about the different palaces of Roma. Marsiglio and he had spent all afternoon in the library of a priest called Borso. The priest's residence had once belonged to a long-dead Roman noble, and its interior, with its mosaic floors and walls that had been dressed with marble, was pleasantly cool. And Borso had been most welcoming. He had even agreed to Coenred's request to lend him his precious *Evangelium of Nicodemus*. He would take it back to Lindisfarena, where it would be copied, and then returned the following year when more of the brethren made the journey back to Roma. Coenred thought it likely that Borso had only agreed because Martinus himself had introduced them directly. There might be dissent among certain factions of the Church, stemming from complex differences in theology, but it seemed the Pontifex Maximus, the Bishop of Roma, still had considerable influence.

Whatever the reason for the bishop's generosity, Coenred was pleased with the arrangement, especially after the catastrophe at Priano's villa.

Marsiglio trotted across the wide road, darting into the shade of a narrow street on the other side that would take them most of the way to the Lateran *Patriarchium* and the *Archibasilica*. Coenred hurried to keep up, flicking a glance left and right as he crossed the dusty cobble stones. His nervousness at travelling across the city had lessened in recent days. From experience he knew the *Disabitato* was dangerous, but since that trip to the catacombs of Callixtus and the church of Saint Sebastianus, he had travelled safely to several other catacombs, churches and palaces without incident. Now, with the sun setting, the inhabitants of Roma were preparing for night and the wide road was empty, save for a single rider far off to the east and a pitifully scrawny stray dog nearby that raised its head from where it lay in the shade of a straggly olive tree.

It would be dark soon. Coenred could hardly believe this

would be his last night in Roma. His stay in the Eternal City had certainly been eventful, and not without profit. He had made good friends, like Marsiglio, who he would miss, and he had secured several important artefacts and books for the minster at Lindisfarena. He did not dwell on what might have been if Wilfrid had not caused such a commotion at Priano's villa. The past could not be altered, and at least Beobrand had returned the day before with the tidings that Wilfrid would not be travelling with them.

Coenred stepped into shadow, following Marsiglio between two high crumbling walls. He paused, allowing his eyes to grow accustomed to the gloom, then pressed on. Marsiglio was already some way off and he did not want to lose him. He was sure he could find his own way back to the Lateran *Patriarchium* from here, but the thought of being lost in the *Disabitato* after nightfall lent him an extra spurt of speed.

Knowing that Wilfrid would not be with them when they left was a relief. Coenred was not sure how he would have dealt with his feelings towards the novice if they had been forced to journey together. After they had left Priano's, he had berated the young man, but Wilfrid had been uncaring of Coenred's anger, ignoring his furious diatribe. All Wilfrid seemed able to think about was that book. Even now, when Coenred recalled the book's gem-encrusted cover, he still felt the ghost of the yearning that had gripped him when he had first seen it, and the stab of envy he had felt when Wilfrid had told him he had read several pages.

His jealousy had turned to worry and consternation when Wilfrid told him some of what he had read.

"It is the words of a prophet called Mani," he had said breathlessly as they'd ridden through the dark streets and tumbled ruins towards Eugenius' home. "Mani tells of the battle between light and darkness." Wilfrid's euphoria was palpable.

Coenred had believed it to be from his coupling with the thrall, but now he was not so sure. "I cannot begin to explain the power of what I read within those pages," Wilfrid continued.

"It sounds like heresy," Coenred said, thinking of the force of his own attraction to the book. "That book has the Devil in it. We are both best off without it."

"There is no devil in learning," jeered Wilfrid. "I seek knowledge wherever it may reside. Knowledge is the key to everything. That book can unlock such mysteries. I am certain of it. I would read more of this Mani's teachings. Once I have studied the tome fully I will decide its worth, and whether it is heresy."

"But you do not have the tome," Coenred reminded him.

Wilfrid scowled. "No, I do not."

They had ridden on in angry, brooding silence until Coenred had left him outside Santa Prisca. Since then they had not spoken, and for his part, Coenred was glad of that.

A dog barked behind him, probably the dusty hound he had seen lying beneath the tree. Glancing over his shoulder at the sound, Coenred thought he noticed a movement in the shadows of the alley, where a bush overhung the cracked plaster and broken bricks of the wall. He peered at the place for a few heartbeats, but nothing moved.

A cat or rat perhaps. Startled by the dog's yapping no doubt.

"Come on," called Marsiglio from a bend ahead. "We will miss Vespers if we do not make haste."

Coenred hurried after his friend. He had formed a warm bond with Marsiglio over the course of the fortnight spent at the *Patriarchium*. Despite their very different backgrounds, they each found in the other a sympathetic listener. Both of them, in their own way, had always felt like outsiders in their communities. They had talked long about it over several cups of wine, many more than the abbot of Lindisfarena would have permitted.

The heat made sleep difficult, and Coenred and Marsiglio had frequently sat outside and talked long into the night.

Coenred recalled their conversation of the night before and hoped Marsiglio would reconsider. It had been some time after Compline, long after darkness had fallen and the city lay still and sleeping under the blanket of clouds that the locals said were unusual for this time of year. The two monks had been sitting with their backs against the warm stone of the palace wall, sipping from a skin of wine Beobrand had given them, when Coenred had asked Marsiglio if he would make the pilgrimage to Lindisfarena one day.

Marsiglio had not answered for a long time and Coenred had grown uncomfortable. He'd looked askance at his friend but his dark face was in shadow and it was impossible to make out his expression. Just when he had thought Marsiglio would not reply, he spoke.

"I would like to see your homeland, Coenred," he said. "You speak with such passion of the white sand of the beaches, and of the cliffs over the cold North Sea. I can picture the fortress of Bebbanburg and the minster of Lindisfarena and would like to see them with my own eyes. And if I were to visit I would surely pray before the relics of your holy king, Oswald."

Coenred was relieved that his friend had finally broken the awkward silence, but there was a cautious manner about his speech, like a barefoot man nervously tiptoeing across a floor strewn with shards of broken glass. He uttered each word carefully, making sure it was correct and had not caused offence before moving on to the next.

"You say you would like to see these things," Coenred said, "and yet you do not say you will do so."

"We are friends," Marsiglio said, "and I do not wish to hurt you. But friends must be truthful, so no, I will not travel to far-off Albion."

"Oh." Coenred didn't trust himself to say more without giving away the pain he felt at Marsiglio's outright dismissal of his proposal.

"I did not wish to cause you distress," said Marsiglio, placing a hand on Coenred's arm, "and yet I have done so. I am sorry."

"No need to apologise," Coenred muttered. "We can always write." The transportation of letters was an uncertain business, reliant on the goodwill of merchants and other travellers, and even if the letters arrived safely at their destination, it would take weeks, or even months for them to travel the distance between Bernicia and Roma.

"We can," said Marsiglio, "and I promise you that I will. Please do not be angry with me for not wishing to travel the vast distance to Northumbria."

"I am not angry," Coenred said.

"Ha! And I am not darker-skinned than you," said Marsiglio, his teeth showing briefly in the gloom.

Coenred smiled.

"Honestly," he said. "I am not angry. Not really. I just wished to see you again."

"I know, Coenred," Marsiglio replied, "and I you. But I have travelled a long way in my life to get here, to Roma. This is my place now. God is not calling me to journey for weeks to visit a small, distant minster on an island in the North Sea. I hope you understand."

"I do." Coenred had taken a large swallow of wine, enjoying the sensation of the sweet liquid trickling down his throat. "But you must write."

"You have my word on that," Marsiglio had said, taking the wineskin from him.

Coenred rounded the corner of the alleyway. Trees grew either side of the long walls here, shrouding the alley in thick shadows. Coenred scoured the alleyway, searching for Marsiglio. He had not been far ahead, and yet Coenred could not see his friend anywhere.

Some distance away, something was moving up ahead. For an instant he wondered if Marsiglio had decided to rest, leaning against the wall beneath one of the towering pines. Moving closer, Coenred's eyes became more accustomed to the darkness. Something was writhing beneath the tree.

"Marsiglio?" he said, his voice uncertain and small.

A sound reached him then and in the instant he heard it, he understood what he was seeing. All around him the world seemed to slow and he felt suddenly cold, despite the oppressive heat of the alley.

Marsiglio was locked in a struggle with a figure dressed all in black. As Coenred watched in horror, the tall figure shoved Marsiglio against the wall. Coenred saw the flash of metal and the attacker punched forward. Marsiglio let out a cry and slumped to the ground.

"Marsiglio!" shouted Coenred in dismay.

But his friend did not reply. He lay motionless in the alley, amongst the refuse and rubbish and weeds.

The man who had attacked him peeled away from the shadows and stepped towards Coenred. He was tall and broad-shouldered. Coenred could not take his eyes off the long dagger in the man's hand. There was bright blood on the blade. The man's face was hidden by a dark hood, but Coenred's imagination conjured up a leering grin like that of the evil spirit who had come to him in the forest. The man moved closer and Coenred felt as though his feet were nailed to the ground. He stood there panting in fear, unable to move.

Then the hooded man sprang forwards, breaking into a run towards Coenred. The moment of indecision was shattered. Coenred turned and fled the way he had come.

He sprinted straight into the grasp of another hooded man.

Coenred struggled, but he was no match for the man's strength. Coenred was almost lifted off his feet as this new assailant slammed him hard against the wall, driving the air from his lungs. The attacker pressed a callused hand roughly over Coenred's mouth as the first man drew close. The bloody knife was still in his hand and Coenred went faint at the sight of it, imagining what it would feel like to have it plunged into his flesh.

But he did not feel the sharp knife split his skin and spill his entrails. The man who held him against the wall punched him savagely on the side of the head. The shadows around Coenred grew darker and the shapes of the hooded men swam out of focus. A second blow struck him, but Coenred did not know which of his assailants had dealt it. Perhaps he had fallen and hit his head against the ground, he mused, his thoughts spiralling and confused. Whatever had happened, the pain was mercifully short-lived. Coenred could feel his strength ebbing away.

Was this death? Was he destined to remain in Roma forever, buried amongst the martyrs and saints?

Coenred wanted to speak, to recite the paternoster for Marsiglio and himself, but no words came. The world around him blurred. Coenred's last thought was that night had come very quickly, for all was darkness.

Chapter 26

Cynan sat by the window and stared out at the night. A faint glow lingered in the western sky, the memory of the fiery sunset. As he watched, lightning flickered far away. Cynan held his breath, listening for the sound of thunder.

Behind him, Eadgard let out a roar, and the other men laughed. They were playing a game of knucklebones that Lucifrido had taught them, gambling whatever silver they had left. The men were in high spirits, and Cynan thought how unlike was their mood to the dejection that had fallen over them when they had left Liyon. Of course, they had not spent as long here in Roma, and they had not created the bonds that had tethered them to the Burgundian city. Now they were excited at the prospect of returning to Liyon. Beobrand had planned not to stop in the city, fearing that Wilfrid might once again cause problems. But when he learnt that the young man would not travel with them, he had relented. Cynan had let the men know and they were overjoyed. Even though they were no strangers to the brothels of Roma, they still yearned for the women they had met in Frankia. Grindan in particular had not stopped grinning since Cynan had imparted the news. In Liyon, he had been smitten by a pretty young girl called Suriyah, and the prospect of seeing her again had made him giddy with excitement.

Ingwald too was brimming with anticipation. He had hurried out to purchase a gaudy necklace of silver and green glass beads from a merchant who frequented the square outside the *Archibasilica*.

"Emma will like this," he'd said, admiring the jewellery in the dying sunlight. "It matches her eyes."

Cynan did not have the heart to tell him the redhead's eyes were not green, but brown. He doubted Emma or Suriyah would be as excited to see Ingwald and Grindan as the warriors expected. Months had gone by and the women were whores. The men had conjured in their memories images of them as their sweethearts, no doubt imagining their reunions filled with laughter, tears and lust. They pictured the women, overjoyed at their men's return, throwing themselves into the warriors' arms and desperate to make up for wasted time, taking them eagerly to their beds.

Cynan glanced at the men seated in a circle, leaning over to watch the throw of the small goat bones. He shook his head. He supposed their welcomes might be warm, if they kept some of their silver.

Bleddyn looked up and offered him a thin smile. Bleddyn's was a deeper affection, Cynan thought. And the woman he pined for was not in Liyon, but with Queen Balthild at Cala, or perhaps Paris. He had been beguiled by the queen's maidservant, a dark-haired beauty called Alpaida.

Bleddyn rarely spoke of her, but Cynan knew Alpaida was ever in his thoughts. It was not certain they would see her as they travelled north. Perhaps it would be best for Bleddyn if they did not, for the girl would surely not leave her mistress. And yet, Cynan hoped for Bleddyn's sake they would encounter the queen and her maidservant as they travelled through Frankish lands.

Turning back to the window Cynan saw another, distant flash

of lightning, but if the sound of thunder followed, it was once more lost in the noise the men were making.

Cynan thought he understood Bleddyn and the nervous anxiety at the prospect of seeing Alpaida again. His own innards were twisted with the same apprehension; a powerful longing, punctuated with an almost overpowering fear of rejection.

Just like the rest of them, Cynan was glad to finally be heading homeward, but he had been gone for so long he was unsure how Eadgyth would respond to his return. The manner of his leaving, and having to finally face up to her wrath, made the prospect of seeing her again more terrifying than any shieldwall. Eadgyth was his old friend Acennan's widow, and since his death she and Cynan had grown close. Eadgyth had continued her role of managing the estate's affairs, doing the job well. For his part, Cynan had become much like a father to her two children, Athulf and Aelfwyn.

Everything had been going well until she brought up the subject of marriage. It made perfect sense, but Cynan had been beset with a turmoil of emotions, not least of which the powerful guilt at the thought of bedding his dead friend's wife. Not knowing what to do, Cynan had seized an opportunity to flee the question. And Eadgyth.

He had never thought he would be away from Stagga for so long, but wyrd had decided his path and it had led him all the way here, to the ancient city of Roma. He had not seen Eadgyth for over a year. Now, with the prospect of seeing her again soon, all of his doubts and fears returned. He was sure now of his feelings towards her, but was terrified that his actions would have turned her against him for ever.

A sudden gust of laughter from the men made Cynan sigh. He was pleased that Beobrand had decided to leave, but he was in no mood for games, wine and merriment. His head was full of thoughts and memories, swirling like leaves in an autumn storm. He needed peace to think. And fresh air. The room was oppressively hot and he felt the trickle of sweat down his back. Cynan would miss some of the things of this far-off land: the wine, the sweet plump fruit and the salty ham. He would never miss the gods-forsaken heat.

Cynan rose, and another flicker of distant lightning lit the world outside. He paused, leaning towards the open window. A breath of air wafted his hair away from his face and a moment later, despite the hubbub of the gaming warriors, he heard the unmistakable rumble of thunder.

He made his way to the door. Lucifrido looked up. He was smiling and appeared relaxed, but Cynan had spent long enough in the man's presence to know he missed nothing.

"I'm going for a walk," Cynan said. Reluctantly, Ingwald made to stand. There was a small pile of coins and hack silver on the tiled floor before him. Cynan signalled for him to remain. "Stay. You are winning and I would not be the one to stand in the way of luck."

"I thank you," said Ingwald, cheeks flushed with wine. "It is not like me to win against the likes of Grindan. I must enjoy this moment while it lasts."

"It will not last long, old man," said Grindan, throwing the bones clattering down.

Ingwald groaned to see how they fell. The men laughed at his dismay.

Smiling, Cynan opened the door and slipped out into the dark corridor. As he was pulling the door closed, a hand halted it and Bleddyn stepped out of the room.

"Care if I join you, lord?" he asked.

"I fear I will not be good company this night," Cynan replied.

Bleddyn shrugged but made no effort to return to their noisy quarters.

"We can be bad company together, lord," he said with a grin.

They walked along the shaded passageways of the palace, their footsteps loud on the polished stone floor. The sounds of laughter and mirth, muted by the door and distance, quickly receded. Ahead of them, an armed guard stood beside the door to the garden. A small oil lamp flickered by his side, illuminating his face and glittering on the burnished rings of his mail.

The guard pulled the door open for them, and nodded. Cynan thanked him, feeling sorry for the man. All the palace guards were required to wear their armour, no matter the heat.

Bleddyn followed Cynan out into the darkness, thanking the guard by name. Cynan had recognised the man, but had never thought to learn his name. He admired that about Bleddyn; no detail was too small.

"Were you planning on seeking out lord Beobrand?" Bleddyn asked in their native Waelisc tongue when they were outside. Cynan responded in the same language.

"I do not think Beobrand would be glad of my company. If he wants to talk, let him speak with Halinard."

The two men had left their quarters earlier in the evening. Cynan would usually go with them, watching over Beobrand as he walked, talked and drank in the gardens. But tonight his dark mood had already taken hold and he had decided not to join them. In this mood he would surely say something unwise and antagonise Beobrand, as he often did. The gardens were safe enough and the lord of Ubbanford would be less likely to argue with the even-headed Halinard.

Bleddyn and Cynan walked in silence for a time. A light breeze rustled the needles of the pines that grew at the edge of the garden. The scent of wet earth was on the air. For an eye-blink the world was suddenly bathed in bright, white light. The lightning left after-images burnt into Cynan's vision, ghostly memories of the flowers and plants that lined the path. The men stopped walking and stared up at the sky in silence, waiting.

After a few heartbeats, thunder growled, rolling towards them like an angry god.

"Rain might improve my mood," said Cynan. He realised with consternation that he found speaking in the tongue he had learnt from his mother did not come as easily to him as the words of the Anglisc.

"It will clear the air," Bleddyn said. "I just hope it does not flood the streams and rivers, or impede our travel on the roads."

Cynan looked sidelong at Bleddyn.

"By the gods," he said with a chuckle, "you are as cheerful as me."

"Sorry, lord. I want to be content, and I am. Truly. But I worry too."

"What are you worried about?" Cynan asked.

Bleddyn reached for a rose from the nearest bush. The flower was dark crimson. It looked black in the pale light of the waxing crescent moon. He twisted the flower's stem, plucking it from the plant. A thorn stabbed his thumb and he cursed. He sniffed the flower, then sucked the spot of blood from his thumb.

"I worry about Alpaida, lord," he said.

"What worries you?" said Cynan, walking towards the wall that surrounded the garden.

Bleddyn fell into step beside him. He sniffed the rose again, breathing deeply of the flower's fragrance. When he spoke, his tone was listless.

"I do not rightly know. That she won't want to see me. That she will have found someone else."

"We might not even go to Paris," said Cynan. "If we do, the queen may not be there. We might not see Alpaida as we travel north."

Bleddyn chuckled without mirth. "I worry about that too!"

Cynan snorted. "What fools we both are, consumed with

worry over women who are weeks of travel away from us. I know what Bassus would say."

"You do not think he would be sympathetic to our plight?"

Cynan laughed. In the same instant lightning lit up the sky.

"He would tell us that we should not fret for that which we cannot control. That the thing we fear is often not so bad when we face it. Bassus would remind us there is nothing to be gained from worrying about what women might do, for they are as inconstant as the weather, their moods like a tempest, not to be tamed."

"And yet he still moped whenever the lady Rowena was angry with him."

"That he did." Sorrow washed over Cynan as he thought of how Bassus must grieve the passing of Rowena. News of her death had reached them in Bebbanburg before they had travelled south. "Bassus is ever good at giving advice, but most men do not follow their own counsel. Especially when it comes to women."

They had reached the western edge of the garden. Cynan liked this spot. There was shade in the long afternoons beneath the high wall. There were also some cracked, marble steps leading up to a walkway that ran along the wall. The lightning was coming more frequently now, the scent of rain on the freshening breeze.

"Come," Cynan said, starting up the steps, "it seems the gods wish to make our last night in Roma memorable."

Bleddyn hesitated.

"Is it safe?"

Cynan grinned.

"Safe or not, I am not going to miss this view of the city."

As if in answer to his words, the sky was lit in the brightest flash of lightning yet. Barely an eye-blink later came the crash of thunder, reverberating across the garden from the ancient stone of the wall and the palace. Cynan clambered up the steps, exhilarated by the arrival of the storm and glad to be distracted from his melancholy. Some men cowered when the heavens opened and lightning hammered the earth, but not Cynan. He had always revelled in the unbridled power of lightning, and now, with the promise of rain, a cool wind, and a night-time view of the Eternal City lit by the awesome forces unleashed from the sky, Cynan hurried to stand on the wall.

Bleddyn joined him and they each looked out over the shadows of the buildings, trees, hills and ruins of Roma. The lightning was coming regularly now, finally releasing the pent-up energy that had been growing in the clouds and oppressing the city for days. The thunder cracked, filling the world with booming sound.

Cynan let out a barking laugh, unable to contain his excitement. A sidelong glance at Bleddyn in the next flash of lightning showed his companion's features were drawn, his eyes wide and anxious. Cynan clapped Bleddyn on the back.

"Don't you feel it?" he asked, shouting over the cacophony of the storm. "The raw power?"

"I would rather witness such power from inside," said Bleddyn. "Where it is dry. And safe."

"Safe?" Cynan scoffed, filled now with the joy of release the storm had brought. "There is nothing to fear here. We are warriors, not slaves!"

"Yes, lord," said Bleddyn, dejectedly. "We will soon be wet warriors. I just pray to God we will not become lightning-struck warriors!"

Cynan laughed, holding his arms out wide as if to invite the lightning.

"I have longed for the rain these past days. I welcome it now."

As if his words had commanded it, rain began to fall. One moment the wind tugged at their hair, lifting dust from the dry hot cobbles and the grit from the square in front of the *Archibasilica*, the next instant, rain was falling in a torrent, drenching both men and making them gasp with its sudden ferocity.

Lightning struck a tall tree nearby, so close the thunder-crack came at the same instant. The tree shattered with a huge, splintering crash. The noise was deafening. Bleddyn let out a cry of alarm. Cynan said nothing, but he began to question the wisdom of climbing up here. It did not do to tempt the gods or one's wyrd.

Flames were flickering on the broken tree's trunk, despite the force of the rain. Cynan scanned the area around the tree, trying to gauge whether a fire might carry to other trees or buildings. The tree had stood alone and had fallen into an open area of the stone-covered road. Cynan thought it unlikely that the fire would spread, so long as this downpour continued for a time. The yellow grass and weeds that grew in the gutters were tinder dry, but the rain was coming down so hard now the streets were quickly becoming streams, churned water frothing in the gushing gutters.

"Perhaps you are right," Cynan shouted at Bleddyn over the din. "I am refreshed now!"

Their kirtles were plastered against their skin, their hair soaked. Bleddyn smiled.

"About time!" he said.

They turned to make their way back down the crumbling steps when another flash of lightning illuminated the street below the wall. Something there tugged at Cynan's attention. Shielding his eyes from the rain with his hand, he peered into the darkness.

Bleddyn halted at the top of the steps.

"What is it, lord?" he asked.

Cynan held up a hand for silence. He could not be certain, but he thought he had seen... Lightning lit the world once more and then he was sure. He leaned close to Bleddyn so that he could speak directly into his ear without the need to shout.

"There is someone down there."

"Sheltering from the storm, most likely," replied Bleddyn.

Cynan shook his head.

"No, there is something about the way the man is moving. Stealthily. Creeping. He is up to no good, I would wager."

He focused his attention again on the shadows below the wall, pointing out the last place he had seen the figure. Bleddyn looked too, squinting against the rain that pelted from the sky. The tree was still burning; the smell of the smoke hot and biting. But the flames were too far away to offer any light that might help to show the hidden man.

Neither Bleddyn nor Cynan moved, both waiting silently for more lightning. They did not need to wait long. Flickering light bathed the world for an instant. The thunder came a couple of heartbeats later. The storm was rolling over them quickly, borne eastward by the strong wind. But the light had given them what they needed. Both of them had seen the dark-robed figure of a man, creeping along the wall below, making his way towards one of the small entrance gates that were closed and locked after dark.

Bleddyn cupped his hand to Cynan's ear.

"Thief?" he asked.

Cynan shrugged.

"Or killer," he whispered in reply. Cursing, he realised neither of them were armed. The man in the street was surely there for nefarious reasons. Whether thief or assassin, there was little chance he would not be carrying a blade. Cynan held his breath, peering into the gloom and praying for another flash of light. Perhaps he might see the gleam of metal in the man's hand, or some other indication of his purpose.

The lighting was less frequent now and they waited without speaking for what seemed an age. All the while the rain continued to beat down, but such was their concentration they no longer paid it any heed.

At last, lightning lit the heavens again. Cynan had been concerned that so much time had elapsed the man might have moved all the way to the gate, out of the line of sight of their vantage point. But to his surprise, the white light of the storm picked out the stark shape of the man in the same location as previously. He had not moved. Perhaps he was waiting for someone there, thought Cynan. His reason for being out at night might not be as grim as theft or murder. He could be meeting a lover for a tryst under cover of darkness. And he did not appear to be standing any longer.

For a heartbeat Cynan wondered if he might not be coupling with some wench down there. Or perhaps the man was with one of the other monks from the palace. It was no secret that some of the holy men preferred the company of men to women. But he dismissed the idea immediately. Surely the rain would have put off even the most ardent of lovers.

There was something familiar about the figure, he thought, but he could not place it. Then, in a moment of clarity as bright as the lightning, he realised his mind had already told him who he was looking at. The figure was a monk, his dark robes darkened yet further by the rain. The monk's dark skin made it even more difficult to see him in the night-shadows of the street.

Finally, Cynan understood. The man had not been creeping with stealth, he had been leaning against the wall, pulling himself laboriously along, step by painful step. And now, his strength depleted, he had fallen.

Turning, Cynan hurried down the wet steps, careful not to slip on the slick marble.

"That is no criminal," he shouted to Bleddyn, who still stood on the walkway, staring bemusedly after his hlaford. "That is Marsiglio and he is hurt. Go! Fetch help at once."

Chapter 27

The rain seethed outside, filling the night with its incessant roar. From time to time a gust of wind would whistle beneath the gables and buffet the downpour against the wall of the palace, but the room was dry.

Beobrand stood in the doorway, watching as Martinus, kneeling beside Marsiglio, prayed for the wounded monk. On the other side of the bed, Zanobi, the sharp-faced physician applied a poultice and wrapped bandages about the monk's midriff. Marsiglio, his dark skin grey in the lamplight, was stretched out on a comfortable bed. The room was sumptuously decorated with painted walls, hanging tapestries, embroidered cushions and a polished dark-grained wooden table, on which rested a book beside an exquisite bronze oil lamp. Word of Marsiglio's plight had travelled through the palace quickly and as soon as the Pontifex Maximus had heard, he had sent for Zanobi and had ordered the monk to be transported to his own comfortable apartments.

Beobrand had been in the garden with Halinard, enjoying the cool breeze and the rain that had finally decided to fall, when he had seen Bleddyn running past. The Waelisc man had quickly told them what he and Cynan had seen, and Halinard and Beobrand had rushed to help.

They had found a guard to open the gate and then carried Marsiglio into the palace. Marsiglio had been stabbed in his left side and had lost a lot of blood. He had been barely conscious, but when he had seen Beobrand, he had gripped his arm with surprising strength. Marsiglio did not speak Anglisc, nor did Beobrand or the others speak Latin. But they all understood what he said and heard the anguish in his tone. Marsiglio's warm blood on their hands lent urgency to the single word he hissed.

"Coenred!"

They had been carrying Marsiglio across the garden on a blanket brought from their quarters. On hearing his friend's name Beobrand had wanted to halt, but they dared not stop. Marsiglio's wound was dire.

"What of Coenred?" Beobrand had asked, his tone sharp with worry. "Where is he?"

But Marsiglio had fallen silent. For a terrible instant Beobrand thought the man had died, but he was merely insensate. And yet, if the amount of blood was anything to go by, death was not far away.

Beobrand stood awkwardly now, watching Zanobi and the Pontifex tending to the man's physical and spiritual needs. Some time had passed, but Beobrand's clothes and hair were still damp from the rain. In the corridor behind him, the rest of his gesithas crowded. They had come in a rush. Coenred was dear to them too and they were anxious for tidings.

"Has he woken?" asked Eadgard.

"What did he say about Coenred?" added Grindan.

Beobrand did not answer. Nor did he turn from the room, where the dancing flames of the oil lamps made the images on the tapestries and paintings appear to writhe and move, more alive than the monk on the bed. Beobrand too wished for answers. His chest was heavy and tight, weighed down by the fear his friend might be dead or dying somewhere out there in the dark of the storm-ripped night. By Woden, how he regretted not sending guards with Coenred. But regrets would not heal Marsiglio. Or bring Coenred back safely.

Behind him Beobrand heard Cynan's calm voice. He was doing his best to quieten the men, telling them that none knew what had befallen Coenred, save that he had left that morning with Marsiglio. And that the monk from Nobatia had returned alone and wounded.

Beobrand moved closer to the bed, unable to remain stationary in the doorway any longer. Glancing back at his men crowding in the corridor, he spied Lucifrido. He beckoned for the man to come forward.

"Speak for me," Beobrand said.

Lucifrido nodded, his usually smiling face sombre.

Zanobi looked up at them as they approached, his expression stern. He rose, dropping some blood-sodden rags into a bowl. Marsiglio was unmoving and ashen. He looked closer to the afterlife than the land of the living, so Beobrand did not enquire about his prospects. Marsiglio's life was in the hands of forces beyond this world. The physician was skilled and the most powerful Christ-priest was praying for Marsiglio, and still death was close. Beobrand's fear tightened its grip on him as he looked at the stricken monk. If he died, they would know nothing of what had befallen Coenred. It would be all but impossible to find him in the sprawling city. Assuming, he thought bitterly, that Coenred yet lived and was not out there in the rain-rent night, already dead, murdered by thieves.

"Can he speak?" Beobrand said. Lucifrido translated his words.

Zanobi glared at them both as if they were the cause of Marsiglio's injury. Beobrand stared back, frowning at the whip-thin man. After a heartbeat the physician relented, hissing a reply.

"He is sleeping," Lucifrido interpreted. "He has lost a lot of blood. He says he may never awaken. He has done all he can for Marsiglio. His life is in God's hands now."

"Ask him if he has spoken," Beobrand said. "Has he said anything about Coenred or what happened to him?"

Zanobi snapped a terse response to the questions. The meaning was clear. Beobrand's heart sank.

Martinus finished praying and pushed himself to his feet. A young priest who had been hovering nearby moved quickly forward and offered the Pontifex his hand, helping him up. Martinus nodded his thanks and addressed Beobrand.

"Marsiglio is strong," Lucifrido translated. "As is his faith. We will continue to pray for him and maybe in the light of day God will provide us with more answers."

"I cannot wait till morning," Beobrand said. "Coenred could be hurt."

"Your loyalty to your friend is commendable," Martinus said. "And I share your sorrow at what has happened and this uncertainty. But without knowing where to look, what would you do? I know you are not a man to idle, but wandering the streets in this storm blindly seeking out your friend would, I fear, achieve nothing."

Beobrand knew the man was right, but it was also true that he could not imagine doing nothing. It would drive him mad. The need for action was already boiling within him. He must do something. Anything.

"If that is all I can do," he said, "then so be it. Perhaps the gods will smile on us in our search for him. No god looks favourably on men who do nothing in a time of need. Is it known where Marsiglio and Coenred went today? Following their path would be a start."

Martinus offered Beobrand a thin smile and placed a hand on his shoulder.

"I see it will do no good trying to dissuade you, and you are right. Just as the great Euripides wrote: 'he who strives will find his gods strive for him equally'."

The young priest made the sign of the cross and scowled disapprovingly.

"Enough of your outrage, Viaro," said Martinus reprovingly. "I see no reason why the Almighty would not agree with the sentiment of the great poet, for is it not written in Proverbs that 'the sluggard craves and gets nothing'?"

Viaro shook his head, his expression sour, but he made no comment.

"Good," continued Martinus, "now is not the time to be discussing theology, but as lord Beobrand says, the moment for action. I concede it would indeed be best to begin the search immediately. I believe Marsiglio was taking Coenred to visit Father Borso today. I will have some men roused from their beds to help you with a search."

A rasping voice from the bed silenced them all. Marsiglio, eyes narrowed with pain, was awake.

"What does he say?" asked Beobrand. "Ask what befell him. Where is Coenred?"

Lucifrido scooped up a cup of water from a nearby table and offered some to the wounded monk, supporting his head gently so that he could drink. Then, lowering Marsiglio's head back with care, Lucifrido leaned close and they conversed in hissed whispers. Beobrand waited impatiently while they spoke until at last Lucifrido stood. The short exchange had taken its toll on Marsiglio, who had closed his eyes now and appeared to be sleeping once more.

"He says there is nothing to be gained from searching the streets," Lucifrido said.

"How can he be so sure?" said Beobrand, steeling himself to hear the worst possible tidings.

"For Coenred will not be where they were attacked."

Beobrand let out his breath.

"He escaped? Then where is he?"

"No, lord Beobrand," Lucifrido said, a surprising softness in his tone. "Coenred did not escape."

"What then?" Beobrand snapped. "Tell me what you know, man. What happened to him?" Beobrand's anger was rising like a spring tide now, and Martinus placed a concerned hand on his arm, softly muttering words of comfort that Beobrand could not comprehend.

"Coenred was taken," Lucifrido said, his voice flat.

"Taken? By who?"

Lucifrido's brow was furrowed with worry.

"I know not for certain," he said. "Marsiglio described how at least two men attacked them in an alleyway. Their attackers were armed and hooded. They sprang from hiding and struck Marsiglio down. Then they moved to Coenred."

Beobrand interrupted him.

"Marsiglio saw what they did to Coenred?"

Lucifrido gave a small nod.

"They did not slay him. They knocked him senseless and bore him off with them."

On hearing those words, relief washed through Beobrand. Coenred was alive! And yet they still had no idea where he was. So many questions needed answers.

"Why did they not kill Marsiglio?" Beobrand asked.

"I asked him the same, lord. He says they believed they had dealt him a killing blow." He looked down at the still form on the bed. "And perhaps they have," he murmured. "But there is more. He says the men were not mere brigands or thieves. There was a deeper purpose to what they were about than robbery."

"What purpose?"

"They meant to kill Marsiglio and take Coenred."

Beobrand's mouth was dry.

"How can he know this?" he asked.

"That is simple, lord," Lucifrido said. "He heard them speaking while he lay on the ground, unable to rise."

"What did they say? Does Marsiglio know where they have taken Coenred?"

Lucifrido shook his head.

"He heard enough to know they sought the Anglisc monk, but no more."

Martinus spoke to Lucifrido now. The Pontifex's voice was low, but there was a hard edge to it Beobrand had not heard before. As they spoke they looked from Marsiglio to Beobrand.

"What does Martinus say?" Beobrand asked, his frustration at not being able to communicate freely souring his dark mood even further.

Lucifrido muttered a few more words to Martinus before he answered.

"His Holiness says this affair has the stink about it of a fight between the great families of Roma. Though he says harming men of the cloth is very unusual. He wonders whether Coenred's connection to you might not be somehow the cause of this. He asks whether you might have made an enemy in the city, lord Beobrand."

Beobrand fought down the anger that flared within him at the suggestion that he might be to blame for what had happened. Now was not the time to unleash the beast shackled within him. If Coenred had been harmed, that time would come soon enough. Holding tight to the shackles of his fury, he forced himself to think about Martinus' question.

"I have many enemies, it is true," Beobrand said at last, "but I do not believe I have made any here in Roma. Certainly I have done nothing to bring about such an attack on Coenred. Besides, if someone wished to cause me harm, I have travelled alone or with only one or two of my men often in the last fortnight. Why harm Coenred?"

Lucifrido raised an eyebrow.

"I think the prospect of fighting you and some of your comitatus, or even you alone, would dissuade most men. If someone wished to harm you, could they not do so more easily by striking at your friends? Friends who are less able to defend themselves."

Beobrand heard the truth in Lucifrido's words, but still he rejected the idea.

"But I have done nothing in Roma to create such an enemy."

"Still," said Lucifrido quietly, "Martinus is right. This attack does leave the taste of the families on my tongue too. Who might have ordered this, and to what end, I do not know, but I know how we could find out."

Beobrand looked sidelong at him.

"You speak of your friend Stoldo?" he said.

"Stoldo is not my friend," said Lucifrido, "but he has spies everywhere. A purse isn't lifted nor a drunken traveller robbed in Roma without Stoldo hearing about it."

Beobrand turned this over in his mind.

"You think Stoldo will know where Coenred is?" he asked.

Lucifrido nodded.

"If anyone knows what is afoot and where Coenred is, it will be Stoldo," he said. "I can take you to him."

"He would help me?" asked Beobrand. He thought of Tanualdo in Sutri, and how the man ruled the town and its environs.

"For the right price," said Lucifrido, "Stoldo would help the Devil himself."

For the right price.

Beobrand scowled. Perhaps Stoldo could be of use to him, but he did not relish the thought of entering into a bargain with such a man. Then another thought struck him. Could this attack be a plan concocted by Stoldo and Lucifrido all along? It would be an elegant way to extort from him the treasure he had carried from Frankia.

"Why should I trust you?" Beobrand asked, his voice icy.

"I know I do not have your trust, lord," replied Lucifrido. "But ask yourself this. Since we have travelled together, have I once betrayed you? Have I done anything less than help you and guide you?"

"Not that I know of," said Beobrand, wondering what had transpired between Stoldo and Lucifrido on the day he had spent at Stoldo's villa outside the city walls.

"For what it is worth," said Lucifrido, "I give you my word that I mean you and Coenred no harm."

Beobrand held his gaze for a long while, wondering what other options he had.

"You really think Stoldo will know what is happening?" he asked.

"I do," said Lucifrido.

"And can I trust him?"

Lucifrido smiled suddenly.

"If I said you could trust Stoldo, I would be a liar. But for a price, I think he might have the information we seek."

Beobrand still did not like it. No matter that Lucifrido had given his word, he was Tanualdo's man. Such a man's word was as worthless as spit in a storm. Still, Beobrand could think of no better course of action. He was about to say as much when the slap of sandalled feet echoed in the corridor outside.

Beobrand's gesithas parted, allowing entry to a young man. He wore the simple garb of a servant and he must have come at a run, for his face was beaded with sweat.

Bowing to Martinus, he spoke in a breathless rush. Martinus replied, gesturing for the servant to lead the way out of the chamber. The young man walked briskly out of the room. Martinus paused momentarily and spoke to Lucifrido. Then, signalling for them to follow, the Pontifex strode after the servant, Viaro on his heels. Beobrand, Lucifrido and the men from Bernicia followed behind.

"Where are we going?" asked Beobrand, as they hurried through the dark corridors of the palace. "What has happened?"

"Someone has come," said Lucifrido. "A messenger."

They passed an open window. The rain still cascaded from the sky, running in freshets from the tiled roof. Beobrand welcomed the cooler air on his face after the stuffy room. The servant was trotting along and Beobrand noticed that Martinus, not a young man, was struggling to keep up.

"A messenger in the middle of the night must surely be unusual," said Beobrand, his long stride easily matching the pace set by the servant. "It must be more unusual for the Bishop of Roma to give them an audience before dawn. But why ask for us to come too?"

"That much is easy," said Lucifrido, a ghost of his usual smile on his lips. "The messenger asked to speak to you."

They were soon at a reception room near the main entrance of the palace. The room was sparsely decorated in comparison with some of the grander rooms, but still the walls were lined with elaborate tapestries, a statue of a woman holding a baby stood at the far end, and there were dark, polished wooden stools next to a small table. There were small puddles of water on the marble floor, no doubt left there by the messenger who must have travelled through the rain.

As they entered the room, Beobrand took in the occupants at a glance. There was not one but two messengers it seemed and they were indeed both bedraggled and soaked through by the storm. The room was poorly lit, but even from the flickering light of the single oil lamp, he recognised both the people who sat waiting for their arrival. With that recognition the reason for the messenger's request became clear.

Wulfwyn stood. Her clothes were drenched, her hair slick and flat against her head. Her movements were fast and nervous, and she moved close to Aelfwig's side, taking hold of his hand.

"Wulfwyn," Beobrand said, his mind whirling, "what brings you to the palace at such a time of the night? Has Priano done something?" Beobrand did not want to imagine what might have driven her to travel through the darkness and the storm with her blind son. As if there wasn't already enough for him to contend with. Beobrand had been sure that entering Priano's service was a mistake. But when he had rescued the woman, and brought her and Aelfwig to Roma, he had taken on the responsibility for their safety. When he left they would no longer be under his protection, but while he was here, he would not forsake mother or child.

"Lord Beobrand," Wulfwyn said, bowing courteously. "Priano has indeed done something terrible."

Beobrand instinctively reached for his sword, forgetting momentarily that he was not wearing it.

"I will make him regret hurting you," he said, his voice as hard and sharp as flint. He looked quickly at Aelfwig. The boy was withdrawn and sullen and a terrible thought surfaced in Beobrand's mind. "Not the boy?" he hissed.

Wulfwyn held up a hand.

"No, no," she said. "Priano has not laid a hand on either of us."

Beobrand frowned.

"What then? What has he done to bring you here in the dead of night in such a tempest?"

Wulfwyn's face was pale, her eyes huge and gleaming in the lamplight.

"We know why Coenred has been taken," she said.

Chapter 28

"No, not this one," snapped Cynan. Pulling the saddle off the horse's back, he thrust it into the hands of the servant who had brought it from the stables. The servant was young, not much more than a boy, and he cowered, confused and bleary-eyed, before Cynan's wrath.

The wind gusted, violently shaking the trees in the garden. Their branches rocked back and forth and the sound of the leaves reminded Cynan of the rush of waves on a shingle beach. A heartbeat later rain began to fall again. Cynan cursed. The rain had eased for a time, then halted altogether. But now it began to pelt the men and horses gathered in the courtyard. Glancing up, Cynan saw the moon was still hidden behind black clouds. The rain would likely continue for most of the night, and perhaps the next day too.

Cynan smiled at his own fickle anger. Shortly before he had been glad of the downpour, pleased that it would bring some coolness to the land and wash away the arid dust from the air. Such was the way of men. Never content with their lot.

The courtyard was full of people and horses. Several hostlers and servants had been woken from their slumber and ordered to prepare mounts for Beobrand and his warriors. The servants were not happy to be made to work in the middle of the night.

Their dour, frowning faces made that clear. And yet they did not complain, for the order had been delivered by Viaro, Martinus' attendant priest, and the command had come directly from the Pontifex himself.

Cynan looked over to where Lucifrido was already mounted. He was about to call over and ask Lucifrido to tell the stable hand what it was that he wanted, but thought better of it. It would take longer to explain than to simply fetch the saddle himself.

"Take it," he said in what he hoped were the correct words for the servant boy to understand. Cynan waved his hands to emphasise his meaning, then, ignoring the boy's bemused expression, he hurried into the stable building.

It was dark inside, the lamp propped on a stool near the entrance adding little illumination to the dim light filtering in from the open doors, but Cynan knew where the harness was stored and found his saddle quickly. He had bought it from a saddler in Liyon and it was the most comfortable saddle he had ever owned. It was one good thing that had come from this long journey. Cynan took pride in the knowledge he was able to ride any steed, but he saw no reason to be uncomfortable while doing so.

Carrying the bulky saddle back outside, he thought of what had transpired. It had happened so quickly there had been little time to ponder. The men had been in a buoyant mood, preparing to leave in the morning, now they were tense and sombre, wearing their byrnies and bearing shields and weapons.

Like the other gesithas, Cynan was concerned for Coenred. He was a good man and had always been kind to him. But to Beobrand Coenred was like a brother. The thegn of Ubbanford was beside himself with anxiety. And when he had learnt of the plot that had led to Coenred's capture, Cynan knew it was all Beobrand could do to hold his simmering rage in check.

Wulfwyn had told them of how Aelfwig, a smart child and learning the languages of Roma faster than any of the men could comprehend, had overheard Priano in conversation with another man. Priano it seemed had forgotten the boy was in the next room while he spoke, or perhaps he had believed that Aelfwig did not yet have a good enough grasp of Latin to comprehend what was being discussed. Or mayhap he simply had not understood the keenness of the boy's hearing. Whatever the reason, Aelfwig had heard Priano asking after Coenred. On hearing the monk's name, Aelfwig had paid more attention to the conversation. What he heard had horrified him.

Beobrand had softened while questioning the boy, placing his hands gently on Aelfwig's shoulders, speaking in a quiet tone, listening carefully to the boy's replies. Aelfwig was clearly shaken and it would not do to frighten him further. But Cynan had seen how difficult it had been for Beobrand not to shout at the boy; to shake him and urge him to speak more quickly.

"Who was the man Priano spoke with?" Beobrand had asked.

Aelfwig had sniffed, wiping the back of his hand across his nose.

"I don't know," he said. "He came after dark. Turco let him in, but he didn't say his name. Priano sent me out of the room and they didn't speak till he had closed the door behind me. I didn't try to listen. I really didn't. Not at first. I just couldn't help it." He shifted uncomfortably, as if he believed he might be in trouble for what he had done. "But when I heard Coenred's name, I wanted to hear more."

"You did well, Aelfwig," said Beobrand, his tone earnest. "What you heard might save Coenred's life."

Tears welled in Aelfwig's unseeing eyes.

"I remembered Fredegar..." His voice cracked and trailed off. "I should have said something."

"No, Aelfwig," Beobrand reassured him. "What happened in Sutri was not your fault. And you did the right thing going to your mother. She is wise." Beobrand met Wulfwyn's anxious gaze. "And brave."

Reckless too, thought Cynan, though what she had done had taken courage. She had retrieved her horse, Osweald, from the stable, sneaked out of the villa with Aelfwig, then ridden to the Lateran Palace in the dead of night, while lightning split the heavens and rain soaked the land.

"What did you hear them say, Aelfwig?" Beobrand prompted. "What did they say about Coenred?"

"Something about a book," Aelfwig said hesitantly. "That they had sent word to Wilfrid that they had Coenred. Priano said that if Wilfrid didn't return the book he had stolen, they would…" His voice caught in his throat.

"You are safe here," Beobrand said. "What did Priano say they would do if Wilfrid did not return the book?"

"They said they would send Wilfrid pieces of Coenred until he did. And if that did not work, Wilfrid would be next."

Eadgard's voice boomed suddenly in the marble-lined chamber, making Aelfwig flinch.

"I should have killed that nithing back in Frankia," Eadgard gnarled. "If Coenred dies because of Wilfrid's actions, I swear I will take his head. The man is a curse on us."

"Hush, Eadgard," Beobrand said, his voice stern and brooking no dissent. "You are my man and you will slay who I tell you to." He fixed him with a stare. "Or do I not have your oath?"

Eadgard returned Beobrand's stern gaze for a time, then looked at the wet marble floor.

"Aye," he mumbled, "you have my oath, lord. Never question that."

Beobrand nodded.

"I know you are true, brave Eadgard," he said. "And I share

your anger. Never doubt that if Coenred is harmed, I will make those responsible pay."

Eadgard looked up, a sudden light in his eyes.

"If it should come to it, lord," he said, "will you let me kill the whoreson?"

Aelfwig had grown pale with all this talk of killing, and Beobrand signalled for Eadgard to be silent.

"Quiet now, Eadgard. If the time should come for such an act, and if it is in my power to grant it, Wilfrid's life is yours. But you wait for my command on this. Understood?"

Mollified, Eadgard nodded and fell silent. Beobrand turned back to Aelfwig.

"Did you learn anything else from what you heard, Aelfwig?"

"I don't think so, lord," Aelfwig replied, his voice small and wavering now as the emotion of the night caught up with him.

"Think hard, Aelfwig," urged Beobrand, "for anything we can learn might be of use. Did you hear where they are keeping Coenred?"

Aelfwig frowned, shaking his head. Then, suddenly, he stiffened, as if he was hearing anew the voices of Priano and his visitor.

"They did speak of a something they called *hypogaeum*. I don't rightly know what they meant by that, but I think that is where Coenred is."

Martinus stroked his beard when they asked him what this could mean.

"It is a word derived from the Grecisc," he said. "It means simply underground. It could mean anywhere in the city. Or outside," he added after a heartbeat. "The land outside the walls is riddled with catacombs."

On hearing what they had learnt from Aelfwig, Martinus had been shocked, but he did not appear surprised to learn that Priano would stoop to such things.

"I wonder what book they speak of," he'd mused, but none of them knew.

All they knew was what Coenred had told them about the fabulous tome Wilfrid had sought to purchase and that Priano had refused to sell. They quickly told Martinus of the argument that had seen Coenred, Wilfrid and Baducing thrown out of Priano's residence.

"You must go and speak with young Wilfrid as quickly as possible," Martinus said. "Surely there must be some mistake here. He is a God-fearing young man and would never steal from Priano. The man must be mistaken." He clutched at the gilded cross that hung from a chain around his neck. "I can scarcely believe Priano would react in such an extreme fashion, but for many years there have been rumours about the company he keeps. Though I would never have imagined he might resort to such villainy."

They had left Wulfwyn and Aelfwig with Martinus. The Pontifex had kindly offered to keep them both in his household, saying they would be safe there and certainly they could not return to Priano's villa, unless all this could somehow be explained away.

Rushing out of the stable into the rainy darkness with the heavy saddle in his hands, Cynan almost collided with the young servant returning with the other saddle. Cynan nimbly stepped around the startled boy and hurried over to his mount. The rest of the men were already astride their horses and were waiting for him impatiently. The horses snorted and stamped, full of energy and perhaps as glad as Cynan had been earlier for the rain and the cool it brought.

Ingwald held Cynan's horse's reins. Slinging the saddle over the animal's broad back, Cynan reached beneath to tighten the cinch. While he was securing the saddle, Beobrand rode to the front of the group, his horses' hooves loud on the cobbled area before the stables.

"I have decided on our course of action," he said in a loud, clear voice that cut through the wind-whisper of the trees and the murmur of the rain. All Beobrand had said to Cynan earlier was that they would ride immediately, but he had not told any of them what he had planned. "First we ride to Wilfrid," he went on. "How this has come to pass is uncertain; it looks as though Wilfrid is somehow the cause of this. And he must help us to fix it. I pray things are not as they seem. But whatever the truth of it, Wilfrid is involved and I will see he is held to account for his actions."

The men nodded their agreement.

"If you need someone to beat some sense into him, lord," Eadgard growled, "you know I am your willing servant."

"Grindan, Halinard," Beobrand said, ignoring Eadgard, "do you have it?"

"We do, lord," Grindan replied, patting the bulging saddlebags that rested on his horse's rump.

Beobrand nodded his approval.

"Good," he said. "If Wilfrid cannot, or will not clear this up, we will ride for Stoldo's. Lucifrido will guide us and, if the gods smile on us, Stoldo will be able to aid us in our search for Coenred. But let us hope it does not come to that."

Cynan elbowed his horse in the ribs, quickly taking advantage of the animal's reaction to tighten the cinch for a second time. Content that the saddle was secure, he mounted. He shifted, trying to get comfortable, but the saddle was already wet from the rain and the sensation of sitting on the cold, wet leather was not pleasant.

Yes, he thought, let it not come to having to visit Stoldo for information. It did not sit well with him that Lucifrido had suggested such a meeting and now they were preparing to give away much of the silver they had acquired on the journey. That silver had been hard won. Cynan would not begrudge giving it all up to save Coenred, but he could not shake the idea that all this might have been orchestrated by Lucifrido and his criminal friends in order to free Beobrand of his treasure. Treasure that Tanualdo's men had failed to keep hold of in Sutri. Beobrand had the same thoughts, Cynan knew. They had spoken of it briefly as they made their way out to the stables. They both had the same reservations, but Lucifrido knew how close Beobrand was to Coenred. He knew how much Beobrand would sacrifice for the monk's safety. Cynan liked Lucifrido instinctively, but he could not deny he did not wholly trust him.

Gods, how he longed to return to the simple worries that had beset him earlier in the evening. To think he had been anxious about heading home, to his hall, his land, and a comely, warm-hearted woman that he loved. A woman who had sought to wed him. If only he could go back to such trivial concerns. Instead now his mind was full of the fear of losing their silver. And much worse still, the very real chance they might lose their friend.

Beobrand turned to him. His gelding pawed at the slick cobbles, perhaps sensing its rider's emotions.

"Ready?" Beobrand asked.

"I am, lord," Cynan said, wondering how anyone could be ready for the unknown.

"Then let us ride to Eugenius' hall," said Beobrand, his loud voice carrying over the hissing rumble of the rain, "and find out what Wilfrid has to say for himself."

The hostlers opened the gates and the riders cantered out into the night. Lightning still flickered in the distance from time to time, though its intensity had dwindled as the night wore on. Now, a flash in the sky lit the road before them. Cynan saw that the lightning-splintered tree no longer burnt, its fires extinguished by the continuous downpour. But the lightning picked out other details of the path ahead of them. The weeds and bushes that grew at the side of the road. The dressed stones that paved the way. Large puddles and the water that ran in streams along the gutters beside the road. The looming shapes of far-off trees and ancient buildings. And closer to them, picked out starkly against the darkness, a lone rider.

Cynan's keen eyes made out details of the horseman and he kicked his mount into a gallop to catch up with Beobrand.

"We won't need to ride to Eugenius' hall after all," he said, raising his voice to be heard over the rain, wind and the clatter of hooves.

"What do you mean?" asked Beobrand. Not for the first time, Cynan marvelled at how poor his hlaford's eyesight must be, particularly at night. It was a miracle he could see well enough to fight.

"We ride to speak with Wilfrid," Cynan said, "and unless my eyes deceive me, that is him there, riding towards us."

Chapter 29

Beobrand peered into the gloom. Water trickled down his back and he shifted his position to better profit from the scant shelter offered by the high wall and the weeds that sprouted from between its cracked bricks and crumbling mortar. He shivered. It was not cold, despite the rain, but he was on edge. They had been waiting in the dank darkness for a long time. It had rained most of the night and still rain poured from the leaden sky. The dark clouds that roiled over the city gave little hope that the storm would abate any time soon. Dawn would be wet, and it was not far away. Even through the thick clouds the lightening in the eastern sky was clearly discernible.

"You are sure this is the right place?" Beobrand asked, keeping his voice quiet.

Beside him, Wilfrid tensed. He did not turn to look at Beobrand.

"You may think me a fool, lord Beobrand," he hissed, "but I assure you I am not. I know very well the location of the Viminal Hill and the great *Palatium Diocletiani*. And that is the southern gateway." He pointed to a large archway that passed through the wall. "This is where I was instructed to meet."

"You *are* a fool," said Beobrand. "Of that I have no doubt. I hope you are right about the place."

Beobrand did not repeat the threats he had made to the young man earlier that night. Wilfrid knew all too well what would happen to him if Coenred was not brought back to them safely.

Beobrand stared up at the huge shadowed building complex before them. As always, the scale of the Roman constructions amazed him. Wilfrid said that while the locals called this place a palace, it had in fact been a bath house. Beobrand could not believe that. Surely there would never be enough people in all middle earth who would wish to bathe at the same time in one place. Whatever the truth of it, the edifice was as massive as any of the palaces in Roma and for whatever reason it now lay abandoned; overgrown with weeds and crumbling, like so much of this once great city.

"They said to come alone," whispered Wilfrid.

"If you had wished to come alone," snarled Beobrand, "you would not have come looking for me." The young man's tone grated on his nerves. "They want the book. Having me with you won't change that."

When they had met Wilfrid on the road he had blurted out the whole sorry affair. Whatever else Beobrand thought of Wilfrid, the man was quick-witted. When he saw Beobrand and all the gesithas riding in the night, he had quickly understood there was no room for lies and evasions. He had told them how a messenger had come to him, telling him to go to the *Palatium Diocletiani* at dawn. There he could exchange the book for Coenred.

"I never thought anything like this would happen," Wilfrid had said. "You must believe me, lord Beobrand."

Beobrand's tone had been as chill and sharp as a seax blade.

"Do not tell me what I must believe, Wilfrid," he said. "How is it you come to have Priano's book?"

Wilfrid looked nervously at the warriors who had surrounded him on the road. There was no friendship in those faces. Eadgard spat and looked ready to rip Wilfrid's head from his shoulders with his massive hands.

"He would not sell it to me," Wilfrid muttered.

"There is no time for your excuses," snapped Beobrand. "Marsiglio might be dead by morning, and Coenred's life is in the balance." Wilfrid flinched as if slapped. "And you," Beobrand went on, "are responsible. Now tell me plain, how did you come by the book?"

Wilfrid would not look him in the eyes. His horse stepped nervously and shook its mane as a gust of wind swayed the trees that grew beside the road. He mumbled something that Beobrand could not make out.

"Speak up," he said, his voice growing harder and louder.

"Lutozzo," said Wilfrid simply.

He had told the rest of the tale in a rush. Wanting the book he had seen, he had sought out the man he had met at the feast. Lutozzo had said that for the right amount of silver he could supply the book to him.

"I thought he meant to procure it for me. I did not know he planned to take it."

"Steal it, you mean," said Beobrand. "And you did not think that Priano might imagine you were the thief of the book you had been so taken with just days ago?" Surely someone as clever as Wilfrid could not be so naive.

"I never imagined anything like this would happen," Wilfrid said. "As Jesu and all His saints are my witness, I do not wish for Coenred to be hurt."

"Perhaps that is so. But words cost nothing, Wilfrid. Your actions have caused this. Now you must make it right."

"You will help me then?" Wilfrid asked, his voice trembling.

"It is not for you that I do this," Beobrand said, biting back the anger he felt. "It is for Coenred. And you should pray to your God and His saints that he is unharmed. If Coenred is hurt, Priano will not be the worst of your enemies." He reached over from his horse and gripped Wilfrid's tunic, almost pulling him from the saddle. "You have seen what I do to my enemies, Wilfrid," he said. "Do not think your God or anyone else will save you if another of my friends is harmed because of your foolishness and greed."

"I was not to blame for what happened in Frankia," Wilfrid whined. "You know this."

"And yet once again, you are hale while others are in danger. And there is no denying this mess is of your doing." He released Wilfrid, shoving him back so hard that he almost toppled from his horse. "There is no time for this. We will settle our differences when the moment comes. But for now I will ride with you to the meeting place. Perhaps we can reason with the men who have Coenred. Do you have the book?"

Wilfrid looked aghast.

"I would never bring such a valuable thing out in this storm. It is safe. In Eugenius' library."

Beobrand scowled.

"How far is this palace? This *Palatium Diocletiani*?" Beobrand stumbled over the strange words.

Wilfrid did not need to think about his answer.

"We can reach it before dawn," he said, "if we ride immediately."

"Is there time to collect the book first?"

Wilfrid contemplated the idea, then shook his head.

"Not without running the risk of missing the meeting. And I do not imagine these men are forgiving of tardiness."

"They want the book," said Beobrand, "so we must hope they are forgiving of those who don't bring them what they have asked for." He turned to Cynan. "I don't like this. If we cannot free Coenred tonight, I would still wish to know where he is being held. Take the saddlebags from Grindan and ride with

Bleddyn and Ingwald to Stoldo's villa. Lucifrido, escort them and bring me back good tidings." He hated to split his already small band, but he could feel Coenred's time running out, like water trickling from a cracked pot. "And Lucifrido," he added, while the men were transferring the heavy saddle bags to Ingwald's horse, "I am a man with many enemies, do not add your name to that long list."

Lucifrido smiled briefly, then grew sober.

"We will be back as quickly as our horses can carry us," he said. "I give you my word on that. Do not worry, lord."

But the gods knew Beobrand did worry. All the while they rode through the dark thoroughfares of the rain-drenched city, he turned over in his mind what the morning might bring.

He worried that Eadgard, Grindan and Halinard might be too far away to come to their aid should things turn against them. The messenger had told Wilfrid to come alone. By having Beobrand with him, he had already defied that order. Beobrand thought they might well ignore that infraction, but imagined having four mounted warriors accompanying the novice might prove too much. So he had ordered the others to remain with the horses, hidden beyond the wall of the palace grounds. Grindan had said he would climb up the wall and observe their meeting, but it would still take the three gesithas some time to reach them, if things went badly.

Beobrand had often wondered whether the old gods held any sway here, far to the south where the Christ god was all powerful. But the twists of wyrd on this foul night had all the trappings of the madness so loved by Woden and his children. Beobrand could imagine Thunor's chariot rumbling across the heavens while the rest of the gods watched the folly of men.

How the gods loved chaos.

He shuddered again, staring into the shadows of the hulking

building that loomed before him. He did not understand the ways of the gods, but he knew one thing Woden desired even more than frenzy and turmoil. The All-Father wanted blood.

Woden, All-Father, Beobrand prayed silently, *let Coenred live and I will bring you sacrifice.*

"We should have brought the book," muttered Wilfrid, breaking into Beobrand's thoughts.

"Too late for that now," whispered Beobrand.

There was movement on the far side of the open area in front of the palace buildings. Beobrand squinted, trying to make out details through the rain and the pre-dawn gloom. He wished Cynan was there, and cursed that he had grown so reliant on the Waelisc warrior's keen eyes. He would rather not admit weakness before Wilfrid, but swallowed his shame. His pride was of little consequence that night.

"How many do you see?" he asked.

Wilfrid stared for a few heartbeats, shielding his eyes from the rain. When he spoke, fear made his voice so quiet that Beobrand could barely hear him.

"There are four of them."

"Good," said Beobrand, stepping out from the shadow of the wall. "Enough that they will not feel threatened by me."

Wilfrid looked up at him as if he was mad.

"Only a fool would not be threatened by you, lord," he said.

Beobrand scoffed and shook his head at Wilfrid's obvious flattery. Nevertheless, he took some solace from the truth he saw in the young man's eyes. There was respect borne from fear in that gaze. Beobrand might not see or hear as well as he once had, but he was yet a tall and imposing figure; a warrior lord of Bernicia.

"Do not forget that, Wilfrid," Beobrand said. "You told me yourself, you are no fool. Now, come, let us meet with these men. And keep your wits about you. What you say now will decide the path of Coenred's wyrd." He fixed Wilfrid with his icy stare. "And your life is tied to his."

Wilfrid was frightened, his face pale, but there must have been some steel in him, thought Beobrand, for the novice did not hesitate. Side by side they trudged in silence across the broken cobbles towards the four waiting men. Wet weeds and grass swished against their ankles and calves. Beobrand's shoes and leg-bindings were already soaked, so he made no attempt to avoid the muddy puddles, instead splashing through them without slowing his step. Wilfrid, more fastidious than the thegn, stepped around them, or jumped over the dark pools.

As they grew closer, the rain eased, falling in a nebulous drizzle. The light from the east brightened the sky. Beobrand could make out details of the men now. They were all hooded and cloaked and had halted, spread out in a line that set them a distance of several paces from each other. Close enough for them all to speak and hear what was said, but too far apart for Beobrand to attack more than one at a time. Their cloaks were wrapped about them against the rain and their hoods pulled down low. It was impossible to see their faces or what weapons they carried beneath their cloaks.

There was no sign of Coenred.

When Beobrand and Wilfrid were still two dozen paces away one of the men held up a hand to halt them.

"Remember," whispered Beobrand, so that only Wilfrid could hear him, "we each have what the other wants."

"I don't see Coenred," Wilfrid hissed back.

"He might be close by, hidden in the palace." He was going to add that as they did not have the book with them, they must seek to ensure that Coenred was kept safe, but the man who had raised his hand spoke.

Wilfrid replied. The two of them conversed for a time.

Beobrand understood only a few of the words. There was mention of a book and Wilfrid spoke of his friend. Beobrand scoffed at that. Some friend Wilfrid was. To be his friend was to court death and betrayal at every turn.

While they talked, Beobrand cast his eye over the four men. The three who were silent did the same, sizing him up, taking in his size and strength, Nægling's glimmering pommel and tooled scabbard.

One of the men was bulky and broad. Seeing Beobrand appraising him he pushed aside his cloak to reveal a stout cudgel in a meaty fist. A thick dark beard protruded from the hood's shadow. The other three men were taller and gave the impression by their movements and bearing of being younger. They kept their hoods up and their cloaks tight about them, but at least one of them had a sword. His cloak tented to the side in the tell-tale shape made by a sword hanging from a baldric and clasped in one fist, ready to draw the blade forth.

The tone of the conversation between Wilfrid and the leader of the group was becoming heated. Beobrand stepped close and placed a hand on Wilfrid's shoulder.

"What is he saying?" he asked. "Did he ask about me?"

"No," Wilfrid said. "He knows who you are. He wants to know why I have not brought the book."

Beobrand felt a flicker of useless pride at the man's recognition, but shoved it aside.

"Ask him for proof that Coenred yet lives," he said.

Wilfrid uttered a few words. The man shook his head, speaking quickly. His tone was cutting and sharp.

"He says the monk is unharmed. We can see he is well when we come with the book. If we do not bring the book to the next meeting, they will slay Coenred."

"Tell him if they kill the monk so easily, they will not have the book at all."

Wilfrid translated. The man laughed. It was an ugly, throaty sound. When he stopped chuckling, he barked a few words.

"He says his master would rather not have to kill anyone. But if they are forced to, they will take the book by other means and the monk will have no value then. He says if we do not bring the book here after dusk tonight, he will begin cutting him…" Knowing that Wilfrid was interpreting his words, the man leered, his grin wide in the shadows of his hood. "He says they call him Carnifex, The Butcher, and he is good at his job. He says he will start with the ears, then the fingers and toes…" Wilfrid blanched and his voice dried up. Carnifex gave a guttural laugh.

Beobrand clenched his fists at his side. Staring into the man's shadowed eyes, he thought quickly, turning over possibilities.

"I understand," he said. He had met men like this many times before. The Butcher was a man who took pleasure in dealing out pain. Beobrand got the impression the man would like nothing more than to be given an excuse to maim and kill Coenred.

"Tell him," Beobrand said, "that we need more time to retrieve the book."

"But we could collect it—"

"Silence," Beobrand hissed, cutting him off. "Say exactly what I tell you. Say you have hidden the book somewhere safe and need more time to collect it."

Wilfrid hesitated.

"But, lord—"

"Do it!"

Wilfrid swallowed then spoke quickly. Carnifex stared at him, unmoving for some time, weighing Wilfrid's words. Eventually, he replied, his tone terse.

"He says we have till tomorrow's dawn. If we are not here by then with the book, Coenred dies."

Beobrand thought for only a heartbeat. He did not think he could push the man further. He hoped it would be time enough.

"Tell him we agree."

Wilfrid did so. Without another word, the four men backed away. Beobrand, mutilated left hand on Nægling's hilt, watched them go. When they were a spear's throw distant, they turned and disappeared into the shadowed recesses of the palace buildings.

Only then did Beobrand begin to make his way back towards the arched gateway, and his warriors and the horses that waited beyond.

"So tomorrow we will bring the book?" asked Wilfrid. His voice wavered and he sounded very young; his usual self-assuredness had vanished as surely as the hooded men who had been swallowed by the veiled gloom of the ruined palace.

"Perhaps," replied Beobrand.

"What do you mean 'perhaps'?" Wilfrid's confusion was clear. "You heard him. If we don't bring it they will kill Coenred."

"And if that is still a chance by dawn tomorrow," Beobrand said, striding under the crumbling arch, "we will bring the book. And you will pray to your god and all the saints that those nithings hand over Coenred in exchange."

Their footsteps echoed briefly from the arch above them and then they were back out into the misty drizzle of the dawn. Already the rising sun was warming the wet earth and a low mist was forming over the ground.

"But what alternative is there?" Wilfrid asked.

Beobrand could see the shapes of their horses in the distance. He beckoned to Grindan and the others to bring the mounts. Halting, he turned to face Wilfrid.

"Pray to your Christ that Cynan and Lucifrido bring back good tidings," he said.

"Good tidings?" repeated Wilfrid. "How will that change things?"

"If they bring us what Lucifrido said they might, perhaps

there will be a different outcome to this than meeting Carnifex and those whoresons tomorrow at dawn."

Wilfrid frowned.

"What other outcome could there possibly be?" he asked.

A thin smile played on Beobrand's lips and he thought of his silent promise to Woden.

"The best of outcomes," he said. "We kill them all and bring Coenred safely back."

Chapter 30

Cynan was nervous. As they had ridden through the rain-swept night, the land outside the walls of Roma had been devoid of other travellers and Cynan had felt safe enough. Ingwald's horse carried a large portion of Beobrand's treasure in its saddlebags, but even if they had stumbled upon bandits, there was nothing to indicate the four riders were transporting such wealth. Besides, the four of them were armed with swords and clearly not men to be trifled with. They would dissuade most thoughts of robbery from the wolf-heads and brigands who roamed the land.

But now, taking in the scale of Stoldo's villa in the grey dawn light, seeing the numbers of men manning the gates and watching their approach, Cynan realised that Ingwald, Bleddyn and he, no matter how brave and battle-skilled, would be powerless to prevent Stoldo from taking the silver by force should he wish to.

Nothing about this venture felt right and Cynan could not convince himself that they were not heading into a trap. Riding towards the white-walled and clay-tiled villa from the *Via Appia*, Cynan thought of the possibility that Lucifrido had betrayed them. The path was long and as they wound up the hill through olive groves, Ingwald and Bleddyn slowed their mounts, falling back to ride alongside Cynan. Lucifrido glanced at them, but made no effort to ride close enough to join their hurried, muttered conversation.

"Do we just ride into the maw of the wolf?" whispered Ingwald.

Cynan pushed his wet hair away from his brow. The downpour had finally ceased with the dawn and now they rode through a thin mist that gave the land a dreamlike quality.

"I see no other option," Cynan said. "Do you?"

Ingwald sniffed and spat.

"No, but I cannot lose the feeling we are riding like sheep following a goat to the Blotmonath slaughter."

"I am sure nothing bad will befall us," said Bleddyn with a crooked smile. "For is it not said that Beobrand is a lucky lord?"

Cynan snorted.

"So people say," he said. "Though there is a problem with your thinking."

"And what is that?" asked Bleddyn.

"Beobrand is not with us, and you are *my* sworn men."

"Then we have nothing to fear at all," said Bleddyn blithely. "For you and I have the luck of the Waelisc."

"What about me?" grumbled Ingwald.

"We'll protect you, old one," said Bleddyn. "Besides, nothing can happen to us. We have women awaiting us far away. It would not do to die before seeing them again."

Bleddyn's forced cheeriness did nothing to lift their spirits and the mention of the women they missed dampened their mood as surely as if the heavens had opened once more. They fell silent again and spurred their horses after Lucifrido.

As they reached the gates, a man shouted something from the wall. Lucifrido replied with a few words. The man vanished and after a short pause the great timber gates were pulled open. Bleddyn, Ingwald and Cynan shared a look.

"Almost as if they were waiting for us," hissed Ingwald.

Cynan said nothing. There was nothing else to do now but to follow Lucifrido and pray they had been right to trust him.

They found themselves in a large courtyard. It was surrounded by high walls with the main villa building before them. To the right there were several smaller, less grand structures and a long timber stable. Men hurried out of the more humble buildings and several more from the large house.

There were soon ten armed men surrounding the newly arrived riders. The men did not brandish their weapons or threaten the horsemen, but the message they sent was clear. Servants stepped up and took their reins. Cynan and the others dismounted.

A tall, massively shouldered man with a ruddy face and a twisted, misshapen nose spoke with Lucifrido. The man from Sutri removed his sword and gave it to the man with some deference.

"This is Vico," Lucifrido said. "We must hand over our blades before we can speak to Stoldo."

One of the hostlers made to remove Ingwald's saddlebags. Ingwald slapped the man's hands away. The servant let out a small cry of surprise. Vico took a step forward and growled something to Lucifrido.

"Best if you do not strike Stoldo's servants," Lucifrido said. "Vico here would be all too happy to repay you. He is a formidable fist-fighter."

Ingwald jutted out his chin defiantly. He did not look away from Vico.

"Tell the ugly whoreson I would happily teach him what it is to fight a man of Bernicia," he said. "Or does he only like to beat old pilgrims?"

Lucifrido did not translate his words.

"Easy, Ingwald," he said. "Vico is a killer."

"So am I," whispered Ingwald.

In an attempt to lessen the tension, Cynan quickly pulled his baldric over his shoulder and handed his scabbarded sword to Vico. The man accepted the weapon and belt, but continued to glare at Ingwald. Cynan wondered how much Vico had understood of what Ingwald had said. Even without being able to speak Anglisc, the disdain and insult in Ingwald's tone had been clear enough. Helping him to remove the weighty saddlebags, Cynan placed a hand on Ingwald's arm.

"Remember what we have come for," he whispered.

"Sorry," Ingwald hissed. "But after what he did to Sergius, I cannot like that man."

Ingwald had struck up an unexpected friendship with the old Frankish pilgrim after Coenred had introduced them. Sergius had been bed-ridden for several days after the beating he had suffered at Vico's hands. Fridolin, his ill-mannered son, had left his father to recover alone, and had disappeared into the city's murkier depths, where he had spent much of the remainder of his father's silver on whores. Ingwald had sat with Sergius when he could, using Coenred as interpreter. He liked the softly spoken Frank, and felt sorry for the pain his son had caused him with his neglect. But more than that, he despised the brute who had beaten the defenceless old man so savagely.

"You do not need to like him," said Cynan, "just don't start a fight with him. Or would you care to explain to Beobrand how you stood in the way of freeing Coenred?"

Ingwald shook his head and looked away from Vico. With a grunt, he shouldered the saddlebags.

"Give the man your sword," Cynan said.

Bleddyn had already done so, and now Ingwald, biting his lip, unbuckled his sword belt and held it out for Vico to take.

The red-faced fighter stepped close. He grinned, showing several missing teeth. As he took the sword from Ingwald, he whispered something.

"What did he say?" Ingwald asked.

Before Lucifrido could reply, Cynan cut him off.

"Enough of this," he said. "Lucifrido, please, tell Vico we must speak to Stoldo without delay."

Vico listened to the request, then replied.

"He says the master of the villa rises early. He will meet us immediately. But first he wishes to check inside those bags."

Cynan nodded to Ingwald. Vico leaned in close and pulled open the leather covers of the panniers. Ingwald tensed and Cynan gave a slight shake of the head. He had never before seen the older man so incensed by anyone. This was not a good time to discover such a hatred, Cynan thought, watching in tense silence as Vico rummaged in the saddlebags.

Stepping away, Vico whistled and offered Ingwald a wink. Ingwald scowled, but to Cynan's relief, did not react.

Satisfied they were not armed, Vico handed their swords to one of the other men in the courtyard and clicked his fingers for five others to join them as he turned and led the way into the villa.

True to Vico's word they were not made to wait and he led them across a small, shadowed inner courtyard and through a heavy dark timber door.

"I have a bad feeling about this," Ingwald whispered.

Cynan said nothing. He could not be rid of the sense of a trap being closed around them but he forced himself to stand straight and to walk with purpose into the large room. The other men trailed them, boxing them in and adding yet further to the sensation of being caged in and trapped.

The room was cool and clean. There were large windows facing east. The shutters were open wide, giving expansive views of Stoldo's lands and the rising sun. The villa was situated atop a hill, so from the windows Cynan could see seemingly endless rows of olive trees rolling away into the brightly hazed dawn. Above the brilliant sun, dark clouds still cloaked the sky, reminding them all of the violence of the night's storms, and perhaps an augury of darker times ahead.

A table was set before the windows. On it were jugs, cups, plates and bowls. The room's walls were painted white, the floor smooth plain earthen tiles. The food on the table caught the sunlight and gave the otherwise austere room a splash of colour. There were plump figs and shiny cherries, platters of fresh bread and dishes of soft white cheese and rounds of hard yellow cheese. Small bowls of green olive oil and rich sauces festooned the table like jewels, glimmering in the early morning sun.

There was only one occupant in the room. The solitary figure seated at the table rose and faced them as they entered. He was dressed all in black, his clothes as plain as the room's decoration. His hair, at one time as black as his tunic and breeches, was now streaked with grey, as was his close-cropped beard. Deep set, intelligent eyes watched the newcomers as they approached. For a heartbeat, the man's features were impassive, as rigid as stone, and then, in an instant, a broad smile lit his face and he held out his hands in welcome.

"Lucifrido!" he exclaimed.

Lucifrido crossed the tiled floor in a few quick steps and embraced the man. They kissed each other's cheeks in greeting, whispering urgently before parting. Lucifrido indicated his companions and introduced them, saying each of their names in turn.

"This is Stoldo," said Lucifrido. "He bids you join him in breaking his fast."

Cynan bowed. Bleddyn copied him. Ingwald offered the man a curt nod.

Vico said something, and Stoldo's attention flicked to him. Whatever the brawler had said appeared to annoy Stoldo, for he frowned and waved the man away with a barked order. The other guards had remained in the doorway, but Vico was already halfway across the room. Now he hesitated. Stoldo snapped another command, and Vico turned on his heel and walked stiffly from the chamber. The guards followed him and the door closed behind them.

Stoldo smiled at Cynan as if Vico had never been there.

"*Cynan*," he said, pronouncing the name strangely.

"*Ita*," Cynan replied in Latin, nodding and touching his chest. "Cynan."

Stoldo beamed and spoke rapidly, believing Cynan was able to comprehend him. The Waelisc man held up his hands in defeat. He knew only a few words and phrases and was painfully aware that he was at Lucifrido's mercy. More than ever, Cynan hoped the man was true to his word.

"Please tell Stoldo we will need to speak through you," he said.

Lucifrido spoke. Stoldo nodded and replied, indicating with a sweep of his hand the laden table. There were eight stools around the board.

"Stoldo says we are to make ourselves comfortable. There is plenty of food for us all."

"Please thank him," said Cynan, "but tell him we have need of great haste. We would ask for his help and we bring silver as payment." He held out his hand and Ingwald passed him the saddlebags.

Lucifrido shook his head.

"I will not say these things," he said.

Cynan's heart sank.

"So quickly you betray us?" he asked bitterly.

Lucifrido smiled at that.

"Do not think so little of me," he said. "I aim to help you, not bring you more hardships."

"Then speak my words and be done with it."

Stoldo had sat back down at the table and was watching the exchange expectantly.

"I know Stoldo," said Lucifrido, "and you do not. We will get to the matter you wish to speak about, but if you refuse his hospitality, you will do him a great insult. Believe me, that is something you do not wish."

Cynan glanced at the black-garbed man. There was still a smile on his lips, but his dark eyes had grown as obdurate as granite.

"Of course," muttered Cynan, moving to the table and sitting on one of the stools. "*Gratias tibi*," he added, nodding first to Stoldo, then Lucifrido. Perhaps the man was not going to betray them after all.

Placing the heavy saddlebags on the tiled floor, Cynan accepted a piece of crusty bread smeared with soft cheese that Stoldo proffered him. Stoldo's expression had softened and his smile reached his penetrating eyes once more. Ingwald and Bleddyn both sat, each reaching for some of the food. Despite the urgency of their visit Cynan smiled. They had learnt well the lessons of the warrior. Rest when you are able and always eat when food is offered, for you never know the next time a meal will be available.

Lucifrido sat beside Stoldo, who was speaking in warm tones. He pointed out the window as he talked. The sun, still hanging below the heavy clouds, shone through the wisps of mist that drifted between the olive trees, bathing the table in a golden light. A rainbow shimmered far off in the cloud-heavy sky, and Cynan took that as a good omen.

He bit into the bread and cheese. It was creamy and pleasantly sour and he was suddenly aware of how hungry he was. Tired too, for they had not slept. Reaching for one of the pitchers, he filled a clay cup. Sipping the liquid, he was pleased to find it was sweet watered wine. A glance at the table showed him there were enough cups for all of them, and more than enough food. He wondered whether Stoldo's men had seen them on the road. Or had this meeting been prepared since Lucifrido's visit? He would find out soon enough.

Cynan chewed the mouthful of food and washed it down with the fine wine. Lucifrido was talking, demanding his attention.

"Stoldo says that this time, just after dawn, is his favourite moment of day. He likes to eat here and look at the land from this window. He says he can think in this peaceful time before the day is full of noise."

"And what does he think of?" asked Cynan.

Lucifrido translated. Stoldo smiled and replied, Lucifrido speaking his words in Anglisc.

"I wonder what drives men of Albion to ride through a stormy night to visit me."

Cynan nibbled at a slice of hard cheese. The salty tang of it was wonderful.

"My lord Beobrand sent us," he said.

"Ah, yes." Stoldo nodded. "Lucifrido told me about this Beobrand. Why does he send you to my home and why does he not come to visit me himself?"

"He could not come this night. He has a friend in need. My friend too. For all I know we might already be too late to save him."

Stoldo's expression became grave as he listened to Lucifrido's words.

"After family," Stoldo said, "friendship is all. Friends are the family we choose for ourselves. And yet I still do not understand why you have come here."

"Lucifrido thought you might be able to help us."

Stoldo raised his eyebrows and looked sidelong at Lucifrido.

"He did, did he? And how did he imagine I might be able to

do that? I have never met your lord Beobrand, or your friend, as far as I know."

"Lucifrido says you are a man of boundless wisdom. That the great families of Roma do nothing without your knowledge."

Stoldo snorted at that.

"Lucifrido flatters me," he said. "But I am intrigued. Tell me what has happened to your friend that Lucifrido would think I might be able to offer you guidance."

Cynan told Stoldo all he knew about the attack on Marsiglio and Coenred. How a messenger had gone to Wilfrid with the demand for the book that he had stolen from Priano. When he finished, Stoldo stared out of the window for some time. His brow was furrowed and he rubbed a hand over his beard.

"And you say this man, *Wilfrid*," he struggled to say the name, "asked Lutozzo for his help obtaining the book from Priano?"

"That is what Wilfrid told us," Cynan said.

"And the messenger told him to bring the book to the *Palatium Diocletiani*?"

Lucifrido answered that question himself with a curt nod. Stoldo shook his head, chuckling quietly.

"Then it would seem Lutozzo has been very busy," he said.

"What do you mean by that?" Cynan asked.

"Lutozzo controls the *Collis Viminalis* hills. Much of the land of the *Collis Esquilinus* too."

Cynan frowned, confused. "I do not know the lay of Roma well enough to picture that area. What of it?"

"The *Palatium Diocletiani* is on Lutozzo's land," Stoldo said.

"You think Lutozzo has taken Coenred?" Cynan asked. "After stealing the book from Priano?"

Stoldo shrugged. He took a thin sliver of dry cured ham from an earthenware dish.

"I think," he said, chewing, "that Lutozzo would like nothing more than to be paid for stealing something and then paid again for retrieving it." He smiled at the thought and Cynan thought Stoldo looked as if he shared the sentiment. "From what you say of the attack," Stoldo continued, "on the monks and your friend's capture, and the location of the meeting place, I think it would be safe to wager that Lutozzo was behind this."

Cynan felt suddenly overwhelmed by tiredness.

"Lucifrido," he said, "you told us Lutozzo was the most powerful man in Roma."

"*One* of the most powerful," he replied, before saying a few words to Stoldo. Stoldo nodded.

"Lutozzo is not a man it would be wise to cross," he said. "My advice would be to get your friend back as quickly as possible."

Cynan looked at the food on the table hungrily. But he did not take any more. The food he had eaten felt as heavy as a stone in his gut.

"If we hand over the book," he said, "do you think he will release our friend?"

Stoldo scratched at his beard, then drank from his cup.

"He might," he said at last, "but nothing is certain in these things. If your friend yet lives, the longer he is held by Lutozzo's men, the more chance he might be killed."

Cynan took a deep draught of the watered wine. This was not what he wanted to hear. He could not return to Beobrand bearing only these doom-laden tidings.

"But why kill him?" he asked. "Priano wants the book, not Coenred's life."

Stoldo sucked his teeth.

"What Priano wants is not the issue," he said. "If your friend is held by Lutozzo, as I suspect, he will most likely be in the hands of Carnifex. The longer that beast has him, the more likely that even if he lives, he will not be returned whole."

A chill washed over Cynan, though the day was already warm.

"Who is this Carnifex?" he asked.

"A savage man," said Stoldo, his expression grave. "A butcher. He likes to skin men alive, to put out their eyes, to slice off fingers, ears... their manhood. Carnifex takes great pleasure in such things. He is Lutozzo's wolf, and like the wolf, he is wild and cannot be tamed. If he held a friend of mine, I would do all I could to retrieve him."

Cynan let out a long breath.

"I see nothing we can do," he said, despair and weariness making his voice crack, "save giving Lutozzo the book and praying he keeps his word."

Stoldo scoffed.

"Lutozzo's word is meaningless," he said. "But there is another way."

Hope flared within Cynan.

"What way?"

"You could liberate your friend from his captors," Stoldo said.

"Perhaps we could," Cynan replied, his tone uncertain, "but that would place him at great risk. Besides, even if we wanted to, we do not know where he is being held."

Stoldo gave him a cunning smile.

"Ah, but there you are wrong," he said. "For I know where Lutozzo holds his prisoners. And more than that, I have other knowledge that will help you."

Cynan stared at Stoldo, trying to gauge the man's true intentions.

"Why would you help us?" he asked.

Stoldo smiled without amusement. His eyes remained dark and impassive.

"I am no friend of Lutozzo's," he said. "Any blow struck at him brings me joy. Besides, I would not offer you what I know for free. I know much of what occurs in Roma, and this knowledge I possess will help you. But," Stoldo held his hands out palms upwards, "I do not do this for nothing. I am a generous man, but I am also a man of commerce."

Cynan mulled over everything he had learnt. Pouring fresh wine into his cup, he turned to Ingwald and Bleddyn.

"What say you?" he asked.

Ingwald barely looked up from the bowl he had filled with cheese, bread and fruit.

"I say we cannot trust this whoreson, any more than we can trust Lucifrido."

Lucifrido sighed at that.

"I tell you," he said, shaking his head, "you can trust me."

"It doesn't matter if we can truly trust the man," interjected Bleddyn. "As Stoldo said, he is a man of commerce. All he wants is silver."

"He could take it from us," said Cynan, expressing the worry he'd had since they had reached the villa compound.

"True enough," said Bleddyn, "but that might cause him problems. Better to have us give him the silver. The question is then, do we believe he has something that could help us?"

Cynan drank, watching Stoldo over the rim of his cup. The older man appeared oblivious of their conversation. As Cynan watched, Stoldo picked up a cherry and popped it in his mouth with an approving smile.

"I don't like it," Cynan said.

"Neither do I," said Bleddyn, "but that is of no importance."

Cynan bit his lip, trying hard to think of the correct course of action. He could sense time slipping by and knew that back in Roma Beobrand would be growing increasingly anxious. Sensing Cynan's indecision, Bleddyn continued.

"What you must ask yourself is whether Beobrand will be angrier if you spend some of his silver and bring back information that might help to free Coenred, or if you return with nothing to show for our efforts, and nothing to aid Coenred."

Cynan nodded. Bleddyn was right. They all wanted Coenred freed. The thought of the kindly monk held captive by some savage known for butchering his adversaries filled Cynan with dread. The silver was of no consequence. If Stoldo and Lucifrido had played them all along in order to steal from them, so be it. They could be made to pay later.

Sensing he had made his decision, Stoldo turned away from the window and faced him once more. He raised an eyebrow, awaiting Cynan's response.

"Tell him," said Cynan, "that if he has information that could help to free our friend, I have silver."

As if he could understand Cynan's words, Stoldo's mouth stretched in a wide grin that showed his teeth.

PART THREE

SHADOWS OF THE ETERNAL CITY

Chapter 31

Stoldo sat in silence for a long while after the men from Albion had left. It was still early morning, but the quiet of the dawn had departed along with the thin mist that had been burnt away by the rising sun. All around him the house was awakening and the sound of voices and movement pervaded the air. Usually by this time he would be out of this room, perhaps inspecting his lands, or tending to some other pressing task. Often that meant receiving men and women who would come to him, much as the strangers had, begging for his help. He glanced down at the pile of coins and hack silver on the table. Normally Stoldo would not have taken payment for such favours, instead accepting an oath of friendship from the petitioner and an understanding that when the time came, the recipient of his benevolence would aid him in whatever way was necessary. This network of people loyal to him had made Stoldo the force he had become. He might not be the most powerful man in Roma, but he was proud of all he had achieved. And where others relied on violence, torture, extortion and murder, Stoldo was much happier to reap the rewards of his power without shedding blood. Of course, it was not always possible to avoid violence, he thought, taking a coin from the table and turning it over so that the morning sun glinted from its polished surface.

Nor was it always the best decision to accept nothing more than a promise of future service in exchange for his help. He had liked the northerners well enough. They had the solidity and forthrightness of the men of Langobardia. His father had come from such stock. Honest, grave men. But men without subtlety or guile. They would surely honour any oath he might have made them swear, but they would not be in Roma long enough to do so. Either they would be far to the north, once more on their cold, barbaric island of Albion, or they would be dead. Lutozzo and his man Carnifex were not to be trifled with.

These northerners were tough and no doubt deadly in battle. Tales of their tall, fair-haired leader and his exploits on the road to Roma were already whispered among the members of the families. The man was surely a brute. Direct, quick to anger and just as quick to kill. There was always a need for such men, to be the blade wielded by men of worth. Someone to do what others were unwilling, or unable, to accomplish. But such killers were dangerous. And this one was a foreigner; a stranger to the ways of Roma, and unknowing of their customs and laws.

Stoldo smiled grimly, wondering how such a man would make use of the information he had provided. With luck, he would direct his savageness at Lutozzo, whose strength had been waning of late. His judgement was lacking too, it seemed. To accept payment from this ambitious young monk for the theft of a book from Priano, and then to take money from Priano to recover the very same tome, was not the action of the Lutozzo of old. This was as venal and daring as ever, but there was a new recklessness that spoke of the problems assailing his house.

Taking in a deep breath, Stoldo savoured the scent from the open window of the rain-damp soil as it warmed in the morning sun. He shook his head, thinking of the forbidding men of Albion. The man who led the likes of Cynan must be formidable indeed. Lutozzo had made a mistake this time. Perhaps a mistake that would prove his downfall, or at least widen the cracks in his leadership. His three sons were already impatient to be given more control, and Stoldo's spies had told him of the infighting between Lutozzo's three heirs. It was all Lutozzo could do to hold his family together and to provide his sons with enough distractions to keep them from open war. When war came, as it inevitably would, Stoldo would be glad he lived outside the city walls. The streets would be bathed in blood. Remaining distant from the conflict as much as possible was surely the safest option.

Stoldo took a sip of his wine. He had often longed for sons of his own, and had watched jealously as Lutozzo fathered one boy after another while Ammanata had given Stoldo nothing but girls. All four of his daughters were sweet things and yet, love them as he did, they were only women and they could not be expected to take over the family when the time came. This had been a source of worry for him these many years, but having seen Lutozzo's sons recently had given Stoldo pause. They bitterly resented each other and their father.

He scratched his beard and allowed his mind to wander where it had wished to roam ever since the morning's visitors had left. In fact, his thoughts had not been far away from the subject since Lucifrido's visit a few days earlier. Whenever Stoldo saw him, he found himself drawn back into the past and he would brood for days on what might have been.

Lucifrido looked so much like his mother. The first time Stoldo had seen him he had almost wept. Leofrun had been such a beauty and Stoldo had been a young man, full of youth's passions. He had sought out the slim, blue-eyed whore as frequently as he could, offering to travel to Ostia whenever his father needed someone to carry out an errand there. On several occasions he had taken a horse from the stables and ridden through the night for the chance to lie with her. For a few months that summer he could think of little else. He had been drunk with love and lust.

Had his father known of his obsession? Stoldo had never had the nerve to confront the old man with that question. He had been too afraid of his father to ever seriously contemplate such a thing. Not like Lutozzo's boys, who railed against their father so openly. But Stoldo had always suspected his father's hand in what had happened. All Stoldo had known for certain was that one day, a few months after his marriage to Ammanata, Leofrun was not in Ostia when he had gone to visit her. He had enquired what had befallen her, desperately asking the other whores and the sailors along the docks if they had seen her, but none of them could, or would, tell him anything to help him find her. Leofrun had simply vanished.

He had been distraught, but time is the greatest healer. His daughters were born. His father grew old and Stoldo's days were filled with the running of the estate and the family's interests in and around Roma. Slowly, he had reconciled himself to the fact Leofrun must be dead, but he always wondered whether his father had something to do with her disappearance. The old man cared nothing if he ploughed the servant girls, and visiting whores was of no consequence to him. But his father had always counselled him not to allow himself to become besotted with any woman. Such a thing breeds weakness, he'd said, leaving the head of the family open to attack.

Now, as the leader of the family, Stoldo understood that his father had been right. But he had never stopped thinking of the beautiful, shy woman who, before she sold her body to the sailors of Ostia and the impressionable sons of local noble families, had been snatched as a child thrall from a pirate raid in far-off Albion.

Stoldo still recalled the day he had first laid eyes on Lucifrido. He had been attending a meeting of the families in Sutri and had immediately noticed the young man in Tanualdo's employ. There had been something about the boy's features that had snagged

Stoldo's attention. During a break in the endless conversations, he had spoken to the smiling youth, asking him about his past. When he had heard the boy had been born of an Anglisc whore from Ostia, Stoldo's breath had caught in his throat. He had struggled to hold back his emotions for he had long since given up ever seeing Leofrun again, or even that she might be alive. To be suddenly confronted with this handsome young man who so clearly resembled his mother was as unnerving as it was exhilarating. Without giving away his intense interest, Stoldo had asked about Lucifrido's mother's health, only to hear that she had passed away from the flux several years before. He had reeled from that news. Despite thinking her long dead, to hear the truth of it still struck him like a blow to the gut.

He shook his head to remember the shock of it now. Draining his cup of wine, he placed it back on the table beside the silver. His hand was steady, but he remembered how it trembled back in Sutri when he had learnt of Leofrun's death. And he recalled how his mind had whirled as he had watched Lucifrido's movements, focusing on every aspect of the boy's face and physique. The young man did not know how old he was, not exactly, so there was no way to know whether he might be Stoldo's son, which was the first thing that had pierced his thoughts. Stoldo could see nothing of himself in the boy, but he could not deny the possibility. Lucifrido was certainly close to the right age.

Over the intervening years Stoldo had watched the boy whenever he had visited Sutri, or when Lucifrido had come to Roma on business for Tanualdo. Stoldo liked the young man well enough, but he had come to the conclusion Lucifrido was no son of his. He was too light-hearted. He was frivolous and smiled too freely. Stoldo had once toyed with the idea of offering Lucifrido a place in his household, where he would have been able to observe him more closely. He was glad now that he had not done so. Lucifrido was pleasant enough, and yet his loyalties were not clear. Tanualdo had taken him in and given him everything a man could wish for, and yet just that morning Stoldo had again seen signs that Lucifrido's loyalties were divided at best. He seemed truly and inexplicably invested in the fate of this foreign monk. If Stoldo had not known Lucifrido all these years he might have thought the young man had an ulterior motive in helping the men from Albion. He could easily have sought to trick them out of more of their silver, asking for a cut of the wealth for himself. Instead, he had pleaded with Stoldo not to take all of the treasure Cynan had offered him.

Stoldo shook his head. The boy was a fool. It was just as well he had never told him of his love for Leofrun and the possibility they might be of the same blood. Stoldo wanted nothing to do with such softness.

The conversation that morning had intrigued Stoldo. He had watched the interaction between the men carefully. The distrust Cynan and the others felt towards Lucifrido was clear, and yet Leofrun's son still aided them and did not seek to enrich himself at their expense. So like his mother, Stoldo thought. Soft. Stoldo had fallen in love with that softness in the whore. To see it in her son sickened him. The ways of men always surprised Stoldo.

At times, he even surprised himself. He could easily have ordered Vico to kill all four of the visitors, or perhaps just the men from Albion, leaving Lucifrido alive. God knew Vico would have been glad to oblige. The older of the men had insulted him somehow and Vico was furious. And Vico did so enjoy fighting. It was the only reason Stoldo kept him in the family. Every ruler needed his own man of violence. His blade. His butcher.

Or his Beobrand.

If he had given the order to kill them, he would have had all their silver now. Perhaps he was as soft as Lucifrido. Maybe all these thoughts of the man's mother had softened him. And yet, it was not so foolish, Stoldo told himself, to allow the four men to leave as friends. Beobrand, armed with the knowledge Stoldo had provided, might well strike a blow against Lutozzo. And Stoldo had thought of another way this turn of events might profit him.

He wondered how far Lucifrido and the men from Albion had ridden since leaving the villa. They were tired, but anxious to get back to Roma as quickly as possible. Stoldo looked out of the window. He could not see the *Via Appia* from here, but he gauged the position of the sun. It was still a long while until it would reach its zenith. There was time yet to put new plans into motion.

He thought of the other man who had arrived the day before. As far as he knew, his guest had slept through the dawn arrival of the four men. Stoldo had hoped so, but now it was of no matter. He had been unsure how he might help the man sleeping under his roof; how he would repay the debt he owed. Stoldo loathed being in anyone's debt and his visitor had not been gracious the day before when he had held the debt like an axe over Stoldo's head. In fairness to the man though, Stoldo thought he would probably act no better if he were in the same position.

Absently pushing a few of the pieces of silver into a line, Stoldo ordered his thoughts, thinking about possibilities, of how the different players might react. There were many pieces in this game, and Stoldo was aware of others even now sliding onto the board of Roma's intrigues. There would never be a perfect plan, he knew, but he was as certain as he would ever be that with the right move he could further benefit from the current situation, and in so doing, settle his long-standing debt.

He clapped his hands and called for a servant. He felt a pang of regret at what might befall Lucifrido as a result of the decision he had made, but as the door opened and his steward entered, Stoldo pushed aside such concerns. The smiling young man was not his son, and Lucifrido had chosen his own path and his own loyalties. When the time came, he would still be in a position to save himself and return to the family that had raised him. Stoldo hoped the boy would make the right decision. But that was up to Lucifrido.

The steward walked quietly up to the table, knowing from bitter experience not to interrupt his master when he was thinking over his morning repast. He stood patiently until, at last, Stoldo looked up at him.

"Awaken our guest," he said, his voice firm and decisive, "and bring him to me. We have much to discuss."

Chapter 32

Wilfrid's eyelids were finally drooping when Cynan and the others returned. It was mid-afternoon and Wilfrid had not slept all night. Since Beobrand had brought him back to the Lateran Palace shortly after dawn, he had been unable to rest. Halinard, Grindan, and his brute of a brother had all stretched out on their thin pallets and in the way of seasoned warriors were soon asleep. Wilfrid had paced the chamber for a time, until Eadgard had roared at him to go to sleep or to get out.

Wilfrid was happy enough to go into the gardens, but to his annoyance, Beobrand, all scowl and sweating frown, had followed him outside.

"I want to pray, lord Beobrand," Wilfrid said. "To contemplate what has happened."

"You can pray and think all you want," Beobrand said. "But do not imagine I will let you out of my sight for one moment until we have Coenred safely back with us."

The man was insufferable, his presence distracting and overbearing. Wilfrid did his best to ignore Beobrand as he walked along the fragrant paths of the garden. His mind teemed with concerns and questions. And yet, even when he prayed for guidance he found his thoughts tugging him away from the

Almighty, and returning to his own actions, and to how he had come to be in this predicament.

Wilfrid stroked the petals of a rose. The ground was still damp from the storm, the air humid. The scent of the flowers was heavy in the warm day. He had been a fool, he knew, and he berated himself. He should have known better. He must be stronger if he hoped to fulfil his destiny. Even as they had ridden back from the *Palatium Diocletiani*, Wilfrid had begun to regret what he had done.

The warriors all loathed him. They saw Coenred's capture as his fault and, just as in Frankia, somehow they found him to blame for acts taken by others. He would have to get used to such things. A man of vision is always surrounded by lesser minds. Beobrand and the other warriors were not thinkers. They were useful in their way. They could offer protection and mete out justice if needed. They did their lord's bidding and would stand in a shieldwall against those who might harm Wilfrid and others. But they could not grasp matters of great import. They did not comprehend the danger that Martinus, the Pontifex Maximus himself, had placed himself in by confronting the might of the Emperor and the Patriarch in Constantinopolis.

And such simple men would never be able to fathom the power of the book.

The book.

The Treasure of Life, it was called. And what a treasure it was.

The words and drawings within the tome filled his every waking moment and even filtered into his dreams. He had thought of little else since he had first opened the gem-encrusted cover and gazed at the sumptuously decorated vellum pages. Coenred had only glimpsed the book, but Wilfrid had seen the desire in the older monk's eyes. Coenred was no fool. Baducing too, if he came to read the book, would immediately understand its importance.

The moment they had arrived at the palace that morning, Beobrand had insisted on visiting Marsiglio. He had made Wilfrid accompany him. The wounded monk lay in fevered silence, his dark skin wet with sweat. The room reeked of sickness. Zanobi had whispered to them that Marsiglio's life still hung by a thread.

"Pray for him," he said, looking earnestly at Wilfrid.

Wilfrid had nodded and had even offered up a prayer for the injured man. He had not wished for the monk to be hurt. Nor did he want anything to happen to Coenred. He did not like the man. Coenred was too sanctimonious by far for Wilfrid's liking, but he did not seek his death.

Beobrand glared at Wilfrid accusingly after they had left Marsiglio. His thoughts were clear. He blamed Wilfrid for the man's wounds, and if he should die, it would be Wilfrid's doing.

And yet Wilfrid had not held the knife that stabbed Marsiglio. He could not be held responsible for the attack on him. Perhaps Marsiglio, a man of God who valued knowledge and learning, would understand, perhaps even condone, what Wilfrid had done.

Wilfrid had a vision for the future. For his future, and that of Albion. When he saw the book, Wilfrid knew he must possess it. It had called to him, washing away with its power all other desires, wiping away the need for earthly delights such as Priano's slave girl. He had enjoyed her for a time, but the instant he saw the book, he had all but forgotten her soft, pliant flesh and the pleasure he had felt as she wept and shivered beneath him. Thoughts of the book consumed him utterly. And as he walked in the garden a small voice deep inside him whispered that if Marsiglio or Coenred, or even both of them, should die, it would not be too high a price for the possession of the tome. Such a thing was beyond value, and whatever other treasures he might yet find in Roma, Wilfrid knew none would compare to Mani's *The Treasure of Life*.

After spending some time in the garden, with Beobrand as his morose shadow, Wilfrid decided to go to the *Archibasilica*. It was time for Nones and he hoped the familiar liturgy would allow him to order his thoughts.

Beobrand clearly did not wish to attend the service, but when Wilfrid had made it clear he was going, the tall thegn had walked with him across the open area where he and his men often trained with spear and shield, and followed him into the gloomy interior of the great church building. Inside it was cool and shadowed, the air redolent of incense that wafted over the faithful from an ornate silver censer suspended on a chain from the high ceiling.

Wilfrid moved down the long pillared space to stand with other clergy and monks near the altar. Beobrand, stifling a yawn, propped himself against the wall near the large doors. Wilfrid had half-hoped Beobrand might fall asleep. Then perhaps he would be able to slip away. What he needed to do was becoming clear to him, and it would be easier if he did not have to confront the thegn of Ubbanford to do it.

But Wilfrid could feel Beobrand's gaze on him all the while, so he closed his eyes and prayed, lending his voice to the ritual words of the liturgy. He opened his mind for God to speak to him, to give him a sign that what he planned was wrong. But no sign came and when the service was concluded, his resolve had only hardened.

As the morning dragged on, the hot sun drying the streets and slowly sliding into the west, Wilfrid pondered his options. He cursed his weakness that had led him to make rash, hasty decisions. He knew now what he should have done all along and, with his mind made up, his weariness and the sultry heat of the afternoon had finally begun dragging him towards sleep.

Beobrand too succumbed to his tiredness, stretching his tall frame out on one of the narrow beds. But before he slept, he woke Grindan. Beobrand whispered something to him and they both glanced in Wilfrid's direction. Wilfrid cursed silently. There would be no chance to escape the warriors from Albion, so he closed his eyes. He would need his wits about him later.

It was not long afterwards that Cynan, Ingwald, Bleddyn and Lucifrido came noisily into the stuffy room. They made no effort to keep quiet and all the men in the room were soon awake. Wilfrid rubbed at his eyes and looked out of the window. The shadows of the pines below had barely moved. Sighing, he pushed himself up and made his way to where Cynan was speaking to Beobrand. The rest of the gesithas were crowded about them. Wilfrid hung back, but he could hear well enough.

"I hope you feel better than you look," Beobrand said.

"It is good to see you too, lord," said Cynan with a weary, lacklustre smile.

The Waelisc man's face was dusty and streaked with sweat. Beneath the dirt, his skin was sunburnt. His eyes were red-rimmed, the flesh beneath them dark and bruised.

"I am glad you are back," Beobrand said. "Waiting has not been easy."

He told Cynan then of the meeting at dawn, and how they had convinced Carnifex to postpone the exchange until the following sunrise.

"Stoldo told us about Carnifex," Cynan said. "He says the man takes pleasure in his work. He also said Lutozzo cannot always control him." He shook his head. "I do not like the thought of Coenred in such a man's hands."

"None of us like it," snapped Beobrand. Whatever patience he possessed had evaporated sometime during that long, stormy night and the hot, sticky day that followed. "Woden knows there is little we can do but exchange the book with him and hope he has not harmed Coenred."

Cynan looked dubious.

"The longer he has him—"

"Do you think I do not know what is at stake?" Beobrand said, cutting him off. "Coenred is my oldest friend. I cannot abide the thought of what might be happening to him." His fists were clenched and he let out a breath, forcing himself to calm down. "Tell me you bring something that might help."

"I do," replied Cynan. "Perhaps."

"Perhaps?"

"Stoldo thinks he knows where Coenred might be held. But I think it might prove safest to meet Carnifex at dawn as planned and give him the book. Once he has that, he will surely have no reason to keep Coenred."

"And if he has harmed him?" said Beobrand, his tone bleak.

"Then we will know where to seek him out. We can make him pay whatever blood-price we think is right."

Eadgard stiffened.

"If there is blood-price to pay," he snarled, "Wilfrid here will have to pay his share." Wilfrid was painfully aware of the huge man's hateful stare.

"Hush, Eadgard," said Beobrand, but Wilfrid noted how the other men nodded their approval of the massive warrior's words. "There will be time enough for such things later," Beobrand went on. "For now we must focus on getting Coenred back. Cynan, tell us what Stoldo told you." Beobrand's words did little to allay Wilfrid's fears.

Cynan spoke for some time, detailing the location of Lutozzo's lair, the place where he held and tortured his captives, and the secret that might allow them to gain entry.

"You are right," Beobrand said when Cynan had finished. "This knowledge may prove useful. Still, we are few and such a place will be well defended. Even with the secret Stoldo has given to you."

"Not given, lord," said Cynan, accepting a cup of water from Grindan and sitting on a stool.

"How much did you pay him for this?" Beobrand asked.

"Just under half the silver."

"Better than I had hoped," Beobrand said.

Cynan nodded.

"Lucifrido spoke for us. He drove down the price, I think."

Beobrand looked at Lucifrido, appraising him.

"You are a surprising man," Beobrand said at last. "I thank you for your help."

"I want no harm to come to Coenred," Lucifrido said. "He is a good man."

"That he is," said Beobrand. "And from what you say, Stoldo is not. So why give us this information? Such a secret could be useful for him in the future."

Lucifrido shrugged.

"I do not know what is in the man's mind, but I believe he wishes to see Lutozzo's power diminished."

Beobrand looked sceptical.

"And he thinks the few of us can do that?"

"If anyone can," said Lucifrido, "it is you and your Black Shields, lord. Even Stoldo has heard of your battle-skill."

Beobrand scratched the back of his neck.

"I fear battle-skill will not be enough for this," he said. "I believe Cynan is right, much as it pains me to admit such a thing." He offered Cynan a thin smile. "We must retrieve the book. Then pray to whatever gods you think might listen that Carnifex holds up his end of the bargain."

Wilfrid could barely believe what he had heard. To think that Lutozzo would first accept his payment for the book and then work for Priano to retrieve the very thing his own men had stolen! But the more he thought of it, the more Wilfrid admired Lutozzo's ambition and daring.

Beobrand's purpose was now clear, and the thegn barked orders. His men rushed to do his bidding.

"Halinard, Grindan," he said, "accompany Wilfrid to Eugenius' hall and bring back this accursed book. The rest of you, get some sleep. We will all ride to meet this Carnifex before dawn. If he tries to cross us, or if he has harmed Coenred, then we shall show him the battle-skill of the Black Shields of Bernicia."

Wilfrid moved meekly towards the door, keeping his expression blank.

"Forgive me, lord," said Grindan, blocking the doorway, "but Lutozzo may have men watching us, or watching Eugenius' residence. I know you are in need of rest, but if Lutozzo has many men, Halinard and I could be overpowered and the book snatched."

Beobrand hesitated for only a heartbeat, then nodded.

"You are right, Grindan." He rubbed his half-hand across his face. "I am tired. But I should have thought of this."

Grindan smiled.

"That is why you have me, lord," he said.

Beobrand scoffed.

"Certainly it is not for your humility," he said. "But you spoke well. We cannot risk losing the book. We shall all ride with you."

Cynan groaned. He was evidently exhausted, but he pushed himself up from the stool. The others who had ridden to Stoldo's moved towards the door without complaint.

"Get fresh horses from the stables," said Beobrand. "Your mounts must be spent."

Cynan smiled ruefully at that.

"The horses are weary, it is true," he said. "But as luck would have it, *we* are not tired at all, are we boys?"

Bleddyn smirked.

"Not in the slightest," he said. "In fact I was hoping for a nice afternoon ride. It has been too long since I was astride a horse."

Ingwald, apparently too weary for jests, pushed them both out of the door.

"Come on, you fools," he grumbled. "My legs are as bowed as a whore's after pleasuring a whole warband. If I have to spend much more time in the saddle, I'm not sure I'll be able to walk, let alone fight."

The hostlers readied their horses quickly and soon they were riding towards Eugenius' residence and the church of Saint Prisca. Wilfrid thought of all that had changed since he had met them on this road the night before. When the messenger had come to him with the demand for the book and the threats on Coenred's life, he had panicked. He knew now that he had acted unwisely and in haste. But God was providing him with an opportunity to change that now.

They travelled along the wide road, the horses' hoofbeats loud on the cut stones. Most of the rain had already vanished in the heat of the sun, but some puddles remained in the shade of trees, and the channels that ran beside the road were boggy and wet.

The men barely spoke as they rode, each lost in his thoughts, or concentrating on his own battle against weariness. Wilfrid was glad of the quiet. He spent the time going over in his mind exactly what he would do when they reached Santa Prisca.

If Lutozzo's men were watching them, Wilfrid saw no sign, and it was not long until the familiar shape of the church and the adjoining hall loomed before them. The afternoon sun warmed the walls of both buildings, picking out dark shadows beneath the eaves and in the crannies of the architecture.

Rounding the building they found the courtyard thronged with people and animals. Men shouted orders, while others scurried to obey. They had expected the area before the church to be quiet, not this hubbub of activity. Beobrand and the others reined in their horses to take in the scene.

A large contingent of riders must have recently arrived. Several horses were tethered outside Eugenius' stables. One animal in particular stood out from the others: a fine white stallion, its sleek coat shimmering in the afternoon sun.

A dozen men were unpacking two large waggons, carrying heavy iron-bound chests towards the hall. A score of warriors guarded the entrance. Wilfrid recognised their distinctive crimson cloaks. As he looked, a man stepped out of the shadow of the hall. He had half-expected it to be Eugenius, but this was not the priest. This man wore rich silks and his oiled hair was held in place with a circlet of gold. Two huge men flanked him. He ignored them, but surveyed the scene in the yard with a haughty arrogance. Seeing something not to his liking, he shouted an order to one of the servants.

Wilfrid took in a deep breath. He had been hoping for a sign, and now God had not only provided one, but had made Wilfrid's path clear. He had come with a plan, but on seeing the man on the steps of the hall, he saw a better way. There was no time to waste. Beobrand was still taking in the horses and people, but it would only be a matter of heartbeats before he too would recognise the visitor who had come to Eugenius' residence.

Offering up a prayer of thanks to the Almighty, Wilfrid kicked his heels hard into his horse's flanks. The animal sprang forward and Wilfrid was glad of all those times his father had forced him to practise in the saddle. Keeping his seat easily, Wilfrid galloped across the courtyard. Servants scattered before him. Cynan shouted for him to halt. But Wilfrid did not slow until the last moment. The guards by the hall's entrance were moving to block his path. Wilfrid tugged savagely on his mount's reins, pulling the horse to a skittering, skidding halt. Shouts and the sound of hoofbeats followed him and Wilfrid knew there was no time for hesitation.

Leaping from his horse's back, he hit the ground at a run. He had hoped to reach the steps, but the armoured guards blocked his path. Glancing back he saw Cynan and Grindan reining in beside his abandoned horse. Beobrand and the others were close behind.

"Lord Deusdedi!" Wilfrid cried in Latin. "In the name of Jesu Christ and all that is holy, I beg your protection. Praise be to God that you are here."

Cynan sprang from his saddle and ran after Wilfrid. The guards around the novice stiffened. Wilfrid had seen the Waelisc warrior in combat. He was fast, lethal and implacable. If Beobrand's warriors and Deusdedi's guards began to fight, being caught between the two forces would be a terrifyingly dangerous place to be.

Grindan had joined Cynan now. They had drawn their swords and in a heartbeat they would be on Wilfrid. Drenched in sweat, Wilfrid shuddered. Perhaps this plan had not been so wise after all. Beobrand's gesithas would either cut him down or drag him away with them. Wilfrid didn't want to imagine what Beobrand would do to him after he had so blatantly disregarded his command.

Casting about him for some escape, Wilfrid shoved against the iron-knit byrnie of the nearest warrior, but the Exarchatus guard was as immovable as a boulder. Cynan and Grindan were almost on him and, behind them, Beobrand, Eadgard and the others were already dismounting. The courtyard was in turmoil. Some of the servants had dropped one of the chests, spilling its contents on the cobbles, and an hostler was struggling to hold the frightened white stallion that was rearing up and pawing the air with its hooves.

Perhaps sensing the danger of open combat with so many adversaries, Beobrand shouted for his men to hold back. They halted a few paces from Wilfrid. At the same instant, Deusdedi called out and his guards opened their ranks, allowing Wilfrid through.

"Wilfrid, is it not?" Deusdedi said, walking down the steps. "Did you say something about protection? From what?" His voice sounded more amused than concerned, as if the sudden galloping horses, shouting and threat of violence were the antics of unruly children.

Wilfrid saw that Eugenius was at the envoy's side. His smooth skin was furrowed in a scowl as he looked on in disconcerted shock at the sudden turn of events. He frowned at Wilfrid, unspoken questions clear in his expression.

Wilfrid pointed at Beobrand and his warriors, who were now standing in a line before the Exarchatus troops. At their centre, Beobrand glowered, half-hand on the pommel of his sword. The thegn and his gesithas numbered only eight men. Behind them, the servants had retreated, but before them stood more than twice their number of guards, all wrapped in polished byrnies, draped in red cloaks, armed with swords and bearing shields painted with the Christ symbol monogram of the Grecas letters *Chi Rho*. Despite being heavily outnumbered, there was no sign of fear on Beobrand's face. His gesithas stood solidly by his side, ready to fight if their lord should demand it.

Wilfrid swallowed against the dryness in his throat.

"From these blasphemers, lord," he said in a rush. "These heretics and pagans."

Deusdedi frowned and peered between his guards.

"Ah, yes," he said. "I recall lord Beobrand well. A most unpleasant man."

"Yes, lord," agreed Wilfrid. "He follows the old gods of Albion. He refuses to renounce them and will not worship the one true God."

Deusdedi shrugged.

"Alas," he said, "we must allow the word of the Lord to work in the hearts of man. I cannot change a man's mind on such matters. Only the Almighty has that power. I will pray for lord

Beobrand." He seemed bored to be speaking of such things. "But you spoke of protection?"

Wilfrid's sharp mind twisted and turned as he thought of how best to control this situation. God had surely provided him with a saviour, but he still needed to convince the emissary of the Exarchatus to believe him.

"Beobrand is returning to Albion," he said. "He would force me to go with him. He will not allow me to remain in the bosom of the Christian Eternal City. I would visit Ravenna and Constantinopolis, where I could learn more of God's word, but Beobrand would drag me back to his pagan land."

Beobrand was shouting now, his face crimson as his infamous anger took hold.

"Come back here, you toad!" he cried. "Without the book, they will kill Coenred." With an effort, he overcame his fury, forcing himself to slow his breathing and to lower his tone. "I care nothing for you, Wilfrid," he went on. "Stay here if you wish, but give me the book."

"What does he say?" asked Deusdedi.

Wilfrid thought quickly, hoping that none of Deusdedi's men could understand Anglisc.

"He has told me to steal a book from Eugenius' library," Wilfrid said. "He promised if I did that, he would release me."

Deusdedi scowled.

"A book, you say?"

"A rare book indeed. It would fetch a high price in Albion."

Deusdedi held his gaze as if gauging the truth of what Wilfrid said.

"And you agreed to this?" Eugenius asked.

"I feared for my life, lord," replied Wilfrid. "Beobrand is so full of rage. He kills all who refuse him."

"But why steal it?" asked Deusdedi. "There are many who would sell books in Roma."

Wilfrid glanced at Beobrand, unsure how to answer.

"Who can understand the mind of such a barbarian?" he said at last.

Deusdedi contemplated what Wilfrid had told him. He glanced at Eugenius, who shrugged. He was evidently unnerved, but deferred to the man from Ravenna. Beobrand was shouting again now, his temper rising as he demanded Wilfrid bring out the book.

"I would speak with the man," Deusdedi said. "Wait here." On a whispered command from Deusdedi, his two burly bodyguards moved close to Wilfrid, each grasping hold of an arm.

Wilfrid could barely breathe as he watched the line of guards part. Deusdedi stepped out to converse with Beobrand. Eugenius remained on the steps beside Wilfrid, awkwardly watching.

"Lord Beobrand," Deusdedi said. "It would seem each time we meet you are angry. You should seek the peace of the Lord God Jesu Christ in your heart."

Beobrand pulled Lucifrido forward and Wilfrid's heart sank. The man from Sutri would interpret the words between Beobrand and Deusdedi, and all would be lost. What a fool he had been to believe Deusdedi being here was a sign from God. Now Wilfrid would not be able to put into practice the plan he had thought of all that long day.

Lucifrido whispered to Beobrand. The Bernician thegn replied and just as Wilfrid had known he would, Lucifrido spoke his words in Latin to Deusdedi.

"Lord Beobrand says he has good reason to be angry with Wilfrid. He cares nothing for God and His peace. He just wants what Wilfrid has promised him."

"And what would that be?" Deusdedi asked.

"A book," Beobrand replied, speaking through Lucifrido. His tone was sombre. "If he does not give us this tome, someone will die."

Deusdedi looked back at Wilfrid and Eugenius with a raised eyebrow.

"Nobody will die today," he said to Beobrand. "And you will not get the book you seek. Wilfrid tells me you are soon to leave Roma. I would advise you do so as soon as possible and to forget about Wilfrid and this book."

"You do not understand," said Beobrand sharply. "Wilfrid is a liar."

"I understand well enough," retorted Deusdedi. "You are a violent pagan who wishes to steal holy artefacts from the Church. Wilfrid has told me the truth."

On hearing Lucifrido's translation of Deusdedi's words, Beobrand's face clouded.

"Whatever Wilfrid has said to you," he growled, "he is lying."

Lucifrido interpreted and Beobrand continued, furiously cursing Wilfrid for a liar and a nithing.

Deusdedi held up a hand for Beobrand to stop speaking before Lucifrido had a chance to translate.

"Tell your master," he said imperiously, "that I am in Roma on business of the Exarchatus of Ravenna and the Patriarch of Constantinopolis. I do not have time to speak to pagan *barbaroi*." Lucifrido began to interpret the emissary's words, but Deusdedi silenced him with a gesture. "No, I will finish. I am no longer conversing with this man. Have him know that Wilfrid is under my protection. I have pressing matters to attend to and enemies enough in Roma, but if I see him again, your master will be added to that list."

Wilfrid could not prevent himself from grinning at Deusdedi's words. Once more he was convinced that God had placed the man here just for this purpose; so that he might escape from Beobrand and keep the book. He offered up a prayer of thanks and begged forgiveness for his momentary lack of faith.

Deusdedi did not wait for Lucifrido to finish translating.

Stepping back through the lines of his guards, he hissed at their captain: "Do not let them pass. If they are not gone soon, bring the rest of the men and disperse them with force."

The massively muscled bodyguards moved away from Wilfrid. Deusdedi placed a hand on his shoulder and, turning him towards the steps, together they climbed up to the entrance to the building.

"Now, young Wilfrid," he said, "tell me of this book."

"Yes," added Eugenius, "I would hear which of my books lord Beobrand wished to steal."

Before Wilfrid could answer, Beobrand's booming voice carried over the sounds of the men and horses in the courtyard.

"If something happens to Coenred," he bellowed, "it won't matter who you hide behind, Wilfrid. I will find you and you will pay."

Emboldened by Deusdedi and Eugenius standing either side of him, and the score of armed men between Beobrand and the steps, Wilfrid turned back to face the tall thegn.

"You know how to rescue Coenred, lord Beobrand," he said. "There is no reason now to give up the book."

"If he dies," Beobrand spat, "keeping the book will be the least of your concerns." His mutilated hand gripped the hilt of his great sword so hard that the knuckles showed white, and the cold fury in his blue eyes made Wilfrid flinch.

"You would not dare harm me," he said. "You gave your oath."

Beobrand's glare did not waver. There was loathing in that stare and Wilfrid wondered whether he had miscalculated.

"An oath can be broken," Beobrand said, his voice quieter now, but still carrying easily to Wilfrid.

"And so can necks," shouted Eadgard, his angry voice as sudden and loud as thunder.

Chapter 33

Beobrand stretched and rolled his head to loosen the tension in his neck. His bones crackled and crunched loudly. He glanced to his left and could just make out the shape of Cynan in the darkness. To his right, Eadgard stood huge and motionless in the shadows, like one of Roma's statues. All of the men were still and silent. None of them looked in Beobrand's direction. Evidently the sound of his grinding bones was quiet outside of his own head.

Beobrand looked up at the sky. The clouds above the colossal *amphitheatrum* were tattered and torn. The thick canopy of the last weeks had burnt away in the warm day, but if what Stoldo had told them was true, the *hypogaeum* would still be flooded.

Cynan leaned in close.

"There is no movement," he said, his voice barely audible. "How much longer should we wait?"

Beobrand gauged the position of the moon.

"Soon," he hissed.

The plan was a simple one, but it was fraught with danger. They were relying on information given to them by the murky character Stoldo. They did not know the layout of the *hypogaeum*, the disposition of their enemies, or even if the place they planned to attack was truly where Coenred was being held.

So much could go wrong and once again Beobrand felt his ire rising at Wilfrid's betrayal that had forced him into this action.

Eadgard had repeated over and over as they'd made their way back to the Lateran Palace that they should have killed the novice when they'd had a chance. Beobrand understood his anger, but in the end he had snapped at the axeman to keep his thoughts to himself. They needed to concentrate on rescuing Coenred. The time for recriminations and vengeance would come, but now, in the warm Roman night, they needed to marshal all their powers. There was no room for dwelling on Wilfrid's duplicity.

There had been a dreadful moment standing before Deusdedi's guards when Beobrand had thought he would not be able to contain Eadgard, such was the man's fury. Beobrand did not blame him. He himself felt the powerful urge to draw Nægling and throw himself at the armoured men, to fight his way to Wilfrid. Woden knew he would have tried it in his youth. Even now he had been tempted. They were outnumbered, but the Black Shields might have been able to cut their way through. But for what? They would suffer losses against so many armoured foe-men and no doubt Wilfrid would hide within the stone walls of Eugenius' hall. They still would not have the book to exchange for Coenred's life.

In the end Beobrand had ordered Grindan to placate his brother. He was the only one of them who could tame the huge axeman when he was lost to the battle frenzy. Grindan had placed a light hand on Eadgard's shoulder and whispered to him. Beobrand had no idea what Grindan said, but Eadgard listened to his brother and slowly, he relaxed.

As they'd ridden back to Martinus' palace, Beobrand had discussed their options with Cynan and Lucifrido.

"If what Stoldo has told us is true," Cynan said, "we could await in ambush. We know where this Carnifex is holding Coenred. To meet us at the agreed place for the exchange, they will need to bring him out before dawn. It would be easier to take them in the street than in Lutozzo's tunnels."

"We must pray that Stoldo has sold us gold and not turds," said Beobrand. "If not, Coenred is doomed. And that thought I cannot abide."

"Even if what he gave us is the truth," Grindan said, nudging his horse closer as they rode along the stone-covered street, "waiting till they leave for the exchange surely puts Coenred at more risk."

Lucifrido nodded. He had spoken little since the confrontation with Wilfrid and Deusdedi. In the red glow of the setting sun, his face looked haggard and tired. He had not smiled for a long time.

"Grindan is right," Lucifrido said. "We know Carnifex is vicious and not a patient man. And what if Lutozzo had men watching us? He might soon learn that we do not have the book."

They had talked it over for some time, and while there was no way to know whether he had made the right decision, in the end, as the red orb of the sun slid behind the hills in the west, Beobrand's mind was made up.

He bit his lip as he stared at the dark building in front of them. He had led men into battle countless times, but he would never grow used to the feeling of fear before an engagement. He had no qualms risking his own life. The gods knew he should have died many times before. It was the weight of responsibility for the good men who had placed their trust in him that filled him with anxiety. Men who had sworn oaths of loyalty and would follow him into the jaws of death itself if he gave the command.

He looked at the warriors clustered around him. The moon shadow was dark in the arched gateway of the crumbling wall where they hid. He could barely make out the seven figures, but he could well imagine them, armoured and stern-faced, as he had last seen them riding through the night-time streets of the *Disabitato*. These men, whose lives he risked, did so willingly, and he loved them for it. They were brave men, hardened in battle. Men who would stand by his side and give their lives if called upon, as he would give his life for them. These were his Black Shields, his comitatus, and he knew their worth.

All save Lucifrido.

He was still unsure about the man from Sutri. And yet there was nothing for it now. Lucifrido could speak the language and knew the ways of the people of Roma. Beobrand just hoped he had not made a mistake in taking Lucifrido at his word.

He also hoped that eight men would prove enough. He knew his Black Shields would acquit themselves well if it came to a fight, but perhaps he should not have been so hasty in rejecting Baducing's offer of aid.

Shortly after dark, they had armed themselves and ridden to the villa where Baducing was residing. When Beobrand had told him what had happened to Coenred and of Wilfrid's subsequent betrayal, Baducing had been incensed.

"After everything that happened in Frankia," he said, "I should not be surprised by Wilfrid's actions. But at each turn he seems to try to outdo himself. He was difficult to like before, yet still I forgave him." He punched his meaty right fist into the palm of his left hand. "This is unforgivable."

Beobrand was gladdened to see Baducing's reaction. He liked the man. Though of a similar age to Wilfrid, and as interested in reading and the word of God, the two men were as different to each other as a rat is to a boar.

"I thought your priests preached forgiveness," said Beobrand.

"They do indeed," said Baducing with a sigh. "And God is love, and Christ spoke of offering the other cheek when slapped." He held out his large hands and shrugged. "But I am just a man, and a sinner. God can forgive Wilfrid. I will not."

Eadgard had grinned savagely to hear the stocky monk's words.

"You can stand behind me when the time for revenge comes," he growled. "I am first in that long line."

"I will leave the vengeance to you, my friend," Baducing said. "I have no love for Wilfrid, but I am still a Christian."

"We can decide who does what to Wilfrid later," Beobrand said.

"Of course," replied Baducing, taking in the men sweating in their byrnies, their swords hanging from baldrics and belts. "It is late and you are bedecked as for war. What is it you need of me?"

When he heard their plan, Baducing offered to join them on the assault.

"I would willingly take up a sword to help Coenred," he said. "And I am sure Aculf and my father's gesithas feel the same way."

Aculf nodded.

"We would stand with you, lord Beobrand," he said, grinning. "And gladly. We have not had a good fight since coming to Roma."

"I thank you both," said Beobrand, "but I hope it will not come to that. You plan to remain in Roma, but if we live, tomorrow we will leave. If you have fought against the likes of Lutozzo, your lives will be as good as worthless in the city."

"We are not afraid," gnarred Aculf, raising himself up to his full height and thrusting out his chin so his jutting beard bristled.

"I would never think you craven, Aculf," said Beobrand, "and if the need arises, I will call on your sword. But I would ask something else of you."

And so it was that they had ridden through the abandoned thoroughfares of the city, the sound of their horses' hooves echoing from the cobbles and dressed stones of the streets. They halted some way from the vast shadowy presence of the *amphitheatrum* in a large secluded area Lucifrido knew. Cattle often grazed there and it stank of cow shit. The recent rain had left the earth marshy and flies flitted about the men's faces as they dismounted. The warriors swatted at the insects and Aculf grumbled about being left to wait in a dung heap. But they did not dare take their mounts any closer to their destination for fear that the sound of their hooves might reach any guards posted outside.

Baducing gripped Beobrand's forearm before he slipped into the night.

"Godspeed," Baducing whispered. "I will pray for you."

"Pray for Coenred," replied Beobrand.

Aculf clapped him on the shoulder.

"Good luck," he said. "You know where we are if you need us."

Beobrand grasped his arm in the warrior grip.

"Keep the horses safe and be ready to ride," he said.

Beobrand rubbed at his eyes. They were gritty from lack of sleep, but he knew that even if he had been fully rested, he would have been unable to make out any of the details of the plain timber door nestled in the wall some fifty paces ahead of them. He drew in a long breath of the warm night air. The scent of wet earth, not yet dry after the previous night's downpour, lingered beneath the arch. It reminded him of the rich loam of his land on the banks of the Tuidi. His throat was dry and he wished he had thought to bring a skin of water or wine. Unbidden, he thought of Bassus. His old friend would tell him it mattered not what he wished for, only what lay ahead. Glancing up at the sky, he saw the moon had slid across the star-dappled dome of the heavens. Dawn would light the sky in the east soon.

He touched Cynan lightly on the shoulder.

"It is time," he whispered. "You know what you have to do."

Cynan nodded, pulling his dark cloak about him and drawing

it over his fair hair so that when he stepped out from the shelter of the archway he was barely more noticeable than a shade. Lucifrido made to follow the Waelisc man. Beobrand caught his arm, holding him back.

"My trust has been betrayed much of late," Beobrand hissed. "Do not make me regret this."

"I have given you my word, lord," replied Lucifrido, and Beobrand fancied he saw the faint glimmer of the man's familiar grin in the dark. "Do not worry about me."

Beobrand released him. It was easy for Lucifrido to speak those words. If he knew how Beobrand worried, he would not have uttered them so blithely. Beobrand watched the two men move silently across the open ground before the wall and the buildings that loomed behind it. The huge bulk of the arena soared in the west, ominous and dark, as vast as a mountain. Soon the sun would rise, illuminating those towering curved walls and their endless arches. But now was the darkest, stillest time of night, when spirits and nihtgengas stalked the land.

Beobrand touched his Thunor's hammer amulet and peered into the gloom, hoping to see something of Lucifrido and Cynan's progress. For a time he saw nothing. He did not breathe. He could sense the tension in the men either side of him. This was the moment of truth. If Stoldo had lied to them, or if his information was wrong, coming here might well prove to be a disastrous decision.

A dog barked in the night, startling Beobrand. The animal barked a couple more times and then was silent. Beobrand could see little in the darkness. He half-imagined the shadows of the men passing between two trees, but then there was nothing.

Was it his imagination that conjured the faint sound of a discreet knock on a timber door? He blinked and opened his eyes as wide as he could, willing them to better see into the gloom. Still not breathing, he strained to hear any sound.

A sudden sliver of light, brilliant in the total darkness of the pre-dawn, cut into the wall across the road. The door had been opened and Beobrand bit his lip. Stoldo had told Cynan and Lucifrido of this place, a large building complex just to the east of the *amphitheatrum*. Once, he said, centuries before, it had been where the men who fought in the arena, the *gladiatores*, had trained and lived. There were tunnels that ran beneath the road all the way into the labyrinth of rooms and corridors beneath the arena. It was there that Stoldo said Lutozzo housed his prisoners, but in the winter, and when it rained hard, those subterranean rooms and tunnels, known as the *hypogaeum*, flooded. At such times, any prisoners held there would be brought back into the smaller compound.

Stoldo had told them the secret words that would allow the door to that compound to be opened. How he had come by that knowledge, Beobrand did not know, he just prayed to Woden and all the gods that the words were correct; that they had not been changed since Stoldo heard of them.

For several heartbeats the thin slice of light spilling into the silent street did not waver. Beobrand's lungs began to burn, but he dared not breathe for fear of giving away their position or of missing the slightest sound that might indicate what was happening.

The light grew brighter momentarily as the door opened wide, and then, as quickly as it had come, it was gone and the night was dark once more. The only light that remained was the silver gleam of the moon and the after-image left in Beobrand's eyes by the lamp beyond the door.

"By Tiw's cock," whispered Eadgard, "what's happening?"

"Silence," hissed Beobrand. He recognised the pent-up anxiety in the axeman's voice. Forcing himself to breathe, Beobrand let out a long breath and filled his lungs slowly, so as to remain silent.

The scratch of a stone on the cobbles made him start and an instant later a dark figure loomed out of the night. Without knowing he had moved, Beobrand's antler-hilted seax was in his hand and he readied himself to strike.

"It seems Stoldo sold us the truth," Cynan said, pulling his cloak back from his head. "And perhaps we can trust Lucifrido, for he killed one of the guards. There were two of them. We made little noise."

"Good work," whispered Beobrand, letting out a great sigh of relief. The tension that had built up within him was released and he rose up from his hiding place. "There will be more men who need killing this night, I think. Come, there is no time to waste. Let us free Coenred."

As silent and deadly as night-walkers in a mead-hall tale, Beobrand and his gesithas hurried across the dark road. Cynan pulled the door open and, drawing their weapons, the warriors stepped into Lutozzo's lair.

Chapter 34

Cynan closed the door quietly behind them, shutting out the night. Lucifrido stepped out of the small guardroom and offered him a curt nod. Behind him Cynan could see the bodies of the guards they had killed. When the moment for action had come, Lucifrido's coolness had impressed him.

They had waited what seemed an eternity after they had knocked. Cynan had barely been able to breathe. His blood had rushed in his ears, loud in the stillness of the night. He had been about to turn back, convinced that Stoldo had misled them, when a small grille had opened and a voice demanded the password.

Lucifrido had whispered the words Stoldo had given them. Moments later the door had been opened. Lucifrido had entered and waited for Cynan to make his way inside, just as they had agreed. The instant they were both through the door, Lucifrido had struck. The man's speed had surprised Cynan, even though he had been expecting the attack. Before he was able to pull his own seax from beneath his cloak, Lucifrido had placed a hand over the mouth of one guard and driven a long knife into his heart.

The second guard had opened his mouth, ready to scream out in alarm when Cynan had cut his throat. Cynan was strong and fast, and he had made the motion instinctively, his nervous energy lending the cut a savage power. The sharp steel of his seax sliced deep into the man's throat, cutting through flesh, sinews and arteries, silencing him before he could cry for help. The guard let out a hissing moan as his windpipe was severed. Hot blood spurted, splashing Cynan's face and hands.

There was a dark puddle of the man's blood on the flagstones behind the door. Cynan stepped over it, but saw that some of the others had left dark footprints where they had walked through the blood. A smeared crimson trail led into the guardroom where Lucifrido had dragged the guards' corpses while Cynan had gone to fetch the others. A small oil lamp rested on a table in the guardroom. The blood was vibrant in its dim light. After the blackness of the night outside, the lamplight had at first appeared blazingly bright, but in truth it was only the glow of a single flame. Still, even that pale light showed clearly where the guard's blood had sprayed and spattered the wall and pooled on the ground.

Beobrand followed Cynan's gaze.

"We will be gone before anyone sees it," he whispered. "Let's move."

Using his cloak to wipe the blood from his face, Cynan stepped next to Beobrand. Lucifrido joined them. Cynan allowed him to pass. They had discussed what they would do once they were inside, and it had been agreed that Lucifrido would lead the way. Stoldo had told him directly of the layout and he had the advantage of understanding the language if someone should attempt to address them.

Lucifrido held up a hand for them to wait. He stood still for a couple of heartbeats, taking in the courtyard before them. There was no illumination here, apart from the faint lamp light emanating from the guardroom. There were several buildings in the compound and Cynan tried to make sense of them and to remember what Stoldo had told them. Before he was certain of which door they should approach, Lucifrido, clearly having made his decision, hurried unerringly across the open space. Cynan and the others followed. The steel of their blades glimmered in the silver moonlight. None of them spoke. Cynan knew they were moving as stealthily as they were able, but still, the warriors' shuffling feet and heavy breathing sounded terribly loud to his ears.

Lucifrido waited until they had all crossed the courtyard, then opened the door. Its hinges squealed and the solid timber scraped loudly against the stone floor. Cynan's breath caught and none of them moved for a time, listening to the night for any indication they had been heard.

Silence.

With a sigh, Cynan followed Lucifrido into the building. The rest of them followed and pulled the door closed behind them. Once again it grated and squeaked loudly. Cynan expected someone to call out, for the alarm to be raised. Perhaps Baducing's prayers were working though, for the compound remained quiet.

There was another oil lamp in a niche on the wall ahead of them. Lucifrido picked it up carefully and handed it to Ingwald. The bald-headed warrior's face was dour and hard in the flame's flicker. He said nothing, but nodded his understanding. They needed light to guide their way, but Lucifrido and Cynan at the front of the group needed their hands free. Holding the lamp high, Ingwald signalled for them to continue.

Cynan saw that Lucifrido had chosen the door correctly. And Stoldo's information had once again proved accurate. Just as he had described it, a long passageway led to stone steps that descended into the earth.

They made their way to the steps, moving as quietly as possible. Their steps echoed and rasped on the stones of the corridor. The opening in the ground yawned before them and the steps fell into darkness.

Gingerly, Lucifrido began to descend. Cynan could sense the man's nervousness. He shared it. Should they be detected now, they could be cut off from escape, trapped in the very subterranean prison where they believed Coenred was being held. He glanced at Beobrand and saw nothing but steely determination on his hlaford's features. Taking a deep breath, he followed Lucifrido down, increasingly certain that at any moment they would be discovered.

But still their luck held. The old gods smiled on them, or perhaps God had listened to Baducing and wished for His servant Coenred to be freed from captivity. No alarm sounded and all eight men reached the bottom of the steps without incident.

They found themselves in a tunnel, wide enough for two men to walk side by side. It stretched off into the distance in the direction of the arena, just as Stoldo had told them it would. Cynan could still barely believe the man had not sought to dupe them.

The tunnel's ceiling was arched and higher than the height of any man. Noticeably cooler here than outside, the air was dank and humid. The floor was formed of dressed stone, but in places large puddles hid the flagstones. The light from the lamp danced on the dark water of the partially flooded tunnel.

For some distance, the tunnel was completely dark, but thirty or forty paces away another lamp emanated a halo of light, illuminating a small portion of the long passage. A man stood in that pool of light. As if startled from a doze, he jerked upright, then called out something. He did not shout, but his voice was loud, amplified by the stone throat of the tunnel.

Lucifrido did not hesitate. He began walking towards the man, replying to him as he went. Splashing through the puddles, he did not slow his approach. After a moment of indecision, Cynan, Beobrand and the others set off after Lucifrido. Ingwald's lamp did little to illuminate the man from Sutri now as he was some way ahead of them, but Cynan could see Lucifrido clearly silhouetted against the light of the guard's lamp.

He was almost on him and the guard shouted a challenge. There was an edge to his voice now. Lucifrido must have heard it too, for he sprang forward. The two men grappled as Cynan and Beobrand sprinted forward. Their footsteps echoed loudly in the tunnel, as did the guard's shouts of alarm.

An instant later he was silenced as Beobrand plunged his seax into the man's kidneys. The guard arched his back and gasped. Beobrand clamped his hand over the man's mouth and lowered him down where his blood mingled with the water on the partly flooded floor.

There was no other sign of anyone in the tunnel, but they had made a lot of noise. Beobrand held up his half-hand for them all to be still. They stood, unmoving and listening for several heartbeats. The flames of the lamps flickered, reflecting from the pools of water that soaked their feet and making the warriors' shadows writhe and dance on the damp walls.

To Cynan's amazement no alarm came. No cry echoed in the night. No clanging bell. No hastily sounded horn.

"Beo," said a small voice in the sudden hush, "is that you?" The voice was muffled, but recognisable enough.

Cynan's heart leapt and he offered up his own prayer of thanks to whatever god might listen.

"Coenred," hissed Beobrand, stepping over the guard he had killed.

A solid door of timber bound with strips of iron was set into the wall. The tunnel beyond led off into darkness. They were fortunate it had rained, flooding the *hypogaeum*. Cynan could not imagine they would have been able to find their friend so easily if they'd needed to search the labyrinth of tunnels and chambers beneath the amphitheatre that Stoldo had described.

Dragging aside the locking bar, Beobrand pushed the door

open. The cell beyond was darker than a moonless night and the stench that rolled out of the darkness made Cynan's guts churn. It was worse than a midden in the height of summer. The stink of stagnant water, night soil and rotting vegetation swirled in the air. Cynan's gorge rose, and he spat.

But Beobrand did not pause.

"Raise up that light," he hissed and stepped into the cell.

The room was lower than the tunnel and Beobrand's feet splashed into ankle-deep water. A pale figure was crouched in a far corner of the cell and Cynan recognised Coenred's tonsured head and slender frame.

"I prayed that you would come for me," Coenred said, his voice cracking with emotion. "But my faith is weak. I had begun to give up hope. I thought I might become another martyr down here in my very own catacomb."

"You will not be dying this night," Beobrand said.

Coenred clutched Beobrand's arm with sudden ferocity.

"How does Marsiglio fare?"

"He was badly wounded, my friend," replied Beobrand. "But he yet lives."

"Praise the Lord," Coenred said. "I prayed for him too."

"Your god has been busy," whispered Cynan. "But we cannot tarry here."

Coenred squinted into the lamplight.

"Cynan too," he said. "All of you? Thank you, my friends. Thank you for coming for me." He began to weep, pitiful sobs wracking his body.

"Hush now," said Beobrand, pulling him to his feet. "You can thank us later. There is no time to talk. We must leave before we are discovered."

Coenred sagged against him and it was only then, as the light fell on him, that Cynan noticed the blood on Coenred's face and the stained bandage on his left hand.

"What did they do to you?" asked Beobrand, holding the monk at arm's length and staring at him in the dim light. The thegn drew in a sharp breath. By the light from Ingwald's lamp that shone into the noisome cell, Cynan saw that the dried blood smearing Coenred's cheek came from where his left ear had once been. In its stead there was now a scabbed, bloody orifice.

Coenred lifted his bandaged hand tentatively to the ruin of his ear. The bandage was dark with blood. From the shape of the hand beneath the cloth Cynan guessed that at least one of the monk's fingers had been removed.

"It could have been worse," said Coenred, sniffing back his tears. "There is one among my captors who calls himself Carnifex. Gnaeus Pompeius Magnus was given the same name, you know? It means the butcher, or executioner. The name suits him well, I would say." He shuddered. "I am glad you came now so that I do not have to find out what part of me he would slice off next."

Deep in the back of his throat, Beobrand made a sound more animal than human.

"I will kill him," he said. "I will feed this Carnifex his own entrails. We shall see how the butcher likes being butchered."

"Just get me out of here, Beo," whispered Coenred. "Leave the punishments to God this once."

"He's right, lord," said Cynan. "We must go. Can you walk, Coenred?"

"If it means leaving this place," said Coenred with a weak smile, "I will even find the strength to run."

"For now," said Beobrand, "we walk. And pray to your God that we are not seen or heard. But know this, if that whoreson Carnifex should show his face, I will take his life."

Bleddyn allowed Coenred to lean on him, and they made their way along the wet tunnel back towards the steps. None of them spoke and Cynan saw the shock on their faces at the state in which they had found Coenred. The monk was pale and weak from his ordeals, but he had a resolute strength of character they all admired as he stumbled along beside Bleddyn without complaint.

They climbed the steps cautiously, listening for any sign they might have been discovered, but as they reached the corridor above, it was still devoid of movement; as still as a tomb. Cynan let out a long breath. They moved quickly down the corridor towards the door. When they reached it, Ingwald blew out the lamp's flame and placed the lamp on the ground.

"Ready?" Beobrand hissed.

Cynan lifted his seax and nodded. He was not sure that Beobrand could see him in the gloom, but before he could speak, the thegn of Ubbanford pushed the door open with a scraping of timber on stone and the squeal of iron hinges. Outside, the thin light from the moon lit part of the courtyard. The other half was cloaked in impenetrable shadow.

Pale lamplight still oozed from the guardroom. But there was no movement in the yard. No shout. No alarm.

"Come," hissed Beobrand, ushering them out of the door. If Beobrand was as incredulous as Cynan that they had not been discovered, he did not pause to contemplate their good fortune. Hurrying across the courtyard, they made it to the door by the guardroom. The moment that Bleddyn and Coenred reached them, Beobrand pushed the door open and they stepped out of Lutozzo's lair and into the empty street.

Cynan looked up at the sky. Dawn was still some way off, but the sky was already paling, faintly lighting the soaring arches of the amphitheatre.

"We have horses nearby," Beobrand whispered to Coenred. "Not far now. We will be away from here soon."

They started to make their way across the street. Cynan let

out a long sigh. They had done it. Beobrand always loathed being called lucky, but how else could such a feat be explained?

"I did not believe we could do this, lord," Cynan whispered, as they hurried across the cobbled road.

Beobrand did not pause.

"Nor I, truth be told," he said.

And in that moment, as if to remind them of the folly of men and how the gods loved chaos, a dozen warriors, the naked steel of their swords gleaming softly, stepped out of the shadows and blocked their path.

Chapter 35

"Protect Coenred," Beobrand said to Cynan and Bleddyn. "We have not come so far only to lose him now. When the fighting starts, try to get to the horses."

Trusting the two Waelisc men to keep the monk safe, Beobrand moved to stand in front of them. Without needing to be prompted, the rest of the warriors fell into position either side of him. Grindan stood at his right, where Cynan would usually stand in a shieldwall. It was a place of trust and honour, for the man there would use his shield to protect his lord's flank. But the Black Shields had not come prepared for a shieldwall. Their shields were with the horses in the marshy field, guarded by Baducing, Aculf and his warriors.

Beside Grindan towered his brother, Eadgard, his massive axe held ready in his meaty fists. Next to him, at the far end of the line, stood Halinard. He was not as strong as Eadgard, or as fast as Grindan, but he was solid and deadly in battle.

To Beobrand's surprise, Lucifrido stepped next to him to take the position to his left. Ingwald completed the short line of warriors. Beobrand would rather have had one of his gesithas at his side, someone he had trained with and fought beside in countless battles and skirmishes, but Ingwald knew what he was about and Beobrand trusted him at the end of the line. Besides, there was no time to reorder his meagre force. The shadowy figures who confronted them were walking forward.

Beobrand studied them in the gloom. There was little light, but he could make out enough to see that the dozen men, like the warriors from Albion, did not carry shields. However, his gesithas wore their iron byrnies. They had faced much worse odds than these and been victorious. Beobrand was confident they would be able to fight their way out of this. But they would have to be fast. Coenred's escape and the dead guards they had left behind were sure to be discovered soon. When that happened, they would have Lutozzo's men at their rear as well as whoever these assailants were blocking their way.

"Who are they?" Beobrand whispered. He could see few details in the darkness.

As if in answer to his question one of the men spoke. His tone was harsh and though Beobrand could still not make out his face, the man's hatred dripped from his every word like venom from a viper's fangs. There was something familiar about the voice, but Beobrand could not place it.

"It is Agiperto," Lucifrido said.

"Agiperto?" asked Beobrand.

"You killed his son in the hills near Sutri."

Instantly Beobrand recalled the grief-stricken anger of the man who had confronted him at Tanualdo's villa. He had no idea how the man came to be here, in Roma's warm night, in Lutozzo's territory, but this could be no chance meeting.

Agiperto stepped forward and with the searing loathing Beobrand remembered from Sutri, he bellowed, rending the stillness of the night asunder with his fury. Lutozzo translated, muttering the words quickly, his nervousness clear in the wavering of his voice.

"He says when you killed his son, you killed part of him. He cannot allow you to leave these lands with your life when you have taken his."

A dog, perhaps the same animal they had heard earlier, barked in the darkness. Beobrand cursed. Agiperto's shouts would carry far. But perhaps it was not too late. Maybe he could yet quieten him.

"Tell him I am sorry for his grief," he said, "but his son attacked us. Tell him I am a father too. I understand his pain. Let us leave this place and we can discuss a blood-price for his son."

When he heard the meaning of Beobrand's words translated by Lucifrido, Agiperto spat at Beobrand, then hissed a reply so full of spite and bitterness, it needed no translation. Agiperto stepped back and his men closed ranks before him, raising their weapons.

In the distance, behind Beobrand, a cry of alarm came from Lutozzo's compound. A moment later, a clanging bell began to sound, its metallic ring echoing back from the stone walls of the *amphitheatrum*. This was the sound they had dreaded for so long. Beobrand dragged Nægling from its scabbard. He could not allow them to be surrounded by two enemies.

"There is no more time," he said, raising his voice against the clangour that now reverberated in the shadowed street. "We will break these whoresons and make our way to the horses. Black Shields, with me!"

Springing forward, Nægling raised high, Beobrand threw himself at the centre of the enemy line. He was glad then of all the time they had spent training their bodies and honing their battle-skill, for his gesithas came with him. To his amazement, even Lucifrido, who had never trained with them, fell into step, sword-blade gleaming as he shouted something incomprehensible.

Just before they crashed into the rank of Agiperto's warriors, a bright light flared behind Beobrand. He did not have time to look back, but from the shouts of challenge and anger, he knew the door to Lutozzo's compound had been flung open and more men were tumbling out onto the road. Those men must have come with torches, for the night was suddenly lit by the red glow of flames. In that flash of firelight, Beobrand saw details of the large man before him. His shoulders were broad and heavily muscled, his nose twisted and his face scarred. In his gnarled hands the ugly man held a great cudgel.

"Vico!" shouted Ingwald in recognition.

So that was how Agiperto had known where to find them. Vico was Stoldo's man and either he had told Agiperto, or perhaps Stoldo himself had betrayed them. Whatever the truth, there was no time to dwell on it. How these men came to stand before him was of no significance. All that mattered was that they threatened him and his men, and they stood in the way of Coenred's escape from his terrible ordeal. Ever since seeing Coenred's blood-stained face and hand, and hearing of the torments he had been forced to endure, Beobrand had wanted to kill those responsible. Now he allowed the fury that had simmered within him to bubble over.

Letting out a terrible roar, Beobrand swung his sword down. He put all his anger into that blow, already anticipating how the blade would thrum as it split the man's skull. And yet Nægling's steel did not slice into his enemy's head. With surprising speed and skill, the burly man before him sidestepped and parried the powerful blow with his club. Nægling's blade gouged the wood, throwing splinters into the air. Beobrand felt the force of the blow and his forearm throbbed. He cursed his arrogance. He had thought Vico's wooden weapon to be unwieldy, no match for his fine sword. Expecting an easy kill, he now found himself off-balance and vulnerable.

Swinging the cudgel as though it weighed nothing, Vico aimed a blow at Beobrand's head. Overextended as he was, Beobrand barely saw the attack coming. He sensed more than registered the impending blow, his years of experience lending him speed and agility. Throwing himself to the side, the club whistled past his ear and glanced off his left shoulder. Immediately, his left arm grew numb. Beobrand regained his balance quickly, dancing away from a backhanded swing of the club. He wished he had his shield. Beating Vico would have been easy then. As it was, Beobrand was glad the brute's club had not struck him a solid blow. If it had, byrnie or not, his bones would have surely been shattered. If that cudgel had hit his uncovered head, Beobrand knew he would certainly have been killed.

All around him his men were fighting. Lucifrido was holding his own against a wiry-looking man armed with a cleaver-like knife. Ingwald had managed to gut one of his opponents, causing the others to step back, wary of his flashing blade. Grindan was locked in a struggle against a thickset man with a dark beard. Beyond them, Eadgard was laying about him with his axe, scattering men while he bellowed at them.

"Come and taste death, you nithings!" he roared.

Already, a man lay dying at his feet. The metallic stink of blood and the sour stench of spilt guts and piss filled the warm darkness. These were the familiar smells and sounds of battle. Beobrand was dimly aware of approaching footsteps from behind. The light from the torches was growing brighter. In moments they would be surrounded. Beobrand could not see Halinard, and he wondered if the Frank had fallen. But there was no time to think about that.

Vico surged forward, sending another crushing blow towards his head. This time Beobrand was ready for it. Catching the strike on his sword's blade, he pushed the cudgel aside and aimed a savage kick at Vico's groin. It connected and Vico grunted. Doubling over, he staggered backwards.

Beobrand followed, meaning to dispatch him, but another enemy stepped into the breach. Beobrand registered the flicker of steel and without thought, he parried the blade with Nægling. Then, with a twist of his wrist, he swept the long sword into his opponent's face. The man collapsed, screaming and whimpering.

Beobrand risked a glance over his shoulder. At least half a dozen men had come out of Lutozzo's building. Some carried torches. All of them bore naked steel in their hands. Cynan and Bleddyn had already turned to face this new threat. Coenred swayed, unsteady on his feet, unarmed and unprotected.

Another man sprang forward to face Beobrand. He avoided the man's clumsy sword thrust, stabbing Nægling into his chest.

"Death for Woden!" Beobrand screamed, remembering the promise of sacrifice he had made to the father of the gods. They needed any help they might receive now. Their position was increasingly precarious.

Looking behind him again, he saw that the men coming from Lutozzo's compound had halted. Perhaps they were waiting for more men to join them, or maybe they were confused by the fighting they saw, unsure if either side was friend or foe. If they considered both Beobrand's warriors and Agiperto's men to be enemies, they might decide to wait out the fight and then slay whatever weakened force remained.

All around Beobrand was tumult now. Metal sang. Men screamed. Some whimpered and moaned; some, like Eadgard, driven mad with battle-lust, laughed. Beobrand controlled his own ire, allowing it to give him strength and speed, but holding its madness in check. He had given in to it momentarily and the aching pain in his left shoulder reminded him how close he had come to death as a result.

And Vico was still a dangerous opponent. Crimson-faced and spitting his fury at Beobrand, Stoldo's warrior hurried forward now, shouldering his comrades aside. Vico did not take his eyes off Beobrand, and his murderous intent was clear in that hate-filled gaze.

Beobrand stepped in to meet him. His shoulder throbbed from the earlier blow, but he had the measure of the man now. There was nothing to be gained from worrying about what else was happening around them. His men were all killers, trained in the art of war and adept at the task of killing. They would take care of themselves. For now, all he had to deal with was Vico.

"Death!" shouted Beobrand in his battle-voice, hoping that Woden would hear his cry and accept the offering of the slain.

Vico was shouting abuse, spittle flying from his snarling mouth. Beobrand did not comprehend the words, but the man's meaning was clear enough. Vico directed a huge swing of his club at Beobrand, but fast as he was, Beobrand was faster, and he was ready for him now. Avoiding the blow easily, he sent a thrust towards Vico's midriff. With a growl, Vico leapt back and the sword cut through nothing more than air. Pressing forward again, Vico attacked once more with the heavy club. It was splintered and jagged now, but Beobrand was still careful not to take the full weight of it on his blade. Such a hefty weapon might well snap even the best sword. Instead he deflected each strike, pushing the wood out of line and using his speed to avoid the strikes.

Each probed the other's defences, but could find no weakness. Beobrand was sweating profusely, his kirtle soaked beneath his iron-knit shirt. Both men were breathing heavily. Beobrand was aware of other men falling around them, and he sensed that his warriors were evening the odds, and still Vico stood before him.

Beobrand's frustration grew. They needed to move. To stay here would bring defeat and death to them all. Woden might well laugh to receive the blood of the Black Shields as his payment for allowing Coenred to be rescued, but Beobrand refused to allow that. It was not his wyrd to die this night!

Stamping forward, he sent a flurry of strikes at Vico, forcing the brawny man to parry and retreat, giving him no space to retaliate and counter-attack.

Without warning, a cry of anguish cut through Beobrand's resolve and focus. Coenred was screaming out in pain, or fear, or both.

Beobrand hesitated, turning instinctively to see what had befallen his friend. Before he had barely moved, Beobrand made to rectify his mistake. He could not drop his guard against one such as Vico. Beobrand returned his full attention to the cudgel-wielding warrior, but in that instant, he knew he was too late. Seizing on Beobrand's momentary lapse in concentration, Vico had sprung forward, splintered club swishing through the air.

Without thought, relying only on instinct and his innate speed, Beobrand flung himself backward. His sudden movement saved his skull from being shattered like an egg, but still he was not able to completely avoid Vico's blow. The stout oak of the club crashed against Beobrand's forehead. The night burst in a flare of light and Beobrand staggered back, to fall, stunned and bleeding, at Vico's feet.

Chapter 36

"Beobrand!" Coenred screamed.

He watched in shock as the thegn of Ubbanford collapsed onto the street's uneven stones. Coenred had been reciting the paternoster and the Twenty-Third Psalm over and over as the men fought, but he feared now that the Lord had forsaken him completely.

During his incarceration, while Carnifex had delighted in tormenting and torturing him, Coenred had prayed constantly for delivery. When Beobrand had opened the door to his cell, he had thanked God for his deliverance. The Almighty had listened to his ceaseless prayers and sent His instrument, Beobrand, to rescue him, to carry him out of that dank, pain-riddled darkness and back into the light.

When the men had stepped out of the shadows and the fighting had commenced, Coenred had felt his faith crumbling.

In the darkest moments in the cell, when his hand burnt with the agony of a finger that was no longer there, and the side of his head throbbed as he dabbed ineffectually at the ruin that had been his ear, he'd heard the deep chuckling of the malevolent spirit that had come to him in the forest in Langobardia. In an attempt to drive out the laughter of the foul thing, Coenred had prayed and prayed through his tears of pain and fear. In the end, whether his prayers had dispelled the evil thing, or it had merely been in his imagination, the only sound left in his underground prison was not laughter, but the gurgle of water trickling down the wet walls.

Now, as the men fought all about him, he wondered whether the malicious spirit had in fact taken hold of his soul in that dark forest. Perhaps it watched now from the darkness and would never release him until it dragged him down into the hell in which it dwelt.

Coenred was weak and dizzy. Even if he had been hale, he would not have fought. He was no warrior. But he would do whatever he could to help his friends. They had come for him, and he would at least offer whatever aid he could. He exhorted God to deliver them, breathlessly chanting prayers and liturgies.

When the men had rushed from Lutozzo's compound, Coenred's prayers had faltered. Yet he had rallied, persevering and lending his spiritual strength to his rescuers' blades. When he'd recognised the sneering face of the man who had so relished inflicting pain on him, Coenred's prayers had stuttered to a halt and he had let out an involuntary cry. His knees buckled and he almost collapsed at the thought Carnifex might once again take him into the dark and continue his devilish tortures.

It was this cry that had distracted Beobrand, and Coenred watched in dismay as the stocky man fighting the thegn smashed his hefty club into his friend's head. Cynan saw what had happened too and, with a shout, leapt over Beobrand's inert form to defend him.

Coenred dropped down beside Beobrand, reaching out a trembling hand to touch his cheek. Blood ran freely from a gash in Beobrand's forehead and his eyes were dazed, unfocused.

"Beobrand," Coenred said, stroking his cheek. Tears wetted his own face as he remembered how he had found Beobrand all those years before. The tall, fair-haired warrior had been wounded then too, delirious and barely conscious, covered in blood and half-blind. "I'm sorry," whispered Coenred. If Beobrand had not come for him, none of this would have happened. They had each saved the other's life several times over the years. Now it seemed Beobrand's famous luck had run out.

Above them, Cynan battled the man with the club. All around them the other warriors fought. But Coenred could not look away from his stricken friend. He would not. If they were to die here, he would be with Beobrand and they would die together. He wished Beobrand had found the peace of the love of Christ in his life, but he had never been interested in the Lord's teaching. At least he would die in the holy city of Roma. The tears flowing freely down his dirt-smeared cheeks, Coenred began to pray. He would continue to pray for Beobrand's soul until his dying breath. The fight surged and gyred around them, but Coenred did not stop praying.

His pleading words tumbled out of him, begging for God's mercy. Through the tears blurring his vision, Coenred began to imagine Beobrand's body was moving underneath his hands, but surely his friend could not have survived such a blow.

A moment later there could be no mistake. Jerking awake with a groan, Beobrand pushed himself up into a sitting position.

"What are you weeping for?" he asked. "I'm not dead yet." With his mutilated left hand, he wiped the blood from his eyes, wincing at the pain as his fingers brushed against the wound made by the cudgel.

Coenred sniffed back his tears with difficulty.

"Praise the Lord," he said.

"Praise him later," said Beobrand, surging to his feet. Snatching Nægling up from the cobbles where it had fallen, he scanned the fighting around them. Lucifrido and the Black Shields were locked in combat with Agiperto's men. All save Bleddyn, who waited, nervously watching the men who approached from Lutozzo's compound.

Beobrand took in the torch-lit figures until his gaze rested on Carnifex.

"Is that the man who hurt you?" he asked, his voice as sharp and unforgiving as flint.

Coenred could not speak, but he nodded. He had seen Beobrand in battle before, and he knew him to be a deadly warrior. And yet the transformation in him now took Coenred aback, such was the speed with which Beobrand changed, and the ferocity of his sudden rage. Heartbeats before, Beobrand had been stunned, barely conscious, and Coenred had believed him to be dead or dying. Now it seemed his ire had replenished his life-force and given him renewed power.

Screaming his battle-cry, Beobrand sprinted forward, scything his sword before him. Also taken aback by the thegn's rapid recovery, Bleddyn hesitated for an eye-blink, then, adding his voice to Beobrand's, he too charged at the gathering group of Lutozzo's men, leaving Coenred watching in amazement.

Beobrand and Bleddyn covered the ground quickly. Lutozzo's men had not expected the attack and were caught momentarily off guard. One lunged with a torch at Beobrand. Grabbing the man's wrist, Beobrand twisted it to one side and hacked down with his sword. The man fell. Without pause, Beobrand scooped up the burning brand in his left hand and continued on towards Carnifex.

Another man tried to halt him, but Beobrand prodded the flaming torch into his face, causing his assailant to reel away and into Bleddyn's path. The Waelisc warrior sliced viciously into the man's thigh, almost severing the leg, such was the force of his blow and the sharpness of his blade. Following Beobrand's example, he too snatched up the man's dropped torch, then kicked him in the face as he ran past.

The rest of Lutozzo's men were cautious now, wary of these death-dealers with their strange war-cry, blood-drenched swords and spark-flaring torches that drew patterns of light in the darkness as they swept them from side to side, ready to strike whoever was foolish enough to approach.

But Beobrand did not wait for anyone to draw close. With a huge roar, he threw himself at Carnifex. The torturer had perhaps believed himself safe behind the other warriors, but they had been killed with ease and now he cowered before Beobrand's wrath.

A warrior, armed with a long knife, leapt at Beobrand. Bleddyn cut him down. Beobrand seemed not to notice. His focus was on Carnifex. The torturer retreated away from him. His feet tangled with the legs of the man Bleddyn had dispatched, and he toppled to the ground. Carnifex stared up wide-eyed and frightened at the bloody-faced thegn of Bernicia. Bleddyn glowered at the rest of the men, daring them to attack. None were brave enough to face him.

Beobrand loomed over Carnifex. Without warning, the prostrate man drew a vicious-looking blade he'd had concealed from his sleeve and jabbed up at Beobrand. Coenred gasped at the man's speed, fearing he would wound Beobrand. But Beobrand was known as one of the fastest warriors in all of Albion. With the speed and grace of a cat, Beobrand stepped nimbly out of the dagger's reach and as fast as thought, he struck with his sword, severing Carnifex's hand. The torturer let out a howl of anguish. Beobrand stepped forward, stamping down savagely on his bleeding stump.

"You are lucky I do not have more time," he snarled. Carnifex stared up at him, terror and pain etched on his features. The man could not understand Beobrand's words, but from the horror in his eyes, Coenred was certain he knew that death had come for him, just as he had brought it to so many.

Beobrand spat at Carnifex, then brought his sword crashing down to split his skull. The torch light gleamed on the fresh blood, brains and shards of bone that tumbled onto the cobbles.

Coenred shuddered. Unbidden, the words of the paternoster rolled from his mouth. He knew it was wrong to be glad to see a man killed. But he was weak and he was a sinner, and he could not deny that seeing Carnifex slain brought him an unholy joy.

Beobrand stood panting and unmoving, staring down at the twitching body. But there were yet five other men behind Carnifex. And the bell was still sounding behind the compound wall.

"Come, lord," said Bleddyn, his voice tight with tension, "they will attack soon."

"Let them come," growled Beobrand, spitting again onto Carnifex's corpse.

Bleddyn eyed the men around them. If they rushed them together, Coenred thought they might not be able to hold. Behind him, the sounds of combat were as vicious as ever. For a moment, Coenred thought Beobrand would ignore Bleddyn, but then, slowly, he began moving back towards Coenred and the others.

Bleddyn and Beobrand retreated, keeping their eyes fixed on Lutozzo's men. As they reached Coenred, there was a change in the atmosphere of the conflict; it felt to Coenred like the moment lightning and rain had finally come after the storm had been brewing over Roma for days. But now it was not thunder that presaged the change, it was a bellowing cry of utter anguish.

The scream came from Eadgard, and as Coenred looked, he saw by the flickering light of the torches what had caused his distress. Grindan lay sprawled on the cobbles. The warrior's head had been stove in. White bone showed in the massive wound, and black blood pooled about Grindan's pallid face.

Coenred knew instantly that Eadgard's brother was dead. So,

it appeared, did Eadgard. He roared like a beast, swinging his axe with such mad abandon and fury that even his shield-brothers needed to leap away from him. If Beobrand's rage-fuelled attack had shocked Coenred, it was as nothing when compared to Eadgard's ferocious fury. Screaming as loudly as a gale's howl in a winter's storm, Eadgard cut down two men, before the others managed to retreat out of his reach.

In that same moment, the sound of hoofbeats on stone reached Coenred. The shadows of several riders and many horses came into view.

Cynan glanced in that direction.

"It is Baducing," he said, his eyes as keen as ever.

Agiperto still had seven or eight men around him, including the heavily muscled, club-wielding Vico, who had somehow avoided death. Agiperto and his men fell back from Eadgard's furious attack, but they did not turn and flee.

Agiperto swept his gaze across Beobrand's men until he found Lucifrido. Pointing at him with the blade of his sword, Agiperto's lips pulled back in a snarl and he hissed something at the young man from Sutri. Coenred could not make out the words over the clanging bell, the hoofbeats and the shouts of approaching warriors.

Men were streaming from the door to Lutozzo's compound now. There were already a dozen of them on the street, with more joining their ranks. Beobrand looked from one group of men to the other, then at the horses galloping towards them.

"Eadgard!" he shouted. "To me."

The huge axeman either chose to ignore his lord, or did not hear him, lost as he was in grief and battle-fury. Shouting and spitting abuse, Eadgard swiped with his axe at the men before him.

Baducing, with Aculf and the rest of his men, rode up with a cacophonous clatter of hooves.

"I know you said to wait for you, lord Beobrand," Baducing said, "but I decided to disobey you this once."

"I forgive you," shouted Beobrand.

Grabbing Coenred's stained kirtle, Beobrand shoved him towards the horses. Several of the animals were riderless and were being led by Baducing and his warriors. "Get Coenred on a horse," Beobrand yelled at Bleddyn. "The rest of you too. Mount up. We are leaving while some of us yet live."

Bleddyn ushered Coenred towards a small, dark horse and unceremoniously hoisted him into the saddle. Coenred almost toppled over the other side of the animal's back, but clung on tight, ignoring the pain in his left hand. He refused to hold up their escape.

The rest of the warriors were climbing into their saddles too. All save Beobrand, Cynan, Ingwald and Eadgard.

The axeman seemed oblivious of their shouts, deafened and blinded by his sorrow and the madness that often took hold of him in combat. As Coenred watched, Eadgard hacked his axe into the chest of a man who had allowed himself to get too close. The weapon's iron head became caught in the fallen man's ribs. Eadgard bellowed, struggling to free the axe, jerking the foeman's corpse like a dog shaking a rat.

Seizing the opportunity, Vico stepped in quickly and cracked his club against Eadgard's skull. The man's cudgel had snapped or been cut short in the fight at some point, so the blow was not as powerful as it would otherwise have been. Still Eadgard reeled back, staggering and teetering.

Cynan and Beobrand lunged at Vico and the other men with their swords. Agiperto's men fell back, retreating from the Bernicians' bloody blades.

"Get him on a horse," yelled Beobrand.

Ingwald pulled Eadgard to a mount. The axeman was dazed, but still fought against him, wanting to return to the fray.

"Grindan gave his life to protect Coenred," Ingwald shouted at him, his face close to Eadgard's. "If we stay here, Coenred will die. All of us will. Would you let your brother's death be in vain?"

Shaking his head, Eadgard pushed Ingwald away and let out an inchoate roar. Coenred thought he was going to lash out at Ingwald, but instead he hauled himself up into the saddle. Ingwald quickly mounted too.

Beobrand and Cynan rushed back, throwing themselves up onto the backs of two of the horses. One horse remained riderless. Already Baducing had turned his mount and was kicking it into a gallop back in the direction from which they had come. Bleddyn rode close to Coenred, and he held out a hand to him as their horses sped forward into a run, following the others.

Coenred looked over his shoulder. Agiperto's men seemed caught in a moment of indecision as more than a score of Lutozzo's men, torches and weapons in hand, ran along the street towards them.

An instant later, Agiperto barked an order, and his men turned and fled into the night. They were swallowed quickly by the shadows of the walls and buildings, as rapidly as they had appeared from the gloom.

Some of Lutozzo's men sprinted after them, others skidded to a halt to stare after Beobrand and the men from Albion as they galloped away into the pre-dawn dark.

On the cobbles behind them lay several dead, dying or wounded men. Coenred's gaze was drawn to the motionless shape of Grindan's body. Beobrand and Bleddyn had discarded their torches. One of them guttered close to Eadgard's dead brother. The torchlight reflected in the puddle of Grindan's blood. And then, fearing he might fall, Coenred had to turn away to grasp his horse's mane tightly.

When he looked back again, they had rounded a bend in

the road and all he could see was darkness and the colossal, oppressive shadow of the great amphitheatre against the lightening sky.

Chapter 37

Beobrand used the sleeve of his kirtle to wipe sweat and blood from his face. He cursed. Much of the blood was his. Each galloping step of the horse jarred his head, reminding him of the savage blow that had knocked him almost senseless and reeling to the ground. He loathed to admit it, but he had been lucky. Or Woden had aided him, taking some of the sting from Vico's cudgel, in exchange for the blood Beobrand had offered to the All-Father.

Beobrand glanced at the riders ahead of him. Baducing led the way, unerringly guiding them across open areas of land where livestock grazed, then through narrow openings between buildings that Beobrand would never have noticed in the gloom. He clung to his reins and trusted the monk to get them to safety. So far, there had been no sound of pursuit. But both Lutozzo and Agiperto knew where Beobrand and his men were staying. It would be only a matter of time before they sought them there.

The sun was brightening the sky now and there were flashes of lighter grey in the gloom as they sped past trees and buildings. But the street along which they now rode was still dark. Despite the shadows, Eadgard's bulk was clearly visible. The huge warrior was slouched on his horse. Beobrand's head throbbed from the glancing blow Vico had dealt him. The brawler's club might have been shorter when he'd hit Eadgard, but Vico had struck him squarely. That he had remained on his feet was a testament to his strength, or perhaps Woden's hand in the fight. Beobrand could only imagine the pain the axeman felt.

Beobrand thought of Grindan lying in a pool of blood, his head smashed like a dropped hen's egg. He had seen much death in his life, but the cruelty of the gods still shocked him. And whatever agony Eadgard felt from Vico's cudgel, it would be as nothing when compared to the anguish of losing Grindan.

Gods! The weight of the loss had not yet truly penetrated Beobrand's thoughts. Grindan had been so long in his service, Beobrand could barely believe he was gone. It was a high price to pay for Coenred's rescue, and yet Beobrand knew that Grindan would have thought it a good bargain: his life for the monk's.

Beobrand gritted his teeth against the pounding headache, his vision blurring as they rode on, turning along a thoroughfare lined by tall, slender-trunked pines. He was gladdened they had brought his friend out of the darkness beneath Lutozzo's compound. But he could not deny the stab of guilt he felt too. He had promised Woden a sacrifice of blood. He should have known the father of the gods would not be satisfied with the blood of Beobrand's enemies. That was too easily shed to be a worthy gift.

The sky had become the colour of iron heated in a forge. Ahead of them, a stream ran along a ditch beside the road. No doubt it had been swelled by the recent rains, and a small pool had formed there, lapping at the stones of a small shrine that housed a statue of a young boy. The statue's left arm had been snapped off and Beobrand felt a pang of anger at what had been done to Coenred.

Baducing had at first led them back towards where he had waited with the horses. That might throw any pursuers off their trail, for a while at least. Now they had circled round and were galloping into the east towards their destination. Baducing pulled his horse to a halt, and signalled for the others to do the same.

"Let the horses drink," he said. "But not too much. We still have a way to go."

Lucifrido glanced back in the direction from which they had come, as if he expected a horde of enemies to appear at any moment.

"It is not safe," he said. "They will follow us."

"Then they will find death," rumbled Eadgard. His madness had left him and now he scowled, sullen and furious, his expression as bleak as a winter tomb.

Beobrand slid from his horse and led the animal towards the water. His legs were stiff, and his hands trembled. He closed his eyes against the ache in his head and stroked a hand along the horse's long neck. The creature's smooth coat, and its familiar dusty smell calmed him. Opening his eyes, Beobrand drew in a long breath.

"If we face that whoreson Vico again," he said, "we will kill him for what he has done. But we must not forget what our purpose was this night. Coenred is safe now, but our enemies know where we reside and there are too many of them for us to withstand. We had planned to leave Roma today. We must do so now with all haste. There is no time to waste."

Coenred nudged his horse forward. He was an awkward horseman at best and now he moved with the careful stiffness of a man in pain. Beobrand clenched his jaw and his stomach twisted to see the oozing wound where Coenred's ear had been cut off, and the left hand, tightly bound in a dirty strip of cloth.

"I thank you all for coming to my aid," Coenred said. "I had prayed for a rescue, but, truth be told, I was beginning to lose hope. I should never have doubted you…" His voice trailed off as his emotion overwhelmed him.

"There is no need to thank us, Coenred," Beobrand said. "We would never have abandoned you."

The rest of the men nodded. Bleddyn, who rode protectively close to the monk, patted him on the shoulder. Tears welled in Coenred's eyes and he cuffed them away.

"I am sorry," he whispered. "I fear the cost of my rescue has been too high."

"No," Eadgard said. "My brother…" His voice cracked. He coughed, sniffed, then continued. "Grindan gave his life willingly. In service to his lord and to protect you. Any of us would do the same." The men muttered their agreement. Eadgard's voice grew cold. "But there is one who must pay."

"Eadgard," warned Cynan, sensing where this was going.

"We all know it to be true!" shouted Eadgard, his rage erupting as suddenly as summer lightning. "That nithing Wilfrid is the cause of all this," he spat.

"I hear your words," Beobrand said, gladly accepting a waterskin from Aculf and washing the taste of blood from his mouth. "Wilfrid has done us wrong and he should face justice, but we cannot remain in Roma. To do so would be for all of us to die. Our enemies are too numerous, and we are too few."

Eadgard's face was thunderous.

"I will not flee like a craven."

Beobrand held out the waterskin to Eadgard, but he ignored the offer.

"Not like a craven, no," said Beobrand, handing the skin to Cynan instead. "Not like a fool either. Like a warrior, and a man. A man whose brother bravely gave his life to protect those he loved. A warrior oathsworn to me."

"Grindan is dead because of Wilfrid," Eadgard said, his voice not much more than a whisper. "I cannot turn away from that."

"Do you think me a coward, Eadgard?" Beobrand asked.

"Never, lord. But—"

"Do I run from my troubles?" Beobrand continued, cutting Eadgard off.

Eadgard slumped on his horse, lowering his head in abject dejection. The dawn sunlight gleamed in the tears on the big man's cheeks.

"No, lord," Eadgard mumbled.

"No," Beobrand said. "I am vengeful. Men of Albion know not to cross Beobrand of Ubbanford if they hope to live. I will face Wilfrid and make him pay for what he has done. But not this day." He fixed Eadgard with a hard stare. He felt the man's pain, but there were more pressing things now than Wilfrid. He saw in Lucifrido's frightened face that he was right to fear retaliation from Lutozzo.

And Agiperto yet lived. The man burnt with his need for revenge. If Beobrand could have faced the man in combat, or paid the blood-price for his son, that might have been the end of the matter. But the time for that was gone.

Judging his horse had drunk its fill, Beobrand pulled the beast's head away from the stream and turned to Baducing.

"You still mean to remain in Roma?"

"I do," Baducing replied. "We killed no-one this night. Perhaps we were not recognised. And I trust in the Almighty Lord's protection."

Beobrand thought of Marsiglio and Coenred, and the countless martyrs whose tombs thronged the underground catacombs outside the walls of the city. He was not so certain of the Christ god's power to protect his followers. But there was no time for such a debate now.

"Then I thank you for your help, Baducing," Beobrand said. "I am in your debt. I hope you will be safe." He squinted towards the rising sun. "The way to the Lateran Palace is clear from here. It is not far, and I think it would be best if you were to leave us now."

Baducing hesitated, then reluctantly nodded in agreement. Swinging himself back into his saddle, he reached down and gripped Beobrand's arm.

"Truth be told, I think I will feel safer when you are far from Roma. Danger follows you like gulls behind a plough."

Beobrand offered him a thin smile. Baducing's words were close to his own fear that he was the cause of much of the misery that so frequently surrounded him.

"Stay safe," he said.

Aculf strode over, holding out his hand. Beobrand grasped it and clapped the warrior on the back.

"Guard him well," he said.

Aculf chuckled.

"That is easier when you are not nearby." Beobrand frowned and Aculf smiled to take the sting from his words. "May God watch over you on the journey home."

Clambering up onto his horse, Aculf signalled for the rest of his men to ride. Without another word, they wheeled their steeds around and rode away from the rising sun, their shadows stretching before them.

The horsemen were perhaps a spear's throw away when Cynan looked up from where he was watering his horse and let out a cry.

"By Tiw's cock," he shouted, "where is *he* going?"

Halinard turned and cursed.

Beobrand peered at the retreating backs of the riders. His eyesight was not the sharpest, but he recognised easily enough Eadgard's lumbering bulk on one of the horses. The blow to the skull must have made him stupid, he thought. He should have known the axeman would not so easily give up his chance of vengeance.

Cynan had already vaulted back into his saddle.

"I'll go after him," he said.

"Wait," snapped Beobrand. "You alone will not bring Eadgard back. I am the only one who can do that." He spat, wondering if he would be able to dissuade the grief-stricken warrior. "If his oath means anything to him."

"He will be hard to catch," said Cynan, his frustration clear in his voice, "unless we ride now."

"We know where he is going," Beobrand replied. "I will ride after him." He swept the men with his gaze, calculating who would be best to accompany him. "With Lucifrido and Halinard."

"Lord?" Cynan was incredulous. "Lucifrido is not your man. It is too dangerous. We should all go with you." He watched as Eadgard peeled away from the other riders and headed south, in the direction of Eugenius' hall. "And we should leave now."

"All of Roma is dangerous for us," Beobrand said. He chose to ignore the comment about Lucifrido, though it was not without merit. "Coenred is hurt. He cannot chase after Eadgard." He held up a hand to silence Cynan's protestations. "No, I need you to lead the men, Cynan. Take Coenred back to the palace. While you ready the waggon, have Zanobi tend to him. And thank Martinus for his hospitality. But do not tarry, and do not wait for us. Make your way from the city as quickly as you can. With or without Eadgard, we will meet you on the road."

Cynan frowned. Damn the man, he was going to argue.

"Cynan," snapped Beobrand, "you said yourself, there is no time to waste if we are to waylay Eadgard."

"But, lord."

Beobrand glowered.

"Do not defy me on this. You are yet my man, are you not?"

"I am your man, lord," Cynan said. "My place is at your side."

"Your place is to do my bidding." Beobrand moved close to the Waelisc man and clasped his arm in the warrior grip. "Keep the men safe. I will see you soon and I'll bring that rash fool Eadgard with me."

Cynan gave a curt nod, then shouted at the men to mount up and follow him.

"I will pray for you," said Coenred.

"You do that, Coenred," said Beobrand, forcing a relaxed smile. "And do what Cynan says."

They rode away at a canter. The sun had already crested the horizon and the warm air of the dawn was filled with birdsong. Beobrand watched the horsemen for a moment, then pulled himself into the saddle. Lucifrido and Halinard were already mounted.

"It will not be long before Lutozzo sends men after us," Lucifrido said.

"And what about your friend Stoldo?" said Beobrand. "Vico is his man."

"He is, lord," replied Lucifrido.

"And yet without the information Stoldo sold us, we would not have freed Coenred."

Lucifrido shrugged.

"I know not what game Stoldo plays," he said, "but it is clear to me he is no friend."

"Of mine or yours?"

Lucifrido met his gaze steadily.

"Your foe is my foe too, lord."

Beobrand wasn't sure what to make of that.

"I have many enemies," he said. This was no time for conversation, but he felt the need to voice his suspicions. "You had no hand in Agiperto and Vico finding us?"

"None, lord," said Lucifrido, his tone earnest.

"What did Agiperto say to you back there?" Beobrand stared at Lucifrido, looking for signs of deceit in his answer.

Lucifrido sighed.

"He said I should remember who my family is."

"You fought at my side against Agiperto," Beobrand said. "Is he not your family?"

"He is Tanualdo's cousin. Not mine." Lucifrido shaded his eyes against the rising sun. "My mother died long ago. I have no kin now." He looked Beobrand in the eye. "No family but the friends I choose."

Unblinking, Beobrand weighed Lucifrido's words. He approved of the sentiment. Having made up his mind, Beobrand kicked his heels into his horse's ribs.

"There's no more time to waste," he said. "Now we must ride after a good friend, not a foe. Let us see if we can reach Eadgard before someone sends him to the afterlife with his brother."

Lucifrido's horse skittered nervously, but he got it under control and spurred it into a run. But rather than follow the path Eadgard had taken, he rode towards the shadows beneath a row of cypresses that grew at the bottom of a long, low slope. The hill was capped with an ancient temple. The golden sunlight shone bright on the marble columns and the gilded statue that presided over the pediment.

"Follow me," Lucifrido shouted over his shoulder. "I know a different way to Santa Prisca. With luck we can head Eadgard off before he arrives."

Beobrand hoped his trust in Lucifrido was not misplaced. He looked at Halinard, unsure how much luck he might have left. The Frank gave a small shrug of his shoulders.

Gritting his teeth against the pain in his head that he knew would be intensified with his mount's jarring gallop, Beobrand slapped his horse's rump and set off after Lucifrido.

Chapter 38

They sped along alleyways and across pastures strewn with dried cattle dung. Their galloping mounts scattered a small flock of chickens, sending the birds flapping and squawking out of their path. A man in a threadbare nightshirt stepped out of a shack built against the wall of what might once have been a noble's palace, but was now just a hollow shell of arches, crumbling walls and jumbled debris. Presumably the owner of the chickens, he flailed his fist at the riders, shouting abuse at them. But they did not slow.

Three dogs, skinny and dusty, hips and ribs jutting, rushed suddenly from the shade of a fallen statue. They barked loudly, nipping at the horses' legs. Beobrand's mount shied, but continued to gallop forward and he kept his seat. The dogs followed them for a short while, yapping and snapping at their heels, but they soon gave up the chase.

Beobrand had ridden between the Lateran Palace and Santa Prisca enough times to know it was not far. Despite his familiarity with the journey, he did not recognise any of the paths they were travelling on now. But Lucifrido was keeping the rising sun to their left, so Beobrand at least knew they were heading in the correct direction.

Beobrand had previously guided himself by the huge white

marble arch built into the massive building of the circus near Eugenius' church, but so far he had not seen it. They had been riding fast and must surely already have travelled far enough to be past the arch and ruined buildings. He was beginning to wonder whether he might have been wrong about Lucifrido, when they sped around a corner and there before them was the wide expanse of the road he recognised from previous trips.

The familiar walls of the *Circus Maximus* rose before them. The marble arch was smeared with bird droppings and weeds grew in fissures in the stone, but still it gleamed as bright as snow in the early morning sunlight. Sparrows fluttered and chirped in the branches of the pines that lined the road. Lucifrido dragged on his reins and his horse skidded to a halt. One look at the road ahead and it was clear to see why. Beobrand and Halinard reined in their horses, and all three animals stood quivering and sweating from their exertions as their riders stared about them.

They were near to Santa Prisca here. Beobrand had thought it very likely that Eadgard would reach his destination before they would be able to head him off. So early in the morning, Beobrand had imagined the road would be empty, but the cobbled street in front of them was filled from one side to the other with a moving, swaying sea of cattle. There must have been many more than a hundred of the red beasts. They milled about, lowing and jostling, forming a wall of flesh between the circus buildings and the high wall that ran along the eastern edge of the road. The beasts were further compressed by several men on the road to the north and an ordered row of armoured warriors to the south. The men to the north of the herd were dressed in dusty, drab clothes and wore broad-brimmed straw hats. In their hands they carried long staves with which they goaded and prodded the cattle, keeping them in a tight mass on the road.

Two men dressed in similar garb to the rest of the cattle drovers were on the south of the cattle where they leant on their staves. They were locked in a heated discussion with one of the armed men. Beobrand did not know the man's name, but he recognised him and his polished armour as one of Deusdedi's men. Behind the officer a squad of some score warriors, all dressed in the regalia of the Exarchatus, stood patiently, staring ahead and leaning on their spears.

Behind the warriors was a carriage pulled by two fine stallions. The carriage was covered with curtains of silk, protecting its occupants from the sun. At the rear of the vehicle, another score of warriors stood unmoving in the sunlight. Beobrand was impressed with their discipline.

Looking back to the north, Beobrand noticed a rider in the shadow of a pine's wide canopy. He had not seen him at first glance. The horseman was tall and seemed to dwarf the horse he rode. The big man saw him at the same moment and tensed. It was Eadgard. Beobrand held up a hand to him and was pleased when Eadgard did not turn his horse and ride away.

Perhaps his luck, such as it was, had not yet run out after all. Or maybe Woden's power still held sway this far south. The gods knew they had offered up enough blood for him to watch over them still.

"Come," Beobrand whispered to the others.

Nudging his horse to the right, he walked it slowly around the edge of the herd of cattle, careful not to allow his horse to rub along the flaking masonry of the wall. Lucifrido and Halinard followed.

Behind them, the leader of the guards was losing his temper, raising his voice. Beobrand could not understand his words, but the man's anger was clear. The cattle were blocking the road and he wanted them moved. The drovers spoke in calm, hushed tones, nodding as the officer's anger grew. They seemed disinclined to do anything to improve the situation.

The cattle eyed Beobrand and the other riders balefully. The horses were not used to being so close to such animals and they were skittish and nervous. Beobrand thought about dismounting, but discarded the idea. He preferred his chances on horseback surrounded by so many horned beasts. More than once kine moved too near for his liking and he shoved them away with his foot. When a huge cow swung into his path, Beobrand's horse snapped its long teeth at it. The cow moved quickly aside, pushing its neighbours back. Beobrand spurred his horse into the gap and was soon through.

He had been focused on the cattle, and now, when he looked up, his heart lifted to see that Eadgard remained beneath the tree. Lucifrido and Halinard were both making good progress, so Beobrand moved his horse towards the axeman.

The cattle drovers looked up at Beobrand, at first with disinterest on their weather-beaten faces, then, as they took in the riders' weapons and armour, the blood that streaked them, they recoiled, distancing themselves from these men of war. To his surprise, Beobrand saw a glimmer of recognition on the features of the nearest man. He pulled his horse up and beckoned. The man hesitated, then, seeing there was nowhere for him to go, he stepped close.

"I know this man," Beobrand said as Lucifrido rode up beside him.

"You do?"

"He was having trouble carrying some goods down to the river a few days ago. We helped him. Ask him how his donkey fares."

Lucifrido raised his eyebrows. He spoke and the man looked sheepish as he replied.

"He says it died," said Lucifrido.

Beobrand thought of how the man had mistreated the animal.

"Beat it to death, did he?" he asked.

The man listened to Lucifrido as he translated. He shook his head as he answered, a slight smile playing on his lips. Removing his hat, he wiped a hand over his bald head, watching Beobrand's face intently as Lucifrido spoke his words.

"He says it just died." Lucifrido frowned. "Forgive me, lord, but he says he wonders if perhaps you poisoned the animal."

The man was watching him slyly. Beobrand rubbed absently at his arm, remembering how the man's donkey had bitten him. Beobrand did not like the man, but he might need his help now, so he offered him a thin smile.

"Tell him if he had fed that skinny thing better, a single mouthful of the flesh of a man from Albion would not have been enough to kill it."

Lucifrido looked confused, but relayed his words.

The bald man chuckled and nodded, then shrugged.

"If it yet lived," he said through Lucifrido, "I would not have to stand behind a hundred shitting cattle all day with my wife's brothers."

"Ask him what is going on here," said Beobrand.

Lucifrido did. The man spat, then said a few words in a gruff tone. As he spoke he swiped out with his stick at a cow that wandered too close, sending it back into the densely packed herd.

"He says that some lord from the Exarchatus wants to get to the *Archibasilica*."

"Deusdedi?" asked Beobrand.

The man shrugged. The name clearly meant nothing to him.

"Why would he travel with so many guards just to go to Mass?"

It was Lucifrido's turn to shrug, but he relayed the question. Another of the drovers spoke up.

"This one thinks they mean to arrest the Pontifex."

"Martinus?" asked Beobrand.

The man nodded and spoke quickly.

Lucifrido looked incredulous, but relayed the man's words.

"He says he's heard that the Emperor himself ordered it."

"Why would he do that?" Beobrand said.

The cattle drover had no answer.

"Do I look like a man who speaks to the likes of Martinus, or the envoy from Ravenna?" he said.

"You do not," said Beobrand, "so why would I listen to these rumours about the Pontifex being arrested?"

The man chewed his lip. He seemed embarrassed and would not meet the eyes of his fellow drovers. As he finally replied, the other men began to laugh. The man's cheeks flushed.

Lucifrido too smiled as he translated the drover's words.

"He heard it from a whore last night. She works down in the circus. Seems some of the warriors from the Exarchatus were there too and they were none too quiet about their plans."

Beobrand thought of all he had learnt about the differing factions of Christ followers, of how they squabbled over the best way to worship their nailed god. None of it made sense to him, and yet the man's words had the ring of truth to them. Looking over the backs of the densely massed cattle Beobrand saw that the captain of the guards was red-faced and bellowing at the drovers now.

Turning to check whether Eadgard was still under the tree, he saw that his gesith was riding to where Beobrand conversed with the drovers. The cattlemen looked at the hulking man warily. Beobrand nodded curtly to him.

"I would speak with you, Eadgard, but first I must conclude my business with these men."

"Business, lord?" said Eadgard. "The only business I have is wringing the neck of that cocksure bastard Wilfrid."

Beobrand ignored him and turned back to the cattlemen. He pointed across the backs of the cattle, to the men arguing with the warrior from the Exarchatus of Ravenna.

"What is the problem there?" he asked.

Lucifrido spoke, listened to the reply, and interpreted it.

"They want to pass. But they did not ask..." He searched for the right word. "With respect."

Beobrand eyed the drover and the man whose donkey had bitten him. They were solid, thickset men with heavy brows and small, dark eyes. Reaching for the pouch he wore on his belt, Beobrand tugged the strings open. It was full of silver, both coins and pieces hacked from larger items. Shoving his hand into the pouch he pulled out a fistful of metal. Coins fell to the earth as he opened his hand to show them the gleaming silver. All of the drovers were staring at the treasure on his outstretched hand. The dead donkey's owner stooped and quickly snatched up the coins from between the cracked cobbles.

"Would this be respectful enough?" Beobrand asked.

The men nodded, speaking rapidly, their gaze avaricious and unwavering as they stared at the glinting treasure on Beobrand's palm.

"They say for one as respectful as you," Lucifrido translated, "they will move the cattle as quickly as they are able."

"I do not want them to move the cattle," Beobrand said. "Tell them I will give them all the silver in my hand and what is left in my pouch, if they can hold the men from the Exarchatus here. They are to make it look as if they are trying to move their animals, but they must not let the envoy pass for as long as possible. Can they do that?"

The men nodded and Beobrand leaned down and handed them the silver in his hand. There were still several coins and chunks of hacksilver in the pouch, but there was no time to remove the small bag carefully from his belt, so Beobrand reached for the seax that hung at his back and used the knife's sharp blade to sever the leather thongs that secured the pouch. He tossed the jingling bag to the nearest drover.

"Tell them to start right away," he said.

On hearing Lucifrido's words, the drover who had caught the pouch shouted loudly to the two men arguing with the leader of the guards. A yelled conversation commenced in which the drovers shouted back and forth and the Exarchatus guard grew increasingly frustrated. It would not be long before the man's patience vanished. There was no time to waste. Beobrand pulled his horse's head away from the cattle and moved towards Eadgard.

The giant warrior's face was grim. Ever since he had been gripped by fever Eadgard's skin had borne a slightly sallow tinge. Now his face shone with a sheen of sweat, there was colour high on his cheeks, and his eyes burnt with anger. He had yet to regain all the weight he had lost from his illness, but he was still a formidable man, taller than most, with massively muscled shoulders, long arms and the neck of a bull. In battle, his size, coupled with the madness that so often gripped him, made him all but invincible. Beobrand would not like to face him in combat.

"Lord," rumbled Eadgard, "I waited when you asked, but I will delay no further. Wilfrid is mine."

Beobrand frowned. The shouting between the drovers and the guards continued. The stink of the cattle was sharp in the warming air, their lowing loud.

"I do not wish to shout," Beobrand said, nudging his horse closer.

What he wished was to be done with this and away from here. Every moment they remained in Roma, he could feel peril closing about them like a noose. And now he had learnt of a threat to Martinus too.

Beobrand had ridden so near to Eadgard now that their knees touched. The instant before Beobrand attacked, something gave his purpose away. Some warrior instinct or a tiny expression on the scarred features that Eadgard knew so well from his years of service. Whatever betrayed Beobrand's intent, the axeman sensed the danger and made to evade him. Eadgard was huge, strong and fast, but he had not fully recovered from the ague, and he had never been as quick as Beobrand.

As he had ridden towards Eadgard, Beobrand had held his seax down by his right thigh, unsheathed and ready. Now he dropped the reins and lashed out his left half-hand to grab the neck of Eadgard's byrnie. He twisted his fingers into the fabric of the kirtle Eadgard wore beneath it, ensuring the larger man could not easily pull away. In the same instant Beobrand leant over in the saddle and pressed the naked steel of his seax blade against Eadgard's throat.

"You say Wilfrid is yours," Beobrand snarled, "but you, Eadgard, kin of Grindan, are mine."

Eadgard grew very still. He had never before stared into his lord's chill gaze when death rested on the edge of a blade between them. This was the icy glare that had unmanned countless enemies, the last sight seen by so many of Beobrand's foe-men. Eadgard swallowed, his throat bobbed against the seax blade. Beobrand pressed it forward until it cut the skin. A trickle of blood mingled with Eadgard's sweat, where it further stained his already filthy kirtle.

"My brother is dead," Eadgard said at last, his tone bleak.

"I know," replied Beobrand, his voice flat. "And that is why you yet live. A grieving man does not always make the best decisions. But even a man mourning the loss of his brother must still obey his hlaford."

Eadgard tried to turn away, but Beobrand shook him savagely, forcing him to look him in the eye. They stared at each other for several heartbeats and Beobrand wondered what was running through Eadgard's thoughts. Was he thinking of the times when Beobrand had broken his oath to his lord? To their king.

Before Eadgard could utter another sound, Beobrand pressed on. "There is no time for grief now, Eadgard," he said, allowing his tone to soften. "We are all in danger here in Roma, and you heard that man. Martinus has enemies seeking to imprison him. He has been a generous and kind host to us and we must ride to his aid now." Beobrand narrowed his eyes. He felt Eadgard flinch under that piercing stare, but he did not look away. "Wilfrid will have to wait for another time," Beobrand said. "But tell me now, Eadgard, and think hard before you answer. Is your life mine? Do I still have your oath?"

Eadgard stared unblinking into his cold eyes. At last, he let out a sigh.

"You have my oath, lord."

"Good," said Beobrand, removing the blade from his throat. "Do not defy me again, Eadgard. Next time, I will offer you no second chance."

Eadgard rubbed at where Beobrand's seax had nicked his skin. Looking at the blood on his fingers, he nodded.

The drovers were goading the cattle from both directions at the same time now. They were all shouting, their voices loud even above the din of the animals. The bald one who had owned the donkey waved to Beobrand and grinned. Beobrand sheathed his seax and returned the man's wave.

"Come," Beobrand said. "They will not be able to hold the men from the Exarchatus for long."

With that, he took up his reins and kicked his horse's flanks. His mount was already sweating and tired, but there was nothing for it but to urge it into a gallop. Halinard and Lucifrido set off just behind him. Beobrand shot a glance over his shoulder and for a dreadful moment he thought Eadgard would once again break his word. But after a heartbeat, the massive warrior, face drawn into a furious scowl, kicked his horse into a lumbering canter and rode northward after the thegn of Ubbanford.

His oathsworn lord.

Chapter 39

Coenred was exhausted. For a time he had lain in the waggon, vainly hoping for rest. He had slept fitfully for a short time, but the constant creaking of the axles, and the jostling and shake of the vehicle as it trundled over the cracked slabs that paved the *Via Ostiensis* prevented him from any real relief. In the end he had clambered out as the waggon slowed on a shallow incline. Ingwald shouted at the mules and flicked their reins as they strained to heave the heavy vehicle up the slope.

They had originally planned to travel back to Albion by land, retreading the path they had followed south, but Coenred wondered whether the waggon, laden as it was with the relics and goods they were bringing back from Roma, would have been able to navigate the steep mountain passes they had crossed on their way to the Eternal City. As it was, they were now heading for Ostia, the nearest port. There they would seek passage on a ship heading across the Great Sea. They would need to leave the bulky waggon behind. The horses too. Coenred didn't relish the idea of sailing and he wondered briefly what dangers might lie ahead of them. But he was too tired to fret about the future. The past held more than enough perils.

Beobrand saw Coenred trudging beside the waggon and blinking in the bright sunshine. He cantered over, slowing his horse to a walk next to the monk. The sun was high in the sky and the day was once again stiflingly hot. The skin beneath Beobrand's eyes was dark, but Coenred could see no other sign that his friend had not slept for two nights.

"If you are not going to travel in the waggon," Beobrand said, "you must ride. We cannot slow for you to walk." His tone was gruff and even as he spoke to Coenred from the saddle, he took advantage of his position on the hilltop to survey the land around them. The road stretched behind them, dusty and straight, all the way to the far-off walls of Roma. There was still no sign of pursuit, which had surprised them all. Surely it could only be a matter of time before their enemies, or those of the Pontifex Maximus, would rush from the city after them. But Beobrand did not only look behind them for signs of danger. Shading his eyes with a hand, he swept his gaze in every direction, giving particular attention to the eastern horizon.

"You have seen no sign of Stoldo?" Coenred asked. They were not far from Stoldo's land here and they had anticipated he might send men against them.

"Nothing since this morning," Beobrand said, touching the hammer amulet at his throat.

Shortly before Coenred had climbed into the waggon, they had seen three men to the east, sitting their horses and observing the road. They had been on a low ridge, surrounded by gnarled olive trees and had made no attempt to hide. Lucifrido had said they were probably Stoldo's men.

As they had drawn closer, Beobrand had taken Cynan, Lucifrido and Eadgard with him and ridden towards the men on the bluff. Before they reached them, the riders had turned and galloped away, leaving behind them nothing but a thin billow of dust. They had disappeared in the direction of Stoldo's villa.

After that, the travellers had expected not only pursuit from the city, but also to have their path blocked by Stoldo's men.

They were still uncertain as to his true motives in all of this, but there could be no doubt he was no friend of theirs. But they had seen nobody on the road but merchants, tradesmen, pilgrims and farmers.

"Perhaps we are too many for Stoldo," said Coenred.

"Perhaps," said Beobrand, sounding unconvinced and looking along the column of riders, waggons and spearmen that lined the road. Together with Beobrand's Black Shields, twenty spearmen marched behind the carriage that housed Martinus, Viaro and the Pontifex's closest servants. A dozen mounted warriors rode before his carriage. It was a force large enough to dissuade any but the most determined enemy. Sizeable enough, pondered Coenred, to deter even the powerful Lutozzo. But from Beobrand's description of the numbers of Deusdedi's men, it seemed unlikely that it would be numerous enough to avoid the Pontifex Maximus being detained for his perceived crimes against the Church.

"Where is your hat?" inquired Beobrand, his tone curt.

Coenred reached up and realised he had left it in the waggon. He was always forgetting to wear the thing. The pressure from the bandage wrapped about his head had given him the impression his head was protected, but he knew Beobrand was right to be concerned. If he was not in the covered waggon, the hot summer sun might soon work its mischief on him again.

Hurrying back to the waggon, Coenred retrieved the straw hat and placed it on his head. It tugged at the bandage, eliciting a throbbing pain from his ear. Or where his ear had been, he thought gravely. His left hand ached too, but like his head, it was newly bandaged. He shuddered to recall the time he had spent in captivity. And he trembled when he remembered the ghostly voice and horrific images that had come to him in the forest. The women had been sure his addled state stemmed from too much exposure to the sun. The horror of it still seemed terribly real to him, but he had decided not to mention his dark thoughts. He would wear the hat, if that would keep the evil spirit from returning. Besides, Beobrand had too much on his mind already without having to worry about him.

Beobrand's head was bandaged too. Eadgard and some of the other warriors also displayed strips of clean cloth expertly tied around injuries suffered in the fight outside the amphitheatre. Zanobi was thorough, even though there had been scant time for him to work on the warriors before they were again on the road.

The physician was one of Martinus' staff who had remained at the palace. He had tended to them all before they left Roma. Coenred's mind wandered back to that morning's frenetic activity at the Lateran *Patriarchium*. They had not long arrived and the sun was only just showing itself above the hills in the east when Beobrand had returned with Eadgard.

The palace had already been in turmoil. When Cynan had led them into the courtyard, guards had quickly surrounded them. Coenred, shaking and weak from his ordeal, had needed to act as interpreter. Haltingly, he had explained what had happened and was relaying Cynan's instructions to the hostlers and servants to have their waggon hitched to the mules they had purchased, when Beobrand arrived in a clatter of hooves, bellowing in his powerful voice that he must speak immediately with the Pontifex Maximus.

Chaos had held sway in the palace for a time. Through Coenred, Beobrand had insisted that Martinus be awoken, saying that he was in danger and must flee the palace. He must have already been awake, perhaps at his prayers, for Martinus had come to them very quickly. He listened to Beobrand, nodding and stroking his beard as the thegn explained what he had seen. The Pontifex's staff, the priests and clerics who followed him everywhere, were distraught, but Martinus was calm.

"I have nothing to fear from these men," he said. "I only fear my Lord God Almighty, and He knows I am no heretic."

The other priests pleaded with him and a lengthy argument ensued. Beobrand grew increasingly frustrated with the discourse, eventually declaring that whatever the Pontifex chose to do, he would lead his own men out of Roma as quickly as he was able. He would travel with Martinus, or alone, but he could not remain in Roma.

In the end, the priests and clerks had prevailed, and a carriage, a waggon of supplies and a troop of guards had been readied so that Martinus could leave immediately. While all this was taking place, the astute captain of the palace guard, a man called Ghoro, had sent the bulk of his force to intercept the men from the Exarchatus of Ravenna. They had strict instructions not to fight with Deusdedi's men, but Beobrand's warning and the captain's forethought gave Martinus the time needed to escape from the city.

Coenred wished there had been longer to bid farewell to those they had left behind, but he knew the risks of remaining in Roma. Still, he had been overjoyed to see Marsiglio, however briefly. The monk was very weak, but he was awake and Zanobi was hopeful that he would survive his injuries.

"Thank the Lord that you live," Coenred said, dropping to his knees beside the bed in which Marsiglio lay and clasping his hands in his. The white of Coenred's clean linen bandage was bright against Marsiglio's dark skin.

"I praise the Almighty that you live too," Marsiglio said. "I feared for a time we would meet all too soon at the feet of Jesu in His father's kingdom."

"We will meet there one day, my friend," Coenred said, patting Marsiglio's hand. "But thanks to God's grace, you can visit me on Lindisfarena first."

Marsiglio's eyes still gleamed with fever and pain, but he smiled up at Coenred.

"Perhaps I will travel there after all," he said. "It seems Roma is not as safe as I had thought."

Beobrand barked an order at one of the men, pulling Coenred abruptly from his memories. Bleddyn trotted up. He held the reins of a chestnut gelding, which he handed to Coenred.

"I know you do not like to ride, Coenred," said Beobrand, "but you are not strong enough to walk at the pace I will set. Lucifrido says we might yet reach Ostia by sunset, but for that we must hurry."

Bleddyn dismounted to help Coenred up. With a sigh, Coenred stepped into Bleddyn's cupped hands and heaved himself into the saddle. He did not wish to ride, but one look at Beobrand's stern face scattered any thought of dissent he might have.

Nodding his approval, Beobrand swung his mount's head around and kicked it into a trot towards the head of the column. They had been able to take fresh horses from the palace's stable, which was one more thing to be thankful for.

"Will you be strong enough to ride?" asked Bleddyn after he had climbed back into his own saddle. There was concern on his face.

Coenred liked the man. He was more thoughtful than most of Beobrand's warriors.

"I rested a little in the waggon," Coenred said. "I will do well enough."

Bleddyn looked at him askance.

"If you feel yourself tiring, call for me," he said. "You can always travel in the waggon again."

Coenred thought of the bumpy, creaking bed of the waggon. How the heat and the heavy scent of the newly cured leather sacks that carried some of their possessions had churned his stomach.

"Thank you," Coenred replied. "I will tell you if I grow too weak to ride."

"There is no shame in it," Bleddyn said. "You have been sorely treated."

Coenred said nothing, but nodded as they rode on. The sun was hot on his back and he was glad now of the wide-brimmed hat that protected his head and the nape of his neck from the sun's rays.

The relentless pace Beobrand insisted on was one of the reasons they had needed to leave Marsiglio behind. He would not have been able to travel without the risk of opening his wounds. They had left many people in Roma. In fact Martinus had been adamant that most of the guards remain to protect the palace and those who yet resided within its walls.

"Deusdedi comes for me," he'd said. "He has no issue with any of those I leave behind. Still, I have a duty to protect that which the Lord has placed in my care. To that end I command the guard to do what they can to keep the people and the building safe from any harm."

Wulfwyn and Aelfwig were two of those who had stayed behind. Coenred had heard of her night-time ride to warn Beobrand of Wilfrid's dishonesty, and when he saw her watching the horses, waggons and the carriage being prepared for the journey, Coenred felt a strange surge of emotion.

"You will not come with us?" he'd asked.

Wulfwyn's eyes were bright, her skin glowing, in the dawn sun. Her hair gleamed. As always he was impressed with her beauty and resolute strength. He did not imagine the young widow would remain unmarried for long.

"No, Father," she said.

He did not have the strength to remind her he was no priest.

"What will you do?" he said. "Surely you will not return to Priano?"

She bit her lip, nervously tugging at her hair.

"I know not what we will do," she admitted. "But we have come too far and suffered too much to leave Roma now."

"I will pray for you," Coenred said. "That you find happiness here." He glanced at Aelfwig's youthful countenance. "And health," he added. "The Lord God knows you deserve both."

"Thank you, Father." Wulfwyn said, looking at the blood-stained bandages wrapped about his ear and his hand. She was unable to keep the tears from her eyes. "And I will pray that your journey is safe."

It was late afternoon and Coenred was lolling in the saddle, weak and utterly weary from his torture and wounds, when a shout and the sound of galloping hooves dragged him from a doze.

Blinking against the bright, hot sunlight, at first Coenred imagined they were under attack. Turning in the saddle, he stared in the direction from which they had travelled. Back towards Roma. The city walls had disappeared from view long since and now the land about them was dotted with olive trees. The terrain had grown flat as they drew closer to the sea, and with the woods surrounding them, he could not see far into the distance. But there was no sign of any enemies and no sound of fighting. As the day had progressed, it had seemed increasingly unlikely they would be chased and caught before they reached their destination.

The hoofbeats that had disturbed him came from Ghoro, the leader of Martinus' mounted guard. The grey-bearded captain sat his horse as straight as a spear, and despite his age, he seemed oblivious to the heat and the distance they had ridden all that long, sweltering day.

Seeing Ghoro approaching, Beobrand turned his horse and rode back to meet him.

"My master wishes to speak with you, lord Beobrand," Ghoro said.

Lucifrido and Coenred began to translate the man's words at the same time. They both halted. Lucifrido smiled at Coenred and bowed slightly to the older man. Coenred's head was pounding and his legs, lower back and buttocks ached from the day in the saddle. He would have been content to allow Lucifrido to interpret for Beobrand. But he could see the sharp impatience in the set of his old friend's jaw, the tightness of his shoulders. Beobrand was in no mood for any delay. Coenred spoke again, quickly translating Ghoro's words.

Beobrand nodded and without a word he kicked his horse towards Martinus' carriage. The captain of the guard spun his horse around as if controlling the animal with his thoughts, then galloped after Beobrand. Letting out a long breath, Coenred clumsily turned his own mount and followed them.

Martinus stood beside his carriage in the shade of an oak. His priests and assistants had all taken the opportunity to leave the vehicle too. One man was some way off, his robes hitched up before him as he pissed into the bushes.

"What does he want?" asked Beobrand, pulling his horse to a halt, but not dismounting.

Coenred sighed. They were all tired, their nerves stretched and frayed, hearts heavy with loss and pain. But he wished Beobrand would not be so rude. This was the Pontifex Maximus, the most important man in all of Christendom.

Coenred climbed down from his horse. His legs were numb and he almost fell, only preventing himself embarrassment by clutching tightly to the saddle.

"Your Holiness," Coenred said, "my lord Beobrand inquires as to what troubles you?"

"Many things trouble me, my dear Coenred," said Martinus, with a thin smile. "More than I can speak of here. But as to why

I have stopped, I would ask you please to thank Beobrand for his assistance and his warning this morning. But please tell him I shall not be riding further."

"But Holy Father…" Coenred sputtered.

Martinus held up his hand, calming him.

"What does he say?" asked Beobrand.

Coenred told him.

"Ask him why," Beobrand said. "And ask him if he is sure."

Martinus listened to the questions, then spoke in his soft voice.

"I have given this much thought, and I have prayed all this day for God's guidance. I should never have fled. I allowed my fears to be stoked by others, but I should not have run away, fleeing arrest like a thief. God is my shield and I have nothing to fear." Iron entered his voice, an indication of his anger and resolve. "I am the Bishop of Roma, not a common criminal. I thank Beobrand. I know he had only my safety in his mind, but I will travel no further. I will spend tonight at the residence of the local priest. In the morning I will return to face my accusers."

Beobrand listened stony-faced as Coenred translated Martinus' words. Without warning, he swung his leg over his horse's back and slid to the ground. Ghoro tensed at the suddenness of the movement, instinctively pushing his horse between Beobrand and Martinus. Beobrand nodded at the man in acknowledgement that he was merely doing his duty.

"Tell him I mean no harm," he said. For the first time that day, Coenred heard the weariness in his voice.

Coenred spoke and after a command from Martinus, Ghoro walked his horse backward.

"I see there is no reason to debate this matter further," Beobrand said, stepping towards Martinus. "If he has made his decision, I will not attempt to change it." To Coenred's shock Beobrand then dropped to one knee before the Pontifex. "I would merely ask that he gives us his blessing for the journey ahead."

Coenred translated, unable to hide his astonishment at Beobrand's words. Perhaps this pilgrimage to Roma had made more of an impact on the thegn of Ubbanford than Coenred had imagined.

With no sign of surprise, Martinus placed a hand on Beobrand's bandaged head, and quietly recited the words of a blessing. When he had finished, he made the sign of the cross and raised Beobrand to his feet.

"Godspeed on your journey home," Martinus said. "I pray you find the peace you crave."

Beobrand smiled when Coenred translated those words, but there was no mirth in his expression.

"Tell him that I hope his god watches over him in the days ahead."

"He always does, Beobrand," replied Martinus with a grin. "He always does."

They parted ways from Martinus and his retinue there at the edge of the woodland, where a path split from the road and headed due south. The men rode on in silence for a time. The parting had happened so quickly, Coenred had still not quite taken it in. The feeling of safety that he had clung to while surrounded by Martinus' guards had fled, and he looked about him in fear as the shadows lengthened and deepened beneath the trees.

Martinus had asked them to accompany him to the residence of the local priest he knew, but Beobrand had declined the offer.

"We are too close to Roma still," he said. "Too many enemies dog our heels. But I smell the sea, and every gull's cry I hear is the Whale Road beckoning."

Beobrand had set his heart on a ship now, and just as with

Martinus, there was nothing to be gained in trying to change his course. Lucifrido was confident he could find them a suitable vessel.

"I know skippers in Ostia, lord," he said, the setting sun reddening his face, "and you have silver. It will be easy enough to get us passage."

"Us?" asked Cynan. "Surely you will return home." He eyed Lucifrido closely, evidently still not trusting the man from Sutri.

"I have a mind to visit the land where my mother was born," replied Lucifrido.

Cynan frowned at that, but Beobrand said nothing. Lucifrido turned in his saddle, his usual smile replaced by a scowl.

"Have I not done enough to gain your trust?" he asked.

Beobrand stared at him as they rode, his eyes brilliantly blue in the blazing light of the lowering sun. After a moment, Lucifrido looked away, unable to hold that gaze.

"Find us a ship," said Beobrand, "and a buyer for the horses and waggon. Then we can talk once more about trust."

Coenred did not join the conversation. His body ached with every one of his horse's steps, and as dusk began to settle over the land, he simply wished he still had close to fifty warriors around him. Beobrand, his Black Shields, and Lucifrido were all formidable fighters, but numbered only seven.

The gloaming of dusk was short-lived and soon it was dark. The dim light from the stars and moon guided their way. The horses' hooves were loud in the stillness. The wheels of the waggon grumbled and cracked on the road's cobbles. Coenred swayed in the saddle, praying to God he would not fall.

Coenred was about to call for Bleddyn, resigned that he would need to go once more into the waggon or risk tumbling from the saddle, when the Waelisc man, perhaps sensing his need, moved out of the darkness. On his other side, the hulking figure of Eadgard crowded near. Both men rode protectively close and

Coenred smiled in the darkness. Coenred had prayed for God's help and He had sent these warriors to his aid.

"Thank you," he whispered to the Almighty and his friends, unsure if Eadgard or Bleddyn heard him.

Eadgard had barely spoken all that long day. His face was drawn with grief and he had ridden in brooding silence. Coenred remembered losing his sister, Tata, so many years before. The memories dulled over time, but the pain never truly vanished. Eadgard's agony would still be as keen as a blade to his heart now, so soon after his brother's slaying.

"I am sorry," Coenred said, his voice barely above a whisper. He thought neither of his escorts had heard him, when Eadgard's voice rumbled from the gloom.

"None of this was your doing, Coenred," he said. He fell silent for a time, then his voice came out of the darkness again, like the grumble of thunder. "To think all this happened because of a book. I cannot fathom it."

Coenred thought of the book that had caused such suffering. It was a thing of immense value, but there was more than that. He had glimpsed it only for a few heartbeats and felt the invisible pull of its power. Wilfrid had read from its pages and the heretical teachings therein had slid inside his soul, like the talons of a devil prying open a badly secured door.

"Books have great power," Coenred said. "They contain learning and knowledge. This one holds secrets. Heretical secrets. I think Wilfrid fell under its spell somehow, though I cannot explain it."

Eadgard thought for a moment as they plodded on through the night.

"You say it is heretical. What does that mean?"

Coenred was too tired to think of such things, let alone attempt to explain them to the likes of the huge axeman. And yet, Eadgard's brother lay dead on a dirt-strewn street in Roma.

Grindan had given his life to save Coenred. And everything that had happened had started the moment Wilfrid laid his eyes on *The Treasure of Life*. Coenred owed so much to Eadgard. He would do his best to explain what he knew of the cause of his misery.

"Heresy goes against the teachings of our Lord Jesu Christ." Coenred thought of Martinus and Deusdedi; of how Martinus' beliefs concerning the will of God had led to the Emperor and Patriarch of Constantinopolis to send men to arrest the Pontifex. "It can be complicated. But the worst heresies can lead to great conflict."

"What happens if someone is found to be a heretic?" asked Eadgard.

"It depends," said Coenred. "In the most extreme instances, heretics who refuse to renounce their heresy are put to death."

Eadgard made a strangled sound in the darkness. It took Coenred a heartbeat to realise he was laughing quietly.

"Well then," Eadgard said, "let us hope Wilfrid's book is found by that Deusdedi. He does not strike me as a man who would easily forgive a heretic."

The flickering light of torches reached them from between the trees. Shortly after, there came the distant sigh of waves rolling up a beach. The travellers rode out from the sparse woodland and there, where the Tiberis met the sea, lay the old port of Ostia.

Chapter 40

Cynan was still not certain of Lucifrido. The man was a mystery to him and while he had done nothing to disprove his loyalty, there was something about Lucifrido's smirk that needled under Cynan's skin. However, he could not deny the man's value as he led the exhausted group into the shadowed streets of Ostia, with nothing to illuminate their path but the pale light of the moon and a flickering fire that burnt on the harbour's edge. It was late and Cynan wondered if the fire had been set to guide a ship into shore. Perhaps a local fisherman was out later than expected and his loved ones now watched from the beach and the harbour walls, praying that the sea had not claimed another vessel. The blaze reminded him of the fires Mantican's men had set on the beaches of Wessex, luring unsuspecting ships onto the rocks where the wreckers could plunder their cargo and slay their crews.

Cynan shuddered at the memory of the cold embrace of the waves when their ship, *Brimblæd*, had been wrecked on the jagged rocks on the southern coast of Albion. He wished they were not going to take the Whale Road, and yet Beobrand was right that they could cover the distance more quickly that way. If the good weather held and they found a willing skipper.

As soon as they were surrounded by the buildings, the thin

light of the harbour fire vanished and the tired travellers were plunged into a darkness as deep as it had been beneath the trees. But Lucifrido knew the town well and he unerringly guided them through the maze of twisting cobbled streets.

A dog barked, disturbed by the sound of their passing. A shutter opened and a pale face peered out at them. The hooves of their horses and the waggon's wheels were loud on the still streets. Lucifrido hissed something and the shutter was slammed shut.

"We are almost there," Lucifrido said.

Nobody replied. It was as if they feared to awaken the inhabitants of the settlement, though with the dog's loud bark and the echoing clatter of the waggon and the clopping of the horses' hooves, Cynan could not imagine anyone would remain asleep.

They reached a large building near the river's mouth and overlooking the stone harbour walls. From here Cynan could once more see the fire on the harbour. From this distance he saw it was burning in a large brazier and there were several figures around it, their shadowy shapes lit by the twisting flames. None of those people looked towards the land. All stared out at the star-speckled darkness of the sea.

Lucifrido rapped on a timber door set into a high wall. Another dog started to bark, its deep growling giving the impression of a much larger and altogether scarier beast than the previous sentinel that had announced their presence.

After a while, the dog was silenced by a man's shout, then a small window opened in the door. In his weary state, Cynan thought Lucifrido was going to recite the secret words needed to enter Lutozzo's compound, so similar was the grating-covered hole in the door and the gruff voice of the man behind it.

Lucifrido moved close to the door and whispered. After a brief pause, the window was closed, then came the sound of a bar being removed and the gate was dragged open. It was well-maintained, the hinges greased, and it made barely a sound.

"This is Tubbia," said Lucifrido. "He is a friend, and will put us up for the night."

Beobrand dismounted and led his horse into the courtyard beyond. A large dog sniffed at Beobrand, but seemed harmless enough now his master had welcomed them.

"We cannot stay here awaiting our enemies," he said.

"I know, lord," Lucifrido replied. "But we have reached the sea and can ride no further this night. I have friends here. I will find a ship while you eat and rest."

Cynan did not like the way the man called Beobrand "lord". He sensed mockery in Lucifrido's tone, but he could not place why exactly. Still, there was no denying they were all on the verge of collapse from lack of sleep and the ordeals of the previous days.

Sliding down from his saddle, Cynan led his horse into the yard. Tubbia held up a small oil lamp, its flame illuminating his face. He was perhaps fifty, with a bald pate and grey hair bushing at his ears. His eyes sparkled in the lamplight and the deep lines around them spoke of a man who smiled a lot, much like Lucifrido. Two more men came from the building to help with the horses. One was young and beardless, the other several years older than Tubbia.

Beobrand spoke briefly with Lucifrido and Tubbia. Lucifrido went back through the gate and disappeared into the night. Tubbia closed and barred it behind him. Cynan hoped Beobrand was not wrong to place his faith in Lucifrido, but the truth of it was he was almost too tired to care. Even if Lutozzo, Stoldo and the Emperor himself descended on Ostia in that moment, Cynan doubted the renowned Black Shields would put up much resistance. Lucifrido was right. They needed food and they needed sleep.

Bleddyn was helping Coenred down from his horse. The monk looked ready to drop to the cobbles and sleep right there.

"See to the horses," Beobrand said to Cynan, "then join us inside. Lucifrido thinks he can get us a ship and Tubbia here has promised us some pottage and yesterday's bread."

"As hungry as I am," said Cynan, "I would eat last month's bread, mould and all."

He unsaddled his horse and helped unharness the mules from the waggon. Then he set about rubbing down the animals and seeing they had ample water. The men who had come out of the inn knew what they were about, brushing the horses and hanging up their harness in a small covered area at the side of the yard. Cynan trusted they would feed the animals too.

When the beasts were tended to, Cynan turned to Eadgard and Bleddyn.

"Stay out here with the waggon. Laden as it is, we cannot afford to leave it unattended. I'll have food and drink brought to you."

Eadgard glowered, but gave a curt nod and sat on the back of the waggon. Bleddyn said nothing, but Cynan could see he was as tired as the rest of them.

"Even if we travel by boat," Cynan said to him with a pat on the shoulder, "I wager we will still travel through Paris. You will see Alpaida again."

Bleddyn offered him a thin smile.

"I pray you are right about that," he said. "But nothing is ever so easy for us, is it?"

"Do you regret swearing your oath to me?" Cynan asked.

"Every day," Bleddyn said with a chuckle. "Every single day."

Inside the building Cynan found the rest of the men sitting at a table. A rushlight guttered on the board. Tubbia's big dog lay nearby, looking up at the men, hopeful of scraps. At the other end of the room, shrouded in shadows, he could make out the shapes of three sleeping men. As Cynan entered, one rose on his elbow and said something. From his tone, it was not a warm welcome.

"Frankish merchants," whispered Beobrand. "On their way to Roma. They have not taken kindly to being woken."

"I can't say I blame them," said Cynan, scraping a stool on the stone floor and sitting with a grunt. One of the Franks hissed.

"Halinard," Cynan said, "tell that bastard that if he hisses at me again, I'll cut out his tongue and feed it to the dog."

Halinard snorted and relayed Cynan's words to the merchant in the dark. The Frank lay back down and said no more.

"Seems he has grown used to our presence," said Ingwald with a grin. "Now, where is that pottage we were promised? If it takes much longer I will fall asleep with my face in the bowl."

As if in answer to his query, Tubbia appeared, carrying several wooden bowls and half a large loaf of bread. A plump, handsome woman followed behind him with cups and a jug.

It was watered wine and Beobrand thanked them as they served the food and drink. Cynan asked Coenred to tell Tubbia to take wine, pottage and bread out to Eadgard and Bleddyn. That done, he set to eating his own stew. It was watery and barely warm. But it was food, and the bread, while stale, was good when soaked in the salty liquid. The wine was sour, but again, welcome enough after the long day.

They ate in silence until all of their plates were empty. Tubbia brought another pitcher of wine, but Beobrand waved him away.

"Ask for water, if it is clean," he said to Coenred. The monk was barely awake, his bandaged head nodding, but he mumbled something and the chubby innkeeper shuffled away with a shake of his head to return moments later with a clay jug filled with cool water. Cynan poured himself some.

"The wine is bad enough, but better than this piss," he said, after tasting the slightly brackish water.

Beobrand sipped from his own cup and grimaced.

"We must keep our heads clear," he said.

"I hear you," Cynan said. "Rest now. Ingwald and I will take the watch after Bleddyn and Eadgard."

Beobrand sniffed and stared into the wavering flame of the rushlight.

"I will not be able to sleep," he said, "until we are aboard a ship and far from the nest of vipers that is Roma." He looked about at the drawn faces of his men. "But you are right. The rest of you, sleep."

Halinard, Coenred and Ingwald needed no further urging. They stretched out on the hard floor and wrapped themselves in thin blankets Tubbia had provided.

Cynan watched them for a time, then sipped his water. He shuddered, regretting tasting again the bitter, salty liquid.

"You think Lucifrido will come back?" he asked Beobrand, in the quietest of whispers.

Beobrand did not answer immediately. Instead, he took Coenred's cup and, seeing the monk had not finished his wine, offered it to Cynan. Cynan swallowed a mouthful of the sour wine. It was not good, but much more pleasant than that gods-awful water.

"I think he will," said Beobrand at last.

"Can we trust him?"

Beobrand shrugged, accepting Coenred's cup from Cynan and draining the last dregs of wine.

"Perhaps," he said. "Maybe it is as he says. He has helped us, stood with us in the fight with Lutozzo and Stoldo's men."

"But what of Agiperto?" asked Cynan. "Did he lead him to us somehow?"

Beobrand let out a long sigh.

"I think there comes a time when all you can do is take a man at his word and hope he does not break his promise." He stifled a yawn. "I am too tired to worry more about this tonight."

They sat in silence for a time. Their friends were already asleep and one of the Franks was snoring loudly.

"If we are not going to rest," whispered Beobrand, "you and I should let Bleddyn and Eadgard sleep."

Cynan had been dozing where he sat, but snapped awake and grunted in agreement.

Outside Eadgard and Bleddyn were standing beside the waggon, speaking quietly.

"Go get some sleep," Beobrand called as they walked towards them.

Far off, wavering and gossamer-thin in the night, Cynan heard something. He paused, straining to make out more.

"I thought I heard shouting," he said.

Beobrand halted and stood unmoving. The night was still, the only sound that reached them in the walled courtyard was the stamp of the horses and the muffled snoring of the Frank from within the hall.

"I hear nothing," Beobrand said, shaking his head.

"I heard it too," said Bleddyn. "I couldn't say for sure *what* I heard," he added, "but something has happened out there."

"If there is trouble," said Eadgard, "we should stay here, ready for what may come."

"No need, Eadgard," said Beobrand. "There is a wall and stout door between us and the street. There will be time if an attack comes. Sleep, but keep your axe close."

Eadgard scowled, but after a moment, he walked across the yard and made his way into the hall with Bleddyn at his side. They closed the door behind them, shutting inside the rushlight's pale glow. The courtyard was in almost absolute darkness now and Cynan wished they had thought to bring a lamp out with them.

"He will barely look at you," Cynan said.

Beobrand sniffed.

"Eadgard is ashamed," he said. "But I, of all men, cannot hold it against him for wishing to avenge his brother. And you and I both know that a man's wyrd can lead him into conflict with his hlaford."

Cynan thought of how he had ridden to Sulis' aid and remembered Beobrand's fury.

"I am sorry," said Cynan.

Beobrand placed a hand on his shoulder.

"As long as the men who swear their oaths to me are true, I cannot judge them too harshly." He made a sound in the gloom that sounded like a sob, but might have been a snort of laughter. "Woden knows I have tested my own oaths to the point of breaking."

Cynan said nothing. He recalled the times in which Beobrand had faced dilemmas posed by oaths he had sworn in good faith. Cynan's eyes grew accustomed to the gloom and he realised he could pick out shapes and details in the courtyard. The stars and moon would provide enough light to watch over the waggon's contents. The gate was barred and was the only way in. And even if someone were to scale the wall, Cynan would see them from where he stood.

Beobrand and Cynan remained in silence for a long time, listening to the night, each lost in his own memories. Cynan's thoughts turned away from Sulis and broken oaths and moved to Eadgyth. He pictured what it would be like to be sleeping beside her in the hall at Stagga. It was a good thought and he clung to it, building the details of the image in his mind; the scent of her hair, the texture of the bear pelt on his bed, the soft sound of Eadgyth's breathing. Someone scratching on the timber door of the hall.

It was only when Beobrand moved across the yard to the gate, that Cynan realised he had been dreaming, half-asleep on his feet. Shaking himself awake, he put his hand on the hilt of his sword and followed Beobrand.

The scratching sound came again. This was not a dream, but outside in the street of Ostia, someone was scraping against the yard's thick wooden door.

Beobrand dragged Nægling from its scabbard and held up his left hand. Cynan drew his own sword and they stood together in silence. A voice hissed from the other side of the door.

"It is me. Lucifrido."

Cynan saw Beobrand relax slightly.

Fumbling at the latch of the small hatch that permitted a view of the street beyond, Cynan pulled it open and peered outside. All was in shadows. He could just make out Lucifrido's shape, but nothing else.

"Do you come alone?" Cynan asked.

"Yes," replied Lucifrido. "And I have found a vessel. We can leave with the tide. There is no time to waste."

Beobrand moved to the thick wooden locking bar, but Cynan halted him with a hand on his arm. It was possible someone could be hiding out of sight, too close to the wall to be seen from the grate-covered hatch.

Stepping back and dropping into the warrior stance, holding his sword high, he nodded to Beobrand to show he was ready. If Lucifrido had betrayed them, whoever stepped through those doors would meet Cynan's blade.

Beobrand slid back the bar, dropping it noisily to the cobbles and jumping back from the doors. From inside the hall, the dog barked. After a heartbeat, the door was pushed open and Lucifrido slipped inside. As soon as he was through, he closed the doors behind him. Sheathing his sword, Cynan picked up the bar and dropped it back into place.

With the door safely secured again, Cynan let out a relieved breath. It seemed his fears were unfounded and once more Lucifrido had proven his worth.

"The man who will help us is on the harbour wall," Lucifrido explained. "His brother's boat had not returned and his family were waiting for him. Shortly after I arrived, the brother's boat sailed out of the night. He had found a huge shoal of mackerel and such was the weight of his catch he was slower returning to port than usual." Lucifrido wiped sweat from his brow. The night was warm. "I was already speaking to the skipper," he continued, "about taking us along the coast, and I was not sure I was going to convince him. But perhaps God smiles on us, for his attitude changed upon his brother's return. His other brothers, cousins and their families were all shouting and singing. His brother's wife was crying with happiness. When they saw the size of the haul of fish, they could not believe their luck. At that moment the skipper accepted my request for passage. And for a reasonable price too." He grinned, clearly pleased with himself.

"How much?" asked Beobrand.

Lucifrido told him. He was right, thought Cynan grudgingly, it was a fair price and they would have ample silver left over.

"He will take us as far as Pisa," Lucifrido went on. "I told him we wished to be gone as quickly as possible and he said that we should leave with the tide. Today it will turn just before sunrise. So we must hurry."

"You have done well," said Beobrand. "But what about the horses and the mules? The waggon?"

"Let me speak to Tubbia. He might be able to aid us."

Beobrand clapped him on the back.

"See that he gives you a cup of wine and some bread too. The wine is not good, but you have eaten nothing." Lucifrido made to leave, but Beobrand pulled him back. "And have him send his son and that servant to help with the waggon and the loading of the ship."

Cynan watched Lucifrido go, the glow of the rushlight from the open door suddenly bright in the darkness.

"You see?" Beobrand said, smiling. "Sometimes you just have to trust a man to do what is right."

"I would rather ride north than sail," said Cynan, "but I will not deny Lucifrido has done well."

Cynan set about hitching the mules once more to pull the waggon. Soon, the others, bleary-eyed and rubbing sleep from their faces, came out into the yard. Lamps were brought out and soon the waggon was turned around and ready to be taken to the harbour. The other horses were still tethered beneath the lean-to at the edge of the yard. Cynan saw to it that their saddles and bridles were loaded onto the waggon.

Tubbia oversaw his son and servant as they helped, making sure they did not take anything of his. Not much remained that did not now belong to him. Lucifrido had negotiated as best he could, but there was little time and Tubbia, sensing their urgent need, made them an offer for their mounts and the waggon that could barely be called fair and certainly not generous. Still, the silver he gave them would almost cover the cost of their passage to Pisa. Once there they would need to find new mounts, but that was a worry for another day and Cynan would at least have his good Frankish saddle.

It did not take them very long to prepare. Beobrand thanked Tubbia and then they pulled the doors open. The sky was still dark, but looking towards the east Cynan could detect a faint lightening, turning the sky the iron grey of a sword-blade.

Tubbia's old servant drove the waggon expertly along the street and out towards the harbour. Beobrand and Cynan walked in front of the mules, Lucifrido leading the way. Coenred, still weak and dizzy from injury, the hard ride and lack of sleep, rode on the waggon. Eadgard, Bleddyn, Ingwald and Halinard trudged along behind with Tubbia's son.

Several boats were moored in the harbour, lifted now by the incoming tide from where they had lain canted on the sand.

Now their masts swayed gently in the swell, reminding Cynan of spearmen on the march. The fire in the brazier was nothing more than embers now. Most of the people who had been gathered there had gone. There were still some figures on the harbour wall though. Cynan watched as a man clambered out of a ship moored some way past the brazier's glow. The man raised a hand in welcome. Lucifrido responded with a shout.

"That's the skipper who will take us," he said.

Glancing back, Cynan saw the waggon and the mules trundling slowly onto the harbour's stone perimeter. There would be little enough room for the vehicle and they would no doubt have to unhitch the mules and then push the waggon back by hand once it was unloaded. There would certainly not be enough space to turn the vehicle. But the waggon would be empty by then and much lighter. Besides, he thought, that would be Tubbia's man's problem, not his.

Turning back towards the waiting skipper, Cynan saw several men step out from the shadows closer to the brazier. He wondered if they were the ship's crew. But almost before that thought had come to him, something about their bearing gave him pause. Beobrand sensed it too, for he slowed his step and placed his hand warily on Nægling's pommel. Cynan halted, his keen eyes searching the night for a sign of what had unnerved them both.

In that instant a breeze blew life into the embers. The ruddy glow reflected from steel in the men's hands and the brazier gave just enough light to illuminate the faces of the foremost men who stood in their path.

Cynan drew his sword.

"I wish you had been right about Lucifrido," he said to Beobrand.

On the harbour wall, at the head of a dozen men, he could make out the heavily muscled shape and unmistakably ugly features of the killer, Vico. In his meaty fists he carried a club even larger than the one he had used to kill Grindan.

Beside him, the wind-fanned embers shone red on the hate-filled face of Agiperto.

Chapter 41

Beobrand's weariness was bone deep. On seeing the ship's skipper on the harbour wall, his mind had turned towards the future. He was already imagining the swell of the waves beneath the keel as the tide bore them away from the shore, away from Roma and its twisted intrigues and perils.

His tiredness had made him complacent and slower to react than he would otherwise have been, but he still had time to draw Nægling and to ready himself as Agiperto, Vico and the men behind them closed in.

Beobrand surveyed the harbour wall they stood on. The stone was smooth and damp, slick from the fish that had recently been unloaded. Cursing, he realised the waggon blocked the path behind them, almost filling the width of the wall. He would have to stand with only Cynan and Lucifrido at his side against more than a dozen warriors.

Agiperto shouted at Lucifrido. Beobrand glanced at the young man. Lucifrido's expression was stern, unreadable. He did not look away from Agiperto. Beobrand cursed. Had Lucifrido led them here to this ambush?

But there was no time for such concerns. On the seaward side of the harbour, the wall was raised. If they could put their backs against that wall, making it impossible for them to be encircled, they would fare better.

He opened his mouth to give the command to Lucifrido and Cynan, but Vico must have sensed his intention, for he let out a bellowing roar and rushed at them. The rest of the attackers surged forward, as if dragged along on Vico's rage. Agiperto ran beside Vico, sword raised, loathing contorting his face.

When they had clashed in the street outside the amphitheatre, their opponents had been unarmoured. Now, some of them wore thick leather jerkins. Iron armour gleamed on others. Several of them carried shields.

Not anticipating this attack, Beobrand had left his shield, byrnie and helm on the waggon. Cynan had been less convinced of their safety. Despite the warm night and their proximity to the harbour, the Waelisc warrior had donned his byrnie and carried his black-daubed shield. Beobrand had scoffed at the precaution. He was not laughing now.

Gulls shrieked above them, disturbed by the noise perhaps, or gorging on remnants of the earlier fisherman's catch. The birds' cries sounded like laughter to Beobrand.

For the briefest of moments, he had thought he might yet be able to talk with Agiperto, to negotiate with the man and pay the weregild for his son. But if that possibility had ever truly existed, one glimpse of the man's fury-filled features told Beobrand the moment for conversation had long since passed.

Crouching into the warrior stance, Beobrand readied himself to receive the charge. Vico sprinted towards him. Beobrand fixed his gaze on the bald man, his head throbbing with the memory of Vico's cudgel blow. Wearing no helm, Beobrand knew he would have to avoid the stout wooden club. A solid strike from that weapon would break bones or crush a skull. Instinctively, Cynan moved close to Beobrand, protecting his left side. Lucifrido was to Cynan's left, but Beobrand could not drop his focus on Vico to look at how he fared.

With the roar and rage of their assailants' attack, all Beobrand's weariness washed away in a flood of battle-fury. Now, as ever in combat, it seemed to him that his adversaries moved slowly, enabling him to dance around their blows. And so it was, that he was able to duck beneath Vico's huge club. Beobrand lunged with his sword, hoping to disembowel Stoldo's ugly brawler, but the blade scraped harmlessly against Vico's jerkin of hardened leather. Vico did not hesitate or slow his charge. He had expected to connect with Beobrand, and the force of his swing put him off-balance. His momentum sent him colliding into the Bernician, knocking Nægling's blade aside. Beobrand was ready for him. He caught Vico's weight on his shoulder and heaved him up, throwing him over his back and onto the stone walkway of the harbour behind him.

Vico crashed into the paving slabs and Beobrand was set to leap on him, to plunge his sword into the brute and finish him, when another man sprang at him from the gloom. This one had a shield and Beobrand lashed out and grabbed it, twisting it so that the man had to release it or risk breaking his wrist. The shield fell away and Beobrand punched Nægling's hilt into the man's mouth, smashing his teeth. Taking hold of the stunned man's kirtle, Beobrand slashed his sword's blade across his face, then yanked the stunned man hard towards him. Using his assailant's weight, Beobrand twisted his hips and half-threw the man behind him. Vico had been on his knees and rising when the bleeding man crashed into him, sending him sprawling again.

All around them was chaos now. Beobrand thought he could make out Eadgard's roaring shouts from behind him. He imagined the axeman and the other Black Shields fighting to climb over the waggon, or perhaps to struggle around it. But he had no opportunity to look. The man he had sent spinning into

Vico was badly wounded and probably posed no further threat. Vico though was uninjured and the nape of Beobrand's neck prickled to think of the man's club swinging at his unprotected back.

He wanted to turn and face Vico, but there was yet another enemy standing before him now. Beobrand slashed a feint at his face and the man stepped away, giving Beobrand time to snatch up the shield his previous foe-man had dropped. The grip inside the pommel was slick with the man's sweat. Beobrand hoped he would not drop the willow board, his left hand not being as strong as it had once been.

The dark shapes of the men around him seethed, grunting and screaming. The clang of metal on metal, and the thump of blades connecting with shields was loud in the night. Above them all, the gulls cried. Beobrand could make out little of the action in the darkness except that Cynan still lived. The Waelisc fought furiously on his left. But men had swarmed past them and he could sense them as much as see them grouping with Vico, ready to press in from the rear.

Beobrand could see nothing of Lucifrido.

His new opponent had regained his footing now and came forward again, demanding Beobrand's attention. The thegn of Ubbanford spat at the man. He could not fight so many and hope to live, and yet if it was his wyrd to die here, he would take many souls to serve him in Woden's corpse hall.

"Death!" he bellowed, as his attacker advanced. Dimly, through the din, Beobrand heard his men take up the battle-cry.

The man before him was almost his height. He had long black hair pulled back from his angular face and fastened in a plait. He was young. And fast. Perhaps as fast as Beobrand himself. But his movements showed a lack of experience, and in the instant the young man lunged Beobrand knew he would kill the man. The stab was aimed at Beobrand's chest. He caught the blade on the shield's edge, then, as fast as a viper, he flicked out Nægling and opened up the artery in the man's groin. Blood gushed, a hot fountain to add to the fish gore and further slicken the harbour wall.

"Back to back," Beobrand yelled, hoping Cynan would hear him and be able to obey. But Beobrand did not wait to see if he had. Shoving his dying enemy hard into his comrades, Beobrand spun around, certain that danger loomed behind him.

His instincts, honed in countless battles, were right. Vico's club came whistling out of the darkness and it was all Beobrand could do to deflect the murderous swing. His arm jarred from the impact and for a dreadful instant he thought he would lose his grip on the shield. With difficulty, he maintained his hold on the iron boss' handle and was able to soak up Vico's next thundering strike.

Beobrand felt a sudden pressure on his back. He tensed, expecting to feel the burning agony of a knife in his ribs. Instead of pain, it was relief that he felt, as he heard Cynan's voice.

"I'm not sure how much longer I can hold off so many," Cynan panted. Then, raising his voice so that the other gesithas would hear him, he shouted, "Hey! If you are done resting, we could use your swords against these whoresons!"

Beobrand grinned savagely in the gloom. If they were to die here, he could ask for no better men with whom to share his wyrd and the journey to the afterlife.

Just as quickly as Cynan had appeared at Beobrand's back, he was gone again, pulled away into the fierce fighting and leaving Beobrand exposed. In the same instant Vico pressed his attack. Beobrand sliced at him, but the bald warrior pushed his blade away with his club, then, with great skill and strength, he reversed the direction of the blow, aiming the stout cudgel at Beobrand's outstretched sword arm.

Beobrand retreated, narrowly avoiding the attack and

skittering out of range. As he moved backwards, his left foot slipped in the gore on the stones. He fell to one knee, the impact sending a jolt of pain shooting up his leg. Grinning, Vico, flanked by two swordsmen, came in for the kill.

But Beobrand still railed against the weft of his wyrd. He would not die easily here, so close to escape. Surging up, Beobrand caught one sword on his shield and parried Vico's cudgel, pushing it just far enough out of line that it hissed past his face. Vico's missed swing hampered the other swordsman and their weapons clashed.

Beobrand's knee screamed in protest. He ignored it. It would be badly bruised, but the leg held his weight.

Behind Vico, Beobrand made out the shadowy shapes of his men clambering over the waggon. His heart leapt at the sight. If he could keep his opponents occupied for a few heartbeats more, and avoid their stabbing swords and swinging clubs, perhaps he would survive this night after all. For surely these ruffians were no match for his Black Shields.

Bleddyn was the first down from the waggon. He was sprinting towards the back of Beobrand's opponents, sword held high. By the gleam of the embers and the paling sky in the east, Beobrand saw that Bleddyn was not looking at Vico and the swordsmen he faced, but past him, over Beobrand's shoulder. Bleddyn was staring in shock at some new danger. As he shouted a warning, so Beobrand's attuned senses and battle-instinct told him it was too late to save him from the peril that loomed behind him. The relief he had felt turned to horror. The gods had been toying with him all along.

"Lucifrido," Bleddyn screamed. "No!"

Chapter 42

Beobrand tensed. So Cynan's fears had been proven correct. He had trusted Lucifrido and now the bastard was going to strike him down from behind. Knowing it was futile, but still determined to fight, Beobrand flung himself forward, smashing his shield towards the men in front of him.

Something hit Beobrand hard between the shoulder blades. He staggered forward, gritting his teeth against the agony he knew would come. But instead of the blade slicing into his vitals, and the warm flow of his lifeblood running down his spine, Beobrand felt the weight that had hit him slide down and away. There was no real pain.

Glancing down he saw that Agiperto lay dying at his feet. The man's lips were pulled back in a snarl of bitter hatred, his dead fingers clasped around the hilt of a wicked-looking dagger.

Lucifrido wrenched his sword from between Agiperto's ribs with difficulty and stepped beside Beobrand, adding his blade to defend his right side.

"Trust me now, lord?" Lucifrido asked.

At the sight of their leader struck down, and the appearance of reinforcements from the waggon, the men before Beobrand faltered.

"You have earned your place at my side, Lucifrido," said Beobrand, baring his teeth. "Now let's kill these nithings."

Seizing on their enemies' moment of hesitation, Beobrand bellowed his battle-cry and, with Lucifrido beside him, renewed his attack.

He dispatched one swordsman with a vicious downward cut. Lucifrido jabbed at the other man, forcing him to retreat towards Bleddyn, who hacked him down without hesitation. The Waelisc man continued past Beobrand and Lucifrido, rushing to assist Cynan. Halinard followed him, vaulting over the fallen, skidding in the blood on the rocks momentarily, then hurrying to Cynan's aid.

"Help them," Beobrand said to Lucifrido.

"Are you sure, lord?" Lucifrido asked, looking warily at Vico.

"This ugly whoreson is as good as dead already," Beobrand said. "Go."

With a curt nod, Lucifrido turned, joining the rest of the warriors as if he had trained with them for years. Beobrand did not take his eyes from the broad-shouldered bald man before him.

Seeing the men around him fall, Vico growled and spat like an animal. He slapped his cudgel into his left palm and bared his teeth. Beobrand chuckled and goaded the man, holding his shield to the side and beckoning him forward.

"Come on, you turd!" Beobrand spat, opening his arms wide as if for an embrace. Behind him he could hear his gesithas slaying the remaining men. "Think you can take me, Vico?" he hissed, not sure how much the man would understand, but knowing he would hear his name. "Then do it, you whoreson!"

Vico roared and leapt forward, swinging his huge club towards Beobrand's head. He was deadly fast, and even though he had been expecting the attack, Beobrand almost didn't get his shield up in time. The cudgel clattered against the willow board and

Beobrand took a quick step backwards, sliding his feet across the wet stone, careful not to slip again. His knee throbbed.

Normally, he would have sprung back with a deadly riposte, taking advantage of his balance and speed and Vico's overreach. But instead, Beobrand remained motionless. Slowly, he lowered his shield.

Vico lay dead on the blood-slathered stones. Eadgard twisted his axe head in the man's skull, pulling it grotesquely this way and that, until the iron bit came free of the sucking bone and brains.

Eadgard spat onto the man's corpse.

"That is for my brother," he said, his voice cracking with emotion.

The mules were braying noisily, terrified by the fighting and the smell of blood. Tubbia's man and his son had both fled, leaving Coenred, pale-faced and frightened, on the waggon's driving seat.

Looking towards the ship, Beobrand saw his gesithas had killed the rest of Agiperto's men. The eastern sky was brightening by moments and the grey wolf-light of dawn was enough to make out details of the scene. The skipper had climbed back aboard his vessel and now he stared at the aftermath of the battle and the blood-soaked warriors on the harbour wall with an expression of horror on his face.

"Lucifrido," Beobrand said, "tell the skipper to be ready to sail. I'll pay him extra for his trouble. He can see why we need to leave as soon as possible."

Lucifrido hurried to do his bidding. The skipper was pale and he shot them furtive glances, but he set about readying his vessel.

"Seems you were wrong about him after all," Beobrand said, clapping Cynan on the shoulder.

Cynan grunted. He was covered in blood and limping from some injury sustained in the fight, but seemed hale enough.

"I'm glad to be wrong this time," he said. "But don't get used to it, lord," he said with a grin. "It doesn't happen often."

Beobrand scoffed.

"I'll ask Eadgyth about that then when we're back in Bernicia."

Beobrand drew in a deep breath, taking in the carnage on the harbour wall.

"Strip them of anything of value," he said, "then toss their bodies into the sea for the crabs and the gulls." He stared out over the dark waters of the Great Sea. The sunrise was just beginning to soften the hue of the waves, turning them from black to a murky green. "Then get that waggon unloaded. The tide, like wyrd, waits for no man."

Chapter 43

Beobrand stood at the prow of the ship and watched the land slide by in the distance. The vessel was no wave-steed. It was sluggish and broad bellied and every part of it, from the rigging to the strakes, stank of old fish. The sail luffed and flapped as the wind swung into the east and a rolling wave caught them broadside, making the vessel yaw and roll perilously. Heavily laden as it was with the men from Albion and their gear, treasure, and the relics and artefacts that Coenred had bought in Roma, the ship was slow and it was certainly not smooth sailing. At first Beobrand had believed the ship's tortuous pace and stomach-churning rolling was due to the heavy load in the hold, but increasingly he thought it might be down to the skipper's lack of skill.

Bleddyn was leaning over the port-side, retching and spitting. The others were slumped between the thwarts, drowsing as best they could while the boat lumbered onward.

Beobrand knew he would need to sleep soon. But he enjoyed the feeling of the cool sea breeze on his face. Every now and then, the bow splashed into a wave, sending surf up in a soothing cool spray. The sun was already high in the sky and it reflected bright off the swell. Licking the salt from his lips, Beobrand looked back along the ship at where Coenred snoozed. Sunlight fell directly onto the monk's face. He would burn if he didn't move into the shade. The sight of his friend's pinched features, his bruised face and the blood-stained bandage wrapped about his head, twisted Beobrand's stomach. Coenred had come so close to death.

Beobrand let out a long sigh, hoping that Grindan's was the last death he would have to contend with on this journey. As they had left the safety of the harbour at Ostia, Beobrand had taken a gold bracelet and the good dagger that had belonged to Agiperto and thrown them into the sea, offering them as tribute to whichever gods governed the waves. It seemed Woden had been satisfied with the blood they had spilt, and with Grindan's sacrifice. Beobrand prayed his offering of treasure would be enough for the gods of the sea to grant them safe passage.

Lucifrido had been conversing with the master of the ship, but now he made his way to the bow.

"He says we will put in at a cove he knows for the night," Lucifrido said. "We will continue on our way towards Pisa at first light tomorrow."

Another wave washed over the low wale, sending more water swilling into the bilge and ballast. The stench of rotting fish was overpowering.

"We might have been safer taking our chances on land," Beobrand said.

"No, lord," said Lucifrido, his habitual smile returning. "You have made enemies of Tanualdo, Stoldo, Priano and Lutozzo, not to mention the emissary of the Exarchatus of Ravenna. The sooner we are in Lombardia, the better."

Beobrand watched as seabirds flocked behind a smaller fishing boat further out to sea. The birds swooped and dived in the boat's wake. He listened for their keening cries, but they were too far off. He stifled a yawn. The shaking that always followed battle had subsided and now, crashing over him like a wave, came the dreadful weariness that had led to them walking into a trap like lambs wandering into a pack of wolves. He smiled to himself. That is, if lambs bore swords and axes.

"You should get some sleep," he said. "I can barely keep my eyes open and you have been awake as long as me."

Lucifrido's smile broadened.

"But I am younger than you, lord," he said.

Beobrand snorted. He was too weary for jibes. He turned to make his way down the ship, but Lucifrido halted him with a touch on his shoulder.

"Lord," he said, "will you take my oath now, before you sleep?"

The young man had asked if he might swear his allegiance to Beobrand soon after they had left the harbour. Beobrand had said nothing then, merely nodding non-committally. Now he halted and met Lucifrido's gaze. The young man's smile was gone, his expression earnest.

"Are you so sure you would give me your oath, Lucifrido?" Beobrand asked. "We head towards war in the north. And even at peace, you have seen for yourself, it is dangerous to be my man."

"Being anyone's man is dangerous," replied Lucifrido, the corners of his mouth twitching. "I am not afraid of that. And if I am your gesith, at least I doubt I will ever be bored."

Beobrand stared at him for a long while. He fought well and had risked his life for Beobrand and his men when he could have slipped away.

"Very well," said Beobrand. "I will take your oath, but such a solemn act needs witnesses."

"I will be witness."

They both turned to see Coenred, rubbing sleep from his eyes and once more wearing his wide-brimmed straw hat. The wind gusted and threatened to blow it off his head, so he held his hat in place with his bandaged left hand. Beobrand wondered how long it would be until he lost that hat.

"If there are oaths to be sworn, I too would hear them." Cynan was limping towards them.

"I thought you would want to rest that leg," said Beobrand, nodding at Cynan's blood-stained breeches. The cut to his thigh was not deep, but it had bled a lot. It was bandaged now, but would still be painful.

"I'll rest as soon as you've taken this man's oath," said Cynan.

And so it was that Lucifrido knelt on the swaying deck of the fish-smelling tub of a ship, and placed his lips upon Nægling's cool blade. He swore to be true and faithful, to love what Beobrand loved and to shun what he shunned and never to displease him through deed or word.

When Lucifrido was done, Coenred made the sign of the cross and prayed to the Christ god that both oath-maker and oath-taker would uphold the solemn vows they had made. As ever when he heard a man's oath, Beobrand's memory turned to the hall of Bebbanburg what seemed like a lifetime before, when he had knelt before King Edwin and given the first of his many oaths. And, as usual, Beobrand could barely believe any man would wish to bestow upon him such an honour.

Cynan offered Lucifrido his hand. After a brief hesitation, the man from Sutri grasped Cynan's arm in the warrior grip. Cynan pulled him to his feet. Lucifrido grinned and thanked Coenred awkwardly for his blessing. Then he let out a long sigh. His smile did not fade, but his shoulders sagged, and it seemed to Beobrand that he could see the tiredness of the last two days and nights suddenly catch up with Lucifrido, as if he had been holding himself alert and awake until this act had been completed.

"Get some rest," Beobrand said, smiling and slapping Lucifrido and Cynan on the back. "Both of you. That's an order."

Lucifrido beamed, then offered his shoulder for Cynan to lean on. Together they limped back to where the others dozed.

The ship lurched as they hit a wave. A shudder ran through its timbers. Coenred steadied himself by grasping the taut bowline with his right hand. His bandaged left hand was still firmly on his hat. The wide brim lifted and flapped in the strengthening wind, emulating the ship's sail.

"The Almighty truly works in mysterious ways," Coenred said. "You lost a good man not two days ago, and today you hear the oath of another."

"Lucifrido cannot replace Grindan," Beobrand said, leaning both hands on the wale and staring out to sea with his icy blue eyes. "The price of this journey has been too high. Grindan, Gram, Attor."

"You are right, of course," said Coenred. "And I fear we have lost Wilfrid too."

Beobrand spat over the side of the ship, careful to do so away from the wind.

"Wilfrid will find his way," he said. "His kind always do. He'll be a bishop one day, Coenred, mark my words. You'll have to bow and scrape to him. Tell me then what you think of your God's mysterious ways."

"You might be right," said Coenred, his tone tinged with sadness. "But bishop or not, Wilfrid will have to be careful should he ever meet Eadgard again."

Beobrand laughed at that thought.

"Yes," he said. "An axe to the head might well interfere with his plans." He glanced at Coenred, sombre again. "I'm glad we did not lose you, old friend."

Coenred reached his bandaged hand up to the cloth covering where his ear had been.

"No, just parts of me," he said with a thin smile. "I am glad too, Beo. Thank you for coming for me."

There were tears in both men's eyes and they fell silent for a time. Beobrand cuffed at his cheeks. His knee pained him as the ship lurched against another wave.

"I will be pleased to see Lindisfarena again," said Coenred. "I had so long dreamt of visiting Roma, but I will be glad to be home."

"I will be pleased too," said Beobrand. "It has been much too long. I fear for my kin. For Ubbanford. For Bernicia. If what we heard in Roma is true, we are travelling towards war."

"I pray that your loved ones are all safe," said Coenred. "You must be looking forward to seeing your first grandson."

"I am," Beobrand said, though in truth he had thought little of Ardith's child. To think of it made him feel old. What he thought of more, he did not dare to say out loud, not even to his oldest friend.

Even more than Ubbanford and his kith and kin, he longed to travel to the fortress of Bebbanburg.

To Eanflæd.

He had tried his best to push her from his mind. He had hoped that his absence would have made his desire for the queen wane. If anything, his yearning for Eanflæd had only strengthened. The thought of seeing her again burnt within him; a flame he could not extinguish no matter the time or distance they were apart.

Coenred was staring at him. Beobrand wondered if he was able to read his thoughts. The monk was intelligent and perceptive, but surely Beobrand's longing for the Queen of Northumbria was not so obvious.

"I wonder what we will find when we reach Northumbria," Beobrand said. "If the tales of the Picts waging war have reached all the way to Roma, things could be very bad."

"Perhaps Oswiu no longer rules," said Coenred, raising an eyebrow.

Beobrand shot him a sharp look.

"I pray to all the gods he is yet the king," he said. Part of him wondered if that was true. Oswiu was not the warrior king his brother, Oswald, had been, but if war had broken out with the Picts, the king would be called to stand in the shieldwall with his fyrd. And the Picts were fearsome foes.

"Whatever awaits us, Beo," said Coenred, "I am sure you will face it as you always do."

Beobrand gave a lopsided smile.

"Like a headstrong bull?"

Coenred returned the smile.

"With honour," he said, "and the bravery of a boar."

Beobrand shook his head. Yawning loudly, he turned away from the prow.

"I am unworthy of such praise," he said. "But I'll worry about what waits for us in Albion another day. Now, I need sleep."

He squeezed Coenred's shoulder, then made his way down the rolling deck towards the ship's broad belly. He was certain of little about the future except that his wyrd was calling him homeward.

To Bernicia.

And to battle.

Historical Note

The pilgrimage of Wilfrid and Baducing (more commonly known as Benedict Biscop) to Rome sometime in the 650s is a matter of historical record, and I intended to have Beobrand and Coenred accompany them on the journey ever since my initial planning of *The Serpent Sword*, when I naively imagined Beobrand's entire life would be covered in a single novel!

Wilfrid was a divisive figure in his lifetime and frequently clashed with other ecclesiastics, nobility and royalty. He is often accused by modern commentators of being more interested in his own power than any true dedication to spirituality and learning and I have seized on that facet of his personality to drive the narrative. Historical records frequently show that if an opportunity to further his career or influence arose, Wilfrid was quick, and often ruthless, in grabbing it with both hands. He was also seemingly uncaring of the enemies he made as a result. Nevertheless, I feel compelled to apologise to Wilfrid's memory for impugning his character quite as much as I have in this series of books.

Some of the events described in the previous novel, *Forest of Foes*, were directly inspired by the writings of Stephen of Ripon, who wrote Wilfrid's hagiography, *Vita Sancti Wilfrithi*, or the *Life of Saint Wilfrid*. The incidents that take place in *Shadows of the Slain* owe more to my imagination than to the accounts of Wilfrid's life.

In both novels, Wilfrid's appetite for the fairer sex leads him into scrapes. It was not uncommon for priests to marry at this time, but there was already conflict within the clergy when it came to celibacy. Many, like Coenred, believed that celibacy was the correct course for any man wishing to dedicate himself wholly to God.

This would ultimately be a contributing factor in the Great Schism of AD 1054 when Pope Gregory VII attempted to mandate priestly celibacy. Five centuries later, celibacy was once again at the forefront of debate and it became a significant factor in the Protestant split from Catholicism during the Reformation.

As with all the Bernicia Chronicles, I have set my imagined tale of Beobrand and his Black Shields within the very real world of the mid-seventh century, and I aim for the places and people they encounter to be as close to the realities of the time as possible.

The route they follow is based on the traditional pilgrim's way from France, known in Italy as the *'Via Francigena'* ('the road from France'). It was also documented as the 'Lombard Way', and was called the *Iter Francorum* (the 'Frankish Route') in the *Itinerarium sancti Willibaldi*, an eighth-century record of the travels of Willibald, a Bavarian bishop.

Just as I have found when researching the early medieval period of other European countries, what is now modern-day Italy was then a patchwork of kingdoms and provinces. Italy did not become a single nation until 1861, at which time less than 10 per cent of its citizens spoke Italian.

The northern part of Italy was ruled by the Langobards. Much of this area is now the province of Lombardy and still retains much of its uniqueness, such as the millions of people who speak the Lombard language across Northern Italy and southern Switzerland. Modern Lombard has evolved from many different linguistic roots, and still retains clear connections to Lombardic (or Langobardic), an extinct West Germanic language that was spoken by the Langobards (Langobardi), a Germanic people who settled in Italy in the sixth century. The language was already in decline in the seventh century as the invaders adopted the Latin vernacular of the local population, but Lombardic was probably still in use in scattered areas until as late as AD 1000.

Most of the details of Lombardic are lost to us. It is a language preserved only in fragmentary form, with only individual words and personal names cited in Latin law codes, charters and histories. However, from those fragments, and the origins of the people who spoke it, and the similarities in their religious and cultural heritage, it is very likely that Beobrand and other English visitors would have been able to understand at least the gist of what was being said. They would certainly have recognised the old gods the Langobards had worshipped before converting to Christianity.

The various disparate regions of Italy were frequently in conflict, and some of that strife stemmed from religious differences, even when everyone involved professed to believe in the same God.

The Langobard Christians adhered to the Arian theology. This belief was that Jesus Christ is the Son of God, who was begotten by God the Father, but that the Son of God did not always exist, instead being created by God the Father. Despite believing in essentially the same God, Trinity, and all the other tenets of Christianity, this was seen as heresy, and in fact Arianism is most commonly known as the Arian Heresy.

The religious picture of the Christian Church was further confused by the split between the Eastern (Byzantine) and Western sides of the Roman Empire. The pope, or pontiff, resided in Rome, but the patriarch of the Eastern Church, and the emperor himself, were both based in Constantinople.

The Eastern Empire's influence in Italy was centred in the city of Ravenna and controlled what was known as the Exarchate of Ravenna, essentially a Byzantine province governed by an Exarch.

To further muddy the waters, while ostensibly all being part of the same Christian Empire, there were also emerging theological frictions between the pope, patriarch and emperor.

All of this is complex and I have tried to steer clear of the most convoluted aspects of it, but a short background of the issue will explain some of what transpires during Beobrand's eventful stay in Rome.

Pope Martin I (Martinus) had clashed with Emperor Constans II by not waiting for imperial ratification of his consecration as pontiff. Martin then proceeded to infuriate the Patriarch of Constantinople by summoning the Lateran Council of 649 where over a hundred bishops condemned Monothelitism, its authors, and the writings by which Monothelitism had been promulgated.

If you haven't heard of Monothelitism before, you are not alone! It is another seemingly minor theological point that was taken exceedingly seriously by everyone in the clergy for a couple of hundred years. You might be forgiven for thinking they had more important things to worry about, but I doubt the likes of the pope and the patriarch would have found it easy to forgive you! In essence, Monothelitism holds Christ as having only one will, as opposed to having two wills (divine and human).

The Lateran Council's condemnation of Monothelitism did not sit well with the Patriarch of Constantinople, or Emperor Constans II, both of whom were Monothelites and had pushed for the doctrine to be adopted by all factions of the Church.

Martin must have felt strongly about all of this, because he quickly published the decrees of the Lateran Council in an encyclical, a letter from the pope to all bishops across the world.

Constans responded by ordering the Exarch in Ravenna to arrest Martin.

In the novel, I only wanted to give a flavour of the intrigues and machinations, and jockeying for position there must have been within the Church. It was a strange world, fraught with danger, where you could never be sure of who was friend or foe.

With his knack for sensing which way the wind would blow, Wilfrid becomes close to Eugene (Eugenius) who, when Martin is eventually arrested and taken to Constantinople to face his enemies, would become Martin I's successor as pope. It is documented that Eugene was the pope who received Wilfrid on his visit to Rome, and it is highly likely that in reality Wilfrid never actually met Martin.

At this time, the pontiff's Roman residence was the Lateran *Patriarchium*. It was extended and refurbished extensively in the late eighth century into a true palace from which the pope could exercise not only spiritual but also temporal authority. The papal household would not move to the Vatican until 1279.

By the mid-seventh century pilgrimages to Rome were becoming more common, and there was already a trade in pilgrim guidebooks and itineraries, such as *Notitia Ecclesiarum Urbis Romae*, that described all of the churches, shrines and catacombs to visit while in the Eternal City. Roman law forbade burials within the city's walls and by the second century AD, the huge numbers of dead led to vast subterranean catacombs being carved from the volcanic *tufa* rock. These catacombs, some with several levels and literally miles of tunnels, became a huge draw for visitors.

As the years progressed, many of the basilicas were enlarged and the remains of martyrs and saints removed from the catacombs and housed in more luxurious surroundings within the city limits. In the seventh century though, while the number of pilgrims was growing, they had not yet become the big business of the later medieval period. That did not stop enterprising people from making money from wide-eyed visitors, selling them everything from the aforementioned guidebooks, to collections of *ampullae* – small vials of oil from the lamps burning in the tombs of saints and martyrs.

Rome in the early medieval period was very different from the image popularised by films such as *Gladiator*. That depiction is of the city when the Roman Empire was at its peak. However, multiple sacks and sieges, floods, earthquakes and plagues, had seen an incredible decline in the city's population. Rome went from over a million inhabitants in AD 300 to fewer than 50,000 in the seventh century. The aqueducts were destroyed during the Ostrogoth siege in the mid-sixth century, and the subsequent lack of fresh water was partly to blame for the city's contraction closer to the Tiber, leaving great swathes of land as *disabitato*, 'uninhabited'.

It is this landscape of historic monuments in ruins, cattle grazing between the crumbling columns of once majestic temples and palaces, that Beobrand and his friends encounter. It would still have been remarkable and on a scale like nothing they would have encountered before. Testaments to the grandeur of the past were around every corner. The great domed Pantheon that had been converted into a church, the Baths of Diocletian (so huge and elaborate the building was believed to have been an emperor's palace), the massive track of the *Circus Maximus*, with its splendid white marble triumphal arch, and of course, perhaps the most iconic of all Rome's buildings: the amphitheatre that we know today as the Colosseum.

The Hypogeum (or *hypogaeum* in Latin) is a series of tunnels and chambers beneath the arena, and it is connected by a subterranean passageway to the Ludus Magnus, the gladiatorial training barracks just to the east of the building. These tunnels do flood during the winter and bad weather, but as far as I know there is no evidence they were ever used by organised crime gangs.

Of course, even if they had been, the rule of *humilitas* (humility), which evolved into *'omerta'*, the code of silence practised by the modern Mafia, would surely mean we would never hear of it.

At the end of *Shadows of the Slain*, Beobrand and those pilgrims who have survived the ordeals of the journey to Rome, are at long last on their way back to Bernicia. They have been away for over a year, have suffered much at the hands of brigands, criminals, bishops and corrupt officials. They have heard rumours of war with the Picts and are filled with unease about what they will find on their return.

Perhaps Northumbria will be riven by war once more. Or maybe they will have a rare moment of peace in which they might be able to reunite with their kin and those they have left behind. It is even possible that Beobrand might find the love he has craved for so long.

Whatever the future holds, one thing is certain. Beobrand will face whatever his *wyrd* places before him with bravery and stalwart friends by his side.

But that is for another day, and other books.

Acknowledgements

As ever, my first thanks must go to you, dear reader, for taking the time to read this tale. If you've been with me since the beginning of Beobrand's story, thank you for sticking around. If not, and if you've enjoyed this book, go back and read the rest of the series to date and find out how the thegn of Ubbanford and his Black Shields got to be on the pilgrimage to Rome in the first place!

Extra special thanks to Jon McAfee and all my other patrons on Patreon for their generous support. To find out more about becoming a patron, and what rewards you can receive for doing so, please go to www.matthewharffy.com.

Thanks to my trusty test readers, Gareth Jones, Simon Blunsdon, Shane Smart, Jacqui Surgey and Alex Forbes. Their early input was invaluable as ever.

Thank you to my editors, Nicolas Cheetham and Greg Rees, and everyone else in the great team at Aries, Head of Zeus and Bloomsbury. They never disappoint in converting my imaginings into beautiful books.

Thank you to the community of historical fiction authors and readers who connect with me regularly on social media. I love to hear from readers, so don't be shy and let me know what you thought of the book.

For listening to me moaning about publishing (off air) and for some inspiring chats and interviews on air, I must thank Steven A. McKay, author and co-host of *Rock, Paper, Swords! The Historical Action and Adventure Podcast*. Steven is a great guy, and a wonderful writer too. Read his books and listen to our podcast!

And finally, as always, my endless love and appreciation go to my lovely daughters, Elora and Iona, and my wonderful wife, Maite.

Matthew Harffy
Wiltshire, April 2024

About the Author

MATTHEW HARFFY grew up in Northumberland where the rugged terrain, ruined castles and rocky coastline had a huge impact on him. He now lives in Wiltshire, England, with his wife and their two daughters. Matthew is the author of the critically acclaimed Bernicia Chronicles and A Time for Swords series, and he also presents the popular podcast *Rock, Paper, Swords!* with fellow author Steven A. McKay.

Follow Matthew at @MatthewHarffy and www.matthewharffy.com.